# THE
# BURNISHED
# BLADE

# THE
# BURNISHED
# BLADE

## LAWRENCE SCHOONOVER

New York

THE MACMILLAN COMPANY

1948

To

GEORGE L. SCHOONOVER

my father

# THE
# BURNISHED
# BLADE

# CHAPTER

## ✻ 1 ✻

TO TRAVELERS destined to die at the hands of bandits, death came silently in fifteenth century France. The weapons of the period did not make a sound.

Almost within hearing distance of the cathedral bells of Rouen, covering the hills that rise abruptly from the river Seine and fall away again toward the fertile plains of Normandy, an ancient forest had stood since Roman times.

Late in the Tuesday night that followed Trinity Sunday—it was the springtime of 1431—when thousands of people were converging on Rouen, a small cavalcade in too much of a hurry to stop at an inn pressed on through the gloomy old trees. A torchbearer picked out the obscure path before them. A noble knight, armed cap-a-pie, rode behind him. Then followed a richly clad lady.

A woman had no business riding abroad at such an hour in such a place. No one but a distraught mother would have insisted on doing so. Then came the men-at-arms, surrounding the mule-borne litter that carried the sick boy.

There was in Rouen a chirurgeon whose fame had spread beyond Normandy into France. The parents believed that if anyone could, he could cure the intermittent fever that periodically wasted the lad. They had thought they detected the onset of another attack: there would be a day or two of extraordinary good spirits and activity, then nausea, apathy, and burning fever; and then the weeks of slow convalescence. Hence their haste.

The long journey had made them extremely tired. The men-at-arms relaxed their vigilance a little.

I

Suddenly a metallic snap and a hiss split the air like the spit of an angry cat. The ominous sound was followed by other hisses, and the air filled with crossbow quarrels—missiles so deadly and effective that the Church had repeatedly forbidden their use against Christians.

The knight and his lady died instantly in their saddles.

Whoever was shooting at the little party was well armed and accustomed to weapons. It was banditry to shoot a woman, but banditry was not uncommon. The roving bands of outlaws that infested the forests were constantly decimated by punitive raids organized against them by the nobles and outraged citizens of the towns. But they were as constantly reenforced by deserters from the armies.

Some of the men-at-arms were killed, too. Seeing their lord and lady both slain, the others fled into the forest. Nobody paid any attention to the litter.

The man with the torch had flung it away from him so as not to attract attention to himself and had run away from the scene. The torch continued to blaze smokily in the path. In its uncertain light the attackers, a good-sized group of them, cautiously approached the bodies of their victims. The outlaws worked systematically, as if they were familiar with such details. Every article of clothing was stripped from the bodies. What was useless they piled into a heap. What was valuable they kept. The lady's jewelry, the knight's purse and armor and the weapons of the men-at-arms were loaded on a sumpter mule.

"They are French," the bandit leader said pleasantly. "That is curious, so close to Rouen; and very fortunate for us. No one would expect a French nobleman hereabouts. I don't think we even have to worry too much about the escape of a few of the servants. Undoubtedly they'll scamper back to France." They heaped dry branches on the clothes and burned them. Finally, deeming it prudent to destroy the identity even of French victims, they threw the naked bodies into the fire. Then the bandits disappeared into the forest.

The abandoned mules had overset their litter. The boy saw the gleam of the fire and stumbled toward it. He was terribly frightened and confused. He saw, or thought he saw, his parents without any clothes on, burning. He approached the pyre and tried to drag his mother's body out of the flames, but he burned his hands. He saw that his father's eyes had melted out of their sockets. All his mother's yellow hair had burned away and she was turning black. The boy shrieked and began to run.

He ran at great speed on long legs, to which terror and utter deso-

2

lation gave wings, following the path that led through the forest and out to the highway that dropped down toward the Seine and Rouen; and he did not stop until a pain in his chest made breathing so difficult that he had to. His fatigue and confusion increased. In a little while it was impossible to go on.

There was a hollow place between a rock and the roots of a great old tree. Into this shelter the boy wedged his tired, trembling body and lay sobbing until, just before dawn, he thought his father and mother came to say good night to him, as they always did, and told him to be a good boy and go to sleep. There was nothing wrong with his father's eyes, and his mother's yellow hair had all grown back again.

# CHAPTER

## ✳ 2 ✳

WHEN THE BOY AWOKE, his head was hot with a fever and the terror returned as if there had been no interval of sleep. Again the urge to run came upon him. He thought he did run. Actually he walked with a stumbling uncertain gait. He was thoroughly wet with the dew that had gathered on him while he slept. His teeth chattered in a chill he did not feel. His hands began to pain terribly.

After a little time the sun dried out his clothes and his teeth stopped chattering. Some strength returned to his legs. The landscape stopped twisting about. He saw that there were many people on the highway, all going in the same direction.

He was midway between two groups. Ahead of him on a richly draped litter slung between two horses was an old man with a haughty face. He was speaking English to a younger man in a short jacket. From time to time the younger man nodded his head respectfully to the old gentleman, while his nimble legs in their tight hose executed as close an approximation of a genuflection as could be accomplished if he were to continue to keep up with the litter. When he did this, the incredibly long points of his soft leather shoes licked up little whirlpools of dust in the road. Around the litter rode knights in new armor, and both before and behind were archers with long English bows. That the old man in the litter was a great lord bent on a mission of importance was apparent even to the boy, who knew that men were seldom carried in litters like women and sick children.

A group of friars, dusty as from a long journey, was directly behind the boy. One who walked a little apart from the rest and whom they appeared to be following glanced casually at him. With the

4

instinct that some dogs and most children have for manifest kindliness, the boy approached a little unsteadily and very respectfully.

"I am going to Rouen, Father," he said, falling into a walk and looking up at the man.

The priest nodded, but did not speak.

"I am hungry, Father."

The priest nodded again. People were always hungry, and everyone was going to Rouen.

"My father and mother were slain and burned last night." It was almost a question, as if the too bright-eyed boy doubted the terrible words he was pronouncing.

The priest started and looked down at him sharply. The solemnity of the day struck him with an intensity that seemed to have grown with every hour since he and his group had left the cloister during the night, to be present in Rouen where they would make a retreat in the cathedral, offering their thankful prayers for a judgment of the ecclesiastical court which rejoiced their hearts; the commutation of the sentence of the Maid of Orleans to life imprisonment. She had put off her man's garments, recanted her errors, prayed mercy of the court and received it. It is always good to give thanks when mercy is shown, as it always is shown, the priest assured himself, by Holy Mother Church; and, moreover, the Maid was French. Now, however, since dawn, rumor had spread from group to group along the road, swiftly, like pain traveling from the extremities to the heart, that the Maid had recanted her recantation and put on her sinful garb again, and that the original judgment of burning had been reaffirmed, to be put into execution forthwith. If this boy were jesting . . .

"You're not an English lad? Nay, I perceive by your speech that you're not. Perhaps you are telling the truth. What is your name?"

"Pierre."

"Pierre what?"

"Just Pierre."

"How old are you?"

"I do not know, Father."

"How many times have you observed the feast day of your patron, St. Pierre?"

The boy shook his head.

It was not uncommon for children not to know their own age, especially among the peasantry. The boy who called himself Pierre was big enough to be ten, but he spoke like a much younger child. The good,

5

but undistinguished clothing he wore might have belonged to almost any class of person, and it was torn and dirty from his night in the open.

"I am telling the truth," he said.

"No doubt, no doubt. You've the stigmata on the hands to prove it. Who murdered your parents, you poor boy?"

Pierre shook his head.

"Nay, how could you know! You don't even know your own name or how old you are. Where do you live, lad? In Rouen?"

"No."

"Do you live in a city? Are there walls where you live?"

"There are walls."

The priest pondered. There were walls around all cities and all castles. Even the huts of peasants sometimes stood within manorial walls.

"You have made me talk too much, boy," he said severely. "Since dawn my brothers and I have bound ourselves to preserve silence and the custody of the eyes—why I looked at you I do not know—and not to eat at all this sad day. And part of my vow, by my own fault, I have already broken for you. May I be forgiven, and I think I may, for here I can do a good work."

"I do not understand you, Father."

"Probably not. Did you say that you were hungry?"

"Yes, I did."

"It wouldn't hurt you to fast this day, of all days. But your stomach is young, and you've suffered a great loss, and no doubt you'll fast aplenty in the future. Look you, lad; I am only a poor priest, devoted to Our Lady and St. Augustine. Already I have broken a vow for you, and my mind is troubled whether 'twas an angel or the Devil that prompted me to do it." He glanced apprehensively back over his shoulder at the company of splendidly dressed knights that followed his own little group.

"Directly behind us—do not appear to look now—is the great Baron de Retz and his retinue. The baron is the tall young man on the white horse. He is a marshal of France and a brave cavalier. South of the Loire he lives in greater splendor than a king. He is reputed to be interested in orphans. Nevertheless, I do not want him to see you. When I cease talking to you, you are to go to the side of the road and pretend to extract a pebble from your shoe."

"Why, Father?"

6

"Do not ask me why. Probably you will have a pebble in your shoe."

"Yes, Father."

"Above all, you are to avert your eyes so that you cannot see his face, and so that he cannot see yours." Here the priest looked at the youngster with sad, wise eyes. "Do you understand?"

"No, Father, but I shall do as you say. Is there something wrong with my face?"

"There is nothing wrong with your face. That is the trouble."

"I do not understand."

"I do not want you to. I want you to obey me. You understand that, don't you?"

"Yes, Father."

"After the baron and his men have passed, you will continue to extract the pebble from your shoe until the next group of men arrives."

"Yes, Father," said Pierre, half smiling at the notion that it would take him so long to shake out his shoe. The priest smiled, too, liking his quick apprehension, and continued:

"The short, fat man is an armorer of my acquaintance. He is called Hugh of Milan. The tall man with the dark face and the heathen head-gear is his servant. They are both good Christian men. Tell the armorer that you are sent by Brother Isambert de la Pierre and that he will be doing a good work to take you home and care for you until such time as it may please God, my vows of silence having been renewed and discharged, to allow me the leisure to consult with him—"

Pierre's face was a study in confusion.

"Oh, tell him, lad, just tell him to take you home and feed you. I'll speak to him later. Now go." And he signed the cross over the boy. Pierre hurried to the side of the road. There, a little off the beaten way, averting his face and squatting on the ground amid the wayside vegetation, his head looked like a golden flower on a slender stalk. Dutifully he extracted the pebble which the monk had seen bulging under the soft leather of his shoe.

"He should have worn a hat," sighed Isambart. "Oh, well."

The Baron de Retz looked neither to the right nor to the left. He certainly did not notice the boy. His intense face had an odd look of concentrated indecision. He called for a cup of chilled wine. Instantly a page ran to one of the pack mules, raised the lid of a small traveling chest and drew out a silver goblet that appeared to be frosted with dew. This he presented to his lord, who quaffed it delicately and tossed

7

back the cup with a gesture. The man caught it deftly, from long practice.

Pierre had never heard of chilling wine, nor had anyone else in France since the Romans. It was one of the baron's oddities. He had many. Nine years later they dug the little skeletons out of the cellars of his castle and hanged him for, among other things, one hundred and forty murders. But this day he was remembering how he had fought with the Maid against the English and wondering how her execution would affect him.

Isambart and his monks were now far down the road. Once again breaking his vow to preserve the custody of the eyes, he shot a quick glance back at Pierre, noted that he was still extracting the pebble, that the baron's cavalcade had entirely passed, and that Hugh of Milan and his men were approaching. He sighed again and addressed a prayer to the Virgin, thanking her for what he had been the means of accomplishing—if indeed it had been anything, for it was not in his heart to believe all the evil spoken against the baron—and then for the boy, and then for the Maid, and then for himself and for strength to do the things that a galloping courier had just announced were to be demanded of him that day.

Ugo, onetime armorer to Filippo Maria, last of the Visconti dukes of Milan, had found himself exiled to France in the year of our Lord 1427. He had been heard to remark that there were handsomer men in the duchy than Filippo Maria, and the unhappy duke, who was spectacularly ugly and very sensitive about it, banished him forthwith. In Rouen, where he had set up shop, he was known simply by the name of Hugh of Milan.

He watched the boy detach himself from the group of monks and run to the side of the road and squat among the bushes, perhaps to relieve himself. The reputation of the Baron de Retz was known to him, and for a moment his agile mind speculated on the possibilities of the situation. But in view of the high drama about to unfold at Rouen, he anticipated no accosting of the boy. His speedy, accurate interpretation of the psychological factors involved was the product of a curious, inquiring intellect. He was interested in the behavior of men, in the nature of plants and animals, and, most of all, in the working of steel, that wonderful metal of his craft. The universities did not teach these things. No one in Christendom had ever wondered about them. Thus

Hugh of Milan, although he did not know it, was in a minor sense one of the first humble prophets of the Renaissance, which, still without a name, was already burgeoning in Italy.

Hugh of Milan considered himself an unfortunate exile in a backward country. His Turkish slave had caused gossip among the townspeople, and his enormous purchases of olive oil at the market, far more than his household could consume, gave rise to all sorts of rumors. But his regular appearance at Mass with his slave, who was soon discovered to be a free man and a Christian, quieted the gossip about his orthodoxy.

The turban, it is true, was thought to be out of place in church, where it troubled the conscience of some of the worshippers. But on discarding it the Turk was discovered to have no ears. His head was bald and covered with scars so deep and horrible that it seemed no man could have lived to recover from the wounds which had caused them. This was even more disquieting than the turban, and he was quickly encouraged to bind up his head again with a rag. But Abdul had worn many folds and layers of cloth on his head for sixty years. He was cold and ill at ease under a mean little bandage. Thus, as time went on and the people got used to it, the covering assumed more and more the shape of his old turban. But the badge and feathers were gone, and so it had no religious significance. It was even pointed out by Isambart that such a headpiece, worn by a baptized and converted Turk, should serve to the faithful as a sign of eventual triumph of true religion over the heathen. That quieted the rumors about Abdul.

Other things troubled Hugh: the barbarous manners of his customers and the poor quality of the bread. Once he had burned a loaf of it in the fire and saved the ashes and leached them with water. There remained an insoluble quantity of pulverized stone. He was too wise to confront the miller with the results of his experiment, for he knew he would be accused of sorcery. So he quietly surmised that a new grindstone which had recently been delivered to the mill, being poorly surfaced had disintegrated at first, to the great disadvantage of the flour. He assumed that the quality would return, to French standards, at least, as soon as the stone wore smooth; in any case, there was nothing he could do about it.

Then, the olive oil was expensive. Often there was water in it, which had to be removed by boiling. Or there were little sticks and bits of bark that had to be filtered out. Sometimes the oil was contaminated with salt, and this he could never contrive to remove; and since salt ruined the oil for his purposes, he was frequently forced to renew his supply.

Hugh, with his Turkish servant and his two clumsy French apprentices, was returning home after a week spent in the castle of a rich English client who had refused to have his armor repaired in the shop in Rouen. The castle had an inadequate forge and a soft anvil. *Gesù!* Did they expect him to carry his own beautiful casehardened anvil with him on a journey of ten leagues? Well, he almost wished he had done so. The job would have been smoother. But the English lord had paid well, and expressed his satisfaction, especially with the sword. Hugh sniffed contemptuously. Now, if he had been in his own shop with his own equipment around him—ah! there he would have shown him swords to make the English lord's eyes pop out of his head. Hugh carefully explained to Abdul that the sword was good enough for the Englishman. Abdul majestically inclined his head and said that his thoughts were ever the same as the thoughts of his master.

After the passage of the Baron de Retz and his men, Hugh noticed that the boy cautiously turned his head toward the road again and, seeing the way momentarily clear, ran out into the center of it. Here was no beggar boy. Here was a phenomenon which fraternized with the clergy, hid from the gentry on horseback, and was now approaching a burgher on a mule.

The set face of the armorer and the dark foreign countenance of the Turk frightened the boy and caused him to forget the simpler message and to stammer out parts of the complicated one.

"When it please God to discharge and renew," he pronounced, "it is a good work to be silent until such time."

Hugh and his servant crossed themselves. No, no beggar, poor lad. Just a mad little boy.

"Out of my way, fool!" cried Abdul, laying his hand on the jeweled dagger at his waist and bending his turbaned head toward the lad in an exaggerated gesture of menace.

Pierre began to cry.

"But the monk said maybe you would take me home. I'm hungry, and I haven't any home."

"What monk, boy?" asked the armorer.

"The monk Isambart."

"Who is Isambart?"

"Father Isambart de la Pierre. He is with the other monks just beyond the Baron de Retz."

"That is true," said the armorer.

"He told me to speak to the armorer Hugh of Milan, and he will talk to him later."

"Oh, ho! He told you my name!"

"He said it would be a good work, but he also said," here Pierre determined to tell the worst, "that it would not hurt me to fast this day because it is a sad day. But I'm hungry on sad days, too."

Hugh of Milan smiled, but he answered: "I must say, you don't look it. Never have I seen such good bright eyes."

"That is a fever, master," the Turk interposed.

"Fever, lad? There is no sickness about. And look at your hands. Have you been setting fires?"

The reaction to his banter was more than the words or the tone of their speaking could warrant. Pierre began to sob again, with heart-breaking abandon.

"Take him up, Abdul," the armorer ordered. "I meant only to plague him a little."

The servant crooked a mighty arm around the boy's waist and drew him up onto his mule.

"There, my laddie. Hush, my little one. Quiet, thou golden-haired Frank, or the wicked baron will——"

"Careful, Abdul!"

"Pardon, my master. A thousand pardons. I ought to have known better." He wiped away the boy's tears with his sleeve. "Are you all right now?"

"I'm all right. I was crying about the fire."

"What fire, child?"

Pierre told them, jerkily, what had happened during the night. After the tragic recitation both men were very quiet. "That is how I burned my hands," Pierre added, as if he had been guilty of something.

"You're a good boy," the armorer said in a comforting voice. "And even if you were not, I'd help you for the sake of Father Isambart."

Abdul addressed Hugh of Milan with dignity.

"Master!"

"Yes, Abdul?"

"I have a confession to make to you. I have dates in my turban."

"For shame!"

"I am ashamed. It is an old habit."

"How many times have I told you not to carry food about in that barbarous fashion! Haven't you had trouble enough on account of your turban? Do you want people to think there is magic in it, producing strange tropical fruit at any time of the day, untouched by corruption and dripping with sweetness that is not honey? Half the people in France are still terrified by dates. How many have you left?"

"Not many, master. I have been eating them at night."

"By all means give the boy some. But first, I'd better try one or two to make sure that they are not spoiled."

"That is a wise precaution, master."

Abdul soberly reached up to his turban and drew out a small package wrapped in glazed leather of exquisite thinness. When he opened it, Pierre saw a dozen or so curious brown fruits which were certainly not attractive to the eye. But out of the package spread a delectable aroma of such enticing sweetness that his hungry stomach seemed to turn and contract within him. The armorer ate one, and then another, and then a third. "They are not spoiled," he said regretfully. Abdul put one into Pierre's mouth and held the package firmly in his other hand, as if further testing were unnecessary.

"There is a stone in each one," said Abdul. "Do not eat the stone, but do not throw it on the road either. Many people have never seen the stones that lie in the heart of this harmless nourishing fruit, and they might be afraid of them. Save them, as the master has done, or at least let me hurl them into the bushes when nobody is looking."

"That is a wise precaution, Abdul," Hugh said with a sly smile. Master and slave, master and servant, they had been so long together that they could almost read each other's thoughts.

Then in the distance, ahead of the Baron de Retz and his men, they descried another courier, gorgeously clad in the ecclesiastical livery of the Bishop of Beauvais, leading a horse without a rider and rapidly bearing down upon Isambart and his monks. He halted only a moment. Isambart mounted the horse, and together they disappeared in the direction of Rouen, showering the people with the dust and stones that flew from the thundering hoofs.

# CHAPTER

## ✳ 3 ✳

THE MONOTONOUS RHYTHM of the mule's slow walk and the flesh of the sweet fruit in his hungry stomach, the solid body of Abdul to lean against and the hot sun on his unprotected head all acted as a soporific upon the boy and he slept as they entered Rouen.

All the streets were crowded with the young and old, strong and infirm, burghers with their wives and children down to the smallest infants, monks of many orders, ragged students, beggars, thieves, peasants from the surrounding districts, and marching groups of pike-men and archers, principally English, whose duty it was to preserve order among the multitude. Their duty was easily done. Shops were closed. Ordinary life was suspended as for a holiday, yet there was none of the holiday spirit that customarily showed itself at an execution, for most Frenchmen believed that the mission of the Maid was divine.

Just as sincerely, every Englishman present was convinced that she was a witch, and even some of the Frenchmen joined them in their belief. King Charles himself, whose throne she had secured by her victories, was more than half convinced of her diabolical possession. Pierre Cauchon, the Bishop of Beauvais, categorically affirmed that Jeanne was an instrument of the Devil. By all the rules, the ecclesiastical court which tried her had acted with scrupulous fairness, condemning her not to death but to life imprisonment. And who knew but that she might be set free in a year, in two years, when the times grew less disturbed and the people forgot her spectacular career?

To the somewhat lethargic temperament of Charles VII, now that his throne was safe, it seemed no more than just that she be punished if, in the opinion of the most learned judges of two realms, she deserved

13

it. Her apostasy removed her from the jurisdiction of the ecclesiastical court and threw her upon the mercy of the secular arm, which was resolved in advance upon her destruction.

Hugh sent his apprentices with the pack mules to the shop. He considered sending Pierre along with them, but it occurred to him that the sudden appearance of an unknown boy with a claim on his hospitality might prove upsetting to his wife. After all, a wise man does not absent himself for a week and then turn up with a strange, new, and perhaps permanent member of the household without preliminary negotiations of the most serious order. Therefore he kept the boy with him.

The crush about the Old Market, the fish market, was even greater than in the side streets. Satisfied to be no closer, not only for himself but especially on account of the boy, Hugh and his servant took up a position at a corner of the square almost as far from the center of the drama as it was possible to be and still witness what took place.

Then, to his astonishment, a guard who was conducting a priest through the press of people seized hold of the reins of the mules and addressed him.

"Your pardon, Master Hugh, but I must use your beasts as a battering ram to make a breach in this wall of people in order to take this good father to the judges' platform. I'll never get him through alone. Just stay on your mounts, my friends, and I promise you'll have the best view in Rouen."

"*Peste!*" muttered Hugh. "I am perfectly content with the view as it is."

"Well, you're at liberty to dismount, but then you'll see nothing at all," and without more ado he propelled the mules through the crowd, which was forced to part or be trodden upon. The monk who followed raised his head, which had been bowed almost to his breast. His face was deathly pale and the knuckles of his clasped hands were white. It was Isambart.

"Do as the man says, Master Hugh. I shall be closer than you will, and I am not permitted to close my eyes. Let it be a penance for our sins. I am commanded by the bishop to witness the Maid's death."

"Why in the world did he choose you, Father?"

"It is not my place to question the bishop's actions, but perhaps by his choosing me the English will learn that no French priest thanked God that the Maid was to have been saved. Of course, the retreat could not have been conducted anyway, as things turned out; but now even the intention will be forgotten."

"He is a wicked man," growled Hugh.

"Nay, do not say so. It is I who am wicked for talking thus of him; may I be forgiven. The bishop dwells more in the world than I, and he must deal with kings and princes and great affairs which I do not understand. I only wish he had chosen someone else."

"Here is the young man you sent me, Father," Hugh said. "What am I to do with him?"

"Restore his health, Hugh; and in a day or two I shall visit you and speak further of him. My heart is too full today."

On one of three platforms erected at the center of the Old Market stood a royal throne for the English regent, the episcopal chair of the Bishop of Beauvais, and the throne of the English cardinal, more imposing than the others but, of course, no higher than the regent's. Many English and French clergymen and nobles of Burgundy sat or stood around their respective princes in places allotted according to their rank. On the arrival of Hugh and his mules at the cordon of guards that kept the people away from the center of the square, Isambart walked slowly across the open space and took his place among the lesser clergy on the royal platform.

On another platform, smaller and lower than the first, were gathered the active principals of the tragedy: the lawyers, the judges, the scribes, the bailiff, and the condemned Maid herself.

The third platform was white with a thick layer of fire-resistant plaster, as was also the stake, planted in its center. Actually the stake projected through the platform and was firmly anchored in the earth. In a well engineered structure of this sort, the stake is the first piece to be erected and the last to fall.

A huge pile of dry wood had been amassed about the stake, and the executioner noted with satisfaction that there was scarcely a green branch to be seen. Almost always someone attempted to introduce green, slow-burning wood into the pile at an execution, whether as a prank to embarrass him or from a cruel desire to prolong the torture he did not know. But it almost always happened.

Nicolas Midi, a canon of Rouen and one of the lights of the University of Paris, preached a sermon that was a part of the ceremony: *Si quid patitur unum membrum, compatiuntur alia membra*— if one member of the Church be corrupt, all the Church suffers. It

15

seemed interminable to the crowd. Jeanne d'Arc came to kneel at the feet of the bishop. He exhorted her to pray, to repent, and to confess her sins. At length he began to read to her the long sentence of the ecclesiastical court in which her crimes were all remembered: heresy, schism, idolatry, the invocation of demons, her imperfect repentance and her lapse again into heresy, ending with the dread formula by which the Church delivered criminals to the secular authorities to administer any punishment which was foreign to the spirit or beyond the jurisdiction of the ecclesiastical court. "We cast you off, separate and abandon you," and the more merciful qualification, "nevertheless praying the secular power to moderate its judgment toward you."

This formula was so ancient that men had forgotten how it originated. For centuries it had been the means of softening the fate of many wretched criminals. But the terror which it inspired in the fifteenth century bespeaks both the ferocity of secular justice and the ease with which the formula could be perverted by unscrupulous prelates.

Kneeling before the bishop who had abandoned her, Jeanne was heard to murmur: "Bishop, I die because of you. Had you sent me to a prison of the Church, this would never have happened."

She asked that she might be given a crucifix to hold, but there was none at hand. Even the English thought it odd that a bishop who provided such a mountainous pile of wood, which was not his business, had failed to provide a cross, which so distinctly was. An English soldier made a rude little cross out of two small branches and presented it to her. She kissed it, and placed it under her rough criminal garment. But it was an ungainly thing, fashioned hurriedly, no doubt by sinful hands, and she begged for another which had been blessed by the Church she loved and which had stood on an altar close to the Blessed Sacrament. Even the Bishop of Beauvais wept and granted her request. It fell to Isambart to hold before her eyes the cross which the bishop directed be brought from the near-by Church of the Holy Saviour.

Now, indeed, the crowd began to grumble at the protracted nature of the proceedings, the English soldiers especially, and one of them shouted: "How now, priests? Are you going to keep us here till supper-time?" Then, losing patience and not waiting for the bailiff's order, two sergeants hustled her away from the platform where she knelt and delivered her to the executioner, saying, "Executioner, do your duty."

By what Isambart always considered a special grace, it was not his lot to accompany the Maid to the top of the pyre or to hear the desperate prayers she uttered when at length she realized that she must die. But by order of the bishop he stood at the foot of the stake to witness her death and perhaps to be seen by the English authorities.

With the assistance of two soldiers the executioner bound her to the stake. He was given a flaming torch, and he plunged it into the heart of the dry wood.

Pierre, of course, was fully awake by the time the guard so aggressively split the crowd with the mules. The drama being enacted before his eyes made no sense at all, though the colors were pleasing. Little by little he began to feel the undercurrent of tenseness in the crowd and in the great personages sitting so solemnly on the platforms.

"What is happening?" he asked.

Abdul was silent. The armorer mumbled, "It's just a play, lad."

"What is a play, master?"

"It's a sort of game. They just pretend."

"What are they going to pretend?"

"They are going to pretend to burn up the bad woman," Hugh answered.

"Is she really bad?"

"They pretend she is a bad witch, and then they pretend to burn her up," the armorer replied miserably.

"Oh."

But when the torch was applied, the boy stirred uneasily and looked very frightened. Abdul glanced questioningly at his master and Hugh shook his head.

"It's just a play, Pierre. I tell you they're just pretending. Do not be afraid."

"Oh, I don't like it!" Pierre cried, covering his face.

The armorer muttered: "Good. Maybe he won't look."

But the fire roared up and burned the garment off the girl, and ten thousand people saw the battle wounds on her body as it rapidly changed color before their eyes.

"Water! Water!" shrieked the tortured victim, though Isambart later affirmed that it was holy water she called for, and he was closer than most.

Pierre suddenly wrenched himself loose from Abdul's arm and ran screaming toward the stake.

"It is real! It is real!"

Before the guards could lay hands on him, he seized a long branch from the pile and attempted to beat the fire out. But his childish blows

17

served only to overturn a large smoking faggot tottering at the very apex of the pyramid of wood that was visibly sinking as the roaring mass of flame consumed it. The faggot, made almost entirely of twigs, blazed fiercely. The burning twigs fell apart and scattered as the faggot rolled down the mound, and then the whole fire blazed higher and more horribly than before. A great cloud of sparks and smoke rose into the air, startling the pigeons on the church. It appeared as if the boy were poking in the fire to kindle it to greater intensity. One of the guards drew him roughly away and struck him smartly on the forehead with the flat of his sword.

"Bloodthirsty pig! Go away," he snarled, "or I'll throw you in, too!"

But the Maid, who was no longer struggling in her chains, looked out of the flames directly at Pierre. Perhaps she knew what he had tried to do. Perhaps she was thankful for what he had actually done, for assuredly it shortened her torture. One of the birds that the sparks had startled wheeled through the smoke, almost touching the Maid's face, and circled quickly out of the heat. Its wing brushed Pierre's forehead and for an instant the soft touch of its feathers felt like a cool caress where the guard had struck him. Hugh of Milan always maintained that it was one of those pigeons, but there were many in the peasantry who swore it was a dove, which they had seen issue out of the mouth of the Maid and fly up to heaven.

Hugh approached as rapidly as his short legs would permit and carried his fainting charge back to the mule, but it was some time before he and Abdul could get their beasts out of the surging, weeping crowd.

Jeanne d'Arc was still alive, but beyond all suffering, when the Bishop of Beauvais, quitting the dignity of his episcopal chair, walked over to the foot of the stake to examine more closely the condition of his victim, nineteen years old, burning naked in the flames. All the flesh had broiled off the feet. The blackened bones began to separate and fall.

# CHAPTER

## ❖ 4 ❖

T HE HOUSEHOLD of Hugh of Milan was furnished with an opulence which startled his neighbors. In the apartments back of his shop he was known to have chairs with backs to lean against like a bishop in church. Instead of chests that formed such convenient catch-alls for most people of the period, Hugh had brought with him from Italy the idea of the chest of drawers which had doors that opened horizontally, so that there was no need to take everything out of the chest and then pack it back again every time something was wanted.

The great bed in his house was raised two feet off the floor, and it was provided with curtains against the chill night air of France. Even Abdul's bed, in his own small room, was elevated above the cold of the stone floor and warm with a magnificent panther skin that a duke might have envied.

Hugh could not afford the expensive wood paneling with which a few of the richest lords were beginning to decorate their mansions, but he could buy the hides of old farm animals. And so, like many another well-to-do bourgeois, here and there on walls that were likely to be drafty in the wintertime he hung up the well tanned skins of oxen, fur side out. The effect was somewhat barbaric, but the practical results were undeniable.

Opening upon a court in the rear was the spacious kitchen where the whole family dined. Here was a huge fireplace which Hugh himself had taken great pains to equip in the most complete manner imaginable. The hooks that held his stewing pots could be swung out of the fire on ingenious hinges that worked so smoothly that never a drop was spilled and Maria could lift them off without burning her fingers. Because she complained that the fat dropped into the fire when meat was placed on the grill, Hugh had contrived a new grill into each bar of which was forged a V-shaped trough, so that the juices of the meat were canalized into a wide pan. The rich gravies that his wife made contributed not a little to his corpulence. These gravies were poured over the meat and absorbed by the slice of bread which was always placed underneath to soak up the fluid, and which otherwise might have spilled out of the concave, polished slabs of wood that served as dishes, and soiled the table.

Hugh had also constructed a spit, which was long enough to roast half a dozen geese at a time; and, though there was always one of the apprentices to turn it, it had pleased Hugh's fancy to devise a mechanism of gears, powered by a heavy iron weight, that could be wound up like a clock to turn the spit for a long time without attention. But Maria usually forgot to wind it, and so it was seldom used. Hugh considered that it might perhaps be attached to a windmill and so turn forever, but he did not deem the project worthy of further study.

Although tapestries were luxuries that could be purchased only by the very rich, Maria was adept at plaiting the slender rushes sold by the street vendors. She made a delicate screen of them and placed it between the fireplace and the table to temper the heat as they dined. She also made mats for the floors, which were pleasant to walk upon and imparted a clean fresh fragrance to the air. The neatness of her housekeeping and the extreme cleanliness of the place were thought eccentric at a time when most women were content to let the dust and litter accumulate until one stumbled over it.

Maria would have liked to go to the burning, since everybody else would be there, but the apprentices suddenly appeared and blurted out that Hugh and Abdul had returned. They stabled the mules and unharnessed the chests. In their haste and excitement they would have run off at once to the Old Market without feeding themselves or the beasts.

Maria, who could not bear the thought of hunger, thrust a prodigious piece of freshly cut bread into their hands.

"Your stomachs will be sick enough, you savage creatures. Eat something."

Ambrose, whose face was deeply pock-marked and rendered no more attractive by the fuzzy beard which had lately replaced the pimples of his adolescence, said he did not think he would be sick.

Clement, somewhat older, who had shaved for a year and who might have been handsome but for his unfortunately crossed eyes, replied that he had seen a man sewn in a sack with an ape and thrown into the Seine for his crimes. Certainly he would not be sick.

"And see that the mules are fed," Maria ordered, "or sick or not sick, you shall not go."

Then they remembered Pierre, and as they saw to the mules they informed Maria, between mouthfuls of bread, that the master had picked up a strange, sick boy on the road and was bringing him home forever.

"Is he indeed now! We'll see about that!" Maria exclaimed. "Though it would be like my Hugh. Very like," she added to herself. She busied herself in her kitchen, contented at the prospect of getting back to her regular routine after living alone in an empty house for a week. *Gesù!* Not a sound from the shop at night! No hammering! How could a woman sleep?

There was a noise in the court when the master returned, and she saw Abdul place the limp form of the unknown boy in Hugh's arms. Abdul gave the mules a tug at their halters and the intelligent animals entered their stalls of their own accord and snorted their satisfaction at being home again. They were Hugh's own beasts, docile and work-worthy, very unlike the pack mules he had rented for the journey. Hugh carried his burden across the cobblestones of his court and entered his house.

When Maria looked at the boy's face, her vast Italian heart melted like butter.

"Holy Mother!" she cried. "What has happened to that poor child?"

"I found him on the road, Maria. He begged for a mouthful of food. Father Isambart talked to him, too, and told him to ask shelter of us. It seemed only right to bring him home for a day or two until he is rid of his fever."

"And look at his hands! They're covered with blisters."

"His father and mother were both slain in the forest—by brigands, of course, who seem to have been more than usually cautious this time. They burned the bodies. The lad was fighting the fire with his hands when he burned them so."

"And you took him to an execution after a thing like that? Why didn't you bring him straight home?"

Hugh's face began to beam like a warm, round, harvest moon.

Apparently there was to be no difficulty securing a welcome for Pierre.

"My dear wife, he seemed better on the road. Abdul gave him a whole fistful of dates. He slept most of the way. I didn't want to send him home with the boys. We had to go to the execution, of course, and rather than alarm you I kept him by me."

"Oh, Hugh, you silly man. We must get him to bed at once."

Pierre looked from one to another as they talked, but his feverish eyes held no comprehension of what they said, and when he saw the fire on the hearth he began to whimper.

"Would it not be well to put him in my bed, master?" suggested Abdul. "It is warmer than the garret."

"That is a kind thought, Abdul," Hugh replied. They loosened Pierre's jerkin and wrapped him in the panther skin, and Maria brought him mutton broth in a copper bowl. But his teeth were chattering in a chill again, and he could swallow only a mouthful.

"We had better fetch a chirurgeon, Maria."

"Yes, I think so, too. A good one. An expensive one."

Abdul frowned slightly at the mention of a doctor. Their treatments were always the same. He remembered the Persian chirurgeons of Isfahan, the subtle herbs that had soothed his own wounds, and the wonderful chirurgery that had patched up his terribly mutilated skull. But he knew better than to question the decision and he went to summon the doctor.

Maria spread a thick layer of butter over the burns and bandaged both Pierre's hands with fine linen cloth that she had hoped to make into a cap. The unguent was soothing, and Pierre dozed.

Abdul returned with the physician, who promptly bled the boy, exactly as Abdul had feared. After the operation the chirurgeon remarked: "I shall not insist on the iron cautery. I do not doubt there is fire enough in his system already. But I charge you, do not loosen the bandage for three days, or the vein will open. The blood I have drawn from his arm will balance the humors in his body. Who is he, Hugh?"

"He is our son," Maria answered.

"Indeed?"

"He is my ward," said Hugh. "He is an orphan boy that was sent to me by Father Isambart with the very highest recommendation. He is to live here for a while. Until his health is restored at least. Is he not, Maria?"

"He is indeed."

The chirurgeon handed to Abdul the brass cup of blood. Abdul poured it into the night chamber and cleaned the cup with some of Maria's scouring sand and gave it back to the physician, who placed it in the sleeve of his long robe together with the lancet which he had stuck into a sheath of cork.

"He is fallen into fortunate hands, Master Hugh. And the physic of Madame your wife," he observed with a grave bow toward Maria, "is almost the equal of my own. There is nothing, or almost nothing, so good for burns as our good Norman butter. Of course, I do have some rather extraordinary preparations, if you should ever unhappily suffer a really deep burn."

"The reputation of Nicol the Chirurgeon is well known," replied Maria with courtesy.

"And spotless," Hugh added.

"I trust so," sighed the chirurgeon. "It is sometimes very hard to keep people alive. And it is difficult for an old man to be called at all hours of the night to the bedside of the sick. But those of us who honor the oath we take, no less than a priest, must go at once, whether they can pay or not. I have read that in the East the people pay their doctors only while they are well, and, if they fall sick, the doctor's fee is stopped."

"That is true," said Abdul.

"It is a strange custom, Master Hugh. Let us hope it will never be adopted in Christian countries."

"At any rate, we shall not start it in this house," Hugh said, digging in his purse for the doctor's fee. Without appearing to notice this commercial aspect of his visit, the doctor's sharp eye instantly diagnosed the coin as a heavy English piece, a golden rose noble, a generous fee indeed. His skilled fingers, so deft with the lancet, slipped the coin unostentatiously into the purse at his belt. Though the mouth of the purse was worn shiny with such use, the long leather body was flat as a flounder, for the doctor avoided the appearance of prosperity.

"Keep the lad quiet. Let him drink plenty of nourishing broth and plenty of water to quench the fire in his blood. His blood is very hot. I felt it through the cup." The doctor paused. "But this boy is less sick than you fear, good people. His fever is temporary, caused by his exposure to the elements and the sorrow that has afflicted him. I am sure he never had a fever before. His heart beats mightily; his chest is round and strong." Nicol differed from most of his colleagues in that he cheerfully admitted encouraging symptoms when he honestly observed them. "In a day or two, with the help of God, I have no doubt he will be on his feet again," and with that the doctor gravely saluted them and departed.

Pierre slept until noon the next day and awoke strong and well and with an enormous appetite, as if he had never had a fever. The burns, of course, were painful for several weeks.

Shortly thereafter Father Isambart visited Hugh to implore his continued help for the boy, whose parentage remained a mystery. Isambart was prepared almost to preach a homily on the subject; for here, if ever, a man had an opportunity to do a good work for one of God's poor. He had even thought to touch on the delicate subject of Hugh's own childlessness, if necessary, and on the strong probability that Maria, now fifty or close to it, would never have a child.

But he discovered that Pierre himself had accomplished even more than he had come to request. It appeared that Hugh was thinking of legal adoption.

Abdul had nursed him as tenderly as a mother. Even Ambrose and Clement did not exhibit the jealousy that might reasonably have been expected of them. And as for Maria, the only thing that she feared was that Pierre might be taken away again.

"Adoption is a serious matter, my friend," said the priest. "It entails the same responsibilities and obligations that you would have toward a true heir of your body. He is very young and his wants are simple, but over the years even simple wants require money. As he grows older his requirements will be greater, especially if you plan to give him an education and fit him for a career."

"He is a bright youngster."

"I thought so, too. Education is more important nowadays than it used to be. Many common men are advancing themselves as merchants simply by buying and selling. The most successful of them own whole fleets of ships and deal in the products of the East, vain things in themselves, but probably harmless. Such things are very cheap in the Orient, and in Europe they are very costly. I am told that the difference in price represents the profit to these merchants. Such men must know how to read and write and calculate. Perhaps Pierre may one day be a merchant, and you must pay for his education if you adopt him."

"I know it," said Hugh. He added, smiling: "I must say, Father, that you display a remarkable knowledge of these new commercial activities. I never before heard a Frenchman, let alone a priest, describe financial operations so lucidly. It is common knowledge in Italy."

Isambart flushed a little. "I grant you it is very worldly knowledge in a priest. But on rare occasions I am called upon to shrive a merchant with a tender conscience. Usually they are very sick. They tell me what they charge and what they rightly ought to charge. The discrepancy is sometimes astonishing. But it is not usury, no more than discounting loans, and the Church does not forbid it."

"You have suggested an excellent career, Father, and I will bear it in mind. Of course, I'd rather see him an armorer."

"Perhaps I should rather see him a priest. In any event, it is a long time in the future."

# CHAPTER

## * 5 *

LEGAL ACTIVITIES among the petty bourgeoisie were accomplished with considerable dispatch and informality. Before a notary, Isambart, a witness of impeccable standing, deposed that he had found a male child, parentage unknown, age unknown, presumed to be an orphan, on the highway outside the city. In order to adopt Pierre, Hugh had only to inform the notary of his intention of doing so.

The Latin instrument of adoption, written on inexpensive parchment in the slow, heavy, Gothic script of the notary, was almost terse in the concise phrases which transferred the orphan to the guardianship of the armorer.

Hugh could just have managed to write his own name, while Isambart, of course, was a scholar. But nobody ever questioned such depositions and the notary's signature was the only one that was required.

It was decided, after some deliberation, for the sake of neatness, that Pierre was seven years old.

The first winter of Pierre's residence in his new home was one of unparalleled activity for the shop. Never since Hugh had first settled in Rouen had so many men required new armor.

The war had begun to go against the English. Many Frenchmen believed that the spirit of the Maid was still on earth, working in the hearts of the factious lords of France and rallying them round their king. On a higher level the sovereigns of Europe calculated the political significance of the death of the great Burgundian lady who had married the Englishman, John Plantagenet, Duke of Bedford, Regent of France. She was sister to Philip the Good, the magnificent Duke of

Burgundy, which was almost a kingdom within the kingdom of France, and by far the most powerful part of it. While she lived, France was divided. When she died, France moved toward the coalition which was one day to end the war.

Both in times of uneasy truce and in times like the present, when the whole country was disturbed, Hugh was the busiest armorer in Rouen. His reputation was enviable. One of his clients, clad in full plate, was known to have swum a river. Another had saved his life in a melee by jumping over his own horse.

So lightly did Hugh's armor press upon the body, and so freely did the cunning metal joints move, that men forgot they were armed until they felt the snap of an arrow or the stinging impact of a cross-bow bolt that the steel turned aside.

A lance, no matter how well aimed or how heavy the man behind it, glanced harmlessly off his cuirasses because Hugh joined his plates so as to allow no surface to oppose the point, and polished them like Venetian glass.

Even flat on his back a man might still be safe for a while since, for all their smooth working, the joints were so closely riveted that a slender dagger could not penetrate between them.

And as for a sword blow, many a sword had been broken or hope-lessly dulled by the temper of Hugh's Milanese steel.

The forge roared from morning till night. With mighty hammers Hugh and Abdul pounded the ingots of spongy, white-hot iron till the fragments of slag were forced out like seeds from the mass of fruit in the wine press, and the pure, virgin metal remained. This they wrought with constant reheating on a dozen different anvils and stakes of vary-ing sizes and shapes: concave, convex, or intricately curved. Some of them looked like parts of a human body, mysteriously reversed. And indeed it was one of the secrets of Hugh's speed that his anvils were shaped like men.

The pieces altered under the blows. The white heat waned and the iron turned orange and then dull red. To Pierre it seemed that limbs were growing before his eyes, or a head forming on the anvil that was shaped like a pear.

Little by little they had coaxed him into the shop; and though he never forgot the fear of fire, he learned to live with it again.

The final dimensions of each piece were measured with great precision to fit the body of each client, for an ill fitting suit of armor was a source of great fatigue and even danger to the wearer. To

27

accomplish this the edges were trimmed hot with heavy shears. Among his other chores it was Pierre's duty to pick up these dangerous hot pieces with a little metal shovel on a long handle and throw them into the pile of scrap in the corner. They were fine wrought iron, capable of being transformed into steel. They could always be used for gauntlets, which protected the hands, or sollerets, which covered the feet and looked like shoes. These intricate pieces of armor were composed of small parts delicately fitted and riveted together.

It was Hugh's invariable custom, before a suit of plate was hardened and riveted, to try it first on the body of the client. No matter how great the lord or how pressing his affairs, he must perforce stand in his gambeson on the dais in the corner of Hugh's shop while he and Abdul tried the unfinished pieces with temporary rivets for size.

Thus Pierre saw the rulers of the realm in their leather underwear raising their arms and flexing their legs at the command of a commoner or the injunction of a servant. Hugh assumed that such training accounted for Pierre's lack of awe before the great, the noble, and the rich.

At night, during this busy time, the finished parts were packed into a big fire-clay chest with small chips of green wood. A fire-clay cover was placed over the chest to confine the vapors which would be generated inside when the chest was heated till the clay glowed red. Then there would appear over the lid mysterious, dark-blue flames; and that would mean that the iron in the chest was changing into steel. Nobody knew why. But the metal that went in could be hammered, stretched, filed, sheared, and punched; and the metal that came out could not be worked at all.

The process took some time. A breastplate, which was less than an eighth of an inch in thickness, required only half an hour. But the skull of a helm, which might be a quarter of an inch, required three.

This was thick, even for a helm, which ought properly to be thicker than any other piece of armor. But Hugh had observed that his English customers were happier when they could feel honest weight on their heads, and since confidence is half the battle, here at least he let them feel the weight of his steel.

If the hardening went on too long, the metal was brittle. A strong blow of a mace would shatter it like glass. If stopped too soon, the metal retained the characteristics of iron. It was soft to the sword, and a strong man could carve it like cheese.

Red hot, the virgin steel was thrust into a tub of clean rain water.

On emerging it was glass hard, but inclined to be brittle. All good armorers knew this. Then, to render the steel less likely to crack, the temper must be drawn, and to accomplish this most armorers simply held the piece in the fire until the surface appeared deep blue. They attempted to blue it evenly, which was a difficult feat and a measure of their skill, especially when large pieces of unequal thickness were involved.

But at this stage in the process, Hugh locked the door and secured the shutters and sent Pierre to bed, for even his adopted son was still too young to be trusted with the secret of why the armor of Hugh of Milan was so hard and so tough.

Then there would sweep up from the shop an odor of boiling olive oil. It leaked out into the street and caused the neighbors to cross themselves, because the armorer and his Turkish servant were up to their Devil's cookery again.

Boiling in olive oil to draw the temper of steel was a secret which Hugh shared with a few of his brethren in Milan, but with no one at all in France.

# CHAPTER

## ✤ 6 ✤

THERE WAS a young commoner named Jacques Coeur, one of the educated merchants of whom Isambart had spoken. Though a Frenchman, devoted to the French cause, he had come to the English city of Rouen in wartime, just when it was rumored that Rouen itself might soon become the center of warlike operations.

It was not so difficult as might be imagined to gain entrance to the city, since the gates were opened every day for trade with the peasants of the surrounding district. What was more natural than the appearance of another young farmer with a cartload of excellent, late-season cabbages, drawn by a strong fat mule? The honest English guards passed him at once. Nobody carried identification papers because there was almost no paper and hardly anybody could read.

Jacques Coeur with his cabbages did not go to the market place, but instead he led his beast immediately to the house of Hugh of Milan. He stopped in the courtyard behind the kitchen. To the neighbors, who saw him enter, it seemed that he took a long time to sell his vegetables. But when he emerged two days later, his cart was observed to be empty. And the armorer, who consumed such unthinkable quantities of olive oil, was now believed to have developed a passion for cabbages.

Maria took him at first for the peasant that he appeared, but his manners were so good and the speech of his greeting so elegant that she was instantly on her guard.

"God bless you, too, young man. But what do you want?"

"Observe, gracious lady, with what excellent cabbages the Virgin

30

has blessed my little farm! I have come to see whether I could sell some to the illustrious armorer, Hugh of Milan."

"I buy the cabbages in this house, my fine fellow. But my husband you shall see, and this instant, for you are not what you seem."

"Indeed I am not," he answered with an engaging smile. "Shall I follow you into the shop, or shall I wait here in your charming kitchen?"

Maria hesitated. No one was allowed unbidden in the shop, but neither did she want her treasured pots and skillets to disappear.

"I doubt if you've come to steal," she observed. "Nay, wait here and warm your soft white hands before the fire. Your little farm, indeed!"

"It was the only way I could get into Rouen," Coeur said. "I must see your husband."

Maria walked straight into the shop where Hugh was sweating at the forge. Above the hammering of Abdul and the scraping of Clement and Ambrose, who were filing down to the fine guidelines that Hugh had graven on their work, she shouted into her husband's ear that there was a stranger in the house who knew their name and who might be a French spy.

*"Peste!"* muttered Hugh. "These times."

Maria followed him as he strode into the kitchen, the image of a petulant Vulcan. Sweat furrowed the soot on his cheeks. His big hand still held the enormous hammer that, in his haste, he had neglected to lay aside.

"This is my husband, young man. And this, Hugh, is a peddling peasant who talks like a nobleman. And take a look at his hands."

Hugh grunted. "You've been growing inkhorns, from the spots on your fingers. And your nails are very white for a peasant's. Who are you, my young imposter, and how do you know my name?"

The young man laughed. "Good master armorer, everybody in France knows your name. I am Jacques Coeur, a merchant, and the spots on my hands are indeed ink, as you so quickly guessed. It was necessary for me to adopt this disguise or I could never have entered Rouen. My visit is entirely peaceful and commercial, and I pray you, put down that hammer."

Hugh remembered his manners and laid the tool aside. "You came unannounced," he said half apologetically. "I was working, as you see. I am always working these days. You're a Frenchman, by your speech."

"I am the subject of His Grace, the King," Coeur answered simply.

31

"Which Grace? His English Grace, King Henry, or His French Grace, King Charles? Or perhaps the Duke of Burgundy. France is full of Graces."

"I am for King Charles, whom I know," said Coeur. "He has trusted me with a mission of considerable importance in the East. If you had the leisure, I might speak with you at length about the king's good qualities."

"I am an Italian," Hugh replied, "and I am little interested in French politics. The fine armor I make is my whole business in life, and, within reasonable limits, I do not care who wears it."

"It was that that I came to talk to you about."

"A merchant does not generally need armor," Hugh said, appraising the confident young man.

"In the East, he might, Master Hugh. I do not want to go all cased in steel like one of your knights, because my mission is civil, diplomatic, and ought not to be dangerous. But it may become so at any time, and the daggers of the Orient are said to be swift and sharp."

"They are," said Hugh, who knew something about them.

"I have come all the way from France," said Coeur, meaning that he had crossed through the ill defined frontier country between the warring nationalities, "to beg of the art of the most famous armorer in Christendom a cuirass of steel that can be worn under my merchant's gown, and a thin cap, if you can invent one, that will not be visible under the folds of my ordinary hat, but will protect my skull from an unexpected blow. It should be very thin."

Maria saw the glint come into her husband's eye and the lines of his forehead wrinkle in concentration. This was exactly the sort of work that he most enjoyed. It was unusual and it tried his skill. She set a cup of wine before each of the men, and around Hugh's sweaty shoulders she threw a fur blanket so that he would not catch cold. Then he did indeed look like something from the pagan underworld.

"The cuirass I can make for you, and quickly too, Jacques Coeur. Perhaps it had better be a complete jacket, however, so as to protect the back as well. My servant is a Turk, and he has told me some of the habits of the men among whom you plan to mingle."

"A good idea. I had not thought of that," Coeur said.

"About the cap, I am not so sure. My helms are proof against any weapons a man can wield, and so light that I have been asked to make them heavier. But this little cap you desire, this little skin of steel over the top of your head, I do not know."

"If it is a matter of money for the extra work—the extra skill—"

Hugh made a deprecatory gesture. "It is not a matter of money. Not that I despise money, young man. It is simply that your request is so very unusual, so very difficult. Anyone can make you a miserable little steel cap. But one that is thin enough to be comforable night and day, tough enough to turn a determined blow, one that won't fall off— the balance is all wrong you know—I suppose I could thicken the rim just a trifle, and I do have some very unusual iron. . . ."

"You will do it?"

"I will try. But I warn you that the iron fell out of the sky. I polished a patch of it, and it has never rusted. I have kept it for just such an order. Are you afraid of shooting stars, Jacques Coeur?"

"I am not afraid of meteoric iron, Hugh of Milan."

"Nobody ought to be. It's remarkable stuff. Some meteors make exceptionally hard blades. This one I shall forge into your little cap. I hope it protects your head, which appears to be a good one."

Next day Jacques Coeur was allowed in the shop since there was no tempering going on. Clement and Ambrose wondered that a peasant should be ordering armor, but it was soon apparent to them that Jacques Coeur was no peasant, nor was he ordering ordinary armor.

On hearing that the new client was about to embark on a voyage to the East, Abdul whispered something into the master's ear. Hugh laughed and nodded his head, and the delighted servant began some very elaborate preparations such as the apprentices had seldom seem. He cut a quantity of iron wires and thrust them, together with wooden chips, into a small hardening chest of fire clay. In an hour they were steel. He fashioned the front and back of the cuirass, leaving a little extra thickness in two places, which later he stretched with a light hammer and turned on a small rod to form two delicate hinges. While the work was still small and thick, long before the shape was near enough to try on the body of the client, he took the wires, heated them almost to the sparking point and hammered them into the iron so that the two shells which formed the cuirass were surfaced with a tangled web of hard steel embedded in the softer body of the iron. With further hammering the substance of the work thinned and the pattern of steel wires spread and flowed together like watered silk in a cardinal's cape. It was wholly beautiful, even before it was polished, and extremely tough, even before tempering. Jacques Coeur knew that he was in good hands.

Meanwhile Hugh heated the small lump of meteoric iron to white-

33

ness before he could dent it with the heaviest of his hammers. It behaved in a very refractory manner, as if reluctant to heat at all, but once hot, it continued to glow fiercely long after ordinary iron would have cooled. Though it yielded slowly to his blows, it gradually assumed a bowl shape under the hammer. Hugh spent the better part of the day at it and was stiff in all his joints with the protracted exertion before the cap was fitted, brought to a surface that could be polished, and ready for tempering. In fact Hugh wondered if it needed to be tempered at all. His hardest file would just touch it. He guessed it had better be hardened a bit more, but he decided to sleep on this important question. Before he bade his guest good night, he wrapped the cap in several folds of oxhide, out of habit; for Hugh was meticulously careful of smoothed surfaces, and it would never do to have Pierre or the apprentices scar it when they cleaned out the shop.

Everyone went to bed early that night, because they were all very tired. Jacques Coeur slept in Pierre's bed, and Pierre, the last to leave the shop after it was cleaned, crawled into the great bed with Hugh and Maria after supper.

Nobody knew how the accident occurred, but in the night Hugh smelled smoke. Instantly awake, he rushed into the shop, and there, piled too closely to the forge, a stack of wood was burning. There was no danger to the house, since the wood was stored on a stone shelf which was actually a part of the forge, but the pile of wood represented a whole day's supply of fuel and the cost of wood was higher every year. Hugh cursed noisily and thrust the whole mass within the opening of the forge, using a long iron rod so as not to burn his hands, and in doing so he noticed that the small fire-clay chest had been close to the pile, and now it, too, was in the fire. Well, there was no harm in that. He began to work the bellows to hasten the burning so that the fire would be safe to leave and he could go back to bed again. Just then Maria appeared at the door and reproached him for working so late.

"Saints, woman! I am not working. I am just trying to burn this fire out so I can get some sleep without the house burning down. One of the boys piled the wood too close and it took fire. I'll beat them! All of them! Every one, even Pierre. They won't sit down for a week!"

"Calm yourself, Hugh. You said yourself that you had never had the forge so hot as it was today when you were working on that man's silly little cap. Maybe the fire was still alive. The boys are careful. Perhaps the wood wasn't so close."

The fire began to assume more normal proportions, and as it dwindled so did Hugh's anger.

"Well, then, maybe I'll just beat them so they can't sit down for three days. But I maintain that the wood was too close, even though the forge may have been a little warm, as you say."

The figure of Pierre appeared behind Maria. Finding himself alone in the great bed and hearing the angry voice of his foster father, he had come to the shop to see what was the matter. And he thought he smelled smoke.

"Oh!" he cried, looking into the flames.

"Well, boy, look what you've done. There goes a whole day's supply of fuel. You did pile the wood, didn't you?"

"I helped," Pierre answered. "But look at the box!"

"Bother the box. That won't burn. It's the wood I'm angry about."

"But the little cap! I put it into the box to be safe. It was sort of balancing on the edge of the shelf. I thought it would be safer in the box."

"You put the cap—into the box?"

"Yes, Father."

"Leather and all? It was wrapped in leather."

"Certainly, Father. I would not have unwrapped it. I knew it was special. I saw you work all day on it."

Hugh reflected. In justice to the boy he must admit that he had laid the thing rather carelessly on the shelf. Perhaps it had appeared on the point of falling off. Anyway, there was nothing he could do about the matter now.

"Was there any wood in the box, Pierre?"

"I saw a few old burned pieces."

"No green chips?"

"No, just old bits of charcoal."

Hugh groaned.

What this Devil's mixture of charcoal and tanned oxhide might do to the iron of a shooting star better metallurgists than Hugh of Milan might well have refused to conjecture, and Hugh was very tired. A terrible stench was coming out of the box now and little green flames appeared about the lid.

"Well, what will happen will happen," sighed Hugh. "Perhaps the cap will be ruined. I don't even know how long to heat it with all that leather in there."

"Would you know how long if the leather were not there?" asked Maria slyly.

Hugh blurted the truth out miserably. "Oh, plague you, no. Of course not. There are too many unknowns."

"I think we had best go back to bed, my dear, since you don't know what you're doing. Get some rest, dear Hugh, and in the morning maybe the cap will be hard."

Hugh disliked having his wife tell him he did not know what he was doing, but since it was so patently true, he left the cap in the box and the box in the flames of the dying forge and shuffled off to bed, his feet chilly on the cold stone of the floor. All night long the box lay hot in the bed of coals, and in the morning it was still warm.

When they opened the box and looked inside next day, the cap lay embedded in a layer of black dust to which the leather had been reduced. It was stained brown with the oils and tanning chemicals that had boiled out of the hide, but there was no scale on it. It was not pitted, and it had held its shape. But there was no telling whether it was hard or soft.

Hugh snapped a fingernail against it. Instantly the room rang with a loud, clear, pure sustained note like a chime. Hugh's face relaxed. So far, so good. He tried it with a hard file, but he could not even remove a patch of stain.

"We must try it for brittleness," Hugh said, with some apprehension. "Much steel behaves like this, and then shatters at a blow."

He tapped it tentatively with a small hammer. Again the loud, clear, bell-like tone. Heavier taps at every point of the surface served only to increase the strength of the note.

"We must try it for bending," Hugh said, "but I dare not. I am afraid it will crack." And just to be on the safe side, he sent everybody out of the shop except Abdul and boiled the cap in olive oil for half an hour. Some of the stain boiled off and the surface appeared brighter than before. Hugh put the cap in a vise and tightened the jaws until the oval that had been fitted to the head of Jacques Coeur became a perfect circle.

"Now may St. Eloi restore it to its former shape again," breathed Hugh, and he loosened the jaws of the vise. The circle became an oval again.

"It is good, hard, tempered steel," he said. "As good as I ever made."

36

"May I try it with my sword, master?" asked Abdul.

Hugh started. The sword Abdul referred to was one he had made in Isfahan more than forty years ago. It was forged of steel from India. It never had to be sharpened and it would cut a rod of hard steel half the thickness of a man's thumb. The blade looked like a blue lake when the wind ruffles it in the sun, yet the surface was perfectly smooth. The steel for these swords had long been impossible to procure.

"You may break your sword, Abdul."

"I may break your little cap, master."

"I should be interested in the results of your experiment, but I cannot be responsible for your sword."

Abdul kept his sword in his room, and when the apprentices saw him bring it into the shop, which he did very seldom, they and Pierre grouped themselves around him with wide, expectant eyes. Hugh placed the cap on the anvil that was round like a man's head. The big Turk grasped his weapon and whirled it round his head with a peculiar twisting motion. The blade sang through the air like a whining wind and flashed down upon the cap with all the force of the arm that had lifted heavy hammers for half a century. There was a report like a bombard, and the air pulsed with the penetrating ring that they had heard before, but much louder this time. The cap spun on the anvil, which it did not quite fit, and as the note died away the edges tinkled clearly as they vibrated against the supporting metal. Jacques Coeur had never seen anything like it. But then, he had expected to be amazed. The apprentices, who were perhaps better judges of what they were witnessing, were awestruck. When the sword and cap were examined, neither had suffered the slightest damage.

Abdul polished the cap with Hugh's sharpest polishing sand and buffed it till it was so smooth that he could see his face in it.

"I had hoped to engrave a circlet of decorations about the rim," Hugh said, "but nothing will grave this steel. Yet, if you like, I can perhaps stencil on a simple design with sand."

"Make it a circlet of hearts, then," Coeur said. The young merchant was very much in love, and, in addition, he had adopted three hearts, a play on his name, as a part of the crest which, if his mission were successful, his king might bestow upon him with a grant of nobility. The hearts were put on.

When Jacques Coeur left the shop, with his mule and his empty cart, he wore under his peasant's disguise a miracle of steel. There was no price for such a thing, for such a thing had never been made

37

before, but Coeur pressed upon the armorer, and the armorer was glad to accept, a sum equivalent to the cost of several suits of full plate.

"He must be very rich," said Maria.

"He probably thinks we cannot repeat the performance," Abdul said. Abdul had serious doubts on this score himself.

"Perhaps we cannot," said Hugh of Milan. He ruffled Pierre's hair with his big, hard hand. "You can put all the caps you like into the hardening box, my boy!"

"We have no more shooting stars," Abdul observed.

"Oh, bother the shooting stars. There are plenty of oxen in the fields, Abdul. And the tanner who tanned the hide still lives in Rouen. Go to the tanner, Abdul, and buy me more, many more of those skins. It was the leather, Pierre. I know it was the leather, and that was your work."

# CHAPTER

## ❈ 7 ❈

IT WAS COMMON KNOWLEDGE among the peasantry that a French army was gathering under the Marshal de Boussac, and the object of his preparations was said to be Rouen itself, the very heart of the English power in France. Such daring on the part of the French bespoke a new confidence in their lazy king, and many of the English shook their heads in wonder. Even Hugh of Milan was incredulous.

Nicolas Midi, canon of the cathedral, who had preached the sermon at the burning of the Maid, had a deep and honest interest in the people and he warned them from the pulpit of Saint-Ouen that the hand of the Lord might come upon them. He exhorted them to search their consciences with extraordinary care. Let there be no soul so sinful and corrupt as to attract the Prince of Darkness and his legions into Rouen. If a man felt troubled, let him come and confess his sins and go away in a state of grace, which is good Christian living at any time, but especially in time of danger. For the Devil within the walls and a French army without would surely prove more than one city could withstand. The people did not particularly fear the French, for they were French themselves, but the horrendous character of the Devil emerged from the canon's perfervid sermons with such dramatic reality that it appeared almost as if the good man had spoken to him personally. The lines at the confessionals were long.

Isambart was now permanently attached to the cloister of the cathedral, and the canon encouraged him to add to his spiritual duties the practical mission of warning the people to lay in supplies of food, particularly flour, grain, fat, oil, root vegetables, nuts, raisins, and large supplies of meat, which could be salted and preserved. Meat was

39

especially important in a siege, but it was always a great luxury among the poor; and now, just when it was needed most, it appeared to have vanished from the face of the earth. For the farmers, who always seemed to know everything first, drove their cattle into the forests and hid their pigs in their cottage lofts under the hay. When the frightened city folk went out into the countryside to do their own buying, they were able to purchase only a few elderly goats, which were suddenly alleged to be tasty, nourishing, and of additional value since they could be milked, if one knew how. One did not, the farmers asserted, milk a pig, of course.

As the year wore away to its end, the tension increased. Long before twilight the gates of the city were secured, the bridges drawn up and the heavy portcullises let down. The burghers who were caught without or the peasants who were surprised within the walls were questioned with great thoroughness by the guards before they were allowed to pass the barriers next day. Even then they were likely to go without breakfast, for the gates were not opened until noon and the inns were not anxious to serve strangers. The markets were crowded; prices were high, but the people bought anyway. Actually the city was bulging with food, though nobody would admit it. Hugh, like everyone else, had a cache of provisions that he never mentioned to the neieghbors, and Maria had a secret little hoard that she never mentioned to Hugh.

Then the French army appeared and the gates were never let down at all.

One day a French herald, faultlessly armed and chosen for his magnificent voice, rode up to the gate and loudly demanded that it be opened forthwith in the name of His Grace, King Charles, who had been crowned king of France and who demanded his city.

An English herald from the walls answered just as loudly that the gate would not be opened and that the city belonged to King Henry, who had also been crowned king of France and who intended to keep his property. With courteous threats the French herald proclaimed that the attacking army was overwhelmingly strong and that resistance was worse than useless, because it was known that Rouen would starve in a week. The English herald replied that Rouen was provisioned till judgment day and could hold out until that time and more. A vulgar pikeman, perhaps a little drunk in all the excitement, threw a leg of mutton at the shining envoy below, in defiance of all the laws of chivalry, to show how much food they really had. The disgusted

Frenchman then shouted the *défi* of King Charles with great feeling, and threw down his gauntlet so hard that they heard it ring even within the walls. His page picked it up and returned it to him; they backed their horses three or four paces, dramatically and skillfully, demonstrating their reluctance to turn their back on the enemy, and then wheeled round in perfect unison and rode proudly back to France.

Except for the unhappy incident of the leg of mutton, the ceremonial preliminaries to death and destruction had been flawlessly executed. No one could get into Rouen and no one could get out. In a few days the stones and arrows began to fall, and here and there on the walls and in the streets men began to suffer wounds from the flying missles. At first Hugh ordered Pierre to remain in the house day and night. However, it was not customary for a determined attack to be made on a city directly following the opening of hostilities. For many weeks activities were confined to long-range shots from bows and arbalests and a few stones from the catapults that had been erected just out of range of these effective hand weapons. When Hugh concluded that no innovation was to be expected in the normal leisurely procedure of siegecraft, he allowed Pierre the same liberty in the streets as other boys, deeming it wise to acquaint him with the dangers of life that everybody else faced and that he would have to face, too, whether he became a monk, merchant, or armorer.

The quasi-military status that his craft accorded him opened many doors to Hugh, for the fighting men of all classes were glad to welcome the expert who made armor that was reputed to be impenetrable. On one occasion Hugh was invited to the castle, which overlooked the walls, and was, in fact, an integral and powerful part of them. Pierre begged so persistently to be taken along, and Maria so inexplicably did not forbid it, that Hugh, at first hesitantly and then with great pride, let him come.

Pierre's first sight of war proved so absorbing that he innocently exposed himself at one of the open spaces of the battlement where the English sergeant took them for a better view. Instantly there was a heavy English hand on his head that sent him sprawling to the floor, and before he had more than half risen, Hugh gave him an exceedingly swift kick in the backside that lifted him bodily behind the protection of the merlons.

"With a head like that you'll draw the fire of the whole French army," the sergeant warned him.

They waited for what they knew would happen.

There was a whirring in the air and a smack against the wall behind them, and something metal dropped to the floor, followed by a noisy little shower of splintered stone. Hugh picked up the bolt. It was a stubby cylinder of iron with a sharp point and a little tail of leather that steadied it in flight. It was a crossbow quarrel, the deadly missile that the Church had forbidden.

"This thing would now be in your head, Pierre, but for the quick hand of the sergeant," Hugh said. "I told you to stay away from the crenels."

Pierre had learned that war could be as dangerous to the rear as to the fore, an important tactical discovery.

"I am sorry, Father," he said, rubbing his rump. "I was watching an arbalester fitting the bolt to his bow."

"Which one?" asked the sergeant, who knew the members of the group against him pretty well by now.

"He has a conical helm with an open face—"

"So have they all," the sergeant replied.

"Well, this one is missing his camail. He came out from behind a rock. I was surprised to see him so close."

"Ah, now, that's something. We must remind him not to expose his neck or he'll catch cold. Ho, there, Albert?"

One of his men came running up. "Yes, sir?"

"There's a Frenchman down there," he said in English, "who wants to start a war." Everybody laughed at his reference to the eighty-year-old conflict. "Behind the rock. You know the rock I mean?"

"I certainly do. They are always sneaking up there."

"He's lost his camail. Do you think you could persuade him to be less careless of his dress?"

"It will be a pleasure," the archer replied with a broad grin, and he selected a long, straight, polished arrow with care.

"What are you going to do?" Pierre asked with a frightened look.

"The boy speaks English, Master Hugh?"

"English from you people; he hears it on the street all the time. Italian from me, and French from his own parents."

"Just tickle him pleasantly," the sergeant said with an exaggerated wink that was lost on Pierre.

With infinite care and great skill the archer took several quick peeks around the edge of the crenel, his arrow ready, his bow half drawn. Then with a sudden quick step he backed away from the wall, leaning his body sideways only far enough to clear the protecting

42

masonry. He snapped the feather back to his shoulder and let fly. There was a twang from the string and a hiss in the air, followed immediately by a great angry shout from below.

"Did you tickle him, Albert?"

"Exactly as you ordered, sergeant."

"Where?"

"In the neck."

"But you didn't hurt him, did you, Albert?"

"On my honor, he didn't feel a thing."

"See, Pierre? We wouldn't hurt the Frenchies. Would we, boys?"

"No, no! Oh, God, no!" came back a chorus of hearty voices.

Pierre tried to laugh at the joke, too, but he had never been closer to war than the shop, and his first taste of killing as an art was disconcerting and suddenly hateful.

"I know what you did!" he cried angrily.

"Well, Pierre," said Hugh, "he tried to kill you, didn't he?"

"Yes, I suppose he did."

"Well?"

Hugh shrugged his shoulders and raised his eyebrows while he extended his expressive Italian hands, palms up. He looked very hard at his stepson.

Thereafter, as long as he lived, whenever he saw men die, Pierre half remembered the utter finality of his foster father's gesture.

# CHAPTER

## ❊ 8 ❊

ONLY ONE IMPORTANT ATTACK was made during the short siege, and it came perilously close to success. Some of the French succeeded in scaling the walls of the castle. There was fighting up and down its old corridors and even the courts within the walls, and for a time it appeared that the fortress might fall.

But the attackers were not reenforced. The ladders were overturned with long poles and the dead and dying were hurled from the walls, the officers being held to ransom, as usual.

Although he had suffered only a minor defeat, with the loss of comparatively few men, the Marshal de Boussac suddenly lifted the siege and marched away with his army. The English felt, with some justification, that the stubbornness of their defense had convinced the French of the futility of the attack. But the captured French officers maintained that the marshal's men were quarreling over the division of the loot that they expected from the fall of the city. The net result of the operation was to leave the city undisturbed to celebrate its deliverance and consume its vast stores of unsavory provisions. Bonfires were lighted in the street, tuns of wine were broached for whoever cared to drink it, and bands of English pikemen and archers linked their arms and staggered through the narrow alleys, kissing the girls and singing that the king of France and all his men had marched up the hill and then marched down again.

On the anniversary of the lifting of the siege, Nicolas Midi preached a powerful sermon on the subject of repentance at a solemn votive mass of Our Lady in thanksgiving for the deliverance of the city.

Within the sanctuary, clad in his white surplice, his head as golden as the cross in the light of a hundred candles, stood Pierre, who had caught the eye of the canon and been taught the elaborate and graceful ritual required to serve at the altar. The canon's sermons were far beyond the comprehension of his ten-year-old intellect, but he knew and understood that the wine which he held in his right hand and the water he held in his left, when mixed in the chalice the canon reached out to him, were miraculously transformed into the blood of God, and that was a wonderful thing. When he raised his head, at the Elevation of the Host, he gazed, as he had been taught, at the pure white wafer in the priest's hands, which Our Lord was that very instant changing into his own crucified body; and if he did not always feel the exaltation that the ancient miracle ought properly to invoke (and he admitted that sometimes his attention wandered), he was told that the exaltation would come in time, when he was older, when he knew more of life, and when the promise of redemption could be understood in all its compassionate fullness.

The canon was vastly taken with Pierre, and along with the Latin responses he had taught him a great deal of Latin grammar and the Latin words for everyday things. Pierre discovered that Latin was not only the language of the Mass, but that it was the daily vehicle of speech among thousands of European scholars and statesmen, so that a man might travel over all Christendom and make himself understood in any country.

"But in heathen countries they speak Turkish," Pierre said. "Abdul has told me many of the words."

"That is good," replied Midi. "Maybe some day you will go to the East and teach them to be Christian."

Midi had been sick intermittently ever since the burning of Jeanne d'Arc. Today he appeared to have one of his attacks of trembling, and as Pierre lifted his eyes to the Host, he thought he saw it flutter like the wing of a bird. He hoped the priest was not going to drop it, though he knew his part in the ceremony if such a lamentable accident should occur.

Then he noticed that there was a scarlet splotch on the canon's thumb, as if blood had dropped on it; and when he bowed his head again, he prayed a frightened little prayer, because he felt that Our Lord might be reminding him not to let his attention wander.

As he scampered home after the Mass, he met Nicol the Chirurgeon with a big bottle under his arm.

"Good morning, Pierre," the chirurgeon called cheerily.

"Good morning to you, Master Nicol," answered Pierre with some

45

apprehension, because the old man always talked too long, and he was hungry.

"God keep you in good health, even though I starve, and indeed you appear to be under some special protection. I never saw you look so well, boy."

"I am well, thank you, sir. So are my father and mother and Abdul and Clement and Ambrose." Had he not quickly said so, Nicol would have inquired about their several healths tediously, one by one, with a separate benison on each.

"Will you run a little errand for me, Pierre?"

"Why, yes, of course. But I ought to hurry home. Father is taking me out into the country today."

"I truly need your legs, Pierre. They are faster than mine, and right now I ought to be in two places at once, which is possible only to an angel, which I am not yet."

"May you be one soon," Pierre replied courteously, and then caught himself in confusion. "Nay, I said the wrong thing. May you never be an angel, good Master Nicol."

"That is hardly better, lad. But I thank you for what you meant to say. I should this moment be in the cell of good Father Isambart, delivering to him this bottle of precious oil, which, with God's help, will restore the health of the canon Nicolas Midi. And I should also be at the bedside of a poor sick woman who is suffering from a violent commingling of the humors, which have so run together and disturbed the temperature of her body that at one moment she is all hot and another all cold, starting at little noises and scolding her husband unmercifully. Many women suffer thus."

"It is a dreadful affliction," said Pierre, "but I do not understand these things."

"Few people do," replied the chirurgeon with great honesty. "But I have a sovereign remedy to uncommingle her humors, which is no less than the essence of a rare Persian herb. It will quiet her temper and put her to sleep. But it is costly and ought properly to be saved for chirurgical operations. Will you take this bottle to Father Isambart?"

"Yes, yes," cried Pierre, who was sure he could have made the short trip to the cloister behind the church and been home again by now. He reached out his hand impatiently. The chirurgeon held back the bottle.

"Take care, Pierre! Gently, gently carry this bottle. It is half full

46

of the oil of the chalmoogra tree. It has come all the way from India and is worth more than the ship that brought it. There is not another drop in all France. Perhaps I had better carry it myself."

"Nay, master, I shall carry it gently," and Pierre took the bottle into his hands as reverently as he handled the sacred things in church. "If it will cure the canon, I shall carry it gently, but I did not know he was sick."

"Do not say that I told you so. You know how people talk about the canon ever since the Maid's lamentable death. Now run along. Nay, do not run. Walk ever so carefully, Pierre."

"Yes, Master Nicol." He was greatly relieved to see the elderly chirurgeon actually start on his way again, his old back straight as an arrow, his tall velvet hat shining in the sunshine, his long staff tapping confidently over the cobblestones.

Pierre found Isambart in his cell, and was surprised to find that the canon was there, too, in a long gray gown such as penitents sometimes wore.

"I have brought you your medicine, Father," Pierre said.

"Where did you get that bottle, Pierre?" the canon asked. His face was flushed, and he looked angry. The splotch was still on his thumb.

"I am sorry if I have done wrong, Father. I met the chirurgeon, Nicol, who was called to uncommingle some humors of a very sick woman. He begged me to deliver this bottle."

"He should have delivered it himself," snapped the canon.

"I don't think he could have chosen a more reliable messenger," observed Isambart.

"How so, Father?" Midi asked.

"Because, Father, this boy has a special, well, let us say a special skill with his hands, which he has acquired in his stepfather's shop. You know how dexterous he is at the altar."

"That is true," said Midi. "Did old prattlemouth say what was in the bottle?"

"No, Father. Nay, I am lying. He did tell me. It is a precious oil with a long name. It comes from India. He said it would restore your health."

"And then he told you not to mention that you had learned I was sick, isn't that true?"

"Yes, that is true," Pierre said in great confusion.

"Ah, well, 'tis but a little lie. Remember it at your next confession, but it will not be held against you."

47

He reached out his hand as if to lay it on Pierre's head in a blessing, but he withdrew it again. Pierre looked a little frightened, for Midi had often blessed him in this familiar manner, and now he felt perhaps he did not deserve it because of his lie. Midi instantly divined his thoughts and signed the cross over him and blessed him so fervently that Pierre knew he was forgiven. "Perhaps I am sicker than anyone knows," the canon said. "Would you like to stay for breakfast?"

Pierre flushed at the honor. He would be the envy of the neighborhood if he could say he had taken breakfast in the cloister.

"Truly I should like to stay, and I thank you for the offer. But Father is taking me out into the country today and I must hurry home."

"Out into the country? Why?" Isambart asked.

"We are going to the farm he owns. The man has not paid the rent."

"Oh, well, then, hurry along. I hope, I hope very sincerely in fact, that you can have breakfast with me some other time."

"I do, too, Father; thank you again for asking me."

After the boy had gone, the canon remarked: "I think I hope it more than he does, Isambart."

From the familiarity of the address, Isambart knew that his superior was very disturbed indeed.

In an hour or so Nicol the Chirurgeon knocked at the cloister gate and was conducted at once into the presence of the canon, who had returned to his own apartments.

"Is my illness so critical, Master Chirurgeon, that you could not bring the oil yourself?"

"I crave your pardon, Reverend Father. I did not know how long I would be detained. I was called to uncommingle the humors—"

"I know all about the poor woman's humors and your uncommingulation, Master Nicol."

"Ah. Pierre then arrived safely with the oil. But he should not have mentioned the condition of my patient. It is not ethical. I trust that is all he said."

"I never knew a boy less prone to gossip," replied the canon.

"Good, good, Reverend Father. And now would it please the Reverend Father graciously to discover his chest?"

The canon opened his garments. The doctor held aside the folds of the robe with a little polished baton. It was the one that he used during major chirurgical operations and with which he pointed to the parts to be cut.

48

"There is a great improvement, a very great improvement," he murmured. "I think I have never seen so sudden a change for the better in all my treatment of these cases."

"What cases, Master Nicol?"

The chirurgeon looked very grave. "Yesterday I felt I knew, and by today I was sure I could diagnose the disease with certainty. I was prepared to impart sad tidings to you, Reverend Father. But today I am not so sure. Perhaps you will not need the oil."

The canon looked as if he were being tortured.

"My bodily pain is often severe," he lamented bitterly, "but I am not afraid of pain. It is the dreadful uncertainty. Sometimes I feel I am under a curse, and yet I have tried to lead a good life. There were others at the trial. Greater men than I. Men of greater learning. Men of higher authority. Last year it was only a little fever. A little scaly rash. For a long time it went away."

"I know, I know, Reverend Father."

"It was never like this before. And this morning," he cried, his voice rising almost out of control, "this morning I could not feel the Host in my hands at the Elevation! Could not feel!" He was shouting now. "I say I could not feel! Man! Man! Do you know what that means?"

"I had not wished to suggest that dread symptom, Your Reverence. But I do not say it is unexpected."

*"Miserere mei!* What is to become of my work? The enlargement of the cathedral? The repairs to the roof? And the people—they ate goat's meat for three months after the siege. Hated it, too. But if the siege had been longer, they would have been glad of the goat's meat, and it was I, Nicolas Midi, who warned them to lay up the stores. I do not deserve this fate. And then, when Pierre brought the oil and you did not come yourself, I said in my weak heart: Behold, even the physician is afraid of me. He has made up his mind, and I am lost."

"The woman's illness was desperate, or so I was led to believe."

"I should not reproach you, Master Nicol. Your kindness and devotion to the sick are too well known. If you cannot save me, perhaps God will, and if he will not, then His will be done." Nicolas Midi and Nicol the Chirurgeon crossed themselves reverently.

"Perhaps He has already saved you, Father. The spots are gone today."

Midi examined his chest attentively, and then held up his hands before his face.

"I would swear there was a mark on my thumb before Mass." He

49

puzzled a moment. "Even later," he said. "Yes, I distinctly noted it in the cell of Brother Isambart."

"It is not there now, Father. And if my art and my prayers can aught avail, it shall never return."

Midi smiled for the first time during the visit. "I like a doctor who says his prayers. Too many of you take all the credit to yourselves."

Nicol the Chirurgeon bowed in acknowledgement, and asked, "Are you sure the spot was there this morning?"

"I can tell you exactly when I last saw it. I was going to lay my hand on the boy's head in a blessing, and I saw the spot and I did not touch him."

The doctor shook his head. "I think you had best take the chalmoogra oil, Reverend Father. All you can retain. It is nauseous stuff."

When he went out, he was still shaking his head in bewilderment, which was common among his brethren of the long robe but sufficiently rare in Nicol, a truly great chirurgeon.

It was toward evening next day that Hugh and Pierre returned from their visit to the farm. As they approached the wall of the city, they hurried the last part of the way for fear the gates would be closed.

The sun was sinking behind a rounded mass of piled-up clouds that looked solid enough to sit upon. The whole countryside was ruddy with a suffused, shadowless glow; the walls of Rouen shone like copper, and the details of the landscape stood out in the sharp relief that a warm light always produces. Not a leaf trembled on its stem. The wheat stood motionless in the fields, stalk by stalk, individually discernible, so utterly quiet that the eternal work of creation seemed momentarily to have been suspended. Then the great bells of Saint-Ouen filled the empty air with a torrent of welcome sound in which all the other churches of Rouen joined with their lighter tongues. It was Vespers, the hour when a man laid down his work and straightened his back and thanked God, before suppertime, that another day had brought him no harm.

As the deep tide of sound echoed and ebbed away, it was replaced by the persistent ringing of a harsh little bell far down the road. A small group of monks with a man set apart in their midst, followed by a squad of pikemen and crossbowmen, slowly approached. As they came closer, Hugh was startled to note that the monks who were leading the procession held long ecclesiastical candles, but they had been extinguished and they were held upside down so that their blackened wicks pointed toward the earth. The man in the center was clad in a gray penitent's robe. Their faces were all sad and stern.

"Keep your distance!" shouted the monk in the lead. "And keep to windward," he added, glancing up at the leaves which had begun to dance in a slight breeze.

"Saints!" muttered Hugh, and crossed himself. He and Pierre scrambled off the road.

The man in the center of the group, stripped of every garment that distinguished his ecclesiastical position, was Nicolas Midi. The bell was knotted to a cord at his waist and it rang its warning at every step of his naked, red feet. His hands were pressed palm to palm in front of his breast in the attitude of prayer, and the thumbs formed the cross as they did at Mass. Pierre saw the spot on his thumb, bigger than before, redder, and swollen now, as well. During the twenty-four hours that Pierre had been in the country with Hugh, the leprosy of the canon had unmistakably manifested itself. With a speed that was necessary in such cases, the Church had instantly deprived him of his canonicate and designated a solitary distant hospital, where monks who had taken the sternest of vows would care for him as long as he lived, and restrain him, if his mind should wander, from escaping and endangering the world with his contagion. No one knew better than Midi that in time their prayers for his deliverance would become more and more explicitly prayers for his deliverance through death, and that at the end they would push him his food at the end of long sticks, lest his loathsomeness contaminate them and prevent their ministering to others. He would not blame them. He might last twenty years.

His thoughts were too taken up with the enormity of his own misfortune to dwell long on his favorite altar boy, but out of habit he started to raise his hand in a blessing and a farewell to the bright young acolyte who now certainly would never have breakfast with him. But he could see that Pierre was having difficulty recognizing his blotched and altered countenance.

The former canon turned his face away in shame, pressed his palms together again, and walked on, the little bell ringing.

# CHAPTER

## ❊ 9 ❊

THE WAR with England had gone on for so long that generations of men had lived and died considering it the normal way of life. But only a few months after the melancholy affliction of the Canon of Rouen, a colorful conclave of all the kings in Christendom met at Arras to conclude a treaty whose high purpose was to bring peace to the whole world.

But in spite of their feeble hold on their French possessions, the English found the French terms unbearable. Led by the regent, the Duke of Bedford, whose strength, like the strength of his armies, was failing, they walked out of the council chamber with a righteous conviction of outrage, which had so long been a source of strength to that indomitable race of islanders, and stoutly declared their resolution to continue the war.

But the Duke of Burgundy, their ally, remembered that he was French. He forgot his ancient wrongs. In front of all the rulers of Europe, he kissed King Charles, called him brother, and changed sides completely, not without concessions which rendered him almost an independent sovereign, leaving the foreigners without a friend. Vast stretches of France, including Pierre's province of Normandy, remained indeed in English hands; but Bedford soon died, and the fighting languished.

One immediate result of the treaty was the abandonment of Paris to Charles, who for the first time in his life could now enter the capital of his kingdom.

In the absence of the stimulation of war, the people were listless and discontented. Nobody worked very hard any more, and so instead of growing fat they grew lean, and a succession of droughts and poor harvests aggravated their misfortune.

Even Hugh, the busiest armorer in Rouen, noticed a falling off in his business and rarely now was the forge alight after Vespers. But there was always plenty to eat in the house, and under one of the stones in the floor of his shop there was hidden a helm full of golden rose nobles, saved for Pierre's education; and there was another cache as well. Even Maria did not know where that was.

The economic well-being of the nobles ran a vulgar parallel to the fortunes of the peasantry. Many a baron complained that his tenants no longer paid their rents on time, giving as an excuse that there was a blight on the wheat or that no rain had fallen, which indeed he could see with his own eyes, but never lifting a hand to harvest what they might well have saved. The cities suffered especially, not only because trade was at a low ebb, but by reason of the great numbers of farmers who had left their unproductive fields, and multitudes of French soldiers who had been left without a war to fight and who naturally gravitated toward the centers of population. There they were more welcome than on the farms, which in wartime they had been all too apt to plunder.

In the several years of undeclared peace that followed the Treaty of Arras, Hugh found a great deal more leisure to devote to Pierre's upbringing. He initiated him into the secret of the boiling oil and between them they made many experiments in hardening steel, heating it first with leather and bits of wood, then with leather alone, and finally with the ashes of leather. This proved best of all, giving a tough steel of remarkable hardness and even temper, though they could never duplicate the cap.

Pierre suffered a floreate rash of pimples when he was thirteen, but they disappeared when he was fourteen, and a black growth of beard began to smudge his upper lip and his chin, which had recently developed a manly prominence. So had another, less conspicuous member, and what function that might serve bewildered the young man until Hugh explained its utility with great delicacy and considerable enthusiasm. Isambart further explained that it was one of the things of the world that a priest must forego, and thenceforth Pierre was irrevocably lost to the priesthood. Abdul fashioned him a folding razor and made him a double steel mirror to shave in. One side made his face look alarmingly large, and the other ridiculously small. One could also light fires with it in a magical manner. "It is not really magic," Abdul said, "though it looks like it."

It was a habit of Abdul's to sing softly in Turkish as he worked, and often when a piece was done, he would hold it up and express his satisfaction in his own native tongue. Pierre, who already spoke English, French, and Italian, would sometimes repeat the phrase after him, often with such exactitude that Abdul requested and Hugh gave him permission to teach the boy Turkish.

"Another language is always good, my old friend," said Hugh, "though I wish it were Latin you could teach him."

"Latin is the answer to Turkish, master, as the Cross is the answer to the Crescent. Let him learn the lesser first, the greater last, as I did."

"By all means," Hugh agreed. "But are you sure you don't just want company for your heathen tongue?"

"He is very apt," Abdul answered, "but it is partly true that I do long to hear the soft sounds of the East in another than my cracked old voice."

"Listen to Pierre's cracked young one, then," Hugh laughed.

"It hasn't cracked for a year!" Maria objected with feeling, and indeed Pierre's voice had settled permanently two octaves lower than the voice of the boy who had once extracted a pebble from his shoe during the passage of the Baron de Retz and his elegant, refrigerated wine.

"It is no treason to the tongues of Christendom," said Abdul, "to point out to you that Turkish is the most courtly, pious, and scientific of all the languages in the world. Men are more fastidious, manners are gentler in the East than here in the West. Your speech must always be polite. And your speech must always be pious. The priests of the Prophet pray five times a day on beautiful little rugs, facing the city of Mecca, which is a holy place. I must teach you the false and iniquitous phrases, for without them you cannot speak correct Turkish. Also, there is swearing: by the Prophet's beard, by the fig, by the olive, by the daybreak and ten nights, by that which is double and that which is single, and many other curious objects. And then there is the art of proper invective. A Turk is accounted dull if he calls a man a dog. The man must be last in a long line of dogs, all undistinguished, sired by a mangy mongrel at least, and preferably whelped by a scrofulous bitch of a mother after returning to her vomited meal of the filth of camels. And I shall teach you all I know of our elegant system of numbers, which is the same as great Christian scholars now teach in the University of Paris."

54

Abdul, though he did not know it, also imparted to Pierre a certain dignified conservatism of phraseology that had crept into his speech with advancing years, as happens so often among elderly men of all tongues. Before Pierre ever talked to another Turk, he spoke like a pious old gentleman of the last Turkish reign.

One novelty of the new peace was the first appearance of pageant armor. Tournaments, of course, required proof armor, as hard and honest as battle plate. But there were also occasions, when more splendid attire was required, and several rich nobles had recently ordered suits which Hugh considered extravagantly decorated and dangerously thin, as if they expected him to duplicate in metal the weight and style that the tailors wrought into their clothing. Such suits of mail were designed to be seen in, not to fight in. Hugh wrestled with his conscience, for it was not in his heart to make functionless armor. Partly as a result of his new tempering technique and partly by dint of excessive hammer hardening, which was a great labor, he was able to turn out pageantry suits that were only a little less safe than his wartime best.

The most elaborate was for the Baron de Retz.

A lisping ninny of a page appeared at the shop one morning in the hot, dry autumn of 1438, and announced that his master, Gilles, Baron of Retz, Lieutenant of Brittany and Marshal of France, was in the market for an especially fine suit of parade armor. He himself was the physical duplicate of his master, and he had come to be measured, by Jove!

At the "by Jove!" Hugh instantly pricked up his ears. Had culture come at last to France? It was true that in Italy certain of the literati were beginning to swear by the old Roman gods, almost as if they were alive again. It was considered a mark of distinction to be familiar with the classic mythology. Even clergymen sometimes swore by an ancient Latin deity, since it was scholarly, emphatic, and not at all impious; for the Renaissance was still young, and the old gods had not yet come back to visit on mankind their subtle curse of skepticism. Hugh had not heard the oath in France.

"By Bacchus! Your master shall be well served!" cried Hugh in an explosive gesture of welcome.

"Poof!" said the page. "He could teach Bacchus new tricks. With his wine. Venus, too," he giggled. "But I shan't say with what."

Hugh began to recover from his first spasm of cordiality. He was not too familiar with the heathen pantheon, but this well muscled young page seemed to have a mind like a sink.

Hugh's painstaking measurements for a suit of armor might well have fatigued an impatient client like the baron. First, the page lay on a large slab of slate, on his back, like a figure on a tomb. Hugh outlined his silhouette with chalk. Then for hours he stood on the dais as Hugh and his assistants meticulously measured the breadth of his shoulders, the length of his limbs, and the segments thereof down to the smallest joints of the hands and feet. This was done with a series of calipers, some tiny, some huge, that opened and closed like lobster claws. The measurements were transferred point by point to the rough chalk outline on the slate. There was no need for writing in such a method, and gradually the plane figure came exactly to duplicate the original. For thickness the process was repeated with the page lying on his side.

Poor, clumsy, pock-marked Ambrose, now old enough to leave the shop, had remained a few months longer with Hugh at his own request, hoping to acquire the skill to set out on his own. He was assigned to the comparatively simple rear of the anatomy where the measurements are few and easy. His calipers tickled the page and made him giggle, or prodded him and made him furious. After a few such accidents Hugh let Pierre take over the hinder measurements as well as the chest, which he had almost finished anyway. Hugh worked exclusively on the helm and gorget measurements. Abdul busied himself with the intricate hand and foot work while Clement, whose crossed eyes were no straighter than ever, measured the page's limbs. It grew hot in the shop toward noon. The page was tired of lying and standing and being breathed upon by five pairs of healthy lungs whose exhalations were laden with the odor of one of Maria's hearty breakfasts, so tasty with the seasoning of garlic. He turned a little pale, and complained that he was being suffocated and buffeted past all endurance. At this point Abdul, who was also warm and fatigued with bending over the feet, removed his turban to be more comfortable. The page saw the skull and shrieked.

"I beg your pardon, young man," said Abdul. "Sometimes I forget how alarming my bare head is."

"Cover it instantly! I'll dream of that crown for a week!"

Abdul sighed and bound up his head. Pierre, who should have kept his place, flashed back at the page: "Are you afraid of scars, delicate man? Abdul's scars are marks of honor!"

"Quiet, Pierre!" Hugh commanded. "You will lose me a client with your stupid chivalry."

"Nay, he will not, Master Hugh. He has a good spirit. Come here,

56

young man." Pierre stood at the foot of the dais and looked up at the customer.

"You are a handsome peasant, lad. You might do well in my master's service. He cannot abide ugliness in any form." The page glanced at Abdul, who looked pained. "And you are very deft with your hands. I shall undoubtedly speak to the marshal about you."

"I am very happy here, sir," said Pierre.

"The marshal will be here tomorrow," the page continued, addressing Hugh. "Let this one attend him, by all means, and not those creatures" (that was for Clement and Ambrose), "nor the terrible Turk," and that disposed of Abdul. "When is his time up, Master Hugh? Who is he?"

Maria had come to the door of the shop with half a dozen small cups of wine on a little wooden tray. She heard most of what the page said. A deep, unreasoning instinct whispered secretly in her heart, and she was suddenly aware of the nearness of great danger and terrible evil, like an old mother hen that hears without ears the footpads of the weasel, the sucker of blood.

She bustled into the shop and walked straight to the dais, pushing Pierre aside with her elbow, and offered the page a cup of wine.

"Do taste a drop of hippocras," she urged. "The armorer will keep you standing all day with never a rest. I know how tired you must be. But he concentrates so that he forgets how time flies. Saints alive! It's time for lunch right now. Pierre, Clement, Ambrose! Go into the kitchen at once and eat something. Hugh, how can you keep this noble young man standing all morning without a rest? Did he give you a rest, noble sir? Nay, I know he did not. He never does. Will you taste the wine, noble page?"

"You are an angel from Heaven, madame," replied the page. "Indeed, I have been doing penance to these secular persons all morning. I think I have never been so tired, even after a battle."

"I'll warrant you laid them low with those strong arms!" Maria said brightly. Hugh sniffed inaudibly. Pages did not fight, and she knew it. "Will you stay for lunch, sir page? You will not eat with the apprentices, of course."

"Thank you, no," the page replied with courteous finality. From Maria's kitchen a new wave of garlic odors was palpably enveloping the shop. "Though I should enjoy talking with the fair-haired apprentice. Who is he, madame?"

"The fair one? Oh, he is no member of this household. He is a neighbor boy, whose parents have gone on a journey. They will be back in a day or two, won't they, Hugh?"

"Oh, yes, indeed. A week at most."

"Then there is still a chance for the marshal to see him. He is so like me in his tastes," the page said with unmitigated smugness, "as well as in his physical measurements, that I am confident he will want to offer the boy a place."

"Perhaps his parents will agree," said Hugh, who began to see what Maria was about.

"They always agree," said the page.

"Of course they do," Maria added. "Such a distinguished service. Let us hope his parents do not return unexpectedly and take him away."

Later in the day, when the page was gone, she had a serious talk with her husband.

"There is something about that man that bodes no good, dear Hugh. Who is his master?"

Hugh, too, was troubled. "His master is the Baron de Retz. The baron has a bad name. Many strange tales are circulated about the magnificence of his establishments, his elaborate theatrical performances, and his affairs with the players. There are also ugly rumors that the pretty peasant girls on his estates run away from home rather than submit to his embraces, which puzzles me because such girls are usually flattered by their lord's notice. Perhaps his attentions are unusually brutal. That also is rumored." Hugh opened his mouth as if he were going to continue, but he shut it again.

"Are you keeping something back, Hugh?"

Hugh made a gesture. "Nothing of importance. They do say that he is a great artist and that he likes his pages and men-at-arms to be as handsome as possible. That is not uncommon in a great lord who loves display."

"Would you like Pierre in his service, Hugh?"

"God forbid!"

"I thought not. Don't you think we ought to talk to Father Isambart about this?"

"Indeed I do. I was just going to suggest it. We should be helpless if a marshal of France really took a fancy to Pierre and made him an offer, shouldn't we? How could we refuse?"

Father Isambart could not come at all during the day, but after dinner he appeared at the door of Maria's hospitable kitchen. His habit was wrinkled; there was the dust of the country roads over his shaven pate and in the graying circle of his tonsured hair.

"What a day, what a day!" he sighed, tasting the cup that Maria put before him. "I have shriven three sick women and four sick men and annointed a child that I fear will never live to grow a beard. There is much illness about, Master Hugh. That is excellent wine, Madame." Maria filled the cup again to the brim. "Why did you send for me? I trust Pierre is well. Nay, he is always well. Has he ever been sick a day since he came to live with you, Hugh?"

"Not a day. Not a fever. Not a cold. Not even a fleabite."

"That's because I taught him to bathe," Maria said. "Fleas do not bite clean people."

"They bite me, Maria."

"Ah," replied his wife.

Hugh continued: "It is about Pierre. Today there came to the shop a page of the Baron de Retz. The marshal wants a new suit of armor, with long points on the sollerets, if you please."

"Just like real shoes," nodded Isambart. "I have heard of the silly new fashion."

"You can't walk in them, of course, but then, you're supposed to ride handsomely and be admired. The page appears to have the same measurements as the marshal, and so we measured him."

"Not to fatigue His Excellency. I see, I see," said Isambart.

"Then my fine fancy page observed that Pierre is a handsome young man and began talking about recommending him to his master for a place in the marshal's service."

"What did you say?" asked the priest.

Maria answered him: "I did not know what to say. I told a great lie, Father. I said Pierre was a neighbor boy, that he did not live here at all. I denied him completely."

"St. Peter denied Our Lord once," Isambart observed. "He was afraid. Why did you deny Pierre?"

"I was afraid, too, Father. I did not like the page."

"Neither did I," added Hugh. "And I don't think I shall like the master."

"You won't, Hugh. He is probably a very bad man. By no means let Pierre be here when he comes."

"He is coming tomorrow," Hugh said, "and the page was particularly insistent that Pierre be here."

"Then Pierre must be sent away," the priest said sternly.

Maria nodded her head. "That is exactly the way I feel."

But Hugh was inclined to belittle the baron's menace. "After all, he may not even notice the boy. And he cannot simply lead a member of my household out of the door by the nose. Suppose I say: 'My Lord, Pierre is my son and he is to be an armorer. We aspire to no higher station. Now take your fancy page and foolish armor and get out of my shop!'"

"One does not talk that way to a marshal of France. Do you know, Hugh of Milan, that the peasants on his estates do not even have their children christened for months and months for fear the baron will hear there has been a birth in the family? Boys and girls disappear from his farms with alarming regularity. Some of them turn up in his service later; some are never heard of again."

"What happens to them, Father?" Hugh asked.

"There seems to be no special age at which the children disappear, but as a rule they are very young. When they are as old as Pierre, they are always extraordinarily beautiful."

"Pierre is beautiful," said Maria.

"Before the baron married, nobody suspected him very much. He was only a boy himself. After he married, there were comparatively few disappearances. But two years ago, Katherine of Thouars, his wife, left him; since then the kidnapings have doubled and redoubled, until I am told that every parent on his estates now lives in mortal terror."

"What does he kidnap the children for?" Hugh asked.

"A priest of my acquaintance," Isambart replied, "who is also a great chirurgeon, had occasion to visit the baron a year ago. As you know, De Retz is a generous patron of the arts, and has sponsored many miracle plays to the great benefit of the Church. In the course of their talk about the mystery, as they sought some reference or other in the library, the baron showed my friend a book which he had illuminated."

"I knew he was an artist," said Hugh.

"He had also bound the book, Hugh. He is an accomplished amateur in the art. The binding was of singularly soft, transparent stuff, of exquisite texture. It was so lovely," he continued, "that my learned friend—remember that he is a chirurgeon as well as a priest—came to the conclusion that no animal had ever grown such a hide."

"Merciful Saviour!" breathed Maria.

"In his opinion," Isambart said, "only the skin of a young child could possibly have supplied such leather."

60

"Saints!" muttered Hugh. "Are you sure? Who would do such a monstrous thing?"

"It is the lot of us priests, Hugh, to know men in their degradation as well as in their nobility. At the confession the soul is naked to the priest, or at least it ought to be, and it would be strange if we did not come to know its anatomy; though, of course, I am telling you nothing that was imparted to me under the seal. I merely assure you that I am in a position to know that there are men in the world so foul that surely the Devil finds a congenial home in them. Some men kill for the pleasure of witnessing pain. Perhaps one of them binds books with the skins of murdered children."

"Holy, compassionate, beautiful Mother of God!" cried Maria. Hugh looked as if he were going to be sick.

"Rumors have existed among the peasants for years," Isambart continued, "and from time to time tangible bits of evidence, like the unusual leather of the binding, have come to the knowledge of responsible persons. But there is nothing substantial enough to build a lawsuit upon, and one does not lightly indict a great patriot and a marshal of France. But in addition," and here a cold, blue, steely glint came into the priest's eyes, "there has lately been some evidence that De Retz is dabbling in black magic and sacrilege. All in all," he concluded, "I am sure it would be wise not to let the baron set eyes on Pierre. In fact," he added with a smile, "I think this is the second time I have been instrumental in clearing the boy out of the baron's way."

"You brought him into my life," Hugh said, "and now perhaps you mean to take him out again?"

"Nay, it will be only a little trip," Isambart said. "To Paris, perhaps. I could even arrange a little mission for him. There is a certain wealthy widow here in town who every year vows a quantity of candles to be burned for her husband, who was a lusty old sinner and will undoubtedly profit thereby. The good lady thinks that the candles from the Sainte-Chapelle in Paris are particularly efficacious. That is nonsense, of course, but if she faithfully thinks so, perhaps they will prove so. At any rate, they will add fervor to her prayers, and that is the main thing. I promised to procure them, and now I must do what I promised. I think Pierre might well bring them back."

"Had not Pierre best go this very night?" Maria suggested.

Isambart pondered. "The gates are up by now. Of course, almost anybody can have them lowered, but if Hugh did it, it would cost bribe money, and if I did it, it would cause comment. If I know the baron's nature as well as I think I do, he will not show up until midday at least. I think there is plenty of time. May I see the lad?"

"Certainly," replied Maria. "He's asleep, though."

"I shall not wake him."

They tiptoed to Pierre's bed. He was sleeping heavily and snoring in great satisfaction under the panther skin that Abdul had given him long ago, saying that he did not need such a heavy cover now that he was getting along in years. Hugh held aloft the lamp. Pierre's feet projected far beyond the panther skin, and the breadth of his shoulders was remarkable.

"He's almost a man," Isambart whispered, and blessed him softly as they tiptoed away.

That same night Isambart wrote a letter to Auguste de L'Isle-Adam, a brother priest of his order in Paris, attached to the Sainte-Chapelle. He set forth the pious object of Pierre's visit and begged his colleague to accept a portion of the widow's alms. The amount much more than defrayed the actual cost of the candles, and he prayed that the remainder be used for such charitable purposes as his colleague might designate, thus benefiting many souls without diminishing the benefit to the soul for which it had already been offered. "How happy are we," he wrote in his concise Latin, "who can, by a continuation of the power which multiplied the loaves and fishes, multiply into a score the blessings which are singly implicit in the donations of the faithful!" And as he rolled the parchment and sealed it in a little cylinder of horn, against Pierre's falling into a puddle, it occurred to him that it was well for the world that one good prayer or one good deed could be so spread out and subdivided in its beneficent consequences. If it were not so, what chance would there be in eternity for men like the baron? Clement brought the sealed letter back to the shop, and he, Maria, Abdul, and Hugh began to assemble what they considered necessary for Pierre's trip.

Maria laid out a complete new suit of linen underwear, his Sunday hose of fine, soft wool, and the new shoes that he would not ordinarily be given until his old ones were beyond all repair, besides the broad hat which he hated but which protected him so efficiently from the sun. She also chose several fat sausages and two big loaves of bread, a cup of tasty fat, which did not melt like butter and could be spread on the bread, a salt smoked carp, and a bottle of strong sweet wine. Abdul decided that he should be armed and contributed a small sword, which was hidden in a short staff of unfinished wood, thus constituting an extremely dangerous, concealed weapon. He also laid down on the growing pile of necessities his own jeweled dagger, which was very ancient and valuable, as well as Pierre's razor and mirror.

Hugh looked at the pile, and observed that Pierre was going only to Paris, not on a crusade, and that there was no reason to burden him with such a mountain of supplies, especially the food. So most of the food went back to Maria's kitchen, and in its place Hugh supplied a thin, deceptive purse, which could be seen, and a fat money belt, which could not. "There are plenty of inns on the way," he remarked, "and the roads are safe." While the razor was retained, the dagger, which might have caught the eye of a thief, and the mirror, which Pierre could shave without, were among the items thought unnecessary.

Early next morning, to his great surprise, Pierre was told to put on his Sunday clothes and prepare for a trip on foot alone to Paris. He was apprised of the mission, which appeared reason enough, and he did not connect it with the baron, though he was at a loss to understand the anxiety of his foster father's expression and the nervous, unusual way in which Maria constantly interrupted her speech and said, "What was that?"

The notion of a few weeks away from home appealed to him. His razor, the hidden sword, and the substantial sum of money he carried stamped him as a man, and the letter in its sealed horn lent a pious urgency to his mission.

"As for the way," Hugh said, "there are many roads to Paris. Anyone can direct you. But if you should ever become lost, you have only to seek the river and the road that runs along its bank. Walk against the current and you will finally come to the city of Paris. By shorter roads you should be there in a week. By way of the river it will, of course, be longer."

The sun was just rising, clear, red, and full of the promise of another day of dry, unseasonable heat, as Pierre left the armorer's house with a burden of blessings, money, sharp steel, and sausages, for all the discarded, superfluous food had been smuggled back into the pack which he slung over his shoulder.

Promptly at noon the Baron de Retz rode up to the house to confer with Hugh about the details of the armor. He was courteously ministered to by the entire household, though the parents of the fair-haired neighbor boy had, of course, unexpectedly returned and reclaimed their son.

# CHAPTER

## ❧ 10 ❧

THE ROAD to Paris led him south along the Seine. It was easy walking and Pierre was fresh and strong. Toward noon the highway ended abruptly at the river, and Pierre knew from the ropes that arched across its wide expanse, the stables, and hut of the ferryman, that he had come to the crossing two leagues from Rouen, and that he was almost halfway to the twin towns of the Andelys. He had hoped to arrive there by nightfall, but the ferry delayed him, and in the afternoon the highway swung away from the river and led across hilly country where the going was slower.

It was after dark that night when he came to a mean little inn with a rude sign fashioned into the shape of a golden angel hanging by the door, shining in the light from the windows. The innkeeper noted his tired face and new clothing, and calculated quickly what the traffic might bear.

"At the Golden Angel," he announced, "we are always paid in golden angels."

"That is a great deal of money," said Pierre, who knew that Maria could feed her household for a week on the gold coin that bore the stamp of an angel on one side and the cross and the ship on the other.

"It is the custom of the establishment," said the innkeeper, "and the house is full anyway. For all I care, you can fare on to the Andelys. I dare say a young man like you could arrive there before sunup."

Pierre's feet suddenly turned to lead in his sweaty shoes. The surrounding forest was very dark, and there was a great cavity in his middle regions.

"I think perhaps I shall go on," he said, his young face quite ex-

64

pressionless, "unless, of course, one is given supper as well as lodgings for one's golden angel."

"Why, yes, young man," the innkeeper replied, fearing that the boy was less tired perhaps than he looked. "Supper, of course."

"And I dare say there is a simple sort of breakfast?" ventured Pierre. He was more interested in food at the moment than shelter.

The innkeeper balanced the possibilities. Actually there was not a guest in the house. The times were very bad. "A simple sort could be arranged, young man."

"Say three or four simple eggs and butter and bread and a bit of fish? The river is so close."

"Oh, come in, come in; you shall be properly served. But I must say, you haggle as if you came from Italy."

"Perhaps I did," Pierre said, and the innkeeper replied, "Oh, well then," with a helpless gesture.

Pierre stuffed himself with supper. He took off his shoes and loosened his clothing and threw himself upon the comfortable straw in the corner of the room that was given him. But first he unsheathed his sword and used it as a wedge to keep the ill fitting door from squeaking back and forth on its rusty hinges. Much later, when the innkeeper came to ascertain whether the young guest who had gold on him was sleeping soundly or not, he found himself confronted with the sharp point of a sword projecting six inches into his hall beyond the door. He decided to leave well enough alone.

Pierre knew that he had been monstrously cheated, and he made a mental note never to stop at inns after nightfall if it could be avoided.

Next day he stopped at the Little Andely, an inn under the great frowning castle that England's lionhearted Richard had built in the days when the frontier of Normany penetrated less deeply into the kingdom of France, and he was given better accommodations for a silver franc. Commerce was a strange and wonderful thing.

Past Vernon, past Bonnières and the city of Mantes, where the tolls of the river traffic had reared the stately church of Saint-Maclou, he walked, covering the long distances each day with ease and arriving at the inns in plenty of time to drive a good bargain with the innkeepers. The river was his guide.

But after Mantes the way grew rough and the cottages of the peasants took on a neglected look. Many of them were deserted. Pierre calculated that he had been on the road the better part of a week, and he knew he was approaching the frontier between Normandy and

France, a region that had been so repeatedly devastated by the armies that it was no wonder few farmers could prosper long in it.

In an effort to better the speed of his travel through this depressing and rather frightening country, he turned away from the river where a fork divided the road and struck overland in the direction where he had been told was the monastery of Saint-Germain in the forest of Laye.

Toward nightfall he came to a cloister near a castle that was blackened by the fires of old sieges. He could see workmen working on the battlements in broad daylight, a sure sign of peace. He guessed that he was in France and that this was the monastery of Saint-Germain. If it were true, his journey was nearing its end.

CHAPTER

\* 11 \*

AS HE APPROACHED the postern gate he heard the melancholy chant of a Requiem being sung in the chapel, and he knew from the lateness of the hour that it must be a very solemn occasion. He knocked softly. After a full two minutes the door was opened a cautious crack and a chubby, moonfaced young friar looked up at him with fear in his face.

"May I come in?" Pierre asked. The door swung wide, and the man's expression relaxed.

"Anyone may come in, of course, any time," the friar replied. "But I must say I am happy that your skin is clear."

"I thought perhaps I might spend the night here," Pierre explained. "I can pay."

"This house is always open, whether one can pay or not. Though, of course, your alms are welcome."

"I do not know how much I can give," said Pierre with some hesitation. The habit of bargaining with innkeepers was new and strong. "I want only a little room and perhaps a bite of supper."

The friar began to chuckle audibly. He took Pierre by the arm and led him across the courtyard into the main building. There was a strong odor in the air as if someone were pickling cucumbers.

"I took you for a much older man, my friend. Such height as yours often deceives me, for my own measurements, as you see, are the same in all directions. The Cloister of Saint-Germain is not an inn. If you can pay for your rest here, that is good. If you cannot, that is all right, too. And you can stay as long as you like."

"Oh, I am going on to Paris tomorrow."

"To Paris, did you say?"

67

"Yes."

The friar shook his head. He walked before Pierre down a long hall, and at each step the odor grew stronger, and then Pierre saw the cause of it all. Just outside the door of one of the cells was a great hogshead of steaming liquid with a broom stuck into it.

"Most people are getting out of Paris if they can possibly do so," the friar observed. "Here is your room. Not so luxurious as an inn, perhaps, but I can vouch for its cleanliness. I have just scrubbed it down with hot vinegar. Now I must do the hall."

"I come from Rouen," said Pierre, "and I am not acquainted with the custom."

The fat friar glanced sharply at his guest, but there was no jest in Pierre's face. "It is not a custom as a rule," he said in a serious tone. "It is not a custom to offer Requiem Masses just before Vespers, either. Both prayers and vinegar are needed in large quantities, both in and out of season, if the house is to be kept free of the sickness. Did you know that the plague is in Paris?"

"Nay, I did not. If I had known, I think I should have stayed in Rouen."

"Probably you had better go back right now."

Pierre explained something of his mission, and the friar agreed that since it was for the Church, perhaps it should be gone through with. "But at least talk to the abbot. I shall tell him about you. For myself, I think I should rather go without candles a hundred years in purgatory than journey to Paris right now. Of course, the abbot may feel differently. And now I must go back to my work."

He rolled up his sleeves, tucked the skirts of his habit under the knotted cord about his waist, and whisked the streaming broom over the walls, the stones of the floor, and even the vaulted ceiling as high as he could reach. Pierre felt conspicuous standing idle by the door of his cell while the fat little man worked so hard.

"Can I help you, good friar?" he offered.

"Now that is a kind thought," the friar answered with evident relief. "You can and welcome. I'll fetch you a broom!" In a few moments Pierre found himself wielding the counterpart of the young monk's besom, a very heavy object, he soon discovered. Before he mastered the technique of swinging it, he dripped a great deal of the hot vinegar on himself, so that he began to itch all over and steam like a horse that is ridden too hard. But the hall had not had such a cleaning in a century.

After supper the abbot himself took Pierre aside. He was a kindly old man, but he had an icy sort of fire in his eye that Pierre had sometimes seen in Isambart's. It was also a little like the sheen on the steel of some of Abdul's better work.

"Your scrubbing companion," the abbot said smiling, "has told me how valiantly you wield a broom in the service of the Church and for suffering humanity. I am afraid I cannot advise you, young man, whether to go on to Paris or go home to Rouen. Probably as you get older you will have to make many decisions like this. I have often been asked to resolve such a question in a man's mind, but of course, I cannot. It is not cowardly for you to go home now, and if you decide to, I shall write a letter to your priest. No one will ever blame you for avoiding the plague."

"Suppose I go on, Father?"

"You will be doing just about the finest thing I can imagine, sir."

Of course, there was nothing Pierre could say after that; and if the wily old fisher of men had snared another soul for God, he was well within his ecclesiastical rights and doing, indeed, only his duty. The "sir" rang in Pierre's young ears all next day.

Quite a little group of friars gathered at the gate to see him off next morning, and he found that they had remembered him in more than their prayers. His pack was lumpy with sausages and loaves of bread. They had made him a sort of leather sling to go over his shoulder; it crossed his back and breast and met again over his right hipbone, and there, in the spot where great nobles sometimes pinned the badge of their order, hung a jug of the smelly vinegar. The abbot refused his alms and gave him a handkerchief. Pierre had never owned one before. "Wet it often in the vinegar," said the old priest, "and breathe the fumes constantly. The doctors say it wards off the plague. Now go, and God keep you safe."

The morning was the pleasantest of Pierre's whole journey. The road to Paris was clearly marked, and the going was mostly downhill. The little traffic was all in one direction, and consisted mostly of small groups of mounted men and women, obviously well-to-do families, many with heavily laden pack mules, who had left Paris much earlier in the day. They were intent and serious, but there was no panic about them. He was impressed with their preoccupation, however. Nobody greeted him or even looked at him.

The little farms, which were more and more numerous, had a strange air about them. There was smoke in the chimneys, and so there

69

were certainly people in the houses, but the doors were all shut and nobody was working in the fields. In the afternoon Pierre began to come upon commercial establishments on the outskirts of the city, but they were all idle. Several mills, a tannery, a metal-founding shop, a stonecutter's yard, all were deserted and boarded up. Nothing but a dog moved in one great enclosure, full of kilns and piles of unfinished bricks and tiles, where scores of men must ordinarily have worked, and the furnaces were all cold.

Pierre had passed several inns, but they, too, were closed. And suddenly he realized that he was just as glad, because he should have hesitated to enter one. Like everybody else in the great city of Paris, he wanted to be as alone as possible. He was afraid of contact with other people, and his strongest impulse was to dash into the city and get his candles and dash out again. He could see the walls, but they were still very distant. Far to the right and far to the left beyond the walls, he saw the river. It was hard to realize that the same river also flowed under the walls of Rouen, so far away in time.

Pierre was, of course, familiar with the way Rouen spread beyond its walls, but he was not quite prepared for the vast extent to which the city of Paris had outgrown its fortifications. The cottages of the peasants stood in smaller and smaller fields, until they lost their fields completely, becoming little groups of houses separated by vacant lots that this year were not even gardens. He was actually in Paris, though far outside the walls, before he was completely aware that he had entered it, and he had not had his lunch. To judge by the sun, it would be an early supper. He decided to ask the way to the Sainte-Chapelle. Since the inns were closed and there was no one to talk to on the street, he knocked boldly at the door of a cottage, and when there was no answer, opened it. Instantly there was the sickening odor of death in his nostrils. Two corpses lay rotting on the floor. Pierre slammed the door and ran a little way to the next house, but before he could knock, the door was opened a crack and the wicked point of a pike was thrust into his face.

"Go away!" a man's voice commanded.

"But there are dead people in that house!"

The man laughed. "You fool! Of course they are! Can I help that? Go away instantly, or I'll run you through." The door opened a little wider, and Pierre saw that the man meant what he said.

Pierre took to his heels and skipped all the other houses in that group. A small brook with a sturdy bridge separated him from the

next cluster of houses. He stopped at the bridge and soaked his handkerchief in the vinegar before knocking at the door of the largest and
neatest of them. It happened also to be the first, and the brook ran
under its windows, which were generous for the time. They indicated
either the wealth of the owner or the security of the city, or both. There
was no answer, and so Pierre knocked again, and when the silence
continued, he tried the door, which yielded readily. There was no one
inside. The four, well furnished rooms were utterly deserted. There
was a loft under the roof and Pierre called aloud to whoever might
hear that he was not trespassing, he simply wanted to know how to get
to the Sainte-Chapelle. But there was no answer from the upper room
and Pierre climbed the ladder and looked around. There was no one
there either.

It appeared to be a storage room. There were some simple pieces
of furniture, but not a scrap of food, not a spare pot nor pan, not a
drape for a bed nor a length of linen to make into clothing, no sign of
any of the thrifty supplies of odds and ends that the people of the
period put into their lofts to keep safe or to use at a later date. The
dwelling had been systematically stripped and abandoned, as if the
owner meant to stay away for a long time.

Pierre backed down the ladder and sat on a stool, his pack still on
his back, his vinegar-soaked handkerchief still in his hand, and pondered his next move. From the reception he had received so far in the
capital of France, there would be no use going on to the gate that night.
If the people of the suburbs were so suspicious, what would the guards
be like? He decided to wait till morning. Vespers rang out from more
church bells than he had ever heard in his life, and Pierre ate his first
meal since leaving the monastery.

As dusk began to fall he heard the rattle of wheels on the crudely
cobbled street and saw a small, two-wheeled cart drive over the bridge
and stop a little distance beyond the brook. Two laborers quickly
loosened the harness that held the tongue of the vehicle parallel to the
road. The pole tilted up and the cart spilled whatever it carried into a
heap in the road.

As if by magic people began to pour out of the houses and the air
was filled with angry curses and frightened cries. "Take it away! Take
it away! Not here again!"

Pierre was appalled to see in the road perhaps half a dozen dead
bodies. The dreadful odor filled the air again. The drivers were obviously drunk, but they brought down the tongue of the cart again and

secured it to the harness with considerable expertness, notwithstanding the menaces of the crowd, which got bigger all the time but kept a cautious distance.

One body, that of a woman, had got caught on a nail by its dress of rich material, but they tumbled it roughly out upon the pile of corpses. Pierre joined the group out of a frightened, overpowering curiosity. The workmen jumped on the cart again. One whipped up the mules, and the other bowed a low, mock-elegant bow to the people, holding his greasy hat over his heart and answering the curses of the crowd with such a torrent of drunken obscenity as Pierre had never heard. Instantly the air was full of stones, and the cart rattled back over the bridge, the men ducking and swearing and laughing, the missiles bouncing off their dreadful vehicle.

A purposeful activity now animated the group around the bodies, and one man, whom Pierre recognized as the person who had thrust the pike in his face, said: "We'll have to do what we did before. Hurry, now!" Without touching the quiet mass of disfigured humanity, the people began to throw sticks and straw and split logs of firewood over the bodies, and someone came up with a large bucket of liquid tar and poured it over the corpses. When it touched the woman Pierre thought he saw her move. The man called for a torch. At that moment the woman did really move, quite perceptibly, and Pierre was sure others saw it, but nobody did anything about it. From one of the houses a man came running with a great flaming brand.

Pierre had seen two women burned, one of them burned alive, and he did not purpose to see another. "Wait a moment! Wait!" he cried, running heedlessly up to the very edge of the heap. "This one is alive!"

"She is not," the man of the pike replied. "Go away, you fool! Don't touch her." Then he lit the pile.

Pierre forgot his loathing and picked up the woman. The crowd drew back in horror and let him pass. In back of him the fire blazed fiercely up as the people gathered to windward and, for a moment, watched it burn. Then they remembered the danger of one another and they disappeared into their houses and shut the doors, leaving the street deserted again with the balefire burning.

Pierre's first thought was to get the poor creature in his arms safely into the house which he had appropriated, but she was so loathsome from contact with the corpses and so covered with spots of filth that he stopped on the bridge and eyed the brook speculatively. Decidedly that was the thing to do. He laid her gently on the ground. Then he

72

dipped his handkerchief into the water and washed her face. All the spots washed away. Then he washed her hands, and in an instant they were clean, too, and white, like a lady's, with no sign of work on them at all. Her lips moved and she muttered something, but it made no sense and Pierre supposed that she was delirious.

Her dress was torn and incredibly filthy, and whatever jewelry she might once have worn had all been taken from her. Pierre looked at the smeared dress distastefully. The smell of it was frightful. With a guilty feeling he decided to take it off, noting that the bushes on the bank of the stream effectively screened the spot from all view of the road, though if he had thought longer about the matter of privacy, he would have realized that nobody in Paris was quite so safe from molestation as he was at that moment with such a companion. Pierre had never taken off a woman's dress before and he was not sure how it was done. After some examination he discovered that the lacing of the bodice could be undone and the belt about the waist could be unhooked. The rest was easy. He held up the belt for a moment, wondering how so ridiculously short an object could actually go round the waist of a human being. He washed the dress thoroughly in the water, and succeeded in cleansing it somewhat, although the tar, of course, would not come out.

Her white shift was just as dirty as her outer clothing, and Pierre decided to make a thorough job of it, leaving her quite naked on the grass as he did so. When the clothing was wrung out and deposited in soggy little heaps on the ground, Pierre realized that he could not put the wet things back on her, and so he carried her into the house and laid her on the bed, and brought in the clothes and spread them over the furniture to dry. She was still babbling in her delirium and trembling violently, from the chilly water, Pierre supposed, but he could do nothing about that. He went back to the stream and removed his own clothes, which had become dirty during the rescue, and scrubbed his body clean in the water and doused his clothing thoroughly. The cold bath felt good on his skin, which was still itchy from the fumes of yesterday's vinegar. Stark naked, and much more ashamed of his own nudity than hers, he went back to the house, his clothing under his arm. In the presence of the woman, who appeared to be regaining consciousness, he flushed and put on his wet, uncomfortable drawers. His outer clothing he spread out to dry, as he had done hers.

The odor still clung to the woman's body. A man of Pierre's station in life was none too familiar with the romantic laws of chivalry, but he doubted whether the subtle decrees which dealt with almost every conceivable situation that might arise between a man and a woman had ever established how the white body of a naked lady, newly snatched from a pile of plague-ridden corpses, ought properly to be sweetened. It certainly seemed unchivalrous to pour vinegar over such an exciting object, and besides, he knew from experience that it made one itch. He bethought him of his strong, sweet wine, and that surely would be preferable. He took the bottle from his pack, but first it seemed the part of wisdom to try to get her to drink a little of it as a restorative.

He lifted her head and held the bottle to her lips, and she took a great gulp, instantly drawing back with a shudder. The stuff did not smell like wine, and Pierre tasted it himself. He was rewarded with such a sting of fire in his throat that he fell to choking and coughing violently. By an act of carelessness, Maria, perhaps in her haste and excitement, had provided him with a bottle of fiery old brandy. Pierre did not like it and poured it all over the girl, rubbing it in well and wiping her with his handkerchief, which he threw away. At least it was not sticky like wine, and it was certainly cleansing.

Brandy internally and externally applied revived the woman somewhat, and she sat up on the bed in an extremity of fear.

"Holy Mother!" she cried. "What are you doing to me? What is this place? Who are you?"

"I am Pierre," Pierre answered in great confusion.

"Pierre of what?" the girl asked, "And why haven't you any clothes on?"

"Just Pierre," said Pierre. "Though sometimes they call me Pierre of Milan."

"Milan is a lovely place," said the woman dreamily. "Did you leave there recently?"

"I have never been there. I am of Milan only by courtesy, because my foster father, the armorer, is Hugh of Milan."

"Oh," said the woman. "I am Louise," and she did not add, noblesse oblige, that it was also De la Tour-Clermont, who would one day probably be a countess in her own right.

Then, with blinding clarity of thought, she recovered her senses; she realized that she was far more naked than Pierre.

"Holy Virgin!" she cried. "Where are my clothes? I have been kidnaped! I shall be ravished! Or is it money you want? Nay, it is always both," she lamented, and indeed such things were not unknown. She crouched back in the straw.

"I never raped anybody," Pierre protested indignantly. "If you care to look out of the window, you will see a fire, and if I had not pulled you out, you would be there now, with the other corpses."

Louise did look out of the window, and there indeed was the fire, and they were not so far away but she could distinguish the bodies.

"What a dreadful thing," she said. "How did I ever get there?"

"I am sure I do not know. Perhaps they thought you had the plague. Are you hungry? I have food."

The woman now had a measure of the man she thought was her abductor. With a quick eye she appraised him as perhaps half, no, surely two-thirds (with such shoulders) her own age, which was crowding thirty for all her slenderness.

"I beg your pardon," she said. "I did you a terrible injustice in my thoughts. Yesterday we were riding to see a doctor, my kinsman and I, for of course they won't come to see you any more. I had a fever and my head ached and naturally Father was perturbed. Then I remember feeling very faint and looking around for my cousin. He was gone, and I do not remember anything else until I woke up here."

"Perhaps you fainted on the street, madame. You ended up on the death cart with those others. You were dreadfully dirty, and I, too, thought that you were a victim of the plague. You were covered with spots, but they all washed off."

"Who did that?"

"I did."

"You are a very daring young man, Pierre."

"Oh, I wasn't really afraid, madame."

"That isn't precisely what I meant. And please do not call me madame. It is mademoiselle. Did you say you had something to eat? I am dreadfully hungry. I wish I could put my clothes on."

"They are all wet, mademoiselle," Pierre replied. "Look." He held up the shift.

"I think I shall put it on anyway."

"Very well," Pierre said, and handed it to her.

It was growing dark in the house, and Pierre looked for some means of striking a fire, but there was none. Then he fished in his pack and brought out bread and meat and cut it with his sword, while Louise watched with a fascinated gaze, and put it on the table and invited her to eat.

75

"You carve with a precise hand," she said. "I am glad you turned out not to be a kidnaper."

Pierre found himself hungry again, too, and he took a big bite of bread and a big bite of meat at the same time, stuffing them together into his mouth with his fingers and chewing mightily, while Louise ate just as much, but with far more delicacy.

"I have an uncle," she observed, "who teaches the science of mathematics at the university, and once he told me that two bodies cannot occupy the same place at the same time. I must tell him that your bread and sausage have disproved his theories, Pierre of Milan."

"I beg your pardon, mademoiselle. I am hungry all over again at the sight of you alive and well, and I am not used to eating with gentry."

"I was only joking," she said, "but your answer was turned like a troubadour's. It would be singular if my savior turned out also to be a poet."

"Nay, I know nothing about those things," Pierre replied very miserably.

The lady Louise sighed. "I dare say."

It was quite dark now, and the house was cold. Louise, who was, of course, bruised and very tired from her exhausting experience, retired again to the bare bed of straw. Pierre, who was always tired after his day's walking, supposed it was his lot to lie down on the hard, un-inviting floor, and for a while he tried it. But he was cold, and there was nothing to throw over him but his own wet clothes, and he began to think jealously of the warm straw. He listened to her breathing and, because it was regular, he knew she was asleep; and so, since it could no longer alarm her, he lay down contentedly beside her and went to sleep himself. But the chill of the September night struck through the house, and the warmth of the two close bodies worked its unconscious magic. Louise was unaware that she had put her arm around him, and Pierre in his sleep was not conscious of it; but he began to glow with a strangely localized warmth and, though it only half awakened him, the animal movements of his body it roused into being wakened Louise completely. She was perfectly chaste and had every intention of remaining so. "Go away, you pig!" she whispered. Pierre suddenly sat up.

"*Gesù!*" he said. "I dreamed I was drowning!" Then he lay back and went to sleep again. Just before dawn, however, they both experienced different versions of the same guilty dream, and, for an astonishing

76

moment, out of all space and time, Louise remembered again to argue with her uncle, and Pierre resolved to learn more about the science of mathematics, with particular reference to the question whether two bodies can or cannot occupy the same space at the same time. Since it was only a dream, they did not mention it in the morning, of course.

# CHAPTER

## ❖ 12 ❖

PESTILENCE in those days meant a booming business for the soothsayers, the astrologers, and the necromancers. They sold philtres to drink and amulets to wear and charms of written gibberish to be disposed about the body in unlikely places for the purpose of warding off the plague in a magical and impious manner.

To one old witch, with an immense clientele of panic-stricken souls, Bernard de Coucy, kinsman of Louise, had secretly repaired a few days before. For more gold than his impecunious estate could conveniently bear, she had hung below his well tapered loins and a little above the chafe marks of the saddle so that he would not sit on it and destroy its power, the dried skin of a small rat, stuffed with odorous herbs and exotic nauseants that were privy to her and the demons that instructed her. The odor of his protection was not discernible to the unprejudiced nostrils of his relatives, and he rode with Louise to seek the doctor with a show of courage that even old Sir Robert was bound to admire.

Yet in the streets he had kept a prudent distance from the lady, because he thought he detected the signs of a rash on her skin and a swelling on her throat. When she was seized with an attack of nausea between the Temple and the Hôtel des Tournelles, where the king lived, Bernard withdrew to an unchivalrous distance to examine the condition of his mount, which seemed unaccountably to stumble over a cobble. For that moment he lost her from view, but he loudly encouraged his men to hurry to her assistance, which they appeared to do. When he mounted again, his ailing fifth cousin had disappeared. He hurried to her father's house, but his retainers had already spurred speedily home and explained that the lady was lost.

Thereupon De la Tour-Clermont called his entire staff together and sent them into the Town, the City, and the University of Paris in such numbers and with such curses that the plague itself seemed less menacing than the angry old nobleman, frantic with fear for his eldest and dearest daughter.

Bernard offered to cross the Seine and seek in the University, and even in the infected region south of it, taking with him only a couple of men because he was loath, as he said, to expose too many to the contagion of the district where everybody knew the sickness was most prevalent. He chose the two whose consciences were already guilty with the dereliction of their duty the day before.

Scheming was easy for Bernard de Coucy, and he knew that of all the count's men, they would be the least likely to gossip when he did what he planned to do. Sir Robert thanked him with feeling. Bernard instantly galloped through the stricken area and out beyond the walls.

But he discovered to his chagrin that this pleasant, unpopulous suburb had been used as a dumping ground. Spurring far beyond one horrible heap of bodies, he came to a brook with a bridge over it, and drew rein when he saw another gruesome pile only a little way beyond, still smoking from the efforts of the intelligent citizenry to burn the corpses.

Louise saw her kinsman on the bridge. Her headdress was gone, and her undressed hair fell in a careless cloud around her shoulders, streaming away from her spotless face and unswollen throat as she ran to meet him.

He watched the pale, pretty lady with tar on her gown run out of one of the houses, followed by a tall youth in the dress of a commoner. Then to his unfeigned amazement, he recognized her.

"Louise!" he gasped. "Whatever happened to you, my cousin?"

"I do not know," she replied. "I lost you in the street."

"You seem to have found the doctor alone, Cousin Louise. I never saw an illness so quickly cured. Surely this young man is not the doctor, however!" He favored Pierre with a petulant look that Pierre was to see often, even in the eyes of handsome men, and nobody could accuse Bernard of being ugly.

"No indeed; this is Pierre of Milan," and she told him how Pierre had rescued her, deeming it maidenly, however, to suppress the details of how she got so clean after her ride in the dead cart.

"That is amazing," said Bernard honestly. He scrutinized Louise's skin attentively. It was always clear and fair, but never more so than

79

now. "No doubt it, was only a little fever you suffered from, my cousin," he said. "How fortunately my steps were guided to save you from this gruesome district. Undoubtedly the lady Louise's noble father," he said, looking at Pierre, "would add a substantial monetary reward to his thanks for your part in her assistance, if he were here."

"I thank you, sir," Pierre said, "but I came to Paris only to fetch a few candles back to Rouen."

Bernard laughed. "Even I can give you all the candles you want, Master Pierre. I did not know Normandy suffered such a dearth of them."

"These are special, sir. They are holy candles, blessed by the Sainte-Chapelle, for a widow in Rouen to burn for her husband."

"Oh. That's different. I shall be glad to show you the way. No doubt you are anxious to get out of Paris at once."

"I certainly am," Pierre said.

Bernard's attendants dismounted at a word from their master and gave their horses to the lady and Pierre, whose sword, the only touch of chivalry about him, was hidden in his staff. His coarse sack and his mean dress made a drab and common contrast to their colorful apparel.

But Louise said No. "I should never forgive myself if I let you go home, Pierre of Milan, without allowing Father the opportunity of thanking you. Unless you really insist on leaving now, I beg you to come home with us."

Pierre went, of course. Never, he thought, had he seen such a lovely lady. He was ashamed of his youth, his ignorance, his manners, and his clothes. He wished a devil, or a dragon at least, would suddenly materialize in the street, so that he could unsheathe his sword and slay it before her eyes while the people cheered and the glittering highborn men about him took to their trembling heels. He was not the first in the world nor the last to dream such a daydream of daring in the presence of his first, and always older, love. But nothing miraculous happened.

They rode away from the neat and hospitable dwelling, which Louise thought she would remember as long as she lived, and entered the walls by the Porte Saint-Jacques. Here the houses were as close as Pierre had ever seen them in Rouen, except for the military areas immediately adjacent to the fortifications, where there were shops and stalls of flimsy construction usually occupied by merchants and street vendors. They were deserted during the plague, and there were few people on the street even within the walls. The squires attempted for a while to keep pace with the horses, but of course they could not. Yesterday they had arrived home first with the bad news; today Bernard determined to arrive first with the good.

They passed a short bridge over the river. It was lined with tiny houses, wall to wall, directly over the stream. The doors were all open. Many people were inside doing business as usual.

"These are the shops of the money-changers," Louise said. "Here one can exchange any kind of money for any other kind of money in the whole world."

"And borrow as well," Bernard added.

Louise said a little maliciously: "You can believe what my cousin says, Pierre of Milan. He is well known on the Pont-au-Change."

Bernard scowled. "Your humor is as sharp toward your cousin," he complained, "as your heart is cold, dear Louise. Confess that I have done fairly well financially in my work for the new master of the mint."

"That is true," Louise replied. "De Coucy has profited greatly at times in the employ of the king's minister."

"Who is that?" Pierre asked.

Louise answered, "His name is Jacques Coeur."

"He has made the French coins the heaviest and the purest in the world," said Bernard. "His ships sail over all Christendom, and beyond. Of course, I am not actually in trade."

"Of course not," said Pierre. Even he knew that noblemen were not in trade.

"Sometimes my work might appear commercial, but there is nothing ignoble about it. The details are confidential."

Pierre rummaged in his memory. "I think I once met a man named Jacques Coeur in Rouen. But he was selling cabbages."

Bernard began to snicker. "Coeur is a commoner, though he has a title now. But bless me! I never heard the story about the cabbages. It is quite possible."

"Perhaps it is not the same man," said Louise.

In one of the stalls Pierre caught a glimpse of a friar. The house was a little better than the rest, and a curious device like three great, golden balls hung conspicuously over the door.

"Do monks have to borrow in Paris?" he asked in genuine amazement. "Is this big rich city so niggardly with its alms?"

Louise laughed so loud that the friar looked up in surprise and smiled pleasantly. Neither the times nor the nature of the bridge was conducive to laughter.

"No, Pierre; he is lending, not borrowing. The Church's rates are said to be lower than anybody else's."

"It's the only good thing about the bridge," Bernard said gloomily. "The rates of the Church keep the rates of the usurers down."

The bridge ended on the Ile de la Cité, and to the left Bernard pointed out the magnificent chapel that St. Louis had built nearly two centuries before to house the holy thorns that bloodied the brow of Christ. "There is the church you are looking for, Master Pierre. The living quarters in the cellar are usually occupied by servants and cleaning people. But in times like these some of the clergy live there, and I dare say if you stopped now you could get your candles and be out in the country again by nightfall."

"Pierre is much too tired," said Louise. "He told me so this morning. Didn't you, Pierre?"

"Yes, mademoiselle. Indeed, I am worn out with yesterday's long walk." And he made a mental note to cast this lie and his other sins, which one commits interminably both night and day, into the ear and unto the bosom of the Church at his very next opportunity.

The bridge continued over the other branch of the river, and if Pierre had known Paris better, he would have realized that they had traversed the University, fief of the Church, and the Ile de la Cité, first, oldest, and once the only part of Paris, and were now approaching the commercial and royal domain which was fashionable, better defended, and known as the Town.

Here, when the capital reverted from the English invaders' hands into the hands of his master, King Charles, Sir Robert had purchased a stately hôtel, as near the king's residence as the cluster of great mansions belonging to the higher nobility would permit. It was built more like a medieval castle than the new secular Gothic structures of the period, which were so full of windows that it seemed that their walls could hardly hold together, and the windows had glass in them. Sir Robert's had almost no windows at all, and when it rained, there was nothing to stop it coming through the few that it had except the leaky old wooden shutters. But he had got the place at a great bargain, and he found its architecture quite compatible with his old-fashioned tastes.

Ages ago the moat had been filled almost to the brim with the refuse that large dumpcarts making their rounds constantly threw into it. Sir Robert's men had completed the filling, and the rich organic material below, seeping up through the new soil above, had made possible a large border of luxuriant flowers that were the envy of the neighborhood.

He was sitting alone in his bedroom, utterly disconsolate, when his old steward came running with the news that his daughter was at the gate with De Coucy and a tall, unknown young man. If he had waited to hear the rest of his gossipy servant's keen observations, he would have learned that the squires were evidently lost and probably fallen victims of the plague, and one had better, perhaps, pray for their souls, but he did not wait.

Twenty-three years had passed since an English foot soldier had swung an iron mace and shattered his knee bones at Agincourt. Sir Robert had kept his seat despite his agony, and had his horse rear up and trample the churl into purgatory. As for the havoc Sir Robert then wrought on the English before they captured him in that shameful defeat, one had only to listen and the old nobleman would relate it at length. His knee had mended stiff as a pikestaff and remained painful ever since, but he forgot about it when he heard his daughter had returned.

"Now, thanks to Our Lady!" he shouted. "She watched over my baby! Ah, thanks, thanks!" as if it were a personal favor to him from the Mother of God. He ran down the crooked ancient stairway with all the speed, if not the grace, of a man forty years his junior. "Adèle!" he cried. "She is back!"

Adèle d'Épinal, the countess, his wife, already had her substantial arm around Louise's waist, supporting her as if she were still faint, petting her, exclaiming at the rents in her gown, wondering at the tar, bewailing the loss of the jewelry. Naturally, she noticed Pierre, and appraised him, whatever he might be to her daughter, as an extraordinarily handsome male, but quite obviously a person of no consequence. Very young, too. Big, though.

Having negotiated one flight of stairs and seeing Louise safe in her mother's arms, Sir Robert decided not to try another, and waited at the door with his old steward. Behind them unobstrusively gathered the cook, the sergeant of his personal guards, his wife's maid, Louise's maid, and even a cleaning woman, whose proper place was the living quarters in the extensive cellars where the guards and the minor servants slept. It was perfectly dry down there. The air was as good and the rooms were big. She was devoted to Louise, whose rooms were always so neat, and she had stolen upstairs when she heard the excitement. Naturally, she did not stay long.

Another member of the household, however, did not wait at the doorway, but dashed down the worn, old stone steps two at a time, a flutter of yellow curls and a blur of skinny legs—Claire de la Tour-Clermont, sister of Louise.

Sir Robert greeted his daughter lovingly.

Men wept easily in France. It was not considered unmanly. Even in England nobody had as yet discovered that a wooden face can adequately express the intensity of one's emotions, with the gratifying concomitant that one's self-control is greatly admired.

The joyous relief that he felt at the sight of his daughter released a twin current of tears that lost themselves in the wrinkles of his cheeks.

"Child, child! But I'm glad to see you! I was afraid you were dead of the plague."

"She might easily have been," said Bernard. "I found her in the fields outside the walls to the south. The region is a sink."

"That is true," said Louise. "They dump the carts there, beyond the Porte Saint-Jacques."

"Who is the blond young man?" her father asked.

Louise answered, "That is Pierre of Milan."

Adèle d'Épinal pricked up her ears. To be of Milan was to be as good as anybody. Then Bernard said: "We owe, indeed, I think, some debt of gratitude to Master Pierre. The boy seems to have found her first, and he showed commendable ingenuity in separating her from a number of afflicted persons."

When Louise explained that Pierre's commendable ingenuity consisted of saving her life when people thought her a corpse and were going to burn her, the countess decided that whether he was Pierre of Milan or simply Master Pierre, as she suspected, he should eat supper in the great hall. She suggested that perhaps the sergeant ought to relinquish his important place at the lower table in honor of such a guest.

"That he shall not," declared Sir Robert positively. "Think what the boy did, Adèle!"

So the sergeant kept his commanding seat that night at the head of the squires' and pages' table, and Pierre found himself at the exclusive little family table, which was a great honor and almost the closest he had ever been to the gentry.

It was not unusual in the absence of a priest for a distinguished guest to be asked to say the prayer at the beginning of a meal. Bernard suggested that this honor fall to Pierre, confident that Pierre would utter the forthright colloquial phrases with which the common people of France thanked God that they had something to eat. Pierre hesitated for a moment, not quite sure what to do. He could have said graces in French, English or Italian, or, for that matter, he could have thanked Allah, the true, the compassionate, whose prophet is Mohammed, if it had been demanded of him. But he guessed it would be proper to say the Latin words, like Isambart. Thanks to the secular lessons of Nicolas Midi, he was also able to interpolate a reference to the plague, the dry fields, and the scarcity of food without too many grammatical errors. Only Sir Robert happened to have enough Latin to correct him, and, of course, he did not. In fact, he secretly enjoyed the look on Bernard's face, while Louise's eyes began to sparkle at her champion's learning, and Claire whispered, "Mother, he talks like a priest!"

Her mother said: "Hush, child. That isn't polite."

"You do, though," said the lanky girl to Pierre.

Claire's chest was still flat like a child's, but in the last year or so her legs had lengthened and taken on a new and pleasing symmetry. If the blood of the Clermonts and the Épinals mingled in Claire as it had in Louise, there was reason to hope, the mother thought, that the chest, like the legs, would eventually be outstandingly beautiful.

"I learned it from a priest, mademoiselle," Pierre answered.

"Did you learn the part about the sickness and the drought from the priest, too?" Sir Robert asked. "I don't think I ever heard exactly that grace before."

"No, sir. I put that in because I forgot part of the prayer."

"Now I'd have had trouble finding the words, wouldn't you, Bernard? Your priest has instructed you soundly, my young friend."

"Can he teach me Latin?" cried Claire, "Mama, can I learn Latin from Pierre of Milan?"

"Not in one sitting," her mother answered. "It takes a long time."

Bernard suggested that one might start, at least, for he thought perhaps Pierre had shot his bolt and spoken all he knew.

"You begin, mademoiselle, with *amo, amas, amat,*" Pierre said, fumbling a little, "which is a word of action, and signifies preference." Isambart would have turned green. To love, a word of action! This was the result of the canon's secular lessons, not at all Isambart's own ecclesiastical method of teaching Latin. "When you know that thoroughly, you go on to other words."

"Quite a priest!" chuckled Sir Robert under his breath.

"Words that signify the things that one prefers?" Claire asked.

"Latin is very difficult," said her father. "One should not try to learn too many words at once."

The steward entered with an enormous silver platter that seemed to be laden with food. A server took their silver plates and the steward put all the best pieces on them, and what was left, which was little indeed, went to the sergeant and the men at the lower table. It was only goose they ate, which Pierre had eaten all his life, the cheapest meat in Normandy. The turnips were woody; the cabbage was tough. Only Sir Robert's cellars had not been affected by the famine. The wine in Pierre's silver cup was nothing like the wine in the armorer's house, where the cups were all of copper.

"We must leave Paris in a day or two," said Sir Robert. And then turning to Pierre: "No doubt there is plenty to eat in Normandy, but here, as you see, we fast every day. And the steward tells me provisions are harder and harder to procure."

That privileged old retainer took a step forward from his position behind his master's chair and muttered, "There are said to be wolves in the streets, Sir Robert!" and then resumed his accustomed place, shaking his head.

Claire said, "I heard the same story."

Sir Robert looked annoyed. "Henri hears all the rumors in Paris, and there is seldom any truth in them."

"I'm afraid he may be right about the wolves, Sir Robert," said Bernard. "Conditions are worse than you think, sir."

"My supper tells me that they are bad," Sir Robert replied. "But I hesitate to set out for home with the war threatening to flare up at any moment."

"It's been quiet a long time now," the countess observed.

"That's always when it's most treacherous. With a siege on, the trouble stays in one spot. You know what to expect. This lull is very ominous. And their leadership—we fought Bedford for a long time, and we knew his mind. Now he's dead, and we do not know what the English will do. Remember, Clermont is close to the frontier."

"Pierre got through," said Louise, "all the way from Rouen."

"Oh, a boy can easily slip through the forests," said Bernard.

"Did you really?" cried Claire excitedly. "All alone? What a brave thing to do!"

"I would remind you young ladies," Sir Robert said sternly, "that I may not be able to handle a sword quite as well as I did at Agincourt. A man does not lightly risk his entire family on dangerous roads." He looked accusingly at the countess. "Especially when he is encumbered with daughters."

The countess looked guilty, as she always did at this reference, and Claire felt as if she had no right to be alive.

"One cannot help being a woman," Louise observed quietly.

Claire asked: "How did you decide to be a man? I mean, we did not conspire to be women! We did not choose, Father."

"I suppose you did not, child." But he had always suspected that the countess might have done something about it, and she shared his feeling, though what she could have done not even her most intimate friends had ever been able to tell her.

"Undoubtedly we must leave Paris," Sir Robert continued. "To-morrow, perhaps, or surely the day after."

Everyone looked delighted, and the hungry lower table began to buzz with suppressed excitement. One had heard that there was food to the north, and another had talked with a man who said he had heard there was food to the south. There must be food in every direction, they thought, and they were all glad the old despot had finally made up his mind to get them out of the starving city.

"Our learned young friend plans to start home tomorrow, too," said Bernard; "but first he has an urgent ecclesiastical mission to perform. He tells me he came all the way to Paris to get some candles from the Sainte-Chapelle for a widowed woman in Rouen."

"That was foolhardy piety in these times, my boy," said Sir Robert.

"I think it was saintly!" cried Claire.

"Oh, he didn't know the plague was in town," Bernard told her.

"No, I did not," Pierre agreed. "I should never have had the courage."

"That I doubt," Louise said emphatically. "You were courageous enough where I was concerned."

"The lady Louise's beauty can turn the most timorous rabbit into a roaring lion," Bernard replied, inclining his head gracefully.

"I doubt if she was beautiful on the cart," Sir Robert muttered, and her mother shuddered.

"Master Pierre has already expressed his impatience to get on with his mission, and no one can blame him for that," Bernard continued.

87

"I am sure we shall all be glad to breathe pure country air again. I shall willingly show him the way to the church again tomorrow. I pointed it out this morning, but it is hard for a lad to remember directions in a strange city."

"That is kind of you, De Coucy," Sir Robert said a little formally, "and I have already decided to give the young man an escort back to Rouen whenever he decides to leave us. Not a big one, Pierre of Milan," he apologized, turning to Pierre and employing the nobiliary particle for the first time. Pierre knew he did not deserve it, and blushed deeply, but he felt as if the old nobleman had knighted him right there at the table. De Coucy bit his lip. "Most of my men are still with His Grace, the King," Sir Robert continued. "I keep only a few here for my family's protection. I should like you to take two of them with you on your way home. It is so small a thing that I shall be ashamed if you consider it the extent of my gratitude. What you have done for the countess and me is beyond all thanks. I know nothing about you. Are you rich, young man? Can I offer you money?"

"I did only what I felt impelled to do at the moment," Pierre said honestly. "I do not deserve any thanks."

"Do not be foolish, Pierre," said the countess. "We are not rich ourselves, but the count has offered to better your estate somewhat if it needs it. Most men's do. One who gives generously should learn to accept generously also."

Pierre thought a moment. The count possessed only two things that he wanted, and one of them was so utterly unattainable that he dropped his eyes immediately and looked at Claire, who was not in his thoughts. For some reason she averted her eyes from him just as quickly as he had looked away from Louise.

"Could you give me a horse, Sir Robert, for my own?"

There was a dead silence in the room. The men at the lower table were astounded at the daring or the naïveté of the request. The ransom of any three of them, if taken in battle, would just about equal the value of one good horse, and they all knew it. Sir Robert was as astonished as anyone at first. Then he laughed and brought down his fist on the table with a bang that rattled the cups and set the knives and plates to dancing.

"Now that was spoken like a true nobleman, Pierre of Milan! A horse you shall have!"

"Let him have mine!" Claire cried.

"That gentle creature?" retorted her father. "Pierre would go to sleep on her. Besides, I thought you liked your skinny pony."

"I do," Claire said.

"I think that is an excellent idea," said the countess. "Claire's horse is clean bred and has excellent spirit, but it has grown so high that Claire can scarcely mount her gracefully. Of course, the beast has a long back and small feet, but you would not want a great, stubby hulk of a Flemish charger anyway, would you, Pierre?"

"Nay, I should never have asked for a horse at all," said Pierre. "I do not know what I was thinking of. I had forgotten their great value."

"Their value varies, of course," said the countess. "Actually, Claire's horse is a very beautiful one, though not heavy enough for war. I think she is a very proper mount for you to ride home on with your men-at-arms. They will be riding mules, will they not, Sir Robert?"

"Why, yes, of course," he answered.

Isambart's colleague, Auguste de l'Isle-Adam, was a priest and a chirurgeon, with noble blood in his veins. He had moved from the cloister of which he was the head and come to live in the mean and restricted quarters under the Sainte-Chapelle during the sickness.

The churches were all crowded, but none more so than the Sainte-Chapelle. No sooner had Father Auguste concluded his prayers for their souls in the church above than he was called upon to minister to their bodies on the floor below.

Bernard and Pierre arrived early next morning, for the count had decided to leave Paris that day, and preparations had gone forward far into the night. They waited their turn among the people, some of whom looked sick but most of whom were only frightened.

Father Auguste had burdened himself with more duties than one man could adequately discharge. The pleasure that he felt at seeing so many people in church was tempered by the knowledge that most of them would not be there if they had not been afraid. And his gratification at being able to alleviate some of their illnesses was sobered by the realization that most of their ills were imaginary, so that those who were really sick had to wait too long. It was not quite possible for him to separate completely the characters of priest, nobleman, and chirurgeon. The result was a tired, impatient man.

He knew Bernard slightly, but there was no reason for him to spend more time with him than with anyone else.

"Well, De Coucy," he said, "did you just come from church, and do you think you are sick, too?"

"Nay, Father," Bernard replied in a silky voice, "we both heard mass at dawn," which was not true, "and we are well. I have brought you a pilgrim, Father. He says he has a letter for you. I must say, however, now that you mention it, that I do suffer from headaches in the morning sometimes. I trust that is not a sign of the plague."

"Drink less wine," said the priest. "It will do your complexion good. It is not a sign of the plague. Now let me see the letter."

Pierre had it in his hand, with a purse containing the widow's alms. The priest broke the seal, giving Pierre a quick appraising look. "Well, you do look healthy. I'm glad somebody does. Who are you?" He started to read the letter.

"I am Pierre, Father."

Auguste de l'Isle-Adam looked up from the parchment. "Hm, yes, so it says. I can easily give you what you require. It was brave of you to come to Paris."

"I didn't know—" Pierre began.

"Be assured, Reverend Father," interrupted Bernard, "that Master Pierre had no intimation of the danger."

"Let the boy tell it, De Coucy. Of course he did not. Isambart would never have sent him. But you cannot get within ten leagues of Paris without hearing about the plague, and Pierre came on anyway."

"Nevertheless, I shall be glad to be on my way again," Pierre said.

"Isambart speaks highly of you, son," the priest remarked. "I shall go get your candles. You may read the letter." But when he returned with a sizable package, the parchment lay untouched on the table, though Bernard was wrinkling his brow over it.

"I cannot read, Father," said Pierre.

"I can," said Bernard, and indeed he could, and write and calculate as well.

Father Auguste took a pen and began rapidly to write an answer to Isambart, using the swift, new Italian script that had lately begun to replace the ponderous Gothic. Bernard thought he had never seen a letter written so fast, and of course he could not read the slender characters that looked to his eye like elegant serpents coiling across the parchment.

"You should learn to read and write," said the priest. "The Church needs men who are not afraid of the plague. You hear of them all the time, but you can never lay your hands on one. Only this morning I heard of a man who snatched a body from a death cart. The woman was not dead, but she had the plague, and the man is said to have cured her in the space of one night in a manner that is little short of miraculous. The story is all over Paris, and it grows more remarkable every hour."

"I do not think I ought to be a priest," answered Pierre. "Perhaps I shall be a merchant, though first I shall have to study mathematics, as well as reading and writing."

"That woman was my cousin, Father," said Bernard, "and the man who wrought the miracle, as you call it, is Pierre. Actually Louise did not have the plague."

"Now that is astonishing," said the priest, laying down his pen. Except for a lively twinkle in his eye, his face was perfectly expressionless. One never could be sure how much a priest knew, and Pierre was not comfortable under the close scrutiny of the sophisticated Parisian clergyman. Father Auguste added a postscript to his letter:

This bright boy has lightened an otherwise heavy day. I have tried with poor success to interest him in the priesthood, but he will have none of us, and indeed the Calling is not for everyone. Perhaps his talents lie in another direction. He evinces an interest in the science of mathematics. Be sure he learns to read.

Yours in ✝
AUGUSTUS

When Pierre and De Coucy returned from the Sainte-Chapelle, they found the count's household gathering in the courtyard. Sumpter mules, already laden with traveling chests and heavy rolls of mattresses, clothing, kitchen equipment, rugs, draperies, armor, weapons, food for humans, fodder for animals, and tents for the servants to sleep in, waited patiently at the stables, their halters secured to iron rings in the doors. The burdens were neatly secured to their backs with a military precision which the veteran of Agincourt insisted upon. Squires and pages stood ready with the family horses.

Women rode sidesaddle, of course, crooking their right leg over the pommel that was padded and cunningly shaped to fit the anatomy and give a measure of security to their seat. Sir Robert sometimes contrasted these ingenious, delicate saddles with his own functional military equipment, which had elevated forward parts to protect a man's body and a strong, high cantle that supported the loins and added the weight of the horse to the strength that a man's back put into the thrust of his lance. For ordinary riding it was the most comfortable seat ever devised, far more restful than most chairs of the period, while the graceful sidesaddles were vary fatiguing to the ladies and made their right legs go to sleep. But Sir Robert felt that a sidesaddle was quite suitable punishment for anyone who had been so thoughtless as to be born a woman. On the other hand, he was not so old that he was immune to the pretty picture that his friends' young daughters made on their uncomfortable little perches, especially in a breeze. Claire and Louise, of course, he constantly admonished to cover their ankles.

Since the count was obviously at the point of departure, Pierre and Bernard waited in the courtyard, and in a few moments the family appeared. Sir Robert wore his cuirass, for he still considered the roads unsafe, and his sword was buckled on. Indeed, he felt naked without it. But he did not wear his leg pieces, gauntlets or helm in the city of Paris, though his page kept them handy. A squire carried his lance.

This weapon served also to designate the count's rank, since it bore his flag with the green mountain and the white tower. An ordinary knight might fix to his lance a pennon, which was a flag with a forked tail, and even a squire had a pencel, which was a long, narrow ribbon of pretty silk. But only a great noble with a substantial command, or one who had distinguished himself by extraordinary bravery in battle, was entitled to the banner, which was square. Since Agincourt, Sir Robert's had been square.

Louise and her mother wore practical turbanlike headpieces, lower than Sunday dress and suitable for a journey. Louise got onto her horse with easy grace, disposing her skirts about her legs with a practised, elegant hand, and if the jeweled red velvet of her dainty shoes betrayed the smallness of her foot and the slenderness of her ankle, it was the fault of the contrast they made with the emerald-green folds of her skirt, or the breeze that swept round the old stone towers and kicked up the dust in the court. "Modesty cannot command the winds, my father."

The countess's mount was a sturdy, low beast of proven endurance, and Adèle d'Épinal got up on him with great dignity. A squire made a stirrup of his hands, and another offered his shoulder, and the lady came down with a bump, while the horse stood his ground with a fortitude that was a part of his breeding and a certain resignation that was the result of years of training.

Claire had unaccountably elected to wear her tall, tapering conical cap with its heavy, impractical orange veil, and a new gown of rich blue velvet, which was certainly not proper to travel in. But since her new outfit would lend distinction to the cavalcade as they made their way through the streets of Paris and give her daughter some needed practice in managing the cap, the countess let her wear what she pleased. Under Pierre's eye Claire restrained the healthy bounce with which she usually leaped on the horse that Pierre now rode, and mounted with a ladylike ease that compared favorably with her older sister's, her cap perfectly balanced, her eyes shining.

"Claire is growing up," Sir Robert observed.

"It's the horse," said her mother. "She looks bigger on a smaller mount."

Then Sir Robert himself mounted. He had had a stiff leg for so long that it was natural for him to have developed the eccentricities with which people always hide their infirmities. In mounting, he lifted the leg to a great height over the cantle of the saddle, at the same time jerking his body erect with a sudden exaggerated movement. The whole effect was to give the action, which was now second nature to the old man, an air of urgency and determination. It was not at all awkward to witness.

He would have liked to draw up the bridge, as he did when he left his estates in Clermont, but the chains were rusted through and the old planks would certainly have fallen to pieces. Even Sir Robert could find no reason for lifting the bridge over a filled moat that was fragrant with the blooms of late-season flowers. Henri, the steward, double-locked the double doors and hung the heavy iron keys at his belt with the others.

At this point De Coucy, without saying good-by, went over to talk to the countess, while the sergeant detached himself from a group of the more important of the count's retinue and brought the two men-at-arms whom the count had designated for the service and delivered them to Pierre. They each had a mule, like all of the common soldiers, and there was an extra mule to carry their baggage, a further mark of the count's favor. Pierre saw that his sack was neatly arranged between two small traveling chests which were strapped with good new leather harness to the animal's back. The men had honest open faces and were armed handsomely for their class. He knew he was being well treated.

93

He approached Sir Robert to express his thanks, hoping he could find the proper words, but the count relieved him of the necessity by doing all the talking himself.

"I am loath to say good-by, Pierre of Milan, but our way lies north through the Porte Saint-Denis and yours south through the Porte Saint-Jacques, and it is fitting that we bid you farewell here."

Pierre bowed in his saddle with an ease that was the result of his youth, not training, and kissed the hand of the countess, which was already moist with the gathering heat of the day, and the hand of the lady Louise, which was cool as a rose petal. But Claire was still so young, despite her adult dress, that she was permitted to kiss him good-by, on the mouth, like any other child. Her mother eyed the embrace thoughtfully.

"I think perhaps you are right, Sir Robert. Claire is growing up."

Under her breath, as if it were a precious secret, the girl whispered, "I am glad you are riding my horse!"

Then the count embraced Pierre and kissed him on the forehead as if he were a son of his body. "Always fare well, good lad. And if you ever need me, come to Clermont. The gates will open like magic, night or day, to Pierre of Milan."

"I suspect," smiled the countess, "at least one in the family would smuggle you out the keys."

"And keep the men in your service, if you want them," added the count.

"Indeed, I have no service, Sir Robert."

"You will have," said the old soldier confidently. "Return them in the meantime, when they have done their duty."

Then the squire slapped the lance into its holder, and the sergeant shouted a command to the soldiers, and Sir Robert led his men and his women out of the courtyard and onto the street. Pierre and his own two soldiers were the last to leave, except for a couple of the count's servants who barred the gates from the inside with the heavy timbers that fitted into the iron cleats. Then they squeezed through a narrow little door that opened in the body of the larger gate and through which only one man could pass at a time. The steward locked this little door also, and hurried to resume his place behind Sir Robert. De Coucy was riding back and forth among the women, attending courteously to their little wants and making sure that they were comfortable.

Pierre watched the glittering cavalcade as it passed out of his sight, like figures that dissolve when the dream fades away in the morning. He had not felt so lonesome since the night he fled from the outlaws in the woods, and his present desolation partook of the same eerie unreality as that long-ago, almost forgotten tragedy. He looked stupidly up at the high, solid gate that barred all entrance into Sir Robert's house. The rusty noise of the locking bolt still grated on his ears with desperate finality.

Suddenly he was jarred out of his unhappy reverie by a pleasant, gruff voice that reminded him that the noble family were real.

"Now look at that, will you!" said one of his new retainers.

Pierre saw it, too. It was a dainty handkerchief that one of the women must have dropped, lying almost at his feet. For a breathless moment he hoped that it might be Louise's, and intended for him as a memento or a token. Indeed, it might mean almost anything.

But the other man said he had distinctly noticed the countess, who was subject to colds, using it several days ago, and the object instantly lost its appeal.

"Do you want it, young master?"

Pierre did not.

"I'll keep it then and return it when next I see the lady."

"In the meantime," Pierre said, giving an order for the first time in his life, "soak it with vinegar. I still have some that the monks of Saint-Germain gave me. Cover your nose with it, and it will serve to keep away the sickness. We are badly exposed here," he added, forgetting about the bit of lace, "and I think we ought to get out of the city as fast as our mounts can carry us."

"Now what are you sniffling about?" Sir Robert asked Claire in another part of town.

"Oh, nothing, Father," she replied, and wiped her eyes with her sleeve.

"She's probably nervous," said the countess. "Who wouldn't be in these streets? Use your handkerchief, Claire. It isn't polite to wipe your face on your dress like a peasant."

Claire pretended to fish for it in her sleeve. "I think that I lost it, Mother."

"Now did you indeed! That was careless of you."

"Do take mine," said Bernard, riding up and proffering her one almost as pretty as the one she had lost. It had suddenly occurred to De Coucy that if Louise would not have him, perhaps Claire might some day be persuaded to.

Louise looked quietly at both of them. There was great sympathy and understanding in her expression, and her large eyes were perfectly serene.

A few days later Pierre dismissed his escort in the woods outside Rouen, for they were not anxious to enter an English city, and Pierre would not have known what to do with them anyway. But he kept the good pack mule, which they insisted Sir Robert had instructed them to give him, as indeed he had. But it was Claire's doing, for she said she did not want her pony to be burdened with the baggage as well as the body of that big young man.

# CHAPTER

# ✳ 13 ✳

WORD OF THE PLAGUE and the famine in Paris had reached Rouen before Pierre returned. Hugh and Maria had spent a week in exhausting suspense and prayerful anxiety. Isambart called every night for news of his protégé, and shook his head when there was none.

Then one bright morning Pierre turned up in excellent health, tanned from his exposure to the sun, riding a fine horse and leading a sumpter mule that was better than either of Hugh's own, with a load of baggage which, if it consisted entirely of candles, must represent the loot of every church in Paris. The chests contained only his pack, however, and the package which the priest had given him, for his two men had taken their simple belongings with them and the food, which Pierre would no longer need.

Pierre explained how he had come by such valuable property, and the odd manner in which he had met the family of the Count de la Tour-Clermont.

"He had reason to be grateful," said Hugh, and was inclined to attribute Pierre's remarkable preservation from the sickness to the soaking with hot vinegar which he had had the day before.

"Was she pretty?" Maria asked, and Pierre said that she was. But he was young enough to add that that was nothing to him.

In the meantime he displayed a set of alarming symptoms, looking foolishly up at the sky or vacantly down at the river, smashing his fingers awkwardly in the shop and staring for long periods of time at unfinished pieces of work in his hands and never answering when he was spoken to, as if he had suddenly lost his hearing.

If they had had children of their own, they would have spotted the trouble at once and sent him off for a swim in the river. But with the acute sensitivity of foster parents, they consulted Nicol the Chirurgeon, and that wise old man sent them to talk to Isambart in his cell. So it was the celibate Isambart who sent the boy for a swim in the Seine in September.

"The girl must have been most attractive," he said sympathetically, when they saw the light. "There is nothing like good cold water to take the mind off the things of the flesh. Any old priest will tell you that. The young ones might be more reticent. That and prayer, of course. But I suspect Pierre will stay in the world. Even my colleague at the Sainte-Chapelle thought his talents secular rather than ecclesiastical. This same priest, I may add, reminded me of a fault which I have committed too long. I reproach myself that nothing has been done about the boy's education.

"I think it would be wise," he continued, "to take him out of your smoky shop, my friend. We cannot send him to the University of Paris, because we know too well that conditions are not healthful there. But here in the cathedral school he can learn to read and write the several languages he already speaks. Except Turkish, of course. He will also perfect his Latin, which is very shaky, though the poor canon did his best, and he will also learn the science of mathematics. The priest of the Sainte-Chapelle unaccountably noted in a postscript to his letter that Pierre has shown an interest in mathematics. That amazes me."

"Me, too," said Hugh. "I had no idea he was interested in mathematics."

"Neither had I," said Maria.

"And I think," Isambart continued, "that we may be singularly fortunate in being able to acquire a princely tutor for him in the practice of horsemanship, the science of arms, and the art of speaking politely to noble lords and ladies, though Pierre seems to have done great credit to your house already in that respect without formal training. Did you ever hear of the Sieur de la Salle?"

"I think I did," Hugh said, after reflecting a moment. "Was he not a famous French knight of the last century? Quite an adventurer?"

"He was, Hugh. How long the memory of brave men lives! He has a son named Antoine de la Salle, who is now tutor to no less than young John of Anjou, the Duke of Calabria."

"I had not heard that the Sieur de la Salle ever married and settled down," Hugh said.

"Unhappily he did not," Isambart answered sadly. "But he had the son just the same: Antoine de la Salle, a man about your age, Hugh. Like his energetic father he has traveled all over the world, serving many masters, teaching young nobles, and writing lively stories about how to behave toward the ladies. None of my habit could teach Pierre that, of course. La Salle ought to be just the man.

"He has a bad temper and a roving eye, and, at the moment, he is in disgrace with his master. He lives in that bad little inn on the waterfront, spending his days writing letters to his lord, probably begging forgiveness for whatever he did. The duke has a daughter. I have heard that he eats nothing but cabbage soup and has lost much weight since he exiled himself in Rouen. Shall I speak to him, Hugh?"

"By all means," Hugh said. "You seem to have found the very man. Don't you think so, Maria?"

"I suppose Pierre is of an age to learn those things. I confess that I hate to see him grow up. But haven't you chosen quite a rogue as his tutor, Father?"

"He will have to deal with rogues," the priest replied. "And Antoine de la Salle is not a rogue. All teachers of chivalry live by their wits. They teach how to fight, but they themselves are not fighters. Besides, I do not know whether the warrior or his tutor is the greater rogue. But I am persuaded that the great Duke of Anjou has not hired a scoundrel to teach his son."

"Maria agrees. I know she does," said Hugh.

"Yes, I believe I do," Maria answered. "Think of our Pierre being taught by the teacher of the son of the Duke of Anjou!"

"La Salle's fee may be high," said Isambart practically, "but it will still be cheaper than if you sent him to Paris, for Pierre can live and eat at home. The fees of the cathedral school are reasonable. In fact, if I did not know that you can well afford it, Hugh of Milan, they would be nothing at all."

"The clergy giveth, the clergy taketh away," Hugh misquoted impiously. "Blessed be the name of the clergy."

"Who else does even so much?" Isambart asked simply. "But I would not bargain with you over Pierre. Leave that to La Salle."

"Nay, Father, 'twas a bad joke I made. You know I would not bargain either. Not even with La Salle."

"Then I shall, Hugh, with your permission, and with yours, Madame. Incidentally, it has come to my ears that the Baron de Retz is going to be hanged."

"That is perfectly delightful," said Maria.

Within the year Antoine de la Salle grew fat again on the armorer's gold. All Isambart's powers of persuasion could not effect a reduction in his fee, but La Salle compromised to the extent of accepting his pay in installments rather than the lump sum that he had at first insisted upon.

Pierre spent his mornings at the school, because his tutor never got up till noon. The scholastic subtleties that had made the renown of the great continental universities formed no part of the provincial curriculum of the Cathedral School of Rouen. There the hard-working monks drilled into their hardheaded students the essentials of reading, writing, mathematics, and a modest understanding of theology. They knew from experience that when they had done that, they had done all that could reasonably be expected of them. Of course, when they found an ambitious student like Pierre, who had actually experienced the value of what they were trying to teach, they were inclined to make much of him and redouble their pedagogical efforts. For many years Rouen had been bilingual. Pierre belonged to a generation which could not remember when English had not been spoken by the better people of town along with their national French. Some of the teachers at the school conducted their classes in English, and one of the best was an English friar, son of a sea captain, who taught the science of mathematics, with particular reference to profitable trading. As a youth he had gone to sea in one of his father's ships. He had become acquainted with the products imported from the East and the products exported from the West. He taught with a curious crudity, and his classes had no standing among the young French noblemen.

But among Pierre's classmates were several English lads of gentle birth who were not ashamed to listen to their countryman expatiate on elusive mathematical abstractions while he illustrated them with homely actualities of commerce. Could a traveler in time have observed these young Englishmen in their French school at the end of the Middle Ages, he would have detected in their earnest attention the genesis of the spirit with which their remote descendants, in another age and a bigger world, were to found a thalassocracy beside which the proud sea empires of Renaissance Venice and Genoa would shrink to a contemptible handful of islands.

This is how the practical monk taught mathematics:

A crew of a ship can drink up half their supplies of water in a week, three-quarters in a fortnight. In a month they will all die of thirst if the sea stay calm. But if a port be sixty leagues away, and if a fair wind carry them ten leagues a day, they will reach the port before they perish and replenish their stores, with the help of God.

And suppose that a factor in an Eastern port buys a cargo of spices from the heathen caravans and pays £1,000 for it. The cargo will sell for £20,000 in France, and the profit is the difference, minus the expenses, of course, which must be added together and subtracted from the £19,000. It is a profitable voyage.

But if sea water should enter the ship through the carelessness of the crew, or by reason of their sins, and if nine-tenths of the cargo be spoiled, the profit will not equal the expenses, the Jews will take the factor's ship, his children will beg on the streets, and he himself will languish in a debtor's prison.

In a year or two the problems became very lengthy and involved, but they were always practical and easy to visualize. The student who did his work correctly was made to feel that he had personally conducted a profitable and interesting venture.

As for the languages Pierre spoke, it was as easy to learn to write them all at once as it would have been to learn them singly. French and Italian had not diverged from the parent Latin as far as they were to do in later ages, and it was considered little more of a feat to converse in Latin than in Italian. Before he was out of his teens, Pierre could read, write, and speak both. But there was no one to teach him to write Turkish. Abdul was illiterate.

Near the end of his Rouen schooling, Pierre made the momentous discovery that a large empire of almost heretical Christians existed around Constantinople, worshiping paintings, taking Communion in two kinds, and writing the Greek they spoke in an alphabet which was not understood among Western nations. This distant land was very rich in gold and very poor in spirit, which was as much as most Frenchmen knew about the venerable Eastern empire.

The afternoons he spent with Antoine de la Salle, but that noble tutor stayed in Rouen only a year. At the end of a twelvemonth his pleading letters effected their design and he was reconciled with his master. But he left in Pierre's mouth a persuasive flood of pretty words that could be released when the occasion required it. Some things he found that Pierre already knew, and when there appeared no way for him to have learned them, the master put it down to instinct. He had run across precocious lads like that before.

It was swordsmanship that captured Pierre's fancy, however, far more than the art of saying things one did not mean. And since everyone knew that Pierre was not nobly born, La Salle also instructed him in the best methods of thrusting the pike, swinging the mace, and discharging the deadly arbalest. Pierre also became proficient in the English longbow, the fastest shooting weapon of the time. It had humbled the nobility of the continent for generations.

The noblest weapon of all, the lance, Pierre never learned to use. He had a horse, and he could have had scores of lances. Hugh of Milan made them better than anyone in Christendom. But La Salle did not dare subject his student to the contempt of the noble young men who had already embarked on the orthodox way to knighthood and had taken service as pages and squires with their noble kinsmen and influential friends. They were already jealous of a commoner who could afford the tutor of a duke. Cross lances with him they would not. Moreover, La Salle would have ruined his courtly reputation.

"But I'll tell you a secret, young man," he said one day, as if he were whispering treason in the king's house. "The lance is a freak and futile weapon. It has grown so long and armor has become so good that two knights can no longer hurt each other. They break their lances, unseat each other, and fight on the ground with swords. Nobody will object to your learning the sword."

"Lances are dangerous against common soldiers," Pierre objected.

"No, it's the horses. Imagine yourself on the field of battle. You are a footman, say, armed with an arbalest. Suddenly against you there comes charging a line of towering men in shining armor on heavy horses. They fly at you like the wind. Would you not run, even if the charging knights had no lances at all?"

"I believe I would. I'd shoot first, though."

"Naturally you would. But now suppose the knights came at you on foot, with their spears but without their horses. You are armed with a short pike. Would you be afraid?"

"I should not, Master Antoine. My pike could jab faster than their long, heavy lances."

"That is correct. The pike is the grandsire of the lance, Pierre, and a better fighter. There is no chivalry in the pike. No courtly rules restrict its use. Remember, when you come to save your life, that a man dies quickly if you can pierce those soft spots in his head: the eyes, the nose, and the mouth. If your point is struck down, aim for the belly. It is foolish to seek the breast, which is always well protected, and besides, you will get tangled up in the ribs. With a wound in the belly a man dies surely but slowly, Pierre, so watch lest he kill you in his pain and despair. Should your point be struck lower still, aim for his private parts. Thrust quickly. It is astonishing how craven a man becomes at a threat to his manhood. Usually he turns sideways, and then your point has a chance to recover its height, and you can thrust your assailant through the neck."

Then they would practice with their swords.

The day before La Salle left Rouen, he told Pierre something of great importance. "Your swordplay is good, Pierre. I have no fear that my reputation will suffer at your hands. But I hate to see my pupils die. I have come to like you. My nature is generous. I have determined to impart to you my greatest secret."

"How to fight unfairly?" Pierre asked, who was well acquainted by now with some of La Salle's tricks.

"Do not put it so, young man. That is not the proper speech I have taught you. Say rather that it is a cunning means of improving one's advantage when the accepted strokes have been of no avail, especially if it is dark and no one is looking. Now the secret is this: forget that the sword is a noble blade and think of it as a common pike. Seek not to slash, but thrust, boy, thrust! It is my own invention. Not half a dozen men in Christendom know it."

"That is indeed a new thought, noble Antoine. I never heard of thrusting with a sword."

"Oh, it sometimes happens by accident in battle. But our slashing knights want gaping wounds. The more delicate death by internal bleeding is hardly ever thought of. And now, if we can persuade your father to stop his hammering, perhaps we can practice a few of the thrusts. I dare not instruct you in public in this dirty business."

# CHAPTER

## ✴ 14 ✴

THERE WAS a gangling lad with a narrow chest and a pale, intelligent face and a heart that was stouter than his body. He was William, Baron of Strange and Blackmere, the grandnephew of old Sir John, the fifth Earl Talbot, the bravest Englishman in France. William was just the age of Pierre, and so highly connected that it never entered his head to be jealous of a commoner. His friendship for Pierre dated from an incident that had happened in the mathematics class about a year after La Salle rejoined his master.

William had worked hard on a long problem in shipping that involved the computation of harbor fees and the translation of Turkish aspers into English pounds, writing the figures in a clear legible hand on some sheets of parchment, of which he always had an ample supply. (Pierre's store of parchment was so limited that he wrote small to conserve it.) When William left the room for a moment to attend to an urgent call of nature, a husky, acquisitive student sitting beside Pierre furtively pocketed the valuable sheets, which were written on only one side. The teacher saw what happened, but said nothing about it. When William returned, his property was gone. He looked round the room with a pained expression, his face slowly suffusing with red like a leaf after a frost.

"What is the matter, Lord Strange?" asked the teacher.

"Nothing, Friar John," the young man replied. He sat down, toying with his quill as if it were a weapon. There was murder in his black eyes.

"If nothing is amiss, you had best be at your problem," the monk continued. "It was well along yesterday, and you will probably achieve the correct answer today. Fail not to subtract from the profit the tribute that must be paid to the heathen garrison at the Chersonese," and he placidly adjusted on his nose a pair of spectacles which were still so rare in France that many people thought them magical.

Pierre had witnessed the theft also. Without changing his expression or stopping his writing, he lifted his leg under the table and brought down his hard heel crushingly on the toes of the malefactor.

"Yi!" bawled the startled young man in a loud voice. Again the monk looked up from his big folio volume.

"Are you in pain, James Barrow? If you are sick, I shall send for the chirurgeon. But if not, you have no right to disturb the class with such exuberant exclamations."

Barrow nursed his toes under the table, glaring at Pierre.

"Give it back!" Pierre whispered menacingly.

"I beg your pardon, Friar John," Barrow said. "I think a flea bit me."

" 'Twas no flea," muttered William under his breath. Pierre continued to write busily.

Barrow saw that he was outnumbered two to one. The combination of William's position and Pierre's size was too much for him. He reached to the floor, and appeared to discover something.

"Is this yours, William?" he asked, flinging the notes carelessly on the table. "I found it on the floor just now."

The Englishman nodded.

"You did me a service," William said to Pierre after the incident. "I'd have challenged him, if I'd ever found him out. Then my uncle would have beaten me, whether I won or lost. He is forever conserving my precious hide. I think he wants me to be a priest."

"You'd have won," Pierre said. "Barrow is clumsy with his sword. I don't like the sneak."

Many times during their Rouen schooling William of Strange and Blackmere crossed swords in friendly practice with Pierre of nothing, sometimes under the approving eye of proud old Sir John Talbot himself, who saw nothing improper in his grandnephew's friendship with a commoner who had been schooled by the tutor of the son of the Duke of Anjou.

At the Feast of the Holy Innocents in the winter of 1443, when both William and Pierre were nineteen, there occurred in Rouen one of those astonishing holidays called the Feast of Fools. It was an occasion for the relaxation of ecclesiastical discipline, especially among the younger clergy. Both they and the people enjoyed it, and this year the festival promised to be exceptional. A clement season had brought a bountiful harvest, and even the political weather seemed favorable. It was widely rumored that the truce which had been an actuality for so long was about to be ratified into a treaty of peace between the two ancient antagonists.

The English were especially considerate of the French, and the French were extraordinarily polite to the English. All over Normandy and France city gates were left up long after sunset, as a mark of mutual trust and esteem. If, on both sides, men were stationed with sharp axes which could sever the ropes at a single swing and send the ponderous portcullises crashing down at a moment's notice, nobody ever saw them and they had no official orders.

At Vespers time the altar of the cathedral was ablaze with a hundred candles, but a keen eye would have observed that they were not the pure waxen variety that shed the clear, holy light at Mass, but cheap tallow substitutes of the meanest kind, unblessed and unsightly. They smoked, they guttered, and they dripped. Nobody cared.

People crowded into the church. They were dressed for a holiday, and they were all talking out loud, making jokes with their neighbors, cracking nuts noisily with their teeth and munching interminably on large, tasty sausages. Here and there in the aisles little groups played at dice or cards. Women nursed their babies, tradesmen stood on the seats, shouting over the heads of the intervening people, discussing the upswing in trade or debating the likelihood of continued prosperity with the coming of peace. From time to time a bottle of cider or wine would make its appearance from nowhere, and it was hailed as a benevolent miracle and instantly disposed of.

Within the sanctuary, officiating at the high altar in a parody of the sacred ritual, was a young subdeacon, clad in the robes of the Bishop of Rouen. He was not wearing the stole, of course. On his head was a holiday mitre, twice as high as a mitre ought to be, formed of gilt parchment, sparkling with imitation jewels, and decorated with the picture of an ass. The Feast of Fools commemorated the Flight into Egypt, and the ass was honored for a day. Two asses ears projected from the absurdly elevated headpiece, burlesquing the episcopal hat that took its shape from the fire of the Holy Ghost when it rested on the heads of the Apostles and gave them the gift of tongues.

"The Lord be with you," he intoned in a silly, cracked falsetto voice. "Heehaw!"

"And with thy spirit," responded the people. "Heehaw! Heehaw! Heehaw!"

In addition to the spurious bishop chosen by the clergy, a secular authority, the Lord of Misrule, was elected by the people. It was his duty to direct the festivities, and see that nobody kept sober after the mock service in the church.

There was dancing on the pavement outside the portico of the cathedral, and the high arched doorways were full of young couples palpably expressing their admiration for one another.

The Feast was ancient and honorable. No notion of impiety entered the mind of a single witness of such patently impious rites. It was tolerated in every Christian country, and in France it was actually encouraged. Serious priests, like Isambart, always hoped that nothing too dreadful would happen, but it never occurred to him to forbid the festivities, and he had personally seen to the candles on the altar, making sure that the good ones were not burned. Like everyone else, he was in the cathedral, watching tolerantly from an inconspicuous corner, while his clergy and his people enjoyed themselves.

William and Pierre had a prominent place near the altar rail, and they were surrounded by a group of noisy students who seemed to be gathered together for some purpose not immediately evident. Isambart eyed them distrustfully and speculated what deviltry they might be up to.

The high point in all the hilarious nonsense was the entrance of a live ass into the cathedral. The pretty girl that rode him this year was known as Ann of the Inn. She was daughter to the hosteler down on the waterfront who maintained such prosperous lodgings for soldiers, sailors, traveling pilgrims, nobles with their retinues, and anyone else who could pay for his hospitality, which was reputed to be generous and diversified.

She wore a short blue costume, exposing her shapely legs to the knees for everyone to admire, and she straddled the ass like a man. There was a good deal of admirable kicking of the long legs when enterprising young men would reach up and attempt to fondle the big doll that she held close to her breast. This, of course, represented the infant Lord.

Holding the halter as the animal made his progress up the aisle to the altar was the young Lord of Misrule, with a long curly beard, made of a horse's tail and dyed saffron, pasted to his face to make him look like St. Joseph.

The cathedral organ played softly all during the ceremonies. It was the privilege of the parish organist to supply appropriate music for the occasion. It was also his duty to warn the people from time to time by solemn ominous hymns that they were still in church and had better behave themselves.

At the altar the ass was fed a bucketful of oats and the doll was held

107

aloft; its hands were manipulated up, down, and sideways in a blessing to the people.

At this point a couple of the students around William and Pierre broke away from the group and dragged the organist away from his bench in spite of his horrified protests. One of them took his place at the mighty instrument, pulled all the stops, called loudly for more wind in the bellows and struck up the tune of a rollicking popular song that everybody knew, making so much noise that the rafters trembled under the venerable roof and the statues of the saints threatened to fall from their niches. Never before had the cathedral of Rouen been so full of sound and laughter.

The other young men in the group formed themselves into a self-appointed choir around William and Pierre. They raised their hearty voices in a shout of song that could be heard above the thunder of the organ. The words were confused and out of time and pitch, but even a deaf man could have understood from their gestures toward the impersonators of the Holy Family that it was a hymn of praise to the girl or the ass or both. There were several verses, ending with:

> "Hail to the ass who is full of religion!
> Who would not be in his happy position?
> Straddled by that which we know and we hope
> Would Christian the Turk and enamor the Pope!
> Hail to Rouen's virgin astride her good mule,
> And hail to ourselves and the Lord of Misrule!"

The reference to the pope was too much for Isambart. A saintlier man than Eugenius IV had never occupied the Holy See.

"*Malédiction!*" he gasped, laughing in spite of himself. He called to the organist who had been so ignobly unseated at the beginning of the row.

"Ring the Sanctus bell!" he admonished sternly. "This is going too far."

At the deep majestic voice of the great old bell in the tower, which was associated in the people's minds with the holiest of their mysteries, they quieted.

Most of them followed the actors out of the church, where the Flight into Egypt continued up one street and down another, losing more and more of its biblical character all the time. St. Joseph discarded his beard and put on a long false nose, which he waggled eloquently at all the pretty girls, and a jester's cap with tassels and bells, becoming again the Lord of Misrule.

Ann of the Inn, her donkey, and her doll, went back to the water-front, followed by a sizable crowd of sailors, soldiers, students, and other young men. Everybody was thirsty. Ann lived where thirst was a reproach.

Innkeepers were generally as honest as their customers. In spite of their reputation for cheating, overcharging, and other chicanery, they were more often robbed than robbers. For an innkeeper had no recourse if a noble knight forgot to pay or a humble sailor decided unexpectedly to sail away to the ends of the earth, leaving a balance due. It was no wonder they developed long memories and the habit of getting their money first if they could. They suffered under a complicated system of taxes and restrictive laws that protected the customer, while the laws that protected the hosteler were few and ill enforced. Their eyes and their wits were their best protection.

Among this humble fraternity of men who tried to be good but never could were many veterans of all periods of the interminable war. They were often pious men, or at least grateful for divine protection, of which they often stood in need, and since most people could not read, it was their habit to select an angel or a saint and hang the image over the door to designate the business and advertise the character of the establishment.

John o' Leeds had suffered a painful wound in his eye during the siege of Rouen the generation before. After its capture he was sick for several months in the little inn on the waterfront. The unfortunate Frenchman who owned the inn had been killed in the defense of the town, and his bereaved young widow nursed the handsome Englishman back to health and happiness with every means at her disposal. But the eye was blind. John o' Leeds was without a livelihood and the widow was without a husband. He had nowhere to go and she had no one to take care of her. Before the scars of the wound were white it became apparent that Ann of the Inn or somebody would be born, and they were married well in advance of that happy event. The inn had prospered greatly under the unprejudiced management of such a couple.

In its original ownership the inn had gone by the grandiose name of l'Hôtel Saint-Denis, in honor of the patron saint of France, and his image was painted on the sign over the door. St. Denis was depicted carrying his own head in his hands, as usual, in memory of the circumstance of his blessed martyrdom. But the patron saint of France was not popular among the English. John o' Leeds was repeatedly advised to substitute St. George, or at least a dragon. But his vivacious wife refused, and the saint remained. But all the English, and soon even the French, referred to the hostelry as the Inn of the Cutthroat.

John o' Leeds' vision in the eye that happily remained to him was so acute that he earned the ironical nickname, Blind Jack. His business methods were prudent and strict. He had never been known to treat a guest to a free drink. He never forgot a penny of the score. He made honest change in unclipped coins even to the drunkest guests. Inevitably the clientele confused the exacting proprietor with the blessed patron of the house, and he, not the saint, was thought of when the Inn of the Cutthroat was mentioned.

The inn was always busy, and especially so during holidays. Jack had been flattered and surprised when his attractive daughter had been chosen to play the Virgin in the theatrical doings at the cathedral. Now he prepared his house to accommodate the customers that he shrewdly surmised would follow her down to the waterfront.

Above the huge fireplace and in conspicuous places on the walls in the large public room were hung a decorative assortment of lances, pikes, swords, maces, and other weapons of the period, along with banners, pennons, flags, and colorful bunting. They gave a gay martial air to the room. Noblemen did the same in their halls. Great ones, especially the English, mounted the heads of stags they had killed in the chase. Blind Jack, being a commoner, could not hunt, of course, and the custom of mounting large dead fish on boards to look at while one ate had not yet been thought of, and, indeed, would have disgusted everyone.

Blind Jack prudently removed all the weapons, but he left the bunting and flags.

A waiter brought an armful of bottles from the cool cave under the house. This was the good wine. The bottles were heavy and made of glazed earthenware. He brought up a great number of jugs of cider, too, which had been especially good that year. It was cheap, strong, and popular. Then he rolled up a hogshead of ordinary wine and set it on the low wooden horse. Liquor from this vessel was drawn by turning a wooden spigot about a hand's breadth from the bottom. When the level sank to the spigot, it was necessary to tilt the barrel in order to obtain the wine which remained, and at this point the price went down, for the lees of wine are muddy and the flavor is poor. Many thrifty people waited for the barrel to tip before they ordered their drink. This critical little moment was always watched for, and Blind Jack always called attention to it. He would thump the nearly empty barrel with his big hand. A drumlike note would advertise the reasonable price that one might expect for the next few minutes. Cups would be held aloft, the waiters would fill them, and the so-called "darker" vintage would all be sold. Other innkeepers sometimes hid the barrel and furtively tipped it. Not Blind Jack.

The groom threw a big new log on the fire. The cook set a quantity of meats to turning on the spit that was long enough to impale and roast a man.

Blind Jack himself trimmed the wicks and turned up the lights in the ships' lanterns that made his inn bright as a noble's mansion. He speculated whether he should remove the expensive glass shades. They were the pride of his heart. When he heard laughter and voices in the courtyard, he was relieved that he would not have time to mutilate them. He reminded himself that his customers were usually pretty well behaved, and when they were not, he had always been able to handle them.

Ann opened wide the door of her home, and the cold, winter wind blew in the customers. She was surrounded by a group of noisy students so dense as to be almost in bodily contact. She had linked arms with two of the youngest. They were so proud of the honor and looked forward with such anticipation to the good-natured jokes that would be made about the incident that their cup of desire was filled and they wanted no other favors. Ann knew by experience that such boys were a safe, convenient escort.

William, Pierre, and a number of upper classmen followed. Blind Jack showed them to a large table near the fireplace with every mark of respect. Many soldiers and sailors were welcomed with equal warmth, though with less distinguished tables. There was also a sprinkling of elderly, well-to-do townsmen in heavy mantles of costly material and richly furred caps. These old gossips had come to watch, and to be shocked, they hoped, at the dancing of Ann of the Inn, who could sometimes be persuaded to entertain her father's guests. They, too, were given tables near the fire, to thaw them out and restore their appetites. The younger men, the mariners, and the men-at-arms sat anywhere when the tables were filled, even on the floor, which was convenient for the cards and dice that somebody usually produced. If nobody did, Blind Jack would always provide them. He had observed that money once exposed is more readily spent.

The men were hardly seated when they called for the good wine, paying for it by the bottle, pouring their own pewter cups full. Ann circulated among the noisy guests who were still laughing and joking, bringing a bottle to one, pouring a cup for another, and taking an order from a table that had exhausted its supply. She would call the order to a waiter in a loud, clear voice that could be heard over the noise of the crowd. She still wore her short blue skirt.

On every table there were trays of salt smoked fish, cut into small pieces, and little biscuits of bread that were sprinkled with aromatic seeds and large grains of salt. These tidbits were greatly liked, and they were free. Everyone knew why they were served, but Blind Jack made a point of supplying all one could eat, even to the poorest of his guests, so that no one could accuse him of discrimination.

Pierre had eaten a great many salty little biscuits which caused him to drink several cups of wine, like everybody else. The faces of his friends never looked so friendly. Even James Barrow, who was at the same table, seemed a kindly, goodhearted man. Pierre suddenly had an expansive idea. He felt for his purse; it was still there. He felt for his old money belt that he still sometimes wore, and that was there too.

"Gentlemen," he cried generously, "I pray you all to be my guests tonight. Let me be the one to pay for that beautiful joint turning brown before our eyes and begging to be eaten by noble, studious young men like you!"

The joint referred to was the ham of the biggest pig surely that ever had lived. The cook had skewered deep holes in it and stuffed them with the white meat of young chickens and fine-cut pieces of bacon. Some cloves, probably stolen by a sailor from one of Jacques Coeur's merchant ships, dotted the fat and filled the air with an expensive Oriental odor. The cook had given it special attention all evening, and from time to time he drenched it with honey and wine.

The entire table applauded Pierre except Barrow, who grumbled "upstart" under his breath, and William, who protested with all his might: "That isn't fair, Pierre. You are always faster than anybody else. Let me pay for the meat."

"No, I shall not, my friend. You always pay for everything."

Pierre looked up to see if he could catch Ann's eye and give the order. He was delighted to find her looking squarely at him. William, who thought her extraordinarily pretty, could have told him that she had scarcely taken her eyes off him since he came in the door. Pierre raised his hand to beckon her, but before he could finish the gesture she was at his elbow, as if propelled through the air by an arbalest.

"What will you have, my lord?" she asked brightly. "The house is yours."

"Ugh!" said James Barrow.

"The ham," Pierre answered, coloring up to the line of his thick curly hair. "And Master Pierre will do very nicely, thank you, lass."

"Nay, I spoke figuratively," she said saucily. She leaned her elbow on the table for a moment, resting her chin in the cup of her hand so that her face was close to his, and winked at him. " 'Twas my heart spoke," she said. "Is ham all you want?" Her posture caused the loose front of her blouse to drop away from her body, and since she wore no shift she exposed the whole white expanse of her firm, alluring bosom. Pierre could see for himself that the heart was alive and beating.

"*Petrus omnia vincit*," William observed ruefully. "It is a conspiracy! At least I must be permitted to buy the wine."

"Ham is all I shall share with my friends," Pierre said to the girl, who appeared delighted with the compliment. Pierre was visibly moved. He drained his cup and filled it again with so shaky a hand that everybody except Barrow laughed out loud and began making very broad good-natured jokes at his expense.

But Barrow said: "Our Lord Pierre is so recently weaned that one can expect him to gape at the sight of a breast or two."

"Now that was a poor joke," said William. There was black challenge in his level stare.

Pierre's face drained white, and he said: "James Barrow, I am waiting with eagerness to hear you say you meant no offense by your silly words."

"Nay, none at all, none at all, Pierre. How you two stick together!" Some of the men at the near-by tables nodded their heads, and there was a small murmur of agreement. For James Barrow, son of a respected knight, was not without friends. His father held a French viscountcy, though no lands in England, and it was likely that Barrow would one day acquire the French title. Like many new nobles he was touchy of his precarious aristocracy.

The cook gave the ham a final dash of honey, stopped the spit and began to unwind the delicate iron chain that was wrapped round it several times and kept it firmly affixed to the sharp spikes projecting from the body of the spit. Blind Jack himself speared the meat with two large skewers, one in either hand, and a waiter held a large wooden trencher under it to catch the juices that spurted out when the skewers struck home. Then the proprietor gently lowered the precious ham, the waiter cautiously raised the trencher, and the mighty piece of meat was conveyed by the two of them to the table, sizzling, smoking, spitting little jets of fat, and filling the room with a hungry delectable odor.

Blind Jack carved it into their shallow wooden bowls and the waiter placed a ladleful of root vegetables, stewed with a coney and flavored with a piquant sauce, into each dish. They all began to eat, carving the meat with the knives that the proprietor supplied.

Pierre's table manners were as good as a lord's, thanks to La Salle. William of Strange and Blackmere himself speared the vegetables with his knife no more deftly. Pierre held the meat between the thumb and forefinger of his left hand and transferred it to his mouth with grace and dignity, licking his fingers without making a noise. A dry palm was a sign of breeding. A greasy palm betrayed one's ignorance. When one finished, one wiped his fingers on a piece of bread and ate it.

William ordered a bottle of wine for every man at the table.

The ham was reduced to a bone. Pierre threw the bone to a big dog, who had not seen anything like it since he was a puppy, when all bones looked big. He trotted out into the courtyard with it.

After the ham they ate a meat pie, and after the pie a pudding, and after the pudding a wonderful confection of citrons, pale green to the eye, sweet and sour to the tongue, and sprinkled with crystallized sugar, a great rarity.

The man who had bought the ham seemed to have bought the entire larder of the Inn of the Cutthroat, and for an uneasy instant Pierre felt again for his money belt, which he began to suspect he would have to draw upon. But he forgot it an instant later when he saw Blind Jack and a waiter place another of William's bottles in front of everyone at the table.

When Pierre sipped it, his eyebrows went up in surprise. It was a rare, spiced hippocras that he had tasted only once or twice since Sir Robert's table, and then, of course, he did not know what it was.

"This is noble wine!" he exclaimed. "Here's honor to the noble lord who gives it to us!" He raised his cup to William, and they all drank to that.

William answered, "It honors a noble supper, my friend," and they all drank to that, too. And soon they were honoring themselves and their neighbors, the older men at the side tables, and even the honest men-at-arms drinking cider and playing dice on the floor near the door.

The wine was subtle and heavy and unpredictable. It was sweet in the mouth, but its sweetness was tempered by a bitter root that made one long to taste the sweetness again. It had an unusual greenish tinge. It would have been easy to sip all night long, but dangerous.

Barrow leaned back on his stool and gripped the table firmly, his eyes and his stomach a little out of control from the wine he had drunk and the food he had eaten.

"Noble indeed," he remarked, "but dull without music. Will you play your musette for us, Charles of Limoges?" This was the young musician who had performed so vigorously on the organ in the cathedral. He was the son of a seneschal who was highly respected in his native city. Charles of Limoges was studying medicine.

"I don't know if I can," he answered candidly. "The wine of our noble friend has left my lungs quite breathless."

Barrow said, "Oh, there's wind in you somewhere," and he suggested where else it might be available, and this time they all laughed heartily. Charles worked his fingers rather foolishly in front of his face, as if he could not quite see them.

"Would you be kind enough to count my fingers, Pierre?"

Pierre studied the hands closely.

"You are holding up two hands, of course, are you not, Charles?"

"Certainly I am."

"Two at least," said William, leaning far over the table and nodding his head in solemn assurance.

"There are," pronounced Pierre, "on either hand, by the tonsured pate of Friar John, who has taught us the useful science of mathematics, four fingers and one thumb, which is a total for two hands of eight fingers and two thumbs to cover the stops of your musette. I trust my calculation is correct. It was not easy."

"Why, then I'm all right!" cried Charles.

"Not the way I count," William objected, shaking his head seriously. "To my eye there are many more. No doubt a cup of wine will reduce Charles's supernumerary members to their proper count," and he drained his cup to find out. "Alas! They have now redoubled!"

Ann brought the instrument, which had been left with the proprietor when they came in. Charles tucked the leather bag under his arm, placed his eight fingers and two thumbs over the proper holes, and blew the bag full of wind. Then he squeezed the bag with his elbow against his body and played a few tentative squeaky notes, ending with a low-pitched mushy blast.

"There are bubbles in your musette, Charles," said William. "Why is that? What is the matter?"

"My musette will not play," the musician replied, "unless somebody dances to it." Everybody looked at Ann, and Barrow said:

"Come, girl, show us your legs."

Ann pouted. "Your invitation is about as polite as the musette's, James Barrow."

Charles of Limoges looked horrified.

"My musette impolite? My pretty little bag of wind not polite to the lady? Come! I shall punish him!" and he spanked the leather wind chamber smartly. It sounded as if he were slapping a person, and his cunning fingers found notes that almost exactly duplicated the angry wail of a punished child. They all laughed and Ann's pout disappeared. Charles began to play a dance tune and Ann pulled up her short skirt shorter still and began to dance.

She was loosely jointed, which was good for the dance, and remarkably graceful on her long legs that carried her in and out among the tables so that nobody was slighted. But she always came back to the big table by the fire, which took her close to Barrow as well as William and Pierre.

The dance, which they all knew, told the forthright little story of a crusader, who went to the Holy Land, and the lover, who stayed behind. There was the stately farewell, the long, lonesome interval, the meeting with the lover, his repulse, and final acceptance.

Ann's supple body and graceful limbs had an uncanny power of pantomime. At first some of the men sang or tapped their feet in time with the music, but as the dance became more intense, they fell silent and simply watched. Her hands and arms molded in the air the body of her phantom lover; at times one could almost see him. Her body seemed to fight him off, and then grew cold. Her fists clenched, her arms went straight and tight against her sides; she held her head proud and high and appeared to walk in rectitude in the broad light of day, but the man was still there, tempting. Then the mood of the music changed and the stiffness left her body. Her hands moved over the invisible partner again, but this time playfully, her mouth smiled, her teeth sparkled, and her feet tapped out the light quick steps of the lively melody. Then she leaned back, as if the embraces had begun again, and this time the arms did not protest at all, but welcomed the man. The upper part of her body was almost motionless; her face had an intense expression of utter abandon, and her hips and legs moved with such an animal realism that William began to sweat and Pierre gripped the table till his knuckles went white. As for Barrow, a little trickle of wine and saliva ran out of the corner of his open mouth, and he did not have the sense to close it. What the dance did to the elderly burghers one could only conjecture, but one could hear them breathing.

The pantomime ended on a very low moral note, with everyone happy except the crusader, who probably died in the Holy Land. At least he never appeared, even invisibly, again in the dance, which climaxed in a fast blur of Ann's lovely legs, which every man in the room now felt a personal claim to. Even a sober man would have had difficulty distinguishing whether it was one pair or two, and few in the room were sober.

Ann finished her dance close to Pierre's table, close to Pierre, but even closer to James Barrow. Everybody applauded wildly and shouted for more. They stamped on the floor and banged their cups on the tables, and Ann, all aglow and breathless from her exertions, bowed prettily to the table and again to the room, half turning her back on Barrow as she did so.

At this point the foolish young man closed his mouth, swallowed, and ran his hand far up under her skirt.

Blind Jack sighed, rose, and started to walk over to rescue his daughter. This sort of thing sometimes happened after the Dance of the Crusader, and he was prepared to deal with the nonsense.

But he was not prepared for what William did. The young nobleman's mind was hopelessly befuddled by the last bottle of wine. Ann had excited him while he was still sober. Now he was drunk, and her dance had inflamed his imagination beyond all sanity. He thought he had actually seen the lover in the last stages of the dance, ravishing the girl. He now confused Barrow with the lover.

"Begone!" he shouted, mouthing a frightful obscenity. When Barrow persisted before his eyes, astonished and not even withdrawing his hand, William picked up the heavy bottle, still half full, and hurled it with all his might at the stubborn image. His wild, drunken aim chanced to be devastatingly accurate. The bottle hit and broke squarely between the eyes of the unfortunate man. The force of the blow snapped back his head as if he had been struck by a cannon ball, and he toppled off his stool and fell to the floor. A sharp piece of the broken bottle could be seen projecting from his forehead as he fell. He lay perfectly still, his blood mingling with the greenish wine, dying it red on the boards of the floor.

Never in his life had James Barrow been known to have so many friends.

"Foul blow! Foul blow!" went up like a shout from nearly half the men in the room. William might have lost his life if Blind Jack had not had the foresight to remove all the weapons that usually decorated the walls. He was instantly the center of a shower of bottles, fortunately less well aimed than his own. A mug full of cider bounced off his head, drenching him with its cold contents.

But William was not friendless either. As he stood for a moment shaking the cider out of his hair and eyes, most of the students and everyone at his table closed round him in a protecting circle, using their stools as shields and threatening their assailants, who were mostly soldiers, sailors, and townsmen.

The elderly burghers fled at the first blow. They were not anxious to have their names figure in a brawl at the Cutthroat.

When the missiles continued after the first spontaneous shower, the students let fly some of their own, well aimed, with telling effect.

"The lights! The lights!" shouted Blind Jack. "Do not smash the lights!"

James Barrow bled on the floor.

William's senses, aided somewhat by the bath of cold cider, returned sufficiently to tell him that he was in a fight, and he dashed up to the front rank of the students.

"At them, men!" he shouted, brandishing another bottle and charging into the crowd. When they saw his wild face and his weapon, the ranks of the assailants thinned considerably. A good many of them ran out of the door, glad that they were able to save the price of their last drink, an unheard-of accomplishment at the Inn of the Cutthroat. Blind Jack thanked the saints that the knives had not come out. He would have been ruined. Perhaps he was anyway.

The students followed William. The solid charge broke up into a melee of individual fights. Half the stools were kicked to pieces and most of the tables were overturned. In the mixup on the floor, all the students who had been shocked into siding against William had an opportunity to remember their proper loyalties. More than once a student appeared to discover that he was fighting on the wrong side, and would instantly attack a townsman. The townspeople's ranks were thinned even more by these desertions.

Blind Jack had a curious weapon that he reserved for occasions of this sort. It was a stout, short tube of leather that looked a little like a sausage. It was packed hard with sand. When people fought in what he considered a dangerous fashion, he would bring it down heavily on the head of the man who threatened to do the most harm. So far he had not had to use it.

Charles of Limoges abandoned the battle when the tide seemed to turn in favor of the students. He went over to the fallen man who was the cause of the row. Ann had bathed all the blood and wine off his face. He had not moved or moaned since the bottle hit him, and except for an almost imperceptible movement of his chest, there was no sign that he was alive. There was no wound on his face except the one caused by the fragment of the bottle, which still stuck in his forehead. He had stopped bleeding.

Charles was an excellent medical student but he had never performed an operation on a living man. He held his hand to Barrow's heart and satisfied himself that it was beating. Rapidly, he thought, and not very strongly. He touched the bottle fragment, but it was stuck firm.

"I dare not extract it," he said. "His brains may gush out. There is only one doctor in Rouen who can handle this, Nicol the Chirurgeon."

"I have already sent for him," said Ann. At this point her father came up, his weapon in his hand, his face angry and anxious.

"Will he live?" he asked shortly.

"Not with that in his head," Charles replied.

"Then pull it out, man! Nay," he corrected, "do not pull it out. I have seen things like this before. Has a surgeon been called?"

"Of course," said Ann.

A waiter burst into the room from the street. He had ridden hard all the way from Nicol the Chirurgeon's house with the unwelcome news that the old man was sick.

"He said he was sicker than his patients and dared not leave his fire. He said, 'Let them come to me.' "

Just then a wail of pain went up from the other side of the room.

"Saints!" cried Blind Jack, "What was that?" And he ran over to the disturbance.

There he saw Pierre with one of his eyes rapidly taking on a puffy greenish appearance. He was astraddle a man, pommeling him unmercifully with fists.

"Can't you see the man has yielded?" shouted Blind Jack.

"He did once before," Pierre cried angrily, "but then he hit me when I let him get up. Like this!" he said, smashing his fist into the fellow's eye.

Blind Jack raised his weapon and hit Pierre over the head, perhaps a little harder than he meant to, and Pierre collapsed in a sweaty heap. The man he was beating ran out into the street, limping and howling and holding his eye. The angry proprietor tried to pick up Pierre, but he was much too heavy, and he left him lying on the floor.

The students were universally successful by now. Blind Jack and the waiters broke up the few individual fights that remained. The townsmen all took to their heels and the students congratulated each other and compared their hurts, which were not serious.

William sobered considerably when he saw what he had done.

"The man must be attended to at once," he cried. "I certainly never meant to do a thing like that. He will live, of course. Will he not, Charles?"

"I do not know. I do not know how deep the piece went in. I cannot move it with my fingers. Nicol the Chirurgeon is sick and will not attend him."

Blind Jack wailed: "He must not die here! I'll be ruined!"

"You'll be ruined, did you say!" cried William. "I'll be ruined if he dies anywhere! If Nicol will not come here, we shall take him to Nicol."

"There is a litter in the stables," said the intelligent waiter, who fancied a corpse in the establishment no more than his master. "No doubt you noble gentlemen have plenty of horses."

"Yes, yes, by all means harness it up," said William. "Take my horse."

"And mine," cried Charles, and half a dozen others offered theirs.

The groom and the waiter hung the litter between the two horses with great speed and skill. Nobody at the Inn of the Cutthroat wanted James Barrow around. If his guardian angel had personally directed the activities, he could not, short of a miracle, have got him faster out of the house.

"There is another of your group," said the innkeeper, "that you may wish to take with you. A tall man, with fair hair. He is over behind that table."

"Saints!" cried William. "It must be Pierre! What happened to Pierre?"

"He got hit on the head, I think," Blind Jack replied. "How should I know what happened to him? I don't think he is seriously hurt. I certainly hope not."

The two waiters placed the body of James Barrow on a long wooden bench and carried it gently to the courtyard, where they lifted up the bench and transferred him to the litter with solicitous tenderness.

Two students held the bridles while William and Charles attempted to ascertain the condition of Pierre. His eyes were closed, of course, because he was still unconscious, but one was so discolored and swollen that it did not seem possible that he could have opened it if he were awake. Charles ran his fingers through the thick hair. There was quite a bump on the scalp.

"There is no wound," he said, "and I can feel no fracture. The eye looks like nothing worse than the beginnings of a good black eye that will probably disfigure him for a month. It would do no harm, of course, for Nicol to take a look at him."

"Then take him out, by all means," said the innkeeper.

But his daughter said: "Why not keep him here, Father? The other is seriously wounded. He will take all the sick old chirurgeon's skill and time. We ourselves can take care of a black eye and a bump on the head."

"No doubt you are right, daughter, but let these gentlemen decide."

"There is something in what the girl says," Charles agreed. "Nicol the Chirurgeon will not welcome too many patients in the middle of the night."

"He will not refuse the one," said the waiter. "He as much as said so."

"Keep Pierre, then, Blind Jack," decided William. "No doubt your daughter can do as much for him as Nicol the Chirurgeon." Ann said she thought she could. "And here," said William, detaching the purse at his belt. "I am sorry for what I did to your inn. Do not charge Pierre a sou for the dinner. Mind, now. I shall hear about what you do."

"He is my honored guest, noble sir," answered Blind Jack. He caught the heavy purse on the wing. "He shall not be charged a sou, depend on it."

When Pierre awoke, he instantly began to pommel the body next to him, aiming in the dark where he thought the eye was, determined to avenge the perfidy of the scoundrel who had yielded and struck him. But the body was naked, and it spoke with a woman's voice and there was a soft bed under him.

"Be quiet, you big lout! You will wake my father!"

Pierre cried in a loud voice: "Who in blazes is your father, and who are you, woman?" He sat up in great alarm and total confusion.

"Sh-h-h! I am Ann of the Inn."

"Oh, I remember." He also remembered the Dance of the Crusader. His hand explored tentatively in the pitch black of the room, and it was not pushed away. He established to his satisfaction that, while it might not be Ann of the Inn, it was certainly not her grandmother. His voice became almost as discreet as hers. "I beg your pardon if I struck you. I thought I was still hitting a man."

"You nearly killed him, Pierre. My father had to knock you unconscious or you would have."

121

Pierre now felt his own bruised body, the lump on his head, and his swollen eye.

"I trust the room is quite dark," he said, "for otherwise I have been blinded."

"It is still dark, Pierre. But nearly time for sunrise, I think."

"My head aches," he said, "and my eye hurts, and I am most dreadfully thirsty."

"Of course you are. I felt sure you would be. Try to drink a little of this." He felt the cool brim of a cup against his lips in the dark. It was more of the greenish wine and it tasted wonderful. He drained it to the bottom. "Now you'll feel better," she said.

Pierre lay back on the bed. The wine made his head swim, but it chased the pain away and restored his memory and a measure of his discretion, though he knew he was far from sober.

"I appear to have suffered the loss of all my clothes," he said quietly, without a trace of expression in his voice. Actually he was not certain whether he had somehow caught the fancy of Ann of the Inn or been made a victim of some monstrous deviltry of the Cutthroat that had never even been whispered about.

"Naturally. Father took them off himself. You might have had other wounds on your body. One dying man was enough."

"What happened to James Barrow?"

"Nicol the Chirurgeon is attending him."

"Who paid for the entertainment?"

"Lord Strange. Father observed that you were wearing a money belt, and if you had any sense at all, you would realize that you are still wearing it. Not a sou was removed."

"Why, so I am. You probably really are Ann of the Inn."

"How can I convince you?"

Pierre was silent, a little ashamed of the reply that had instantly formed in his mind.

"I think I can read your thoughts, Pierre. Perhaps it is no great matter, but I should like to say that what you have heard of me is groundless gossip."

Pierre felt awkward and uncomfortable and was glad when she continued: "Pierre—I have never had any desire to defend myself from slanderous tongues, nor have I ever had any desire to live up—or down—to my reputation," and in the dark Pierre did not see her smile as she added, "until tonight. . . . Pierre, are you listening? Or have you dropped off to sleep?"

Pierre cleared his throat and said, somewhat huskily, "I am listening."

"Good. Would you like to know me, Pierre? And be the only one to know he knew?"

Pierre let his arms speak for him.

When a little of the cold, late winter dawn came into the room, Pierre saw that it was indeed Ann, although he no longer required the testimony of his eyes. She was sleeping now, but she awoke when he stirred, and looked up at him.

"Incredible!" he whispered.

She nodded and kissed him behind the ear.

"When did you decide on me?" he asked.

"The minute I saw you. I thought of you all the time I was dancing."

Pierre, remembering the graphic realism of the dance, blushed in spite of himself. And because he was confused and excited and tired all at the same time, and hardly knew what to say, he found himself blurting, "Ann, will you marry me?"

He was shocked and a little hurt when she laughed softly, covering his mouth at the same time with her fingertip. "Sh-h-h. You are still drunk. You don't know what you are saying."

"I am not drunk. I mean it," he insisted.

Ann shook her head.

"Say Yes, Ann."

"No. But I'm glad you asked. Now I must get back to my room. Father would kill us both if he were to discover us together, and throw our bodies into the Seine. There is a tunnel in the cellar that leads to the river, you know."

"I dare say."

"Put your money belt back on, Pierre. It is not natural for you to have removed it." Pierre did as he was told. His head began to hurt again and his eye was burning. He dreamed that he was walking down a long damp tunnel under the river; it was paved with tombstones and they all bore the name Ann. But she walked with him hand in hand the whole way, and so did Louise de la Tour-Clermont and also, oddly enough, her skinny little sister, Claire.

Nicol the Chirurgeon slept the shallow sleep of old men. He heard the horses and his eyes were open when his servant tiptoed into the room and cleared his throat and prepared to announce the intrusion of a wounded patient.

"The court is full of men, my master, and a litter has brought the body of one who they fear is dying."

"If he is dying, he should be taken to a priest," the surgeon grumbled. "Send them to the cloister."

"Lord William of Strange and Blackmere threatened me with a sword and swore he would chop me to pieces if I did not announce him. I think it concerns the young man that the waiter from the Inn of the Cutthroat said had been injured."

Nicol said petulantly, "I suppose I must heed the kinsman of John Talbot." He raised himself to his elbow. "Have the sick man brought here. Nay, wait. Did you see the patient?"

"I did, master. It is a head injury."

"Is there much blood?"

"Almost none, master. But something is sticking out of his head."

"Bad, bad, bad," said Nicol. "Give me my gown. Put wood on the fire. Let them not disturb the wounded man. I want them to drive the litter in here."

"Drive the litter in here, master?"

"That is what I said. Must I pump sweet oil into your ears for deafness? Smartly, now!"

The servant went away, shaking his head. Horses in the bedroom! The master's mind was going!

Nicol the Chirurgeon slipped his cold feet into red slippers of Russian leather with fur on the inside. He wrapped a heavy woolen cloak around him and put on his tall velvet hat, waiting with his back to the fire, his bony old hands open to feel the heat, while the men drove the horses in with their burden.

"Set down the litter and get the hacks out of here," he ordered with no very good grace. The frightened, sobering young men unhitched their clean-bred steeds and lowered the litter. "Gently," cautioned Nicol, "gently, gently!" And when the litter touched the floor, he said: "Now everyone go home. Except Lord Strange. I shall need an assistant." They were glad to obey him.

"I should have asked to remain anyway, good Master Nicol. This is my fault," said William miserably.

Charles of Limoges lingered behind the others.

"May I stay, too, Master Nicol?" he asked.

"Who are you?"

"It is Charles of Limoges, a student of your art," William answered.

Nicol said: "That is good. He shall stay. I shall operate at once."

124

Charles gulped. He knew what that meant. The master would not touch the man. The student would do it all.

The servant brought a basin of water, the scalpel, some iron instruments, and several bottles of clear, transparent glass, filled with liquids of different colors and a quantity of unused bandages. He began to heat one of the instruments in the fire. He had also brought several long, strong leather straps.

"How did this happen?" Nicol asked, examining the forehead carefully.

"I threw a bottle at him," confessed William. "I was under the influence of wine."

"Give me the opium, Fernand," said Nicol to the servant. "Open the poor man's mouth, Charles of Limoges," and when Charles forced the mouth open, the chirurgeon poured a trickle of brownish fluid down Barrow's throat.

"Now lift his eyelids," said Nicol, and when he did, the chirurgeon held a candle close to the eyes. "There is no blood on the eyeballs, which is good," he murmured, "but the centers are large, like a man in the dark. That is bad, Charles of Limoges, as I hope you know."

"I did not know, master."

"I thought not," said Nicol, handing him the candle. "Look whether there be blood in the ears."

"There is none."

"Is there water in the nose as well as blood?"

"Only a little blood, master."

"It may not be too bad," said the chirurgeon. "Bind up the man's legs, Fernand. Touch not his arms." The servants deftly strapped Barrows' legs together as high as the knees.

"Now the piece of the bottle must be removed," said the chirurgeon. Charles gritted his teeth and prepared to take it out, but Nicol held up his hand. "Nay, lad, I am too old to be careful of my dignity. Let me do it."

Charles moved away, intensely relieved. Nicol knelt at the head of the unconscious man and placed his fingers on the temples, and with his thumb exerted pressure evenly on the sides of the fragment, not waggling it back and forth the way the barber pulled teeth, but pressing it vertically up and away from the face.

For a moment nothing happened. Then suddenly the fragment lifted with a snap and a dreadful little sucking noise. Blood welled up in the wound. In spite of the unexpectedness with which the piece had suddenly given, Nicol held it firm in his strong, skillful fingers. He did not let it drop. Charles of Limoges knew that he was watching a master.

"Take the stone," Nicol ordered, holding Barrow's head firmly on the floor. The patient had begun to moan and move his limbs.

"Give me my scalpel and probe, Fernand, and then sit upon his knees. Lord Strange," he continued, "you have long legs. Kneel astraddle the man's chest, facing me. Do not sit upon his chest. His breath is already short. Place your knees upon his shoulders so that he cannot move. Watch what I must do, and remember it when next you find a bottle in your hands."

"Is the wound not ready for the cautery, Master Nicol?" asked Charles.

"Many good chirurgeons would say so," answered the old man, "but he would die in a week if I closed the wound at this point, believe me. He may anyway."

"I believe Nicol the Chirurgeon, but I do not understand."

"Watch," said the master.

With his scalpel, sharp as a razor, he slit the skin about an inch on either side of the wound, which was horizontal, parallel to the hairline. He cut to the bone, slowly and carefully, not like the medical teachers, who prided themselves on their speed. James Barrow shrieked horribly and fought against the men and the straps that restrained him. Twice Nicol raised the blade and pushed aside a blood vessel with a steel probe before he resumed cutting. He separated the edges of the wound, which now looked like an extra mouth.

"Give me bandages," he said to Charles. Then he swabbed the blood away, and they could see the white of the skull beneath.

"There are pieces of the bottle still in the bone," said Nicol, "and the bone itself is cracked and ragged. You see that, Charles?"

"I see a brownish bit, like the bottle fragment," Charles answered.

Nicol pulled out the little pieces with a strong pair of iron pincers. Barrow moaned, but he did not struggle as violently as when Nicol had cut the skin. The chirurgeon swabbed the wound several times, looking closely each time to be sure there were no more pieces.

"Perhaps you are lucky, my young lord. The white leather beneath the bone has not been penetrated. His brains will not run out."

"Surely you will close the wound now, Master Nicol," said Charles, almost pleading.

"Many good chirurgeons would do so," answered Nicol, "but a finger of bone has cracked almost off the edge of the slit in the skull. It bends inward and presses upon the brain. And a fine red line extends beyond the area which I have laid bare. The one must be removed, or the man will go mad. The other, even you must know, means that the head is broken. There is no use cutting to see how far the fracture extends, for we could do nothing about it if we knew. Give me the claw, Fernand."

The servant left the knees of the tortured man, who moved them up and down like a fish too long out of water. His struggles were less and less violent.

"The opium has begun to take effect," observed Nicol. "It is a blessing from God's own Mother. Half the things we do could not be accomplished without it. I wish more of it could be procured."

Nicol took the claw, which was a pair of sharp clippers with long handles capable of exerting terrific leverage. He snipped off the finger of bone. Charles put out his hand to pick it up, so that the master would not get his hands too bloody, but Nicol said: "Do not touch it! They sometimes stick to the gray leathery membrane beneath."

He gently took the sliver between the thumb and forefinger of his left hand while with his right he pressed the brain sack away till the bone could be removed without rupturing it. He tossed it into the fire, where it sizzled a moment and then burned. Nicol wiped his hands on his gown and got up painfully from his creaky old knees. He took a bandage and wet it from a bottle that smelled like alcohol. Another he wet from a bottle of thick, heavy liquid with an intense, sweet, penetrating odor. He bathed the wound alternately with first one, then the other, of the wet bandages. The bleeding, never great, entirely ceased.

"Can you close a wound, Charles of Limoges?" he asked.

"I think so, master."

"Have you ever used the cautery?"

"I have watched carefully as the use of the instrument was demonstrated."

"Cold, of course," Nicol said contemptuously.

"Well, yes."

"Then I must do even that myself. Give me the cautery, Fernand." The servant brought the iron. It was white hot.

"Hold him, now, all of you," Nicol commanded. "Charles, approach the edges of the wound as near together as your fingers can push them. I should like them to meet, if possible."

Charles pushed so hard that the wound closed in a bloody ridge of skin.

"Good, good," murmured Nicol, and drew the iron half across the

127

wound. The flesh hissed; the smoke rose right into William's face. Barrow screamed and struggled frantically. William's head began to droop; his eyes began to glaze. It was obvious that he was about to faint. Nicol looked up in alarm. William's knees were performing a vital service.

No one had a free hand to shake him or slap his face to bring him to himself or even to prevent him from falling directly over the wounded head of the patient.

Without hesitating an instant, Nicol touched one of William's noble, useful knees with the cautery. It burned through the striped holiday hose and seared the flesh beneath. William cried out sharply and came to his senses.

"I am sorry, my lord," said Nicol. "This is no time to lose consciousness. The other half now, Charles," and Charles pressed the other side of the wound together and Nicol repeated the cauterization. Barrow moaned loudly again, as if all the breath had gone out of his body at once.

Now only Fernand was needed to hold the unfortunate man down to the floor. His struggles grew weaker and weaker, and after a few moments even Fernand got up and began to pack away the instruments into their little box of clean white sand, which absorbed the blood and kept them from getting rusty.

"Is he dying?" William asked. He was ashamed of himself, and did not even rub the knee, which pained him severely.

"I do not think so," Nicol answered. "Charles, take that heavy blanket from my bed and cover him. He really ought not to move for a week, but of course he cannot stay that long on a cold stone floor. We shall prop up the litter tomorrow, if he is still alive. Bandage the head, Fernand." The servant skillfully passed a clean linen strip several times around Barrow's head, tucking the end under so that it would not unwind.

"Does your knee hurt, Lord Strange?" Nicol asked.

"Not at all," said William. "I am sorry I acted so maidenlike. I had had a great deal of wine."

"Of course it hurts," said Nicol. "Fernand, put my unguent on it."

Fernand daubed the area with a salve that smelled like cloves.

"It does indeed draw the fire, Master Nicol," said William. He reached for his purse. It was not there, and then he remembered where it was. "I left every penny I had at the Inn of the Cutthroat." he explained. "I shall bring you your fee tomorrow."

Nicol the Chirurgeon said it was a matter of utmost indifference to him, but that if he were not at home, it might conveniently be left with Fernand.

Charles and William were both exhausted, of course, but before they left, Charles touched on a professional question which had puzzled him considerably.

"That was unusual medicine which stopped the bleeding," he observed with a cautious note of inquiry in his voice.

"Wasn't it?" Nicol agreed.

"Is a student of the healing art permitted to ask its greatest master what the constituents might have been?" he persisted stubbornly.

"Certainly not, Charles. You know that is not ethical. But I shall tell you, because you assisted me so skillfully. The one should have been the alcohol of the alchemists; I had none, and so I used brandy. The other," he said maliciously, "is a preparation of my own: a distillate of bitumen from the foot of a Theban mummy in a subtle decoction of mandrake digested with white mercury from strong spirit of salt in an elixir of unicorn with as much Phocaean alum as will just cover the thumbnail of an ape. It must be so measured."

Charles nodded his head and congratulated himself on his great good fortune. Not everyone was permitted to share the secrets of Nicol the Chirurgeon. "I see," he said. "I am familiar with the ingredients, of course," and of course all doctors of the period were, "but I never heard of such a measurement."

"It is most important," said Nicol sagely.

The next day Barrow was no better, and the next he was worse, and the third he woke, but he was paralyzed. His father sent four servants, and over the angry protests of Nicol, they carried the litter, a man at each corner, to his home, gently, Nicol had to admit.

"You may be killing the man," Nicol said dubiously. "He should lie perfectly still."

"His father insists," they answered. "Will you continue to attend him?"

"Naturally," said Nicol. "But I doubt whether he will need me long after this foolish disturbance. Shade his eyes, so that he stare not at the sun and go blind."

The people of Rouen watched the serious men with their sad burden progressing slowly through the streets. They were familiar with the face of death. Everyone knew that James Barrow would die with so yellow a skin. He could not blink his eyes, his mouth sagged open, out of control.

"That will make two murders at the Cutthroat," a man in the crowd observed.

When Pierre awoke the sun was streaming into his room at the Inn, and he saw men-at-arms standing around him. There was no perception of depth to his vision, because, like the proprietor of that surprising hostelry, he had the use of only one eye. And so some of the men looked like giants, because they were close, and some looked like pygmies, because they were farther away. He shook his head and rubbed the open eye which presented such an unexpected image to his mind, thinking that perhaps they would dissolve along with Ann, her phantom partner, Louise, Claire, the sepulchral tunnel under the river, and poor James Barrow with the bottle in his head, all of which were hopelessly tangled and confused in his foggy memory of the preceding night. His head hurt him sorely, and he wished the big and little men would go away.

They were persistently real, however, and one of them spoke.

"If you are awoke, young man, tell us whether you are Pierre, sometimes called Pierre of Milan, foster son of the armorer, Hugh of Milan."

"Of course I am." said Pierre. "Everybody knows that. What do you want?"

"We knew, naturally," said the leader of the group, "but we had to hear you admit your identity before we could arrest you."

"What am I accused of?" Pierre asked in some alarm.

"It is my duty to incarcerate you, not to instruct you, Pierre," the sergeant said, "but you will probably hear soon enough from the judges that you killed a man."

Pierre now saw that there were five of them in the room, all armed with pikes and wearing cuirasses. He was naked except for his money belt. He got into his clothes.

"There is some grave error here, gentlemen," he said. "Nobody was killed in last night's scuffle. Not while I was awake anyway. I was unfortunately knocked unconscious before the fighting ended. Who is it I am supposed to have killed?"

But the sergeant had already told more than he should, and he would tell no more.

"At least let me send word to my father and mother," Pierre said. "They are probably already worried because I did not come home last night."

"That is not a part of my instructions," said the sergeant, and they hustled him out into the street without his breakfast, which, of course, he had no stomach for anyway.

Blind Jack happened to be at the door of his inn as the last guest of the night before departed. For some reason he seemed particularly glad to be rid of Pierre.

"Blind Jack!" Pierre called. "Why am I arrested in this unseemly manner in your house? Tell these men that you yourself knocked me unconscious before I did any damage!"

"How do you know that, Pierre?" asked the proprietor, his eye cold as ice.

"Oh, the devil!" grunted Pierre. He could have bitten off his tongue. "I saw you, of course."

"I do not strike my guests, gentlemen," said Blind Jack righteously. "I myself saw no murder. In fact, I see very imperfectly with my one poor eye, as everybody knows. But this man was certainly among those who disrupted my law-abiding establishment last night, and if he has committed a murder, why, I say, let justice be done, as I always do."

"At least inform my father, won't you, Blind Jack?"

"That I will," said the innkeeper.

The men-at-arms walked close to Pierre, as if they were afraid he would sprout wings and fly over the walls, and they directed him toward the castle. In part of that important military edifice lived William, Baron of Strange and Blackmere; in another, the Governor, John Talbot, his great-uncle. And under it were prison cells. Pierre guessed bitterly that they were not taking him to visit his friend, who was probably having his lunch that very minute in the luxurious great hall.

"I do not think Blind Jack will tell my father anything," Pierre said.

"I don't either," the sergeant replied. "He does not seem to like you. I don't blame him. His place is a wreck."

"I suppose so," said Pierre. "I wish I might talk to Father Isambart. Even a condemned man is permitted to see a priest."

"Oh, if it's a confessor you want, I can arrange that," the sergeant said good-naturedly, "although Father Isambart is a pretty important person. I don't know whether he will come himself."

"I should be very grateful if you would ask him, sir," said Pierre, who had once done a great thing when a man called him "sir."

"Now, I'd be glad to," the sergeant said. "Indeed, you don't talk like a murderer. But you never can tell. There are all kinds. Maybe you are one of the educated ones."

Isambart came with a speed which convinced the jailers that the tall prisoner with the fair hair and the black eye was already condemned. He had seen worse cells than the one Pierre occupied, which was reasonably dry, and he would have gone to the worst of those if Pierre had been in one.

Pierre told him everything that had happened at the inn, both during the fight and afterward, and what touched on the girl the good man hid in his heart and forgot about in a few days, as only a trained confessor can, though this was not a confession. It was one of the advantages, Isambart thought, of being a priest.

"Blind Jack is not blind, Pierre," he said, "and not deaf either. Your voice is not noted for softness. He could have saved you with a word or two, but now he will never lift a finger to keep you from hanging. You must not sin, Pierre; but if you do, at least do not compound it by making wicked enemies who will attempt to avenge themselves upon you, thus adding their sins to yours, to the great satisfaction of the Devil."

"If you are preaching me a homily on discretion, Father, be assured I shall heed it in the future."

"The man you are supposed to have killed," Isambart informed him, "went by the name of Thomas Berold. Do you know him, Pierre?"

"No, Father."

"You are supposed to have beaten him to death with your fists."

"It is true that just before Blind Jack hit me on the head I was beating the man who gave me this black eye. He had yielded once, and then, quite unexpectedly, he hit me in the eye when I was looking for someone else to fight. I was angry, of course, and I knocked him down and struck him a few times."

"Hard?"

"Certainly. But he was very much alive and howling loudly."

"I can imagine he howled."

"Blind Jack called for me to stop, and I hit the fellow once more for good measure. Then something hit me, and I did not wake up for a long time."

"Did you observe the activity of the man before you first fought with him?"

"Not particularly, Father. I did notice him once or twice playing dice with some of his friends before the trouble started."

"Before the dance, Pierre?"

"Yes, Father."

"After the dance, Pierre?"

"I think so."

"During the dance, Pierre?"

"Nay, Father, that I cannot tell you."

"Was he winning in the game of dice?"

"I do not know, Father. I was a little drunk. I only remember him playing dice for a long time."

"Was it with the same men, or were they different men, Pierre?"

"The fellow played with several groups, I remember that."

The priest observed thoughtfully: "One does not play at dice with many different men throughout a whole evening while a seductive dance is being performed unless he is winning. Nor will his comrades play at dice with him unless they hope desperately to recover their losses."

"That is true, Father," said Pierre, smiling a little.

"After you fought with him, the unfortunate man must have run into the street, because it was there that his murdered body was found, in a gutter not far from the inn. His head was frightfully smashed and, of course, he had been robbed. At least he had no money on him. But there is no accusation of robbery. Only murder. That is a curious and suspicious circumstance. It is quite obvious to me that the poor man was murdered by someone who knew he had money and wanted to take it from him. You, of course, were in no condition to have followed him into the street, but your own folly has deprived you of the testimony of the man who could most certainly convince the judges of that."

"I am gravely alarmed, Father Isambart."

"You have reason to be."

"Perhaps Ann saw what happened," Pierre suggested.

"That is a vain and foolish thought. She would never dare admit it. Think how afraid she is now of her father. Believe me, she will never mention you. Ah, well, I shall do what I can. God keep you, Pierre."

John Talbot, the gallant old earl, took a serious view of his young kinsman's affair.

"You make me ashamed of the family," he complained bitterly. "The first man I ever killed was a heathen Turk, and I ran him through with my lance. Your first is a Christian, a friend, and an Englishman. And look what you slew him with! Is the Talbot blood so thin in your veins that you can find no nobler weapon than a bottle?"

"Barrow is still alive, Sir John. I have told you that I drank too much wine. I believe the Devil possessed me at the moment. I thought I saw a dreadful vision."

His great-uncle snorted. "Young men did not see visions in King Richard's time, or in the late Henry's reign either, for that matter. We used our swords, and when we got drunk we vomited and went right on fighting. You saw a vision, indeed!"

"I have called every day to pay Nicol his fee. He says Barrow may live."

"It is said in the town that Barrow will die," said Sir John. "And I think he will, too. A broken head usually kills a man, especially when he cannot move after he wakes up. I've seen enough of them in my time. What does the gossipy old necromancer charge you?"

"Well, his fee is about a pound a day."

"A pound a day!" shouted his uncle. "Robbery! You could ransom a prince for that! My own came to little more after Orleans. Of course, I was in prison three years."

"It is what he charges, my uncle. In a sense it is a ransom."

Sir John grunted. "No viscount's son is worth it. He'll die anyway. This is intensely embarrassing to me, William. As soon as James dies, his father will challenge you. He will probably kill you. And, I confess, that will be a source of great sorrow to me."

"I am not so sure he will kill me, my uncle."

"Neither am I. But there is always the chance. He might even run crying to the courts on a murder charge, like the burgher he is. We cannot afford a lawsuit, and the judges would all be French."

"A lawsuit is unheard of, Sir John."

"Not in these times. An English commoner with a French title is a man without honor. He might do anything. Look how a bit of parchment caught his son's eye."

"James is not very noble," William admitted.

"The whole family is a disgrace to England. But they are popular with the Rouenese. Perhaps I ought to send you home. Barrow would never dare bring a lawsuit into an English court."

"You are not suggesting that I run away, Sir John!"

"Nay, nay. Of course you cannot leave a fight. Statecraft is difficult for an old knight. Probably you would be safest in the heart of France."

"I am not worried about my safety, uncle."

"Nor the family, either, apparently. Do not talk so big, young man. Your life may be important to others besides yourself. As a matter of fact, I think I shall send you to France."

"I will not go to France, Sir John."

"You pigheaded clerk! You will go anywhere I tell you to. In fact, I command you to go to France, on a very important mission. One which concerns my own honor. Forget your brawl in the tavern. I have no doubt James Barrow deserved what you gave him."

"The whole world knows that your honor is spotless, my lord uncle. I don't know what you are talking about. And one does not cross over into France in wartime."

"One does if I command one. You and your Frenchified 'ones.' The occupation has ruined the language as well as the men. Listen, grand-nephew. It is not widely known, but some small portion of my old ransom to France has never been paid. A man named Jacques Coeur, who was once only a merchant and later only master of the mint, is now become the greatest power in France. He is the lord receiver of all the moneys of the realm, or some such grand thing. France was always weak and poor till he took over the taxgathering. Now France grows richer every day. I don't know how he does it. The French king is immensely wealthy. With Coeur's money he is raising a large standing army. He actually taxes his nobility, if you can imagine such a thing. He has even quarreled about money with the Holy Father in Rome, all under the guiding advice of this grasping, diabolical Jacques Coeur.

"Coeur has discovered," he went on distastefully, "the small unpaid balance still due on my old ransom, and he stubbornly refuses to go on with the peace negotiations until it is paid. A pretty pass the world has come to when kings haggle over a few miserable pounds! I am not the only one, of course. A number of English knights are involved."

John Talbot drummed with his fingers on the table in vexation over the degeneracy of the times.

"Our sovereign lord, King Henry, has generously taken on himself the financial burden of all these ransoms," Sir John resumed. "Here is a letter that was delivered only today. You can read it yourself."

William unrolled the big parchment. It was beautifully engrossed, and it bore a great golden seal.

William whistled in amazement.

"Why, this is a letter of credit," he gasped, "in the sum of £60,000 in gold! Your name is here, Sir John, with some others. All famous men. Indeed, I had no idea!"

"I believe there are quite a few of us," his uncle said, chuckling with satisfaction. "My secretary read me the names. My sight is not so keen as it was, you know, and I have a little trouble making out the letters."

John Talbot had a superb contempt for anything written. His sight was as good as when he was twenty. But he could not even read his prayer book, and it had lately become fashionable to pretend to be literate.

"This should be sent to Paris at once, Sir John, should it not?"

"Nay, I want you to take it to Jacques Coeur himself. He is in Montpellier, where he can watch his precious ships go in and out of the harbor. Throw it in his face, William! Like a bottle, will you?"

"My uncle, I shall deliver it at once. It is very important, as you say. Surely you are not serious about my flinging it into his face, however."

"Well, I think I should be tempted to," his uncle replied. "You heard about your friend, Pierre, of course?"

"Yes, Sir John. He was hit on the head. I left him at the inn when I paid his score. I admit that I had to wait till he was unconscious before he would let me do it. He could ill afford it, I thought. He is a good friend, honest and loyal."

"Do you think he killed a man with his bare fists, William?"

"Pierre probably could. But of course he did not. Why?"

"That is what he is accused of," Sir John said.

"That is nonsense. Nobody was even seriously injured at the inn except James Barrow, and I was the cause of that."

Sir John sighed. "Yesterday a French priest named Isambart came to me and asked me in my capacity as governor of the castle prison to release the man for lack of evidence. To such tasks am I reduced in these inactive times. I sent him to the deputy, of course."

"Pierre was the last man at the inn, and he was unconscious. Nobody was dead in the house."

"That's what the priest said," his uncle replied. "But a soldier was found murdered, his face all bashed in, not far from the inn. Some of his friends, with whom he seems to have been playing dice, say they saw your tall friend kill him on the floor. The priest very properly observes that a dead man does not walk out of a house and then die a second time in the gutter."

"I should look very carefully into the stories of those men," William said.

"Naturally that is being done. But they hang wonderfully together. Only the priest seems to be working in Pierre's behalf. He has run all over town trying to find witnesses."

"All the students will testify for Pierre," William said.

"Their testimony is suspect. Students always hang together. Of course, if Pierre is guilty he will have to hang, but I must say, if there is still a man alive in this degenerate reign who can kill with his fists, I should hate to have to sign his death warrant."

"The innkeeper's testimony should free Pierre at once," William objected.

"The innkeeper appears to have observed nothing at all," said his uncle. "He has only one eye, as anybody can see, and he pleads his poor

136

sight for his inability to have witnessed the scuffle that went on right under his nose. In fact, he was heard to say that if Pierre were hanged, that would be all right with him. I do not think the innkeeper's testimony will help Pierre."

"That is odd," said William. "But Pierre should certainly not be tried in a Norman court right now when there is probably some feeling on the part of the people against the students. Would it not be possible, Sir John, while testimony is being gathered and the witnesses are being interrogated, for Pierre to be sent with me on the mission to France? Your safe conduct can cover us both, and, of course, I shall give my word that he will appear for trial if necessary."

Many convenient courtesies had evolved during the long, long war. One of them was the habit that sovereigns and great noblemen had of granting safe conduct for their own subjects through the territories of their enemies. The convention was always honored.

"Indeed, that is a very statesmanlike notion," said his uncle. "You would be good at these civil duties, William. I shall be criticized, I suppose, but the priest half convinced me of his innocence. I do not think this is the time for a trial either. And a Talbot's word is good with anyone of course. Pierre never looked like a murderer to me. Probably there is more to the story."

"I'm convinced there is, Sir John."

"I'll get him out of his dungeon. You can write your own safe conduct if you want to. No doubt you will phrase it prettier than I should dictate it."

"Sixty thousand pounds needs no superfluous rhetoric, my noble uncle. I should be proud to carry your own honest words."

Isambart's efforts on behalf of Pierre were successful in high places, but they were unavailing among the people. He found a number of witnesses, but they all affirmed with solemn faces that Pierre had killed Thomas Berold. "With his fists, Reverend Father, most brutally; may I broil a thousand years in purgatory if it is otherwise."

The priest replied, "Trifle not your souls!" but they swore they were telling the truth, and some of them thought they were.

The day before Sir John gave the order that released Pierre from his cell, Isambart knocked at the door of Maria's kitchen. There was a small bag, like a purse, made of waterproof leather hung to the knotted cord around his habit that served him for a belt. The cross slapped against it as he walked.

"My tidings are not of the best," he said, when Maria let him in.

"But at least Pierre will be allowed to leave the dungeon. The governor is releasing him on the parole of his grand-nephew. Pierre is to accompany his friend on a mission to the south of France. In this manner both the young troublemakers will be removed for a time from Rouen."

"But that is wonderful!" Maria cried. "It is almost like a pardon!"

"I wish it were," answered Isambart, "but it is not. Young William has given his word that Pierre will return for trial whenever the trial begins, and, of course, his word is good. We must find some means of removing Pierre permanently from the jurisdiction of the Rouen courts, or at least until evidence can be unearthed that will assure him a fair trial. I am dismayed at the number of citizens who are willing to swear that they actually saw Pierre kill the man. You do not think that Pierre did, do you Hugh?"

"Certainly not, Father."

"Pierre is not a murderer," Maria added.

"I agree with you," Isambart said thoughtfully. "It is not in his nature, and I have talked with him at some length about the whole miserable affair. But I would not have you think I was trying to defeat justice merely because I am fond of your stepson."

He opened his bag and removed from it a letter which he had written in the good, honest, old-fashioned Gothic that any literate person could read.

"Lord Strange and your son are going to Montpellier to see the minister of finance, the receiver-general of taxes, Jacques Coeur, the argenter of France. He was a customer of yours, Hugh."

"Has the seller of cabbages risen so high?" gasped Maria.

"The merchant has done well," said Hugh. "I have heard something of his career."

"It has occurred to me that he might remember your shop kindly, Hugh. This is a letter that will introduce Pierre to him, and I have suggested that Coeur may want to offer Pierre a place in his service."

Hugh nodded silently. His face was set and serious. Maria cried, "How long will he be away, Father?"

Hugh said: "He is a man grown now, Maria. He cannot stay here forever. He could, of course, but Pierre will not be satisfied to. And as you know, dear wife, it is sometimes healthful to leave a place for a time. Think how we left Milan."

" 'Twas your foolish tongue, Hugh," said his wife.

"In Pierre's case, it is his foolish fists," Hugh replied.

"I do not know how long it will be," said Isambart. "I am not even sure the argenter will want Pierre. But we shall find out soon enough."

"How?" asked Hugh.

"Do not assume," the priest answered, "that the slow progress of Lord Strange and his cavalcade to Montpellier is a measure of the speed with which messages now fly over the face of France. The enterprising minister of finance has inaugurated a complex system of relays of horses, so that a courier can ride day and night for as long as he can do without sleep, and in every town he will find fresh horses reserved for the royal service. Jacques Coeur will be appraised of Pierre's coming long before Pierre himself arrives. He will also know what Lord Strange brings him, which, I understand, is a financial document of great importance, confidential in nature and dealing with the coming treaty of peace."

"Pierre is mingling in great events," commented Hugh. "To take part in such a mission is undoubtedly a high honor. It might make his fortune."

"Will it be safe?" Maria asked.

Isambart chuckled. "I am divulging no secret when I tell you that Lord Strange is delivering money to France. And where money is involved, the minister of finance will assure the security of the bearers. Pierre could not be safer in his own bedroom, madame."

"I suppose we should not stand in the way of his future," said Maria.

"In any case, we have no choice," said Hugh practically.

Isambart sealed the parchment in a cylinder of horn and left it for Pierre. He sighed heavily as he placed it in Hugh's hand. "I doubt whether I shall be able to be of much more service to the lad," he said. "Pierre is growing beyond the age when a provincial priest can be of much use to him."

"You have been the boy's best friend," Hugh said stoutly. "I hope your prayers will follow him on his journey."

"Why, of course," the priest replied, with a look of mild wonderment. "I always pray for Pierre."

Before William and Pierre were halfway to Montpellier two letters from the French minister of finance arrived in Rouen. One was read to John Talbot: it thanked him courteously for the money which was alleged to be on the way, commenting gracefully on the deliberate English method chosen for its delivery, and expressed the pious hope that no occasion might arise in the future relations of the two countries when the speedier services of his relays of horses might be required. "Damned upstart!" snorted Sir John.

Isambart read the other letter to Hugh. It was a formal note of thanks and a wary promise to look the candidate over carefully. But it bore a postscript in Coeur's own hurried scrawl, which read:

I remember the armorer well. If his son is as true as his steel, he shall be welcomed here. Pray the armorer to make me another cap. My own is in the East. I have no time to tell you why. The courier is charged to pay for it in advance.

"I took the liberty of returning the money by the same courier," said Isambart. "I knew you could not duplicate the cap."

"That is true," Hugh replied. "Of course, I can make him a pretty good one of ordinary steel."

"I thought perhaps you would offer to do that," Isambart said. He counted out a few gold pieces. "In fact, I told the minister of finance you would do so, and I reserved a few coins in payment. I hope they are sufficient."

Hugh eyed the little pile of gold.

"Abdul shall make him a sword as well," he said. "You kept too much, Father."

"I am not used to trade," Isambart said with a sly glint in his eye, "and I would not have the minister think the armorer's steel is cheap. He compared it with Pierre, you know."

# CHAPTER

# ✤ 15 ✤

CHARLES OF FRANCE was the seventh to bear the name. But only when a king was consecrated or when he died was his serial number remembered. The common people and the chroniclers habitually distinguished one Charles from another by a descriptive word or two: thus, there was Charles the Great and Charles the Bald; there was Charles the Fat and Charles the Simple and Charles the Fair. But nobody could think of a word to describe the colorless seventh Charles, and so he took a name, which the most ingenious of his friends could not invent, from the able character of his ministers, and he was known even in his lifetime as Charles the Well Served.

Many of his closest advisers were men of humble birth, and among them Jacques Coeur shone like a light of prudence, integrity, courage, and originality. Coeur had grown powerful and immensely wealthy in the services of his king. His only vanity, in a world which was fond of display, was a passion for building.

The stately mansions he erected for his own pleasure rivaled the king's in magnificence and outdid them in taste. It was Coeur's custom to have the masons carve on the stone of his graceful balconies and around the high walls of his great halls a motto which was part of his device: *"A Vaillant Coeur Rien d'Impossible.* He firmly believed it; his whole life manifested it; and if the pun on his name was braggart, it was less so than most of the impossible boasts with which his contemporaries painted their shields and bedeviled the stone portals of their castles.

His house in Montpellier was less sumptuous than some of his other residences, but he was fond of it. His favorite room was a library hung with great Genoese charts of every known sea—his ships sailed them all —and detailed maps of France and Europe. Every port where Coeur had a factor was designated by a red heart. Every town in France where an agent represented him was similarly marked. The maps were strewn with hundreds of hearts, from Paris to Trebizond and from the Atlantic Ocean to the Putrid Sea.

From an airy balcony outside his room, Coeur could see a tumble of distant mountains to the right and to the left. These were the Pyrenees and the Alps, which at once protected and limited the growing power of France. Around him spread the fertile plains of the Languedoc and the city of Montpellier, which his own prosperity made richer every year. Below him lay the port of Lates, its wharves busy with his ships unloading their precious cargoes from the Levant; and beyond the river stretched the immaculate blue of the Mediterranean Sea.

King Charles was at Arras, the northernmost city of his realm, awaiting the English delegates. Jacques Coeur was in Montpellier, as far south as one could be and still be in France. The minister fretted at Talbot's delay in delivering the letter of credit.

His agents reported the progress of the cavalcade. They were in Paris at the Epiphany, Bourges for the Purification, Montpensier for the feast of St. Matthias and they arrived in Montpellier just before all the olive trees grew white with the blossoms that promised another fruitful year for the Languedoc.

Coeur had a grove of the scrubby trees, whose culture he fostered because of the wealth they brought to France. He was walking among them one evening, his furred cap in his hand, the fresh spring breeze from the sea whipping the long woolen skirts of his robe around his legs and ruffling his hair, which he wore cut close to his head in the old Roman style, when a steward announced that Lord Strange and his companion had arrived.

"It is certainly time," Coeur said. "Let them come here."

The steward escorted the two young men from the lavishly appointed anteroom to the olive grove. They saw the lord argenter of France stand on tiptoe, reach up and pluck from a tree a small branch that appeared to be just bursting into bloom. He did not look at all cunning or diabolical.

"Welcome to France," said Coeur cordially. "I have been expecting you for some time."

William said coldly: "I came with all the speed I could. My uncle, the earl, thought it wise to send quite a company with me."

"You are all my guests," said Coeur. "It is a privilege to honor the

142

kinsman of France's most distinguished adversary. My house is small, but it can surely accommodate you and your officers. I shall billet your men in the town at my own expense." He glanced at the branch which he had picked and held it out to William. "Look," he said. "I think these are the first olive blossoms of the season. Take them, Lord Strange, and let them be a sign of the peace between our two countries."

In England the factious nobles had begun to pick red and white flowers and to fight over the colors; the first disastrous civil war of the roses was about to erupt and drain off the noblest blood of the kingdom, weakening it for a generation. William was not prepared for the graceful gesture.

"My lord minister," he stammered, "I have a document for you. My choleric uncle intimated I ought to fling it into your face, but your courtesy is so great that I can hardly keep from delivering it on my knees," and he bowed very low and held out the letter.

Jacques Coeur smiled. "John Talbot's message was sure to be sharp," he replied, "like his sword. I honor the testy words of your noble uncle. If you had delivered a courtly message, I should have suspected that the head of your honorable house had fallen into his dotage, or that you had perverted his forthright speech into a mealymouthed compliment. But the scion," he said, bowing in his turn, "is true to the tree, and I honor the uncle in the nephew. Who is your friend, Lord Strange?"

"This is Pierre, my lord, son of the armorer, Hugh of Milan."

"I remember a little boy in the armorer's shop," Coeur said, smiling at Pierre. "He nearly burned the house down, to the great benefit, I was told, of a remarkable little cap that the armorer made for me. Is this big fellow that boy?"

"I believe I have grown very unwieldy, my lord," said Pierre, "since you honored our house with your presence, and," he could not help adding, "with your excellent cabbages."

"Cabbages?" William said in some surprise, looking at the lord steward of the expenditures of the kingdom of France. "Pierre mentioned only that he had seen Your Excellency once when he was a little boy. I know nothing about the cabbages. This sounds like a very treasonable transaction, friend Pierre! Was it not in the middle of the war? Did a loyal Rouenese have to buy French cabbages?"

Coeur laughed heartily. "Now there speaks the proud, English, Talbot blood! If Pierre is one of your officers, or, better still, a friend, Lord Strange, let him dine with us tonight, and it may amuse you to hear how I crossed over from France in wartime to buy some very special armor from Hugh of Milan in Rouen. I did indeed go disguised as a peasant with cabbages for sale, and the armorer fashioned me a helm from the iron of a shooting star."

"Cabbages and shooting stars!" William exclaimed in amazement. "Pierre, why did you never tell me about this?"

"Perhaps he had forgotten," said Coeur. "On the other hand, perhaps Pierre does not waste words on trifles."

With the delivery of the letter of credit, William's part in the mission ended. Jacques Coeur immediately prepared to join the king at Arras. There remained, however, the detail of Pierre's employment, and to settle this Coeur sent word by a page next day that he would see both the young men in the library, if they could conveniently wait upon him.

It was not unusual for the minister to interview his clerks personally. He flattered himself that much of his success was due to the care that he took in his choice of subordinates. Even if Pierre had come less highly recommended, he would have found a minute or two to devote to him, and Pierre came highly recommended indeed.

Pierre had seen luxurious mansions, but Coeur's dazzled him, and even Lord Strange, who was used to the best that Normandy had to offer, was impressed with the exotic richness of the minister's establishment.

They had slept on beds so soft that a cloud seemed to have been conjured into the mattresses. The hangings were heavy silk brought in Coeur's ships from the East, intricately embroidered with figures of fabulous Chinese dragons wrought in thick threads of crimson and silver and gold.

Now they climbed a broad flight of stairs covered from top to bottom with a seamless Turkish carpet with pile so deep that the foot sank into it as if it had no more substance than water, but when the foot was removed, the stuff of the carpet sprang back again, leaving no print, and the flowers that were woven into its patterns rose above them like a living garden.

The balustrade of cedar was topped with a massive silver rail curved to fit the hand. Paneled, pointed arches of sandalwood were let into the body of the railing, imparting a spicy fragrance to the house. Coeur loved light. Windows followed the staircase to the upper stories, high, wide, and glazed with cathedral glass that tempered and colored the rays of the Mediterranean sun.

The library where the page took them was covered with a carpet richer than the one on the stairs, and the room was full of chairs and tables of polished wood, delicately carved. Hundreds of bound manuscript volumes filled the shelves, and in the wall space not so occupied hung charts, maps, and rich tapestries.

At one end of the room was a fireplace, and a literate person could have read Coeur's device worked over the mantle in exquisitely carved letters: Nought Is Impossible to a Valiant Heart. In a corner was a little shrine with a figure of the Virgin in its niche and a well worn *prie-dieu*, startlingly plain in workmanship and material. It contrasted strangely with the other furniture of the room and was, perhaps, a memento of Coeur's humble origin.

"The minister keeps a noble house," whispered William. "My uncle said he was a wizard with money."

"I've never seen anything like it," Pierre answered.

Jacques Coeur was on the balcony drinking something red out of a transparent goblet of Venetian glass. They both thought it was wine till the page offered them each a glass on round, individual trays of polished ebony. When they tasted it, they were delighted at its pleasantly refreshing, slightly acid tang, but they did not know what it was. They looked at each other quickly, each hoping the other might have recognized it and would make some remark that would identify it. Coeur, noticing their bewilderment, said: "You would recognize the ordinary pomegranate at once if you saw the fruit, gentlemen. The juice I express from the pulpy seeds is an eccentricity of my own. I love pomegranates, and I have not the patience to eat them any other way."

"It is wonderful," they agreed.

Coeur went back into the library, motioned them into chairs, and seated himself at one of the tables. It was covered with books, official parchment documents, ink in a well of colored glass shaped like a flower, and quill pens stuck in a silver trough filled with white sand. A small slab of green jade was hung by golden cords through holes drilled in its substance to a frame of carven teakwood shaped like a gate. There was a mallet of felt with an ivory handle with which to strike it. Pierre wondered what sort of Eastern genie would come flying through the air at the summons of such a bell, and his fingers itched to try the sound it would make. Of course he sat perfectly still and respectful and did not even stare at the weird little object.

Coeur was dressed for a journey and he was in a hurry, but he tried not to show it.

"Several letters have arrived since you left Rouen," he said. "I am sure you will want to read this, Lord Strange. It bears the Talbot seal."

William took the letter. He noted that the red wax into which his uncle had pressed the old ring with the figure of the running hound had not been molested, and he snapped it open. The good, thick parchment unrolled like a spring. Coeur watched his face closely, but it required none of the minister's famed subtlety to detect the flush of pleasure and the smile of relief that spread over his features like the sun coming out of a cloud.

"James Barrow will live!" he exclaimed. "That is wonderful news! My uncle says it is almost a miracle."

"I am glad," Pierre said, and he did not add "for your sake," because they were not alone, but he nodded his head and William understood him.

Coeur said, "It is always good to hear that a man will live," and if he knew anything more about the affair, he did not show it. "The other letters concern Pierre here. It seems that he is in your custody, Lord Strange, on a murder charge. Your uncle releases you from your oath, which as the head of your house he has a perfect right to do. He wants you to come home at once. But he attaches the condition that I give my own word to return Pierre to Rouen for trial whenever the authorities inform me that his presence is required. At the same time he recommends him strongly to my service. Knowing the nobility of your uncle's character, I am persuaded that he believes some shabby plot is afoot against your friend."

"I assure you I never murdered anyone," Pierre said.

"The monk, Isambart, also writes me that you are innocent of the charge."

"He gave me this letter for you, sir," Pierre said, and handed his letter of introduction to Coeur, who broke it open and scanned it hurriedly.

"It agrees in substance with what he tells me in a later missive. Isambart is known to the king, who regards him highly and has lately consulted him in an ecclesiastical capacity regarding the execution of Jeanne d'Arc." In deference to William's honest English sentiments with regard to that lamentable burning, he did not use the word "martyrdom," as he might have done to a Frenchman.

"And in addition," Coeur continued, taking up another parchment, "here is a letter from Friar John of the Cathedral School of Rouen. That man is a master instructor. As an ecclesiastic he could have taught anywhere on the Continent, war or no war. I have repeatedly attempted to lure him away from his provincial school. He would be a treasure in the university here in Montpellier, where mathematical instruction, especially the way he gives it, with constant reference to trade, is sorely needed. I have not been successful. He praises your skill in the science, Pierre, and he also adds that you have been known to step heavily on the toes of students caught in the act of stealing parchment."

"That is true, my lord. I saw him do it," said William. "I must say, however, that you are remarkably well informed."

"I have to be," Coeur answered. "But these letters came unsolicited." He turned to Pierre. "Good men defend you, young man. I shall give my word in place of your friend's. I might add," he observed with a smile, "that your choice of weapons was not usual among habitual criminals."

Pierre glanced ruefully at his big hands. Jacques Coeur reached over and struck the green jade gong. The plate vibrated against its golden cords and the high room rang with a note that seemed to come from nowhere and everywhere, like a bell under water.

And before it died away, Bernard de Coucy bounded into the room like a well fed cat."

"Yes, my lord minister?"

And then he stopped dead in his tracks, staring at Pierre incredulously.

"Well, De Coucy, what is the matter?" asked Coeur, looking sharply at him.

"For a moment I thought I recognized this young man," said Bernard.

"This is Pierre," said the minister. "Engross his name, if you will, in the book of the clerks. Not the apprentices, I think. And this is William, Lord Strange and Blackmere. Gentlemen, Bernard de Coucy, my secretary."

Everyone was standing now, and De Coucy said: "It is the same. Do you remember me, Pierre?"

"I remember you well, sir."

"He did a noble thing during the plague in Paris, my lord," said De Coucy. Seeing Pierre apparently in favor with his master, he now decided to be magnanimous about the incident which he had once disparaged. "He snatched my cousin from a pile of burning corpses, cured her of the plague, and restored her to her mother's arms. Sir Robert gave him a horse!"

"I did wash her face," said Pierre.

"Is that how you got your horse?" William asked.

"Do you mean to say that he never told you?" queried the minister instantly.

"Only that a French nobleman had made him a present. It's a good horse. Pierre rode her here from Rouen."

"That is interesting," said Coeur. "Well, Pierre, you have another witness for your character. He will instruct you in your duties while I am away. I must set out at once to join the king in Arras. Shall I mention our new merchant, De Coucy, if I should see Sir Robert?"

"Pray do, my lord," replied Bernard in a courteous voice that lacked expression utterly, like a good servant's. De Coucy always said the right thing, and Coeur was so used to his ritual responses that he never heard them. In that tone Bernard could have said, "Pray stick your finger in your eye, my lord," with perfect impunity.

There was nothing primitive about Coeur's financial organization. Many ingenious commercial practices had been known in principle since Roman times. Venice and Genoa had had a very advanced sort of banking for two centuries. It was the genius of Jacques Coeur that expanded and popularized this knowledge in France at the dawn of the Renaissance. Letters of credit, personal checks, and bank drafts became everyday tools of trade. Credit was bought, discounted, and sold, like any other commodity. Promissory notes and other instruments of obligation were negotiable, and changed hands many times, circulating almost like currency. Interest rates never appeared on their faces, of course, because the Church had forbidden Christians to take interest; but there never was a time before or since when a man in need might not sign a promise to pay two thousand crowns and receive only one thousand, the generous difference representing a profit to the lender. This was not interest but a charge for the valuable service rendered in writing the instrument. Even marine insurance was not unknown. Exports and imports were taxed in a rough-and-ready empirical manner. Under Coeur the revenues were honestly collected, to the great benefit of the king's treasury. Commercial records were kept in an excellent system of double entry which could scarcely be improved upon, though many salutary safeguards that later evolved to protect against fraud had not yet been thought of. Parchment was still used for important correspondence, but paper was known and growing popular among the literate merchants.

But a man needed vigilance and honesty as well as mathematical skill to engage in trade. For if the tools of commerce were modern, their regulation was lax; opportunities for their perversion were frequent and rich. Forgery in particular was a widely practiced art. Some resourceful commercial scribes elaborated their script out of all semblance to ordinary writing in an effort to render their calligraphy proof against imitation, alteration, or substitution, to the astonishment and confusion of future antiquarians.

Bernard de Coucy's knowledge of the business was extensive. Pierre was confused at first, but soon learned to admire the accurate facility with which that literate nobleman could name the country of origin of the products which Jacques Coeur imported into France, their buying price in the East and their selling price in the West: silks finer than those the Roman emperor once forbade his wife to wear; chain mail such as Western craftsmen lacked the patience to link together; Turkish swords and daggers, Persian pepper and spices that Europe had craved since the First Crusade; jewels of a size unknown to Western mines and a luster impossible to Western lapidaries; some very useful things, like ivory; some very foolish things, like apes; many nonsensical Oriental drugs, a few genuine therapeutics, like the mandrake and opium; a vast amount of silver and gold; a few heathen slaves, not to work in the fields, since the peasants were stronger and cheaper, but to add dignity to the domestic service of great noblemen. Some of these servants were eunuchs, and they made excellent chamberlains to the ladies, but their employment was not fashionable in spite of the frequent, extended absences of men from their homes, since a busy order of Christian men, who were not of course eunuchs but noble knights, the Chevaliers of the White Lady with the Green Shield, already existed and were usually on hand, by virtue of their solemn vows, to protect and console the wives and daughters of absent, fighting knights.

It was contrary to French law to export gold from France, but nobody cared how much wood, iron, brass, linen or woolen cloth, pewter, copper, or lead went out of the kingdom, and there was a demand for these things in the East. Coeur's ships never sailed empty. They always carried a profitable cargo both ways.

At Coeur's direction De Coucy set Pierre first to copying manifests of ships' cargoes and then to engrossing the originals. Later, when it became uncomfortably hot on the docks, De Coucy let Pierre do the important, tedious work of checking cargo on newly arrived ships.

It was the custom at the last port of call in the East for the manifests, which contained a detailed inventory of everything the ship carried, to be sealed in a copper tube about the size of a man's forearm. This precaution was taken as a means of protecting the vital documents against spoilage by the damp air or sea water, and it also served to insure the manifests against falsification. In Montpellier the captains delivered the documents to De Coucy. If the seals were intact (and they always were), the tube was broken open and the ship could be unloaded. It was not unusual for a captain to wear the tube strapped to his wrist throughout the voyage.

Since Pierre was not to be an apprentice, he did not live in the barracklike quarters with the younger clerks. De Coucy suggested several inns in a friendly manner, recommending one in particular which he considered just the place for a young man so far away from home. But Pierre was alarmed at the high cost of the hostelry, which appeared very undistinguished from the outside, and chose a cheap, clean little place that happened to be run by an elderly widower of extraordinary piety.

The peace with England was formally ratified at Arras. King Charles returned to Paris, and King Henry returned to London. But both kings were immediately embarrassed by their own turbulent nobles, who now had no enemies to fight and fell to squabbling among themselves, or with their kings, and even with their own families. The incompetent Henry could do nothing about the situation in his realm, and England fell into the Wars of the Roses. In France, Charles the Well Served did better, though at a fearful price of blood. His coterie of irascible vassals carried into their homes the manners that a lifetime of war had corrupted.

Jean of Luxembourg was known to have trained his nephew, the young Count of Saint-Pol, in the ways of war by instructing him how to slaughter bound and helpless prisoners of war in the courtyard of his castle. The uncle pointed, the nephew struck, and the heart's blood gushed out warm over the gravel. Forty men died before the lesson was over. Murder on a more intimate scale was commonplace: the Duke of Brittany assassinated his uncle; the Duke of Gueldre, his father; the Sieur de Guiac, his wife; the Countess of Foix, her sister; the King of Aragon, his son. And so it went.

Charles the Well Served had some of these wicked men slain with a sword before his eyes; some were sewn into sacks and thrown into the river; some disappeared down into dungeons and never came up again.

But many remained. Charles was advised that they might honorably be eliminated in a short foreign war. So with Louis the Dauphin, his son, he formed two formidable armies of the most objectionable of his subjects. One crossed the Alps in Switzerland, the other went north into Lorraine. And under the walls of Metz or in the shivery passes of the Swiss mountains, so many of the troublemakers died in commendable conflict against the king's enemies that the monarch of France sat easy on his throne, unchallenged for the rest of his life, and the monarch of England toppled to his fall.

Not only did Charles secure his position, but the spectacle of French armies on the other side of the broad Rhine and the high Alps inspired in Europe a respect for the power of France that had not been felt for generations.

Jacques Coeur went south to Montpellier, lest the general depravity that accompanied the blessing of peace penetrate his commercial empire also, but he found it healthy under the able lieutenancy of his secretary, Bernard de Coucy.

De Coucy had been instrumental early in Coeur's career in procuring the patronage of a wide circle of influential friends and rich nobles. They would do France a service, he had argued, by furthering the ambitious young merchant's commercial ventures. They had done so, and De Coucy had profited handsomely, on a basis remarkably like the commissions of a successful salesman. But he had long since ceased to be necessary or profitable, and it was a tribute to the great minister's integrity that he continued to employ Bernard in a sinecure long after the middle-aged nobleman's services might better have been dispensed with.

While the great affairs of Christendom molded the shape of history, Pierre went every day to the hot docks of the port of Lates, comparing the cargoes of ships as they unloaded with the written records that the captains prized so highly and kept so safely.

The new peace brought a sort of desolation into the heart of the old Count de la Tour-Clermont, who sensed that an era was ending. He identified his whole life with the restless events of the generation that had fought at Agincourt. He had not fought for twenty-nine years, but now that the world was at peace he felt that he had been deprived of a vocation. While the war continued, even nominally, he bore the pain of his crippled leg as if it were a new wound. When the peace was announced, he fell to complaining as if his discomfort were suddenly twice as severe.

In the province of the Languedoc, to which Coeur's activity and the king's favor brought a thriving prosperity, lived the Seneschal of Béziers, a kinsman of the countess Adèle de la Tour-Clermont. One of his castles was situated near a little village called Lamalou. The castle was small and the district extremely remote and backward. But the countess had not seen her cousin in many years. Now the roads were all open. The frontiers were friendly. Travel was possible, and the seneschal sent a letter to her, expressing his desire to see her again, and invited the family to his country estate. He wrote:

The view of the mountains is delightful, and the woods are full of game. The air is clean and bracing, and if Sir Robert still suffers from his old wound, I can recommend a little spring on my estates that flows hotter than the hand can bear both summer and winter. It is famous hereabouts for its curative powers, which cleanse the body within and without. It will set the roses to blooming in your cheeks, my cousin, and bring, no doubt, springtime again to the body of the count, your husband.

That struck the countess as a capital idea. Sir Robert was always interested in anything that promised relief from his affliction. Louise, who had grown very devout with the years, saw no reason for leaving Clermont, since one place in this transitory world is essentially like another. But Claire was delighted.

Bernard was informed of the family's project, and the news threw him into a nervous flurry of excitement and anticipation. In a rare expensive mirror that he had imported from Venice a year or so before, he examined the distinguished gray areas where the color had begun to fade from the temples. He bethought him of Louise, who had so long and resolutely refused to become his wife. She would approve the mature coloring. Then he thought of Claire, who must be about eighteen by now, and his image stared back at him, flabby and old. Claire would never approve.

There was an old witch that many elderly gentlemen patronized in the bad part of town. She sold little vials of a marvelous potion that Bernard, of course, was still young enough not to have to think about. She could also color hair, for a consideration, in a magical and almost undetectable manner. For weeks De Coucy rode out in the evenings, to exercise his horse, as he said, and little by little the gray disappeared from his hair, so that even Jacques Coeur complimented him on his handsome, youthful appearance.

De Coucy told Pierre, whom he had come to entrust with many of the duties he ought properly to have done himself, that the Count de la Tour-Clermont would pass with his retinue through Montpellier in June, and he promised personally to convey Pierre's humble respects, if Pierre so desired him.

"And that," Pierre thought with a tinge of bitterness, "is supposed to be a great favor!"

"Pray do, my lord," he said aloud, in a perfect imitation of De Coucy's own manner of answering.

"No doubt my kinsman, the count, will send you a greeting," Bernard added cheerfully.

About a fortnight before Sir Robert and his family arrived in Montpellier, as the cool dusk and a gentle breeze brought to a welcome close one of the hottest days of the spring that came early that year, Jacques Coeur descried from the balcony of his library the triple, triangular sails of the *Sainte-Eulalie,* his oldest caravel, the premier ship of his fleet. It was dear to his heart, both because of the sentimental associations which linked the vessel with the earliest memories of his career and the speedy, profitable voyages which she still made. He struck the jade gong sharply.

"The Lady is in, De Coucy!" he exclaimed. "That is welcome news, my friend."

"She is long overdue, my lord," answered Bernard. "I feared she might be lost. The minister is deservedly fortunate again in his enterprises."

"Thank you, Bernard. God is good to France. Let us see what John of Venice brings us this time."

The sails dropped and the sweeps came out with a smartness that told Pierre, who was on the dock, that all the ship's company knew the master was watching and wanted to make a good appearance.

Atop the mainmast fluttered the oriflamme, the holy standard of France, the red silk banderole of the king himself. A little lower was Coeur's own flag, with its scarlet cluster of hearts, and on the aftermast there was a long pennon dedicated to the blessed St. Eulalie, the color of fire and shaped like the flames that refused to achieve her martyrdom.

The waist of the ship was ablaze with the brightly hued shield of John Justin, the noble Venetian who commanded her, and the shields of all the members of her crew who were entitled to bear arms, some of them now straining at the sweeps, rowing the vessel toward the dock.

Galley slaves were not unknown, and many miserable wretches rowed their lives away in coastal waters, but it was neither profitable nor prudent to take them on long voyages. The *Sainte-Eulalie* had returned from Trebizond, beyond Constantinople, from perhaps even farther. Her crew were all free men, the best in Coeur's service.

At the dock the port sweeps were withdrawn at a shout from the master, and the starboard sweeps dropped deep into the water, for the rowers knew where to find bottom in their own home port. Using the oars now as poles, they gently pushed the caravel against the dock and sailors made her fast.

The captain stepped off his ship and bowed to his master.

"I am glad to see you, Sir John," Coeur said. "You are a little late, and I had begun to be afraid some misfortune might have overtaken you."

"We made a long voyage, my lord, and we had a little trouble, too," the captain answered.

"Not fire again, I hope," Coeur said, smiling. Everyone knew the *Eulalie* could not burn.

"Nay, my lord, it was water, and a contrary wind that almost blew us into Africa. We suffered the loss of one of the ship's company."

"Who was that?" Coeur asked.

"Antony, one of the Dineo brothers. A great sea broke over the waist of the ship and carried him off. It was night and very stormy. Naturally nothing could be done about it."

"I am sorry to hear of his death, Sir John."

"His brother Pedro was very attached to him, and mourned his loss in a very sad and moody manner. I excused him from duty for a week, but then I put him back to work again. It's not good to brood too long. He seemed to pull out of his depression."

"If I remember Pedro Dineo," said Coeur, "he was always of a melancholy temperament. Perhaps you will transfer him to one of the other ships."

"He has expressed a desire to remain on the Lady. Unless you order me to transfer him, I think I shall let him stay. It is true that he has always been a glum sort, except on rare occasions, and then he is happy for days at a time, laughing more than anybody on the ship. But mostly he is an able seaman, conscientious and dependable. He never takes a drink, even in port. He says he likes the ship."

"You know your men, Sir John. He shall remain."

"Here are the records, sir. I am always glad to be rid of them." He rubbed the white circle of skin around his wrist that the leather bracelet had kept the sun from tanning.

Jacques Coeur gave the copper tube full of manifests to De Coucy, and De Coucy gave it to Pierre. Pierre had no one to give it to, and he looked at it sadly, for he had already unloaded one ship that day.

"What have you brought me from Trebizond?" Coeur asked.

"The usual condiments, my lord," said the Venetian casually. John Justin was too familiar with the spicy East to wonder at its prodigies.

"There is an exceptionally fine assortment of silks, I think. And I was sent to Chersonesus to pick up some rare Russian skins by Ogli Pasha. That delayed us as well as the storm."

Coeur looked at Pierre, whose face wore a look of comprehension and complete astonishment at the heathen title.

"Baltha Ogli affects the style of a Turkish noble," the minister explained, "because one of the ladies of his princely family married the Sultan. He is a Bulgar, not a Turk."

"Baltha Ogli I know, of course, as the factor in Trebizond," Pierre said quickly. "His name always appears on the manifests. I confess that I was amazed when it seemed that he might also be an important Mohammedan official."

"He's important enough," the captain said. "Ogli has a great castle in the city and large estates outside. I should not be surprised if he were a Turk. Anything can happen in Trebizond."

"Ogli has been in the service almost as long as I have," De Coucy said. "He is high in the emperor's favor there because he delivers such great revenues from the taxes on the trade of our master. But Baltha Ogli is an able, honest, Christian man. No one in Trebizond buys so advantageously from the Persian caravans. He is not a Turk, I know, and if he owns half of the city, as they say, I am sure he deserves it."

"Nobody said he didn't, Bernard. Don't be so touchy," said Coeur. "We all know Ogli," and, indeed, the wealthy Bulgar had once come to Montpellier, and the minister had deemed him worthy of the great responsibilities with which, as a foreign agent, he was entrusted.

Turning again to the captain, Coeur said, "I hope you and your company have kept well?"

Sickness was always a serious affair, for the ships' chirurgeons were never very skillful, and nobody yet had sense enough not to throw slops into the bilges. People reasoned, logically enough, that if one could live with the stuff inside of him, he could live equally well with it a few feet below him. This primitive sanitation was much deplored by later generations with sensitive noses, but every honest sailor aboard the *Sainte-Eulalie* knew that nothing very foul could remain very long in a bilge that was pumped dry eight times a day. For, of course, the Lady leaked badly, like every other vessel of the times, and had to be pumped during every watch.

There was a troubled look on John Justin's face, and he answered: "No one is sick but Ilderim, and he is shamefully sick."

"What does he suffer from?" Coeur asked.

155

The captain answered, "I cannot be sure."

"I shall look at him," said Coeur. "In the meantime, let your company go ashore. The dock guards can keep watch. I had no idea you would be sent to Chersonesus. Everyone will want to go home tonight after so long a voyage."

"That is kind of you, sir," said the captain, looking pleased as a cabin boy with an extra penny. He bowed again and returned to the deck of the *Eulalie,* where he shouted an order that brought a roar of cheering voices, beginning with the cook's galley under the forecastle and ending with the officers' quarters in the aftercastle. The men scrambled off the ship as if it had begun to sink. Actually the vessel rose slightly in the water as soon as it was relieved of their weight, revealing an inch or two of marine vegetation, as if someone had painted a thin, green water line. There were many barnacles in this soft mossy deposit. Everyone knew that barnacles were fruits of a tree that grew in the dark on a tidal flat at the end of the world. There was a little white bird in each one, and when the fruits were ripe, the barnacles burst and the birds flew away. Where else would sea gulls come from, so far away from land? The Lady's bottom would have to be scraped.

Ilderim had been placed on a mattress in the captain's cabin, which surprised Pierre, but Coeur took it as a matter of course.

"That Turk is the best pilot in the East," he said. "I hope it is nothing serious."

The captain remained aboard, but he looked so doleful that Coeur laughed aloud, though a valuable servant lay dying, perhaps, at his feet.

"Follow your men, John of Venice!" he commanded, slapping the captain's arm familiarly. "Since when is a captain the last man to leave a ship?"

"You are very kind, my master," the captain replied. "I confess that there is a sort of fever in my throat, and the land smells wonderful. But I feared you might need me."

"I have plenty of assistants, John. Go to a tavern and cool your fever, and charge the medicine to me. You can unload the ship tomorrow. It is half dark already."

Ilderim lay with his hands folded against his breast. He held a crucifix which, like many converts, he handled incessantly. There was a smile on his lips and a speck of foam. He was mumbling something.

To Bernard he looked as if he were asleep. To Pierre he looked only very pale and tired. But Jacques Coeur had spent years in the Orient, and to him the pilot looked like a very sick man.

156

"Fetch a chirurgeon," he said to Pierre, "the best you can find. Nay," he corrected, addressing De Coucy, "fetch Villanova himself. He will come if you tell him I want him. Go to the university at once, Bernard."

"Surely the Sieur de Villeneuve will answer the master's summons from the mouth of his clerk as well as from mine," De Coucy grumbled.

"Of course he would. But the porters would argue. Do as I say, De Coucy."

"I thought only to help you with the sick pilot," De Coucy protested rather angrily.

"Pierre is all the help I need. Perhaps no one can help." Coeur looked at Ilderim, whose lips continued to move and to smile.

"Oh, yes, Pierre is wonderful with the sick!" Bernard said. His voice was under control again. He actually sounded enthusiastic. "I'll fetch the learned chirurgeon with all speed, I assure you," and he was off with a show of such precipitate obedience that Coeur forgave him his momentary insubordination, in which the minister recognized one more sign of his noble secretary's laziness.

Jacques Coeur knelt at the side of the valuable Turkish sailor and smelled his breath.

"What do you suspect, my lord?" Pierre ventured to ask. He knew nobody got drunk on Coeur's ships, and if somebody did, it was not necessary to send for the Paduan scholar, Giovanni of Villanova, called in France the Sieur de Villeneuve, the dean of the College of Chirurgeons at the University of Montpellier.

"Opium," answered Coeur.

"Opium, my lord? The man has not been operated upon!"

"Some Turks eat the drug, Pierre. Not to render their bodies insensible to the instruments of the chirurgeon, which is what God intended it for, but to deprave their minds and give them sweet dreams. It is a diabolical perversion of a blessed gift. It often ends fatally. I wonder where he got it. Break open the manifests, Pierre."

Pierre broke the seals and scanned the pages hurriedly.

"It is a little dark to read, my lord, but there is a large quantity of the costly drug in the cargo."

"Someone has been very careless with the packing," Coeur said bitterly. "The captain shall hear of this."

Just then Ilderim opened his eyes, the pupils tiny, as if the sun were shining directly into them, and began to speak softly and rapidly. He was not smiling now. He looked terrified. Pierre bent his head close and listened.

157

"The opium," said Coeur, "is always wrapped in leaves, then wrapped in leather, then waterproofed with bitumen, then smeared with tallow, then coated with beeswax—"

"Hush, my lord!" Pierre said it excitedly, holding up his hand in a disrespectful gesture of command.

"What did you say to me, young man?" cried the astonished minister.

"Sh-h-h!"

Nobody but the king had stopped Jacques Coeur in the middle of a sentence for ten years.

"He is calling on Moses," translated Pierre. "He thinks he is in a city in the East. He says he has obeyed the Law and the 'injil of Isa'—that is the Christian Gospel, my lord. Now he is calling on Mohammed, sent, as a holy book says, as a mercy unto all creatures, the seal of the prophets, dispenser of dispensers, whose revelation is Alcoran—he is only half a Christian, my lord—"

"Go on," said the minister, who suddenly realized that his astonishing clerk had somehow learned Turkish in Normandy.

Ilderim's face became more and more terrified in the gathering gloom of the cabin.

"He is giving alms to the poor," continued Pierre, "because his conscience is heavy for a great sin. Now he is in Mecca, kissing the Black Stone and running round the mosque—nay, he is walking—"

"It is the Great Pilgrimage," whispered Coeur. "They run thrice and walk four times round the temple. I had no idea you could speak Turkish, Pierre."

"Many people accompany him," Pierre continued. "Now he is a muezzin proclaiming the *ezan*—he is calling the hour of prayer from a minaret on a mosque, my lord—prayer is better than sleep, God is great, there is no God but God, the Father, the Son, and the Holy Ghost—"

"His theology is composite," Coeur observed.

"He is calling the Virgin to witness that he would have delivered the box if he could have done so; he is calling on St. Gabriel, St. Raphael, St. Michael of Peril because he is afraid he is going to die—"

"What did you say about a box, Pierre?"

"Go forth, Christian soul, he says, into life everlasting, in the name of the Father who made thee, in the name of the Son who redeemed thee, in the name of the Holy Ghost, who sanctifieth thee—"

"Before he blesses himself into purgatory, find out about that box!"

Pierre said something in Turkish, but Ilderim spat in his face and began to mumble again.

"He says I am not an innkeeper, my lord, in the name of the angels and archangels, in the name of the apostles, martyrs, and confessors—"

"Get the name of the innkeeper, Pierre!"

Pierre addressed another question to the Turk.

Ilderim's face contorted. Tears ran down his cheeks.

Pierre translated: "I had already delivered it long ago, as I did before, but for my great weakness. Have mercy upon me, most merciful Saviour, by the soul which accuses itself, by the angels which tear forth the souls of some with gentleness and some with violence, by thy Cross and Passion, by thy glorious Resurrection and Ascension, by the beard of the Prophet, by the barrel and sand of the cook—"

"Now that is something!" the minister cried. He jumped to his feet and rushed out onto the deck. Pierre could hear the quick patter of his velvet shoes on the planks growing fainter and fainter in the direction of the forecastle where the cooking was done in an iron box half filled with sand. This sand was carefully conserved, but when the ashes were cleaned out, some grains always adhered to them, and a barrel of clean new sand was at hand to make up the deficiency.

Ilderim continued his pitiful litany. It was almost dark now. The face of the Turk was so white it appeared luminous. Ilderim prayed to a mixture of Christian and Mohammedan saints, and changed his own identity often. He thought he was a man, a priest, a woman, a crocodile, a child, and an ape, in rapid succession; and he thought he was the slender crescent of the young moon, which had just become visible through the door of the stuffy little cabin.

As the Moon, he was leading the Turks into battle against the infidel *giaours,* whose holy symbol, the Cross, he held so tight to his breast.

His breathing was very slow now, and he stopped talking. Pierre's flesh began to creep and he wished Coeur would return. He stood in the door, where the air was fresher.

The minister was a long time coming back from the forward part of the ship. Pierre saw him finally with a lantern that one of the guards had given him. He walked rapidly aft, the lantern painting a golden circle of light on the deck. He had a sizable box under his arm, and when he entered the cabin, he laid it down beside the body of the pilot.

"Has he said anything else?" Coeur asked.

"He has not spoken for quite a while, my lord."

The box was well made and tied round with a leather strap. There was no lock or hole for a key. Jacques Coeur removed the strap, but the top was attached firmly with nails.

"Can you wrench off those boards for me, Pierre?" he asked.

Pierre tried with all his might, but he could not budge them.

"I shall need a tool, my lord," he said, and fetched one of the spikes that the sailors used to splice ropes.

"If you cannot pull up a couple of boards with your hands, I doubt if you could crush a man's skull with them," observed the minister. "Now let us see what the pilot hid at the bottom of the cook's barrel of sand. It was a shrewd spot to choose."

He held up the lantern. There were several sealed packages which obviously contained opium.

"These are worth about £1,000, Pierre, as you know. You will not find them listed on your manifests. I dare say they would bring several thousand in the northern countries, where the drug is even scarcer. And what is this, pray?"

It was a little leather bag. Something rattled inside it. Coeur drew the string and poured half the contents into his palm. All the stars of heaven shone up at him in the smoky light of the lantern: yellow and red and blue and green and white, sparkling and twinkling with the dazzling brilliance that made the jewels of the East so exquisite and valuable.

"Ilderim appears to have made friends among the jewelers as well as with the poppy merchants," the minister said bitterly. "Nay, this is too much! On my own ship, too! When I set you to calculating how monstrously King Charles is being cheated in taxes by this shameful business, you will be astonished at the sum. It is enormous, believe me. Did you not say that the pilot referred to delivering the box as he had done 'before'?"

"Yes, sir; his words meant that this was not the first time."

"And he spat in your face when he saw that you were not some damnable 'innkeeper.' Is that not correct?"

"That is right, my lord."

"*Peste!*" growled Jacques Coeur. "The town is full of innkeepers. I suppose I shall have to question them all. I fear the racks will be busy, Pierre."

"Then everyone will know about the smuggling, my lord," his clerk objected.

"Do not advise me, young man," snapped the minister. "But of course you are right. I should have thought of that myself. In a quieter moment I should have. You have a cool head on your shoulders, Pierre. I am utterly distracted by this discovery. If only that heathen rascal had mentioned the name of the innkeeper! Wake him up if you can."

Pierre shook the pilot till his teeth rattled in his head, but he remained unconscious.

"Slap his face," Coeur commanded. "Nay, I shall do it myself. It will be a pleasure." And he struck Ilderim hard several times in the face with the palm of his hand. Ilderim opened his eyes dreamily and smiled up vacantly at the lantern.

"I am thirsty," he said in French.

"Come into my tavern," Pierre said quickly, "and refresh yourself. Be my honored guest. Your voyage has been long. Have you no word of greeting for your old friend?"

"Wine and images are forbidden," answered Ilderim in Turkish.

Pierre sighed. "He is the Mohammedan again, my lord."

"Try that in Turkish," suggested the minister, and Pierre did. But Ilderim dozed off again.

"It doesn't ring true in Turkish, sir. I know several words for hostelry, but none of them brings to my mind the picture of an innkeeper with a friendly bottle of wine. My father's servant never taught me that."

"I remember the old Turk in your father's shop. He must have taught you well, for now that I think of it, a pious infidel would not drink wine in a public place. Oh, where is that fat secretary of mine?"

"Shall I put the box out of sight, my lord?"

"Eh? Yes, do, do," the minister fretted. He slipped the bag of jewels into his purse. Pierre put the box into one of the captain's big sea chests. At length they heard the sound of horses hard ridden on the smooth level stones that paved the way to Coeur's docks and facilitated the handling of cargo.

The Sieur de Villeneuve was an elderly man with a grave, distinguished bearing. His dress was rich. He had three assistants with him. He greeted Jacques Coeur with a low bow that was the epitome of pompous self-abasement. His assistant physicians executed the bow with him in perfect unison.

"God keep you in good health, my lord minister," he said. "I hope I have not incommoded you with some slight unavoidable delay in answering your summons."

"God keep you, too, Villeneuve. This sailor is very sick and particularly valuable to my service. Will you attend him?"

"Indeed I will, my lord," the physician answered. He stood quite majestically still, and his assistants clustered round the still, recumbent body of Ilderim, taking his pulse, feeling the temperature of his limbs and peeking under his turban.

"The Sieur de Villeneuve was engaged in an experiment in natural philosophy," explained De Coucy. "It took a little time."

"I was dissecting a newt," the doctor pronounced, "which grew new legs every time I cut them off. The reptile expired today, and I have been attempting to determine the source of its marvelous regenerative powers. It would be a wonderful thing if a man could do likewise."

Every nasty little boy playing in the damp of a castle moat knew that a salamander's leg grew back again if you pinched it off. It was a tribute to the chirurgeon's daring imagination that he could conceive of such a thing happening to a human being.

"Wouldn't it," said Coeur.

"The arteries were all full of blood, as Galen says," continued the Sieur de Villeneuve. "I cannot imagine why so many of my colleagues persist in maintaining them full of wind."

"Neither can I," replied the minister.

He appeared in no very cordial mood tonight. The chirurgeon, who was behaving in a perfectly normal manner for a sick call, looked a little chagrined. Then all the assistant physicians rose and one of them said in Latin, "We do not know what is the matter." The scholarly tongue did not hide their ignorance since everyone in the room except the drowsy Ilderim spoke Latin as well as they themselves.

The senior physician looked shocked, as if he himself had failed in the diagnosis, and went over to take his first look at the patient.

"Open his eyes," he ordered, and one of them did.

He bent and smelled Ilderim's breath as Jacques Coeur had done.

"Put the light behind his head," he commanded, and when they did, he looked carefully at the ears, using his little baton to make them stand out from the head so that the light would shine through them.

"The man is a Turk, is he not, my lord minister?"

"He is," said Coeur, "and the best Black Sea pilot I have. I should hate to lose him. Is the trouble what I think?"

"If you think it is opium, my lord, the answer is Yes. His heart is very weak. His breathing is very slow. The eyes look very bad. I shall do what I can, of course, but it would be wise to send for a priest. Is the man a Christian? I shall inject a stimulant *per anum*. No nauseant will empty his stomach now. I shall burn his toes with the cautery. Someone ought to beat a drum or sing a loud hymn. If he can be kept awake, he may possibly live. If he goes to sleep, he will surely die. When the tips of the ears are so white, there is little hope."

Coeur was tempted to make the doctor an offer of a rich reward if he could save the Turk's life, but he had his wits about him again and he knew it would cause comment if he appeared to value Ilderim too highly.

"I know you will do your best, Messire de Villeneuve," he said graciously. "Good pilots are rare, as you know, and valuable to the king. De Coucy," he added, "be good enough to have a couple of the guards carry this chest of the captain's up to my library. There are some charts in it that I want you to see. Now, if you please."

"Of course, my lord. The whole chest?" Bernard asked in surprise.

"The whole chest," the minister answered positively, and De Coucy scampered off to get the men.

"You, Pierre, will of course want to remain here," he continued, looking hard at his clerk, "to bring me word if the poor man should say anything which might require my attention. Do you understand me, Pierre?"

"I do, my lord."

"A priest shall be summoned, Villanova. Ilderim is a Christian. You can see for yourself how he holds the crucifix. I hope the priest will not be required. It would be a pity if the unfortunate sailor attempted to make his last confession in Turkish, would it not? Would it not, Pierre, I say?"

"I doubt if he will ever confess again," said Villanova, grim as a hangman.

"I have heard that Mohammedan converts at the point of death sometimes slip back into their heathen tongue that no Christian can understand," said Pierre with a wonderful air of naïveté. "I wonder what that does to their souls."

"Ponder the theology while you watch the great chirurgeon," said Coeur. He hoped that his clerk understood as well as he appeared to.

Two big men lugged the captain's chest out of the cabin. De Coucy and Jacques Coeur followed them, and the lord steward of the expenditures of the kingdom of France watched the chest as jealously as an old peasant woman guarding the eggs in the basket on top of her mule.

The doctors lit a little fire in a portable brazier to heat the cauteries and prepared another instrument to inject the stimulant. But nothing they did could keep the patient awake, and after a while he did not even move when they touched him with the red-hot irons.

A priest came wearing the stole, the viaticum in his hand. He was aghast at the sight and thought a man was being tortured till he saw the respectable figure of the Sieur de Villeneuve. He was just in time. He had hardly finished the beautiful prayer, which the unfortunate pilot had so pitifully garbled in his delirium, when Ilderim died, like the newt.

Pierre ran to the castle and was admitted at once. He knocked at the library door, and it swung open as if he had touched a secret spring. There was no one in the room except De Coucy, whose face was almost as white as Ilderim's, and the minister, who had opened the door himself. Coeur closed it again and locked it. It was astonishing to see a minister of France lock his door against his own servants.

"Pierre, does anyone know you speak Turkish? Did Ilderim name the innkeeper? Did he say anything at all?"

"Nay, my lord, I understood your instructions. I am sure that I have never mentioned to anybody that I happen to speak Turkish. I speak Italian and English, too. Latin is the only language I ever studied formally. Ilderim died without uttering another word. I really do wonder what it did to his soul."

"Oh, bother his heathen soul!" grumbled the minister peevishly. "Nay, I did not mean that. Perhaps you were destined to be his confessor, Pierre. It is permitted to confess to a layman *in extremis,* is it not?"

"Well, I have heard that it is, *in extremis.*"

"Was the priest there?"

"He came at the last minute, sir."

"Then I have no doubt that Ilderim's soul is where it ought to be," the minister said comfortably. "As I remember, your translation of his prayer was a bit more Christian than heathen anyway."

Pierre was a little pale himself. "Except for the doctors, I think Ilderim might have lived a while longer."

Coeur shook his head. "It is never pleasant to watch the cauteries."

Pierre said: "They did other things, too. Ilderim nearly burst with an injection of sea water and herbals that they forced into his body."

Coeur shrugged. "Villanova is the best chirurgeon in France. He has traveled widely in the East. Remember how quickly he diagnosed the disease, just by looking at the eyes and ears. Villanova knows what he is doing. But you could do with a cup of wine, Pierre. Being a translator, priest, and chirurgeon all in one evening has shaken your nerves. Sit down, young man." Coeur poured Pierre a cup of wine with his own hand. His kind words and his extraordinary actions astonished Pierre and set him a little on his guard. Pierre sat and took a sip of wine.

"You answered me very shrewdly in the presence of those others, Pierre, when I tried to warn you not to let slip your knowledge of the Turkish tongue. That knowledge may be very useful. Bernard and I have talked at some length about this wicked business." He pointed to the jewels that were all over the table, and the opium packages, which had been broken open to make certain of their contents. "He agrees with me that Ilderim was only an agent, used by some higher persons, both here and in Trebizond."

"The jewels might have come from Constantinople," said Bernard, who had finally found his tongue.

"That is true. But the opium came certainly from Trebizond. That is where all my opium comes from. Baltha Ogli buys it from the Persians. It is almost inconceivable to me that there should be traitors in more than one Eastern port. Nothing like this ever happened to me before. I am convinced that someone in authority there is in secret communication with someone in authority in France. Ilderim was only one link in a chain of at least three—four, if you count the innkeeper. Perhaps there are more."

"Ilderim may not even have known what he was hiding," said Bernard. "It is a dreadful thing."

"Look where the box was hidden!" cried the minister. "The one place on the ship that nobody would ever examine! Whoever thought of that is certainly familiar with the life aboard my ships! And now that Ilderim is dead, we have lost our last chance of identifying which inn the contraband was destined for. Pierre has very properly called my attention to the fact that I cannot question all the innkeepers in Montpellier without causing a frightful scandal and warning whoever is at the head of the thievery."

Pierre looked again at the jewels. Some of them were big as robins' eggs.

The minister said: "You observe no doubt that some of the stones are magnificent. A common sailor would be immediately arrested if he attempted to sell the smallest of them. The disposal of the opium is even more complicated. Someone great, someone evil, is involved at either end of the transaction. There are so many wicked, important noblemen in this realm that it is useless, I think, to seek for the Frenchman who is guilty. Ilderim is dead, beyond our threats and our promises. The box was never delivered. Bernard agrees with me that the mystery may be easier solved in Trebizond than in France. Do you not, De Coucy?"

And De Coucy said, "Indeed I do, my lord."

"The immense value of the jewels is shocking enough," Coeur said, "but the opium, which was obviously destined for illegal sale is truly heartbreaking. Consider how greatly it is needed, how high the legal price is to the chirurgeons. Yet they need it so desperately that they are willing to pay many times what it legally costs. Any diversion of the scant supply of this blessed drug means that many sufferers among the poor will be deprived of its benefits. There is a dreadful sin on the soul of the man who originated this nefarious scheme. I think over and over again how the dying Turk said, 'I always delivered the boxes before'! Who knows how much of it may have been stolen? Were those not the words, Pierre?"

"Words very like that, my lord."

"How will I ever explain to the king! He might ruin me. I should not blame him." The minister spoke as if he were in agony.

"Is it necessary to inform him?" De Coucy asked.

"Why certainly, Bernard. What a peculiar thought."

"I meant, my lord, would it not be kinder to wait until you have discovered the culprit? Not to add to the king's worries in the meantime?"

"No, I must tell him at once, I think." Then he said: "I am going to send you to the East, Pierre. With your knowledge of Turkish, the quietness I have always observed in you, and a continuance of the spirit you have evinced in tonight's events, perhaps you can discover there what I cannot discover here. Above all, you are absolutely unknown. No one else in my service could engage in a secret mission with so good a chance of success and with so little gossip."

"That is true, Pierre," said Bernard. "Imagine how tongues would wag if I should suddenly depart for Trebizond! What a commotion!"

Coeur said, "I can imagine!" Then to Pierre: "When the *Sainte-Eulalie* returns to the East, you shall be aboard her. If you can discover the Trapezuntian, you will doubtless discover the Frenchman who is defrauding the king. And me, too, of course. I shall arrange for you to go in a capacity that will allow you great freedom of action without calling too much attention to yourself. You have a good head, Pierre. You will need it. Perhaps you will also need the strength which appears to have brought you some notoriety in Rouen."

"Indeed!" De Coucy exclaimed delightedly. "I was not aware that Master Pierre's prowess had already got him into trouble! With the authorities? No doubt, no doubt! How very extraordinary! Pierre never says anything, of course. Are you a fugitive, Pierre? Did you waylay a knight or abduct a damsel or two? They thrive furiously in his hands, my lord."

"Oh, hush, De Coucy!" the minister said, laughing a little, while Pierre flushed angrily. "It was nothing so romantic. Your gallant imagination is running away with you again. Someone in Rouen just suspected that Pierre might have beaten in a man's head with his fists."

"Oh, my!" said Bernard. "He is just the man to do it. That is too bad, Pierre. Now they will hang you."

"I did not do it, sir," said Pierre.

Bernard shook his head. "Louise will hate to hear this. She mentioned you kindly, I understand, when our noble master saw the family at Arras. Poor Pierre!"

"If I were you," smiled Jacques Coeur, "I should hate to face De Coucy as one of my judges. You know, Bernard, it is simply marvelous how the prospect of a visit from your kinsman and his two attractive daughters has exhilarated you! You look younger and handsomer every day."

"Oh, I take good care of myself, my lord. Exercise, hard work, regular hours . . ." Bernard straightened his jacket over his comfortable belly and hooked his white, well groomed hands into his jeweled belt with great complacency. He seemed relieved to have steered the interview into a lighter vein. Great matters always fatigued him.

"I think that is all for the present, Pierre," said Coeur. "You will want to get some rest now, because the Lady will be discharged tomorrow."

"My lord minister," said Pierre rising, "I am overcome with this honor. I promise I shall not fail you, while I live. It is a pity that I never learned Greek."

"There is no one to instruct you, even at the university, Pierre. And anyway, you could not learn Greek in a month. You will have to do with your Turkish and Latin."

De Coucy also rose to go. "I shall instruct him," he offered. "I have picked up some extraordinary words from the sailors!" They bowed themselves out of the minister's presence. Jacques Coeur stared gloomily at the fortune in jewels that lay spread over the polished surface of his table. For the first time in his life, he was revolted by the sight of great wealth.

"Pierre," said De Coucy in the hall, "you are a very lucky young man. The women of Trebizond! It is common knowledge that the emperor buys peace from the Turks with the daughters of his noblemen. They are absolutely the most beautiful creatures in Christendom! Let me see, now; Trebizond is Christian, isn't it?"

"They are Eastern Christians," Pierre replied, "now happily united with Holy Church, I believe."

"Of course," Bernard said, "I remember now. The minister apparently trusts you greatly, Pierre. He did not mention it, but you must not say a word of this to a soul. Good night, Pierre."

"I shall be very careful," Pierre answered. "Good night, sir."

The young moon had long set. Pierre shivered a little, remembering the pilot's hallucinations. He said a prayer for the Turk, hoping his soul was where it ought to be, as the minister had so confidently averred. He knocked at the door of his inn, which was closed. Ships' crews did not relax after a voyage in a hostelry run by so strict and pious a proprietor that everyone called him The Friar.

There was a shuffling and a grumbling in the dark inside, and after a few minutes the innkeeper opened the small barred window in the door and held up a cheap tallow candle.

"Go away," he said, "and leave me to my meditations. The house is closed."

"Let me in, Friar," said Pierre, amused at the old bigot. "It is Pierre," and he pushed his face close to the wicket so that he could be recognized.

"There is wine on your breath, Pierre. You are getting just like everybody else." The key grated in the lock. "I shall let you in this once, but believe me, if you stay out so late again, you shall have to go elsewhere for your lodging. What kept you? You can still stand, it seems."

"Oh, come now, Friar. It is scarcely midnight. Are you running an inn or a convent? One of the crew of the Lady died tonight."

"I am sorry to hear it," said the proprietor. "What was his name? I shall pray for him."

"He was a pilot. He was called Ilderim."

"Ilderim? I never heard of him. Of course, the ships' companies do not frequent my reputable establishment. Ilderim is a heathen name. I shall pray for no heathen."

"This Ilderim was a Christian," said Pierre, "and no doubt he can use your prayers."

"Oh, that is different. Then he shall have them. Or one, at least. I am very tired. I saved you a bite of supper, Pierre. It is in your room."

"That was kind of you. Thank you, Friar."

"Well, I won't do it again," the innkeeper said, and he shuffled off to bed. Pierre ate his cold supper and was glad the innkeeper had had the sense to give him a bottle of wine with it. It would appear on the bill, of course, but it felt good in his stomach, which hunger and the excitement of his interview with the minister had set to growling.

# CHAPTER

## ✲ 16 ✲

THE NEXT DAY they unloaded the *Eulalie*. Pierre never inspected a cargo more meticulously. Even De Coucy was on the dock, peering into bales and prying into crates. But everything checked perfectly with the manifests, from the great heavy bales of ermine from Russia to a little basket of saffron strong waters from Trebizond, with a green sprig of Mithrian pine in each of the clear glass bottles.

The day afterward, when the tide was high, the vessel was run into a big tub-shaped depression that had been scooped out of the sandy beach between the high and low water levels. Light vessels could be beached by means of windlasses powered by mule teams that dragged them bodily out of reach of the sea, but not a ship the size of the Lady. A quantity of stone was placed inside her, all on the starboard side so that she developed a slight list. As the tide went out, she gently heeled over on her right side. At low water a man could walk up to her keel without getting his feet wet.

A heavy boom formed of the trunks of trees chained together was dragged across the entrance to the depression and securely anchored. This served to break the force of the swells while the ship was being cleaned, for, of course, the tide would come in and go out many times before the operation was completed. It would strain the hull to have her bump up and down on the sand too hard.

The workmen swarmed over her with sharp iron scrapes and removed the moss and barnacles. Fresh oakum, picked from the strong hempen ropes and impregnated with fragrant Norway pitch, was hammered into the seams to render them watertight. As each workman finished a patch, he painted it with a thick mixture of tallow and tar, so that when the tide came in again the freshly scraped timber would not be fouled.

When one side of the vessel was finished, the ballast was shifted to the other side during the time that the tide floated her; and when it receded, *Eulalie* heeled over to the left and exposed her starboard flanks to be scraped. The whole operation was tedious and time-consuming, but it was absolutely necessary, since it preserved the timber. It was also profitable, because a clean ship sailed faster and maneuvered quicker than a foul one.

Pierre had seen many ships careened on the beach, but seldom one so big and fine as the *Sainte-Eulalie*. And it was unusual for so many workmen to be employed on one ship. Their numbers would have told him, had he not already known, that the minister was anxious to get his flagship speedily to sea again. Her cargo was already piling up in the warehouses. Fresh lines, new sails, and a quantity of provisions were ready to put aboard her as soon as she was clean and tight. Pierre, who had written the manifests, knew that all the cargo was consigned to Baltha Ogli. Not a stop was to be made between Montpellier and Trebizond, except, of course, for water and provisions. This knowledge was common only to the minister, Bernard, and himself. Even John Justin, the Venetian captain, had as yet no inkling that there was anything unusual about the voyage.

The ship was worked on for more than a week before it was ready to be pulled out of the artificial lagoon. During that time Sir Robert arrived in Montpellier. Jacques Coeur's perennial gratitude toward the noble secretary, who had aided him so substantially at the outset of his career, generously extended to the secretary's kinsman. The minister threw open his house to the count and put up at inns in the town the sizable train of retainers that accompanied him. Sir Robert sent Pierre a cordial greeting, which De Coucy had the courtesy to relay almost verbatim to Pierre, and so did Louise. But Bernard brought no invitation to wait upon them, and, indeed, Pierre did not expect any. Nor did he greatly care. It was nearly seven years since he had gone on his mission to Paris. Now a grown man about to sail to the Orient, he had little time to let his thoughts dwell on his doings as an overgrown boy who had fetched some candles back to Normandy. In fact, he did not quite exactly remember what Louise looked like.

On the second evening of Sir Robert's visit, Pierre rode back from his inn to the *Eulalie* to watch the progress of the workmen. The minister kept them busy as long as it was light. They had worked well above the water line, almost to the deck. The moon that excited the moribund dreams of Ilderim had lost its heathen crescent with the passage of ten days and now rose bigger and rounder every night out of the Lombard plain beyond the Graian Alps, bringing high tides that almost engulfed the oval lagoon. The ship would be floated back to the dock tomorrow. Her ballast had been distributed evenly again in her hold, and the masts pointed to heaven. The scraping and painting could be completed from stages slung over the rail.

Pierre was about to ride back to the inn when he heard the leisurely clopping of walking horses behind him on the street along the waterfront. When he turned, he saw that it was De Coucy with Sir Robert and two ladies, whom he took to be Louise and the countess, her mother. When they came a little closer, Pierre was dismayed to discover that the substantial lady was not the countess, but Louise herself, and very handsome, too; but the belt that she wore was surely twice the length of the one he suddenly remembered removing beside a brook in Paris. Sir Robert looked exactly the same as he had remembered him.

The sight of the other lady made him catch his breath and for several seconds he felt as though a cord had been tightened around his chest above the heart. Then all the breath came out of him at once, and he gasped "Claire!" so loud that he instantly feared she must have heard him, and perhaps she did, for she began to look at him curiously.

The party continued in his direction, and he let his horse walk very slowly toward them. When they were so close that De Coucy could no longer politely ignore him, Bernard relaxed his lips and smiled ingenuously and said, "Sir Robert, perhaps you remember Pierre."

"I certainly do," said the count. "I am glad to see you again, Pierre. I heard you were in the minister's service. You could not have chosen a better master. God bless you, young man. Did you give Pierre my greeting, De Coucy?"

"He did, indeed, Sir Robert," answered Pierre. "It was gentle of you to remember me, and kind of him to tell me."

"You look well," said Louise, very cool and remote. "Did you have a pleasant journey back to Rouen?"—as if it had been yesterday. "Did Claire's skinny pony bear your weight courageously?"

"You have let her grow dreadfully fat," said Claire. "Mother always thought she was too high for me when I was little, but now look at her! At least you've fed her well, Pierre."

"The countess is well, I trust?" Pierre asked, looking regretfully away from Claire to Sir Robert for the answer.

"Well indeed," said Sir Robert, "but still fatigued from the long journey."

"Pierre is so busy helping me," De Coucy said, "that perhaps he has no time to exercise his plump horse. Now I give mine a good workout every night."

"That is good management," said Sir Robert, and he added: "We came down to see the *Sainte-Eulalie*, Pierre. Coeur tells me that you are going to make a trip on her."

Pierre looked quickly at De Coucy, who immediately replied: "That is true, Sir Robert. Pierre will leave Montpellier in a few days. The minister is sending him to Constantinople on a matter that deals with the outrageous pilot fees on the Bosporus. No doubt it will be speedily arranged, for Pierre has displayed great aptitude in the mathematical details of commerce."

"That is good progress, lad," said the count, and Louise said:

"I am so very glad for you, Pierre."

Claire reached out to pat the nose of the horse she had given Pierre, but the animal shied away from the strange hand.

"My poor pet," said Claire. "You have forgotten your old mistress. She is thankless as well as fat, Pierre."

"I had thought to exercise her a bit tonight before I go home," Pierre said. "I reproach myself that I have been so careless of her. If Sir Robert does not object, and if it would please you to renew your acquaintance with the horse, I would count it a privilege if you would accompany me on my ride. Perhaps I can show you some of the sights of the city while it is still light."

De Coucy's handsome face grew black as a thundercloud, and Sir Robert was almost as astonished as the night Pierre asked for the horse. De Coucy said: "That is very presuming of you, Pierre, and you know it."

"Why is it presuming, Bernard?" asked Louise. "You talk just like mother. Pierre will not abduct the girl."

"Nay, he will not," said Sir Robert, half smiling. "Pierre has a history of returning young ladies, not running off with them."

"That isn't what I meant," Bernard said.

"I don't know," said Sir Robert. "Your mother will explode like a bombard, of course, Claire, but I do not forbid you to go for a short ride with the clerk if you want to."

"I should indeed like to renew my acquaintance with the horse," Claire said.

Bernard saw how the wind blew and instantly said, "Pierre is a proper enough sort of escort hereabouts, Sir Robert." He hooked his thumbs into his belt. "Everyone knows he is my favorite assistant."

"That naturally gives my common station some standing in this commercial city, Sir Robert," Pierre said, bowing gracefully as a lord in his saddle. There was not a trace of bitterness in his voice, and Sir Robert admired him for that.

"No doubt, no doubt," replied the count. "Well, do not be late, daughter."

"Remember we have a meeting with the minister tomorrow, Pierre," cautioned De Coucy. "Do not get locked outside the walls! Oh, dear me, what am I saying? They never close the gates at all any more, of course."

Pierre bowed again, his face hiding the delight he now felt as his voice had hidden the shame. They wheeled their horses and set off at a decorous pace in the direction of the castle.

"Louise," said Sir Robert, "it will be necessary for you to exercise your wit to find me an excuse to give to the countess for this singular breach of etiquette. You remember how she turned up her nose at the son of a baron last year. Oh, well, I fought at Agincourt. I am not afraid of your mother."

"I shall remind her that I spent a whole night with him and came to no harm," Louise said stoutly. "Besides, I think he looks very noble on his horse. I have always thought Pierre had a noble look about him."

"He and the horse were both younger then," said Sir Robert, shaking his head. "The horse is really too fat. I think I shall give him another. Nay, the bold young man will probably ask for it first!"

If the countess had prayed that Claire might some day be beautiful, the blessed saints in heaven must have bent their tender compassionate ears all at once to the mother's supplication. To Pierre, at least, riding tense and alert beside her through the streets of Montpellier, Claire de la Tour-Clermont was a radiant miracle that a corporate effort of celestial powers had blessed into being. His lonely heart opened like a shrine; the image of Claire floated in on a silver cloud, and a golden key turned and locked it there.

The alchemy of sudden, overwhelming love wrought a mysterious quickening of all his senses, so that he was preternaturally alive to minute and inconsequential phenomena about him. Looking at Claire, thinking only of Claire, he was also aware, like a ubiquitous spirit, that a family of baby thrushes had hatched out of their speckled, blue-green eggs in a tree far above him; the mother had a snail in her beak and was beating off its shell against a cobble so that the babies could eat. A firefly was caught in the ear of a dog half asleep on the street; the ear twitched and the insect flew away, a thin, fast, little line of puls-ing, green luminosity. A latch chain rattled as the breeze blew it against the door of a shop that someone had forgotten to lock, and in the tower of a neighboring church a bell began to creak on its trunnion. To Pierre's distorted sense of time, it seemed like an age before the old verger was able to impart sufficient swing to the ponderous bell to bring its rim into crashing contact with the clapper. The air filled with holy noise and everyone in Montpellier bowed his head, except Pierre, and prayed. Pierre, too, was worshiping.

The tall blonde girl, whose presence so impiously dislocated the senses of her companion, was a very different creature from the skinny youngster who had run down the stone steps of the odoriferous castle in Paris years before. Claire de la Tour-Clermont had grown into womanhood and maturity quickly. She was perfectly aware of her beauty and its disturbing effect upon men. Before her body had out-grown its infantile contours, none of which now happily remained, she had become accustomed to hearing all the eligible young men in the neighborhood praise her yellow hair, her violet eyes, her red mouth, the roses in her cheeks, the lilies in her hands, her little feet, her grace, her poise, her manners. Some of the more impassioned of them touched on the beauty of her body in the direct language that the manners of the period legitimized. These praises she understood and accepted, be-cause anybody could see (and her mother assured her) that they could hardly be exaggerated. Other young men, more intellectually in-clined, composed elegant poems to her wit. Claire had little use for such things. And a few pious ones, hesitating between careers in the Church and careers in the army, the only truly noble profession, talked about her soul. Claire found this very confusing. Claire had never known a merchant, of course, except the great Jacques Coeur and her own noble kinsman, Bernard de Coucy, who of all the suitors was unac-countably the most acceptable to the countess, her mother.

Except for Sir Robert, who was indulgent to the point of negligence where his daughters were concerned, the countess declared in forceful language that both her attractive girls would long since have been wedded, bedded, and bred, and one of them, it did not matter which, to Bernard, whose manners were so elegant and whose name was so ancient and honorable.

Claire raised her pretty head, her curls confined against the breeze by a silver net embroidered with pearls, and observed: "You have not been a talkative guide, Pierre. Where are the sights of the city you promised me?"

Antoine de la Salle had taught Pierre the art of courtly small talk, referring his pupil constantly to a number of lively treatises, some of which he had written himself, among them a penetrating little work entitled "The Fifteen Joys of Marriage." But it never occurred to that illegitimate chevalier to instruct Pierre how to loosen the tongue fifteen minutes after falling hopelessly in love. Perhaps La Salle would not have been able.

"I have not seen them, mademoiselle," he answered. "I cannot believe my good fortune. I cannot believe it is you."

"Nay, you do not remember me either! And to think that I remembered you for so long!"

"I have always remembered your kindness, your generosity, mademoiselle. What you looked like, I confess I did not remember."

"It is just as well, Pierre. I am sure I must have been a great gawk. You looked very old and big and impressive. I know now that you had eyes only for Louise. Isn't she lovely, Pierre?"

"The lady Louise is a noble and wonderful woman," Pierre replied. "It is surprising that she has never seen fit to accept any of the suitors that must surely have laid siege to her heart."

"That surprises everybody. Faithful Bernard still proposes regularly twice a year, at Christmas and Easter time. Mother dotes on him. But my sister has a strong mind."

"He was riding very close to you, I thought," said Pierre. "That was the first thing I noticed."

"Did you really, Pierre? It is true that he has recently transferred some of his attentions to me. Has my kinsman, then, been kind to you?"

"He has given me a great deal to do," Pierre said smiling. "Of course, I am glad of the work. It keeps me very busy, mademoiselle. That is how I let your poor horse get so fat."

"You cannot spend all your time on the docks, Pierre. No doubt you devote your evenings to breaking the hearts of the Montpellier women."

"Actually I live a monkish life here, mademoiselle. The little inn where I lodge is run by an absurdly devout old man. He closes it promptly at Vespers and meditates all evening."

"Do you live in an inn, Pierre? Nay, Bernard has told me that you frequent them and slay with your hands all the customers you do not like."

"That is a vicious story that has followed me all the way from Rouen. Your kinsman has turned gossipy, mademoiselle."

"Oh, Bernard always talks maliciously. Nobody ever takes him seriously. It is his kind of humor."

"I have experienced it often," Pierre admitted. "I do not take it seriously either. Actually, I killed nobody. But one man did die at the hands of an unknown assassin after a harmless scuffle with me at the Cutthroat back home."

"What a horrible name, Pierre! It must have been a frightfully disreputable establishment!"

Pierre told her the pious origin of the bloody name and Claire laughed. There was music in her laughter, Pierre thought, like the music of a bell, transfigured and beatified. It tingled up his spine and tied his tongue again.

Everybody knew everybody else in the little city of Montpellier. The guards at the gate saluted Pierre in a friendly, familiar way, and bowed low to the noble lady, very precisely, in their best military manner.

"Now how did the clerk do that!" the sergeant muttered, bowing with the rest. Montpellier would buzz like a hive tomorrow. They all knew who Claire was. She had been the subject of a good many forthright, ungarnished compliments that she was not aware of.

"There is a very pleasant little road just beyond the walls," Pierre said. "The vista of the harbor is enchanting. I am sure we have time to go up the hill and take a quick look at the view."

Claire smiled. "You conjured me shrewdly away from my father, Pierre. Right under Bernard's nose, too. But I have no desire to go into the woods with you. They are probably full of thieves, and it would not be pleasant to be stolen away and held to ransom."

"There are no thieves in the woods," said Pierre, "but if there were, I verily believe I might kill them with my hands if they attacked you, ma damoiselle."

Pierre split the word instinctively. "Mademoiselle," lost its formal nonentity and became "my lady," with an unmistakable connotation of possession. It was extraordinarily familiar speech. Claire was astonished. But his eyes flashed and his jaws set and his fist clenched tight as if he felt a robber's neck in it. He was not even looking at her.

But Claire was looking at him, in a way that would have disconcerted him exceedingly if he had not been concentrating so hard on choking the life out of the robber, running her glance from shoulder to shoulder, from forehead to chin, all in a second or two, as if she suddenly saw him for the first time.

In that moment she decided to go up the hill, which the intelligent horses they rode, having no other instructions, had already begun to do. Claire had never heard such a yearning in a man's voice. She began to remember more about their first meeting.

One of the millions of wayside shrines that dotted the face of France stood at the top of the hill overlooking the harbor. The sinking sun painted the cross red toward the sea, and the rising moon, which they could not see because of the hill, painted it a softer red toward the land, so that the ancient weathered wood glowed like bronze. There was a place at the foot to kneel, if one felt like it, and a bench to sit on. Both were worn and polished with years of faithful use.

At the crest of the hill they suddenly witnessed the mighty spectacle of a full moon just clearing one distant, black, jagged horizon, while half a sun remained above the other, spreading a golden carpet on the purpling waters from the harbor to the sky.

Claire wanted to watch the sun set, and she honestly persuaded herself that her leg had gone to sleep on her saddle while the horse was climbing the hill, though that had not happened all the way from Clermont to Montpellier.

"I think I shall get down and rest a moment," she said.

Pierre was instantly off his horse, making a stirrup of his hands for her foot to step in, and when he had lowered her to where she could put the other foot on the ground, which caused him to bend his body as if he were bowing, he unlocked his fingers and opened his arms and straightened up a little.

She was so close that they were almost touching. He could feel her breath on his cheek. Something Jacques Coeur imported lent a wonderful fragrance to her hair. His arms closed again, around her waist, and when she looked up in unfeigned astonishment, he kissed her on the mouth.

Pierre closed his eyes; his brow contorted as if he were in pain, so that he did not see that her eyes were wide open and afraid. She was not afraid of Pierre, because she knew well enough that he would not harm her. The man with his long arms around her displayed no evidence of any intention to remove them, ever, while the world lasted. Claire saw in the sky a dreadful vision of half a dozen outraged relatives, and then she shut her eyes and blinked them out of existence. She had been too astonished to struggle; now she did not want to. Her arms went up around his shoulders, one hand stole tenderly round his neck and up into his hair, and she returned his kiss, mentally, at least, for his mouth was still pressed hard upon her own, and she could hardly move.

Pierre could not have helped kissing her if it had cost him his life. When he felt her mouth return his kiss, her body relax and seek his, all the pain went out of his soul and he opened his eyes in wonderment and delight.

"I love you, ma damoiselle," he whispered, moving his lips just far enough away to say the words, and then, very tenderly, he kissed her again.

Something very like Pierre's own image floated into Claire's heart, where it merged with a formless, forgotten duplicate of itself and resurrected it into clear, sharp delineation.

"I love you, too," she said. "I think I have loved you ever since I was a little girl," and she hid her face against his breast at the enormity of her confession.

He thought he was holding her very gently, but Claire could hardly breathe. She was happy enough not to mind the suffocation for a few moments, but soon her ribs began to ache sharply.

"Your arms are hurting me, Pierre."

Pierre opened his arms reluctantly. Claire took a deep breath that sounded so like a sigh of relief and so obviously was not that they both smiled, and he said: "I certainly did not intend to hurt you, Claire. I should rather die."

The horses had wandered away to a patch of grass behind the shrine. The sun had achieved the drowning of itself in the sea. He took her hand and led her to the bench, completing the action that had started so short a time ago by the sun. The sea was aglow with a softer light, not a path but a rosy diffusion, reflecting the light of the sky. Claire looked beyond it, beyond the castle and the town and the ships, and she said: "I am not ashamed to say that I love you. It is the way I felt when I first saw you. Do you remember my handkerchief, Pierre?"

"Handkerchief?" said Pierre. Then he remembered. "Saints! Was that your handkerchief? Of course I remember it. I thought it was your mother's!"

"That is what the man said. He was honest and he brought it back, but I cried for a week. I thought you did not want it."

"If I had known!"

"If you had known, dear Pierre, you would have done nothing about it."

"I would certainly never have sent it back."

"Perhaps not. You are gentle. You would have spared my feelings. But I know exactly what I looked like, and how young I was. You were already a grown man."

"Do you remember that you wanted me to teach you Latin? All I could think of to say was 'I love you.'"

"So Father said. He had a great laugh about it. I actually insisted on a tutor then, Pierre, and Father was willing enough. He is a dear. But Mother said it was nonsense. I had determined to learn Latin so that if I ever saw you again, I could talk Latin to you. But when the tutor came, he also began with *amo, amas, amat,* and I discovered that you had not meant a word of what you said. It was only a lesson after all. So my heart broke all over again and I sent the tutor away."

"I mean it now," Pierre said.

"So do I, Pierre. It is all the Latin I ever learned. Wasn't I a silly goose?"

"Oh," Pierre cried very miserably, "if I had a single drop of noble blood in my veins, nay, if I were only rich like the minister, if I could hope for anything—"

"I know," said Claire. "Do not say it."

"I would go to Sir Robert and ask for you tonight!"

"I would wait behind the curtains, listening for Father's answer! But that is impossible, Pierre."

"Jacques Coeur has a courageous device," Pierre said.

"I know his device. He has written it all over the walls of his castle."

"Men can rise in France, Claire!"

"It has happened. Oh, Pierre, it would be wonderful!"

Montpellier buzzed with gossip. Next morning the countess expostulated so violently with Sir Robert that his head began to ache as well as his leg. He longed for the healing waters on the estates of her cousin, the seneschal.

"Dear wife," he said, "you have reason to be angry. I admit that I permitted an impropriety. Pierre spoke very properly, and before I knew it, I let the girl go with him. I like the clerk. I am mindful of the service he rendered me. You ought to be, too. Now, I warn you, Adèle, I shall beat you with the old leather strap if you continue to annoy me with this minor incident."

"Sir Robert! You wouldn't!" The countess gasped in astonishment. Her husband had not displayed such energy in years. "My dear lord, this gentle climate is putting strange notions into your head."

"Admit that the ride was short. She came home long before dark."

"The moon was so bright that you thought it was still daytime," the countess said sourly, "and Claire looked wonderfully in love. The clerk is a menace, Sir Robert."

"I am not so old that I cannot tell the sun from the moon, Adèle. Pierre is no menace. But there will be no more rides. He leaves for the East in a day or two."

"So I hear," said the countess. "That is good. Maybe that will take the stars out of her eyes. I am highly concerned, my husband. There are convents for foolish young women."

"Nay, was it so bad, Adèle? Perhaps I am an unobservant old fool, as you say."

"I said no such thing, my dear lord. Would you really beat me with the old strap?"

The count grunted a noncommittal grunt.

# CHAPTER

## ❋ 17 ❋

BERNARD AND PIERRE waited upon the minister in the library while Sir Robert threatened his lady in another part of the castle.

"If De Coucy has not already told you, Pierre," Coeur said, "and he probably has, your mission, as far as anybody knows, will deal exclusively with pilot fees. It has sometimes been necessary for me to send agents to Constantinople in order to rectify these troublesome, usurious charges. They become more and more a sort of legal tribute every year. Actually, you may be able to effect a reduction in some of them."

Pierre was, of course, familiar with how local pilots at every port of call, particularly in the narrow waters around Constantinople, were authorized to go aboard every passing ship, at a princely fee, on the theory that they knew the navigable channels better than the ships' own sailing masters. It was often true that they did.

"As my emissary, empowered to treat with the local authorities," the minister continued, "you will be my auditor-general, a person of some distinction." He smiled a little.

"You are not supposed to bargain too effectively, however," Bernard interposed. "If the Greeks conclude that you are inept, so much the better. Do not let the effort to appear stupid fatigue you. Have I interpreted your instructions correctly, my noble master?"

"In a sense De Coucy is right, Pierre. Do not delay or make enemies. Your scene of action, or rather of observance, lies far beyond the capital of the Eastern empire."

"I am sure it will not be difficult to find a plausible excuse for continuing on to Trebizond," Pierre said. His color was high and his voice was full of confidence. Jacques Coeur, probably the only man in Montpellier who was unaware of Pierre's ride beyond the walls the previous moon-drenched evening, was pleased with Pierre's serious, resolute air.

"You will naturally cultivate the friendship of Baltha Ogli in the closest possible manner," he said. "Ogli is a great power in Trebizond."

"Would it not be wise," questioned Bernard, "to apprise Ogli Pasha at once of the trouble, my lord? Pierre could inform him, or I could write him a letter in your name."

"Unless I am to appear stupid here as well as in Constantinople," Pierre interrupted quickly, "I must say that I think that would be the worst possible thing to do."

The minister pondered, and De Coucy's face took on the color of his master's delicious pomegranate juice.

"Ogli could aid you enormously, Pierre," Coeur said. "Naturally my business consumes only a fraction of his time. You will carry more weight in his presence if he knows how important is my reason for sending you. I would not have you land in Trebizond without a friend."

"I do not presume to advise you, my lord minister," Pierre said, "but if nobody knows the secret, the secret cannot leak out. I am willing to take my chances."

"I meant only to better the possibility of the boy's success. But Pierre is resourceful, of course," Bernard said.

"You must be very alert," the minister continued. "Attempt to evaluate the characters of the men who serve me, not excluding the members of the ship's company, regardless of their station. Watch well the actions of my agents that you encounter en route. There may be little fish in the muddy pond I am sending you to fish in. Catch them if you can, but remember, it is the big ones I want."

"I shall fish with a hook, my lord, not with a net—if I am able," Pierre said.

"That is exactly what I mean, Pierre. I am sorry my instructions must of necessity be so general. I am glad that you understand me."

"It is more than I do," admitted De Coucy.

"Bernard," said the minister, "anybody might smuggle jewels. But it is in my heart that this mischief springs from a deep, hellish corruption as well as a desire for gain. Only a subtle, degenerate, diabolical man would think of the opium."

"I see your reasoning now clearly, my lord," his secretary said. "But it is easy for the Devil to hide in hell. And Trebizond! Oh, dear me!"

"By the same token," Coeur explained, "he may perhaps be less careful of concealing his identity there. All in all, if Pierre thinks he needs no help from Ogli, I shall let him do without it. Do not write the factor in Trebizond, Bernard. It may complicate your search, Pierre. You are right, however, in stating that it will stop any possible leak about the object of your mission, though I consider that a very minor possibility. Apparently it is unnecessary for me to warn you to be very cautious in everything you do."

"I shall be exceedingly wary, my lord," Pierre said. "Your instructions are very comprehensive."

"You will need some new clothes," commented Bernard brightly. "You cannot go wandering all over Christendom looking like a dock clerk. I thought of that detail myself, my lord."

"Did you, Bernard? You are perfectly right."

"There is a tailor waiting in the kitchen this minute, sir. It would cause comment if Pierre went to a shop and ordered an expensive wardrobe."

"Nobody would know what he ordered, Bernard. But it was a wise precaution. You have a sword, Pierre?"

"My lord, I could outfit a company of soldiers. I grew up in an armorer's shop, as Your Excellency knows. I am fond of steel, and my room at the inn is cluttered with sharp weapons."

"Oh, my!" said Bernard, holding up his white hands, heavy with jeweled rings. "No doubt he sliced the Rouenese fellow to mincemeat after crushing his skull. I should hate to be the guilty Trapezuntian, my lord minister."

"You had best be getting measured by the tailor, Pierre," Coeur ordered. "Buy nothing too brilliant."

"My lord," said De Coucy, "the tailor has been instructed to bring suitable stuffs. I selected a lightweight, white linen for his underclothing, some bolts of excellent Flanders wool for his hose—they are sober blue and a quiet shade of dusty buff orange, my lord. There is heavy velvet for a formal mantle, miniver for a cap, my lord, and I think the fur will also border the mantle in a very distinguished manner—it is broad enough. There is a handsome green belt of Russia leather to hang a sword on—the brass ornamentation is very pretty, I should say, sir—"

"Bernard, you amaze me," the minister said laughing. "You think of everything. Is it any wonder I treasure my noble secretary?"

The tailor spared no expense in the rapid fabrication of the clothes for the important member of Jacques Coeur's staff that De Coucy had imperiously summoned him and his numerous assistants to serve. When Simonides discovered that it was only Pierre, the quiet clerk who lived at the inn not far from his shop, he was secretly astonished. He cut the goods to an ampler measure and, differing from most of his colleagues, he kept his own counsel.

Simonides was a Jew whose presence in France was connived at because, along with a great many of his race, he was possessed of a skill that Christian brethren of his craft simply could not duplicate. The other tailors of Montpellier would gladly have sewn Simonides into a sack, with their fanciest stitches, and thrown him into the sea. But all the gentry, from De Coucy to John Justin, bought their clothes from him.

Pierre's bill went to De Coucy, who paid it with a flourish, gracefully complimenting the tailor's art, after which, of course, the charge was duly entered in Coeur's books, with a small and perfectly legal commission to the secretary for his services. Pierre's new clothes were packed in cedar sea chests with a sprinkling of aloes to discourage the fleas and cockroaches and other vermin that infested the *Eulalie*, like all ships, and contributed to the wakeful alertness of the sailors.

On Sunday a priest blessed the ship, spurging the bow with a golden spurge, that the *Eulalie* might find her way in the sea, and the sails, that the wind might be fair. The ship's company prayed to St. Peter, St. Christopher, St. Brendan, and other blessed travelers, who, by their own perilous adventures, were known to be attentive to the supplications of mariners.

On Monday the ship sailed, early in the evening, on the breast of a high tide.

It was natural that Sir Robert and his family, whose visit in Montpellier was nearing an end, should want to witness the departure of so large a caravel.

The ship sparkled with new paint; the clean, fragrant odor of pitch and pine hung over her. The decks and rails were polished with salt water and sand, and the raw, clean wood shone like yellow gold in the sun. All her flags and shields were out, brilliant pennons floated from her new rigging, bunting draped from the rails. Many of the wives and families of the ship's company crowded down to the dock to see her off, and so did a great number of clerks, workmen, and citizens of the town. A lively band of musicians played on pipes and musettes, trumpets and drums, but by common practice the plaintive strings of the rebec were never heard in the music for a ship's sailing. Departure was sad enough; ships were unheard of for months, sometimes forever. There was no need to aggravate the general excitement and apprehension by the wail of so melancholy an instrument. Most of the women usually wept. So did many of the men, openly and unashamed.

Sir Robert, the countess, Louise, Claire, De Coucy, and Jacques Coeur were mounted. Pierre wore his sword and one of the least spectacular of the garments that the cunning hands of Simonides and his busy assistants had conjured into a perfect fit at such short notice. Pierre lingered on the dock several minutes after he should have been aboard. A demon was methodically sinking its red-hot claws into the flesh of his heart. He was white as the sheet let down from heaven. He wished the *Sainte-Eulalie* had never been built and that he was back in the armorer's shop in Rouen, and had never gone to Paris or Montpellier or met the girl who was looking down at him from the immeasurable height of her station in life and her horse. Coeur had not suspected that the seriousness of his mission would show on the face of his young emissary so patently.

"Fare thee safely and well, Pierre," he said kindly. "The business you do is important. Fail me not; and if you do not, the king himself shall hear of you. Believe me."

"Thank you, my lord," Pierre replied. He hardly heard the encouraging words, though Sir Robert marked every one of them attentively. The merchant minister did not make idle promises.

Pierre kissed the ladies' hands, and when he came to Claire's, the demon began to gnash with his fangs as well as to claw with his claws, for Pierre dared not hold her hand for a single moment longer than the countess's.

"God keep you, Pierre," she said in a low voice. Her fingers tightened imperceptibly around his own for an instant, and for that instant a bright angel came with silver wings and chased the cannibal imp away.

Sir Robert saw tears in his daughter's eyes, and he began to agree with his lady that it was just as well for the peace of the family that Pierre was departing.

"You are wearing a handsome sword, Pierre," he observed. He had never happened to see Pierre with a sword, though it was common enough for men of all classes to carry them on occasion.

Pierre's sword was a functional, inconspicuous weapon. But the practiced eye of the old soldier instantly noted the thick silver wire wound round its ample pommel to give a man a firm grip, and the blue, curved *quillons* of tempered steel, utterly devoid of ornament, sloping back around the hilt, smooth and long, to deflect a blow and protect the wrist. It was a long time since Sir Robert had seen a sword like that. "Might I examine it a moment, Pierre?"

It was not customary for men to handle each other's swords. But many a greater man than Pierre might have been flattered by the venerable count's attention. Pierre instantly unhooked his new belt (with its very pretty brass ornamentation) and held it up to Sir Robert, the sword still in the scabbard. Sir Robert unsheathed it. He ran his finger over the smooth burnished blade. It was always surprising not to be able to feel the pattern that so strongly resembled ripples on the surface of water.

"Damascus," he said. "They are very rare nowadays." He tried the edge with his nail. "And ye do not strop it like a barber. You know how to take care of steel, Pierre."

"It was made by an Isfahan Turk," Pierre said. "I watched him forge it out of several tongues of thin steel. May I give it to you, sir?"

"Eh? What did you say, Pierre?"

"I should be highly honored," Pierre said very earnestly, "if I could sail away with the knowledge that my sword had been accepted as a gift by the noble Count de la Tour-Clermont. You have always been uncommonly gracious to me, Sir Robert. I have never been in a position to express my thanks. Will you take my sword?"

"Nay, lad, of course not. This blade is too valuable. Anyway, you cannot go to Greece, or wherever it is, without a sword."

Sir Robert held it out to Pierre, but Pierre stepped back a pace.

"I implore you to keep it, sir. I have another in my sea chest."

"That is not true," Bernard said. "I saw the contents of your chests, Pierre, when the tailors packed your clothes yesterday." De Coucy began to feel that Pierre was becoming altogether too acceptable in the eyes of his kinsfolk. Even the countess looked a little impressed. Bernard unhooked his own sword. He removed his ample red leather belt, and he said: "I pray you, Sir Robert, accept the lad's sword. It is valuable, no doubt. But I shall recompense him with my own and you can see for yourself that the jewels in the belt alone will more than repay the generosity of his gesture."

"Ah, but that was kind of you, Bernard," said the countess, and Pierre lost his fleeting favor in her eyes.

Sir Robert wanted the sword. He hooked the belt round his slender middle. It fit him very well and felt very comfortable.

"I shall accept your gift, Pierre," he said, "in the same spirit that you offer it. But only if you accept Bernard's."

"Very well, sir. I thank you."

Pierre took the ornate sword and the jeweled belt from the secretary and tried it around his waist. Claire knew full well that Pierre's waist was only just big enough to put an arm around. The belt was so ridiculously oversize that he instantly took it off.

"It would be a pity to mutilate so handsome and costly a belt," he said, unhooking the sword. "I shall keep the blade, but I cannot accept all these jewels." He gave the belt back to De Coucy, who received it again with that happy relieved expression which must have animated the face of the scriptural father when he sighted his prodigal son.

Jacques Coeur smilingly watched the red leather and the steel and the green leather change hands, and he said:

"Pierre, unless you intend to remain in France, you had better jump aboard the Lady. Her master seems to be getting impatient."

Two sailors had loosened the lines that held the ship to the dock. The *Eulalie* drifted a foot or two away. Her motion would continue. Pierre quickly bowed in a deep semicircle that included them all and ran to the edge of the dock and leaped aboard the ship. Claire thought he cleared the rail very gracefully. Actually, encumbered with the sword in his hand as he was, he miscalculated the distance and barked his leg painfully against a heavy wooden block on the other side. He swore a purple oath at the sharp, sudden pain, endearing himself instantly and unwittingly to one of the common sailors who was coiling a length of line on the deck. Then he composed his face and turned again toward the landing, to watch his world and his love grow small and smaller, merging into unrecognizability as the distance grew. The last thing he saw in France was the flutter of Claire's handkerchief, white like a bird. The last sound he heard was music: it grew fainter and fainter, and finally lost itself in the creak of the sweeps in their locks, the rattle of blocks, the shouts of the sailors who tailed onto the lines, hoisting the sails, and the unaccustomed swish of the cloven water that bubbled and washed along the hull of the swiftly moving ship.

# CHAPTER

## ❊ 18 ❊

PIERRE STOOD a long time at the rail. His face was wet, and the water was salt; but it did not come from the sea, and he did not care who saw it. Suddenly he was aware that a sailor was touching him on the arm.

"It is bad luck to bleed on the deck, sir," the man said respectfully. "Would you raise your foot a moment?"

Pierre did.

"Thank you," the sailor said, and threw a pailful of water under it. Pierre set his foot down.

"*Peste!*" he grumbled. "Now how did I get that?"

"When you jumped aboard, sir. You jumped too far, and hit this deadeye." The man slapped with his hand one of the big solid chunks of oak, pierced through with holes and threaded with lines that steadied a sail.

"I'll take a look at it," Pierre said. He was annoyed at his clumsiness, and he was now thoroughly aware of a very unpleasant pain in his leg. It served to take his mind off Claire, of course, but that only made him angrier. He walked aft to the tiny cabin in the sterncastle that had been assigned to him.

Only the officers had any place at all to sleep. Most of the crew lay down anywhere after their watch in fair weather. In foul, they went below into the stuffy hold. Each man contrived to fit himself a niche in the cargo space. When the cargo was woolens, the men were very comfortable. When it was good French lumber or copper ingots, they were much less happy. By a sort of common law, everywhere understood, these little rats' nests were always respected, and a man might leave his purse, if he had one, or any other possession, with perfect confidence that when he looked for it in a day or a week, it would still be there.

Pierre left a bloody footprint every time his injured member touched the deck. The sailor sloshed water on each one, following him to his cabin. There were fifty men aboard, and of course this singular pollution and ablution was observed.

Pierre stripped off his shoes and his hose and sat down in his drawers on the edge of his bunk, which, with his chests and a small stand with a little rail around it, comprised all the furniture of the cabin. He surveyed the extent of his injury, which was neither large nor deep. But the cut bled with a slow persistence that he did not like.

"I suppose the chirurgeon should cauterize that," he observed with no enthusiasm.

"He is probably heating the iron this instant," the sailor replied. "Master Crispin can smell blood like a vampire. Several of the officers will not even let him shave them."

"Indeed," Pierre said. "I do not think I like your Master Crispin."

"They say he has a theory," the sailor continued cheerfully, "that a wound heals best when the iron burns to the bone."

"I like him less and less," said Pierre, fingering the pulpy edge of the cut gingerly.

"When the sailors cut themselves, they usually bathe the wound in sea water. Shall I fetch you some?"

"By all means do. That is an excellent idea," Pierre answered gratefully.

The sailor knotted a throw line to the handle of a bucket and tossed it over the side. He drew it up full of good, salt, sea water, and Pierre stuck his leg into it. The blood oozed out of the cut in a thin red ribbon, slowing waving and folding back on itself in the clear, cold water that quickly took on a uniform pinkish tinge. Pierre drew up his leg after a few minutes. The bleeding had lessened considerably.

"Your medicine is working well," he said. "What is your name, my friend?"

"My name is Jacques, like the master's. I come from Bourges. I have served him for years."

"I am grateful to you, Jacques," Pierre said.

At that moment an excited man suddenly pushed himself into the cabin which was already overcrowded by only two occupants. He had a red-hot cautery in one hand, and a small smoking brazier in the other.

The sun was low, there was no window in the cabin, and it was already a little gloomy.

"Where is the patient?" he cried. "Did Master Pierre break his leg? Does the bone protrude?"

The ship's chirurgeon stood on practiced sea legs, balancing himself nicely in exact opposition to every roll of the vessel. The little metal pot, full of live coals, suspended from small chains, swung like a thurible.

"I am here, Master Chirurgeon. Be careful of your fire."

Jacques of Bourges had no wounds, but he was very close to the doctor and in mortal danger of receiving preliminary treatment for all the cuts he might ever receive during the rest of his life.

"I am quite well," Pierre quickly assured the visitor, "and I do not need your cautery."

"Certainly you do, sir. Everybody saw you hurt yourself. That was a foolish landlubberly leap. No sailor would have jumped so far as that. We thought you were going to fly clean over the ship. Now let me see your injured foot at once. You bled all over the deck."

"Softly, good Master Crispin," Pierre said. "If I bled a little on your deck, I am sorry. I merely opened an old sore on my leg when I jumped. It has never been cauterized."

"Then we should burn it closed right away! What are you doing with that foolish pail of water, sir? Jacques, did you bring him that?"

"Indeed he did, Master Crispin. I specifically ordered it," Pierre said. "I always soak my sore leg in sea water."

"You are a young man to have old sores on your legs," said the doctor. "And you never had them cauterized?"

"Nay, sir, Villanova himself has forbidden it," Pierre answered solemnly.

The surgeon appeared to lose some of his confidence.

"Of course, if the Sieur de Villeneuve forbids it, it must be all right. I know that he used sea water on poor Ilderim."

Pierre made a mental note that the world is small and the walls have ears.

"Pray what am I to do with the cautery that I heated at such a waste of charcoal?" the chirurgeon complained.

Pierre could have told him, but he was mindful of his instructions not to make enemies.

"If the leg does not improve, Master Chirurgeon," he said very formally, "I shall deem it a privilege to consult your art in a week or two. Meanwhile, I feel honor bound to continue the palliative treatment prescribed by your noble colleague, the dean of the College of Chirurgeons at the university. You are undoubtedly acquainted both with the master and his methods."

Crispin melted visibly and began to ooze.

"Why, naturally, I know Villanova, and sea water does indeed contain some cleansing virtue. Any sailor will tell you that." Jacques was having trouble keeping his face straight. The chirurgeon was notorious among the sailors for his one-man crusade against their homely specific. "In fact," Crispin continued, "I have lately considered making more extensive use of it. But it is slow. All Villanova's techniques are slow. When I see a cut or a sore, I say to myself, Crispin, I say, fix this man up at once. Burn out the corruption! Burn in the healing pus! Get the man back to work in a hurry. No one is sick on the Lady for long, believe me, sir. Even Ilderim might have lived, I think, if I had been called into consultation. I was unfortunately unable to attend him. I was visiting a sick man at a tavern, and I knew nothing about the pilot's illness until after he was dead."

All the heat had gone out of the chirurgeon's cautery; the fire in his brazier was smothering out and very smelly.

"I saw your patient, Master Crispin," said Jacques. "You had to crawl under a table to attend him, did you not?"

"Nay, were you at the tavern, Jacques?" The doctor was somewhat taken aback. "As you know, Master Pierre, there is a superfluity of aqueous humors at sea, whereas, contrariwise, the land exerts a desiccating influence on the organs. I often prepare myself for the sudden change from one dominant principle to the other by fortifying my body with a small draught of brandy, in order that the balance of my humors may be maintained."

"I can well believe it, sir," Pierre said agreeably. "I should consider that a remarkably sensible precaution."

"I would not have you think I drank."

"Certainly *not!*"

"It was while I was attending my patient—"

"Under the tavern table?" asked Jacques.

Crispin favored Jacques with a glare that made him glad the cautery was cold. "A physician must go anywhere. It must have been about that time that poor Ilderim died. All his humors ran into his spleen and it burst. Villanova told everybody, and I share his professional opinion."

Pierre wondered whether the Sieur de Villeneuve had bungled the injection and killed the man, or whether someone had cautioned him to conceal the true secret of Ilderim's death, or whether Crispin knew the Turk ate opium and had reasons of his own for not telling.

"I have heard he was a good pilot," Pierre remarked casually.

"There never was a better one. I have seen him take the tiller himself when the helmsman was slow in answering his orders. That happened off the Caphareus, many weeks' sail from here."

"Ilderim must have been a very unpopular fellow to put on such airs," Pierre said.

"Not unpopular, exactly. But he was a lonely man, never mixing much with the sailors or playing in their dice games. Even I hardly knew him, and his position was such that he might have employed my barbering services. Will you require shaving often, sir?"

Pierre had refused one professional service. He could not politely refuse another.

"My beard grows very slowly," he said. "I shall be delighted to call on you when it gets stubbly, but it may take weeks."

"Oh, I see. That condition often accompanies old leg sores. What a shame. Well, if you should need me, or if you want a haircut, or if a tooth needs pulling—there is no fee aboard ship, you know, but sometimes a distinguished official like yourself—"

"I quite understand about the fee, Master Crispin. My hair will undoubtedly want cutting in a few days, and the minute I have a toothache, rest assured I shall know what to do. Am I correct in my suspicion that your brazier is fouling the air somewhat, good Master Crispin?"

"Nay, perhaps it is. I shall take it away and fetch you a bandage for your sore leg. I have an excellent one that I used on a sailor who suffered a great gash on his shoulder during the last voyage."

Pierre had a mental picture of the rag, all vermin and old blood.

"Be sure you wash it in sea water," he said.

"Nay, but the man cured rapidly. Washing it will remove the healing principle!"

"Wash it just the same, Master Crispin. Remember your colleague's prescription. Bring it to me wet, good doctor."

The surgeon did as he was told. And he cut Pierre's hair, too, when the time came. But Pierre miraculously never required a shave, and Crispin came to the conclusion that he was shaving himself like so many of the other officers. He did not mention Ilderim's death again.

Sailors seldom talk about dead members of the crew. Pierre's leg healed rapidly.

The *Sainte-Eulalie* was lateen rigged. Square sails had been known, of course, since remotest antiquity. The Northmen had come with square sails on their dragon-headed ships from the frigid peninsula beyond the Baltic ages ago to conquer Pierre's home province and give it the name of Normandy.

Men in Cathay with eyes like almonds sailed ships with square sails over the China Sea.

The Romans had used square sails, and the Portuguese were using them again, on their voyages down the coast of Africa and to the Azores on the westermost rim of the known world.

But for the narrow waters of the Eastern seas, strewn with unexpected islands and unpredictable currents, no rig had ever been invented that could compare with the simple, triangular sails of the lateeners. The Lady could sail close to a contrary wind, and, with a little management, take full advantage of one dead astern, which was something of a feat for ships of her class.

John Justin, captain of the Lady, was a knight and a nobleman. He bore a name that was old and famous in Venice, but for two generations his family had had the misfortune to choose the losing side in all the local political struggles of the great Italian republic. Virtually penniless some years before, he had sought service in the growing navy of France, where men of birth, with the habit of command, were eagerly sought. Coeur had engaged him and had never had reason to be sorry. Sir John kept his crews healthy and happy. His discipline was strict and impartial. He was reasonably pious, literate for a nobleman, and on Sundays he read the prayers for the ship's company.

Some of the crew were Italians, Genoese or, like Pedro Dineo, Venetians, countrymen of the captain. Genoa and Venice held ancient animosities, and their history was one long series of wars. But on the neutral deck of a French ship, where they all hoped to rise to prominence, perhaps even to fortune and a command like John Justin, the Italians forgot their jealousies and served King Charles as faithfully as his own Frenchmen, and often more expertly. The captain always referred to them as French.

Best of all, he sailed fast. There was extra pay, for the men as well as for himself, when the Lady made an especially speedy and profitable voyage. He reminded them of that.

He was not a practical sailor, and he was not expected to be. Captains rarely were. Responsibility for the navigation of the ship and the vital calculations of her course, progress, and daily position lay with Tristan Dumont, the sailing master, and his petty officers. Actually, Sir John knew more navigation than he needed to, especially in those landlocked seas where it was unusual to be more than a week out of sight of familiar coasts and islands. He affected to know even less than he did.

His cabin in the sterncastle was three times the size of Pierre's, which made it about the size of a good room in a modest inn. For a ship, that was extraordinarily spacious. With boundless authority over fifty men, with a page to carry his orders and a valet to care for his person, Sir John lived better at sea than he did ashore.

He was held in affectionate awe, and he dined alone in his cabin, though at lengthy intervals he invited the officers to sup with him, one at a time, in exact order of their precedence. Tristan Dumont was the first; Master Crispin would be the last, if, indeed, he was ever invited at all. Pierre's invitation followed the sailing master's after a lapse of many days, but it confirmed his high rank in the eyes of the crew, and reminded Pierre that Coeur meant what he said when he mentioned that an emissary charged with the reduction of pilot fees was a person of some distinction.

It grew warm as the ship sailed south. The wind held steady from the northeast, as might have been expected at that time of year, and the Lady made good runs every day, passing the Strait of Bonifacio and negotiating the treacherous channel between Italy and Sicily under the best possible sailing conditions.

Pedro Dineo heaved a heavy lead, attached to a strong thin line, constantly over the side, trying for the bottom. Once, in the evening as the Lady cleared the Strait of Messina, he brought it up befouled with phosphorescent seaweed that made his hands glow as if there were a cold fire on them. There was a pale gray, ugly fish that had no eyes, tangled in the luminous marine vegetation. He was afraid to touch it, and he cleared the lead with a long heavy fid, a sort of spike that he used to splice lines, and kicked the fish and the seaweed over the side. Nobody was afraid of phosphorescent weeds, which were common enough, but nobody liked the idea that a blind fish had come aboard, because that meant they would lose their way. But Dineo made a joke about the whole thing. His dead brother, Antony, had sent them a present, he said, which everybody considered in very bad taste and a stupid sort of joke.

The Lady slipped round the toe of the long Italian boot and dipped her prow into the blue Ionian Sea. There was no Ilderim to pilot her through the short cut round Cape Matapan, and so Dumont took her south to Cythera, and let go her anchors close to the eastern shore, under the lee of that harborless, desolate Greek isle. The ship had made a wonderful run, but nearly a month had passed and it was absolutely necessary to stop for a day and take on water and fresh provisions.

There was a ruined old Byzantine castle on the shore and a Latin church that the Venetian lords who owned the island had built. They and the gentry went there on Sundays. There was a Greek church, too, where most of the fishers of purple and shepherds went, to kneel on the ancient basalt floor and to stand in the pewless nave, reciting a Christian creed that differed so slightly and so momentously from that of their Western brethren. The fragile unity of the Greek and Roman Churches had not yet been heard of in Cythera.

The Greeks spent their days tending sheep or fishing in the sea for molluscs; and from each sedentary, unpleasant little marine animal they extracted the cyst near the head and squeezed the puslike matter into vials and sold it at a fabulous price. For this was the only source of the famous Tyrian dye. Much of it went to Europe, where it was used to color cardinals' capes and dye the exquisite parchment leaves of holy books, lettered in silver and gold. Kings wore purple robes colored with the dye, and great noblemen, if they could afford it, sometimes affected belts and gloves of purple. But here in the East, where manners were stricter and tradition more faithfully observed, the purple was reserved exclusively for the robes and buskins of John, the sixth Palaeologus, Emperor of Constantinople, and John, the fourth Comnenus, Emperor of Trebizond.

A flotilla of flat-bottomed lighters, propelled by long sweeps in the stern worked by swarthy Greeks in an outlandish costume of short, white, pleated skirts, their heads bound round against the sun with colored cloths in a manner singularly reminiscent of Abdul's turban, sculled out to the Lady with fresh water, lemons, red currants, olive oil, goats' cheese and wine. Some of the wine was yellow, and there was dissolved in it the aromatic gum of the mastic, which was a valuable drug that every good Western doctor, from Villanova to Master

Crispin, knew was a sovereign remedy for toothache, gout, and the spitting of blood.

These stores were hoisted aboard in woven slings of hempen rope, and the ship's English steward paid for them. The crew would have liked to go ashore, even in so uninviting a place, but John Justin had his orders and he took the Lady out again, and Tristan Dumont set her nose to the north-northeast and worked her through the D'Oro Channel between Andros and the Caphareus on the Negropont and out into the Aegean among the Cyclades.

And here her lucky wind failed her. She beat back and forth among the barren volcanic islands for days. The captain sent his page with a friendly greeting and invited Pierre to dinner in the great cabin.

Pierre was conscious of the attention. He shaved his face carefully in Abdul's mirror and put on his new, blue hose with a blue velvet jacket and fur-trimmed shoes, and presented himself at the captain's door, three feet from his own, where the page announced him and let him in.

The windows in the great cabin looked out on a choppy sea. There was a stiff breeze blowing from the north, and the Lady was in one of the numberless Aegean currents, which must have been flowing east, for a pattern of northern waves met a pattern of eastern waves, and where the seas met, they rose in high pyramidal heaps of water that burst into foam on the top. The wind caught the spray and sent it scudding and hissing horizontally off toward the shores of Egypt, six hundred miles away. The Lady was dancing like a new performing bear that the jugglers trained on hot plates of iron. Pierre balanced himself on the sea legs he had acquired and bowed to the captain. The captain returned the bow on the sea legs he could not remember being without, and had him sit in an armchair, an exact duplicate of his own. In a society where there was a nice distinction as to who should have a back and who, arms on his chair, Justin's furniture was very practical, because he never knew whether he would be called upon to entertain a humble pilot or the great logothete of Constantinople.

The page brought them an honest supper of bread and salt meat, nuts, pickles, and a bowl of fruit that had been put on at Cythera, and a bottle of good French wine, with no mystical herbs in it, for neither John Justin nor Pierre was afflicted with the gout, a toothache or the spitting of blood. When supper was on the table and the bottle of wine securely ensconced in the little bracket that had been built to keep such things from falling to the deck, both men rose and the captain said a long Latin grace. He spoke very sincerely, not hurrying a word; Pierre could tell that he meant every word of thanks for the simple supper. Pierre happened to know the response. He said it, in as good Latin as the captain's, and Justin remarked: "They taught you good manners as well as good Latin, Master Pierre. The minister told me you were something of a linguist. Do you happen to know Greek, too?"

"I do not, Sir John. It is a pity. I could use it soon with the pilots. We have made very good time, have we not?"

"Good so far, Pierre, but this," and he pointed with his knife to the choppy sea outside the windows, "this is not good at all. We ought to be in Chios by this time, or very near. Now there is no telling when we'll get there. Do not worry about the pilots. They all speak something they think is French, and if we pick up a stupid one in Chios, we've an interpreter aboard. But I must say, it's a mystery to me how the minister expects you to get the fees reduced. They are established by law, you know. George Phranza, the imperial chancellor, fixes them in Constantinople. In Trebizond they are fixed by the Grand Duke Alexius." The captain chuckled. "He's an enormous fat eunuch, Pierre, and one of the shrewdest men I ever saw."

"Eunuchs are said to have clear minds, Sir John. Perhaps they are able to concentrate better than most of the rest of us. If I should have any luck at all in Constantinople, I have been left free to go on to Trebizond."

"I know you have, Pierre. I don't think the minister ever gave me such comprehensive orders concerning one of his officials. I would read them to you, young man, except that the words would puff you up to bursting. Besides," he admitted, "I threw the orders into the sea. That was also part of my instructions, and I faithfully did it. I am not so stupid, Pierre, that I think the pilot fees are the extent of your mission. Why else are you aboard my ship?"

"The pilot fees are too high, Sir John. And there is the matter of the head tax, also, that goes into the privy purses of the emperors; at least, that is where it is thought to go. There's a gold pound, like a sort of tribute, levied on each of the fifty men on the Lady every time she ties up at Constantinople, and a silver one in Trebizond, as if the men were coming into the empires permanently. In the case of transients, like a ship's crew, the money ought properly to be impounded and returned when the ship sails. As you know, it is never returned."

"Frankly, I did not know. The steward handles those matters.

Well, it is none of my business, young man." He lifted his cup to Pierre. "I wish you good luck with your pilot fees and your head taxes." He took a draught and set down his cup. "I might add, Master Pierre, you speak very plausibly and pump very unsatisfactorily. Perhaps you can actually convince the Greeks of their evil ways. For your own sake, however, not for mine, I hope your business keeps you in Constantinople. It is a far friendlier place than Trebizond and a great deal more civilized."

"Nay, Sir John, I hope just the opposite. De Coucy himself told me that the Trapezuntian women are the most beautiful in Christendom. Is that true?"

"If I were not so young a man, Pierre, I should suspect that now you are the one who is pumping for information. But all Montpellier was talking about your prowess with the ladies and your rides in the moonlight. What they say about the women of Trebizond is true."

Pierre colored up to the roots of his hair at the oblique mention of his ride with Claire. He was very angry and looked it.

"Oh, ho!" Sir John cried very loudly. He was delighted to have found a little chink in the cautious conversational armor of his guest. "Did I touch you there, Pierre? Nay, I struck deeper than I meant to! If I remember my youth at all, and I do, Pierre, that is the face of true love. Do not challenge me on my own ship, young man. It isn't done, and I'm far too old. And I beg your pardon very humbly. Montpellier is a gossipy town. She was a beautiful girl and a noble lady. Whatever you need for your success, Pierre, I wish you." The captain raised his cup again to him. "No wonder you take your mission seriously."

Pierre said: "Thank you, Sir John. My own father could not understand more perfectly. You are very kind, sir. Why does everybody call the *Sainte-Eulalie* the 'Lady'?"

"Oh, that," the captain said. "That's a funny one." He selected a nut and crunched it in his strong teeth. "The *Sainte-Eulalie* was originally the *Saint Lawrence,* and a very sluggish hulk indeed. You remember the lazy saint, Pierre?"

"Wasn't he the poor fellow that they burned on a gridiron, and he said, 'Turn me over and roast the other side'?"

"He was the one. Too lazy to move. Well, the *Saint Lawrence* took fire off Sardinia one time. I wasn't in command of her then. The big old forecastle she carried burned up. She lost one of her masts. She barely got home, and there they rebuilt her with the low forecastle she now has and stepped in a new mast farther forward.

"The sailors all blamed poor St. Lawrence for the fire, which was very unfair, of course. If the blessed martyr had his eye on the ship at all, he would have kept fire away from her. But the sailors don't like ships to carry male names. I was given command of her after she was rebuilt, and we looked around for a new name. Do you remember how St. Eulalie met her death, Pierre?"

Pierre's hagiology was better than most men's but the details of St. Eulalie's martyrdom escaped him.

"I was taught, of course, by a canon of Rouen. He later developed leprosy, poor man. I wonder if he is still alive. All I can remember is that the pagans cut her head off."

"They tried fire first, Pierre, and the flames refused to burn her. So then the pagans cut off her head. Now it seemed to me that if the men wanted a good name for a ship that had nearly been destroyed by fire, there could not be a better one than the name of a saint that fire refused to touch. I suggested St. Eulalie, and that became her name. Nobody thinks she can burn. I believed they would call her by her name.

"But the ship was soon discovered to have wonderful new sailing powers, whether due to the change of celestial patronage or the elimination of the bulky forecastle, I do not pretend to know. She sailed fast, answered her helm quickly, and the men could move her with the sweeps with almost no effort; and the sailors—never underestimate them, Pierre—immediately called her the 'Easy Lady.' The name, with its double meaning, stuck. Of course, it's shorter and more polite simply to say the 'Lady.' "

The captain selected another nut, chuckling. Pierre was about to tell him how the name of an inn in Rouen had suffered a similar amusing transmogrification.

But just then the ship came right up into the wind, an unheard of and dangerous thing.

Instantly there was the rattle of blocks and the thunder of canvas suddenly taken aback. The great long spar that supported the mainsail began to pound like a gigantic hammer against the mast. The ship lost way with the sudden reversal of force applied to her and yawed and pitched wildly, creaking and shuddering in every timber. The mast cracked and groaned as if it were being wrenched out of the body of the ship. Perhaps it was.

It was not possible to jibe a lateener. To shift from one tack to another, the sails had to be lowered, the spars shifted round the masts, and the sails hoisted again on the other side.

There was a great rushing of men's feet on the deck. The master

199

shouted a frantic mouthful of angry orders. John Justin jumped up from his seat at the table and rushed out onto the deck. The Lady had been running under the mainsail, and that only half hoisted. He shuddered to think what would have happened if the helmsman had steered into the wind with the whole surface of the immense mainsail drawing.

Only John Justin and the helmsman did not instantly run to the mainmast. Every other man aboard the ship, the watches above, the watches below, the steward, the cook, the cabin boys, Master Crispin, the marines, the valet, the page, and Pierre, tumbled over one another in a confused and precipitate mass in their hurry to pull down with their hands the sail that would not come down of its own accord. The wind held it tight to the mast as if it were nailed there.

The ship had some sternway on her now—she was going backward in the sea. Green water poured at every pitch through the great open port in her stern which could never be closed because the tiller ran through it to the rudder post. Clutched by so many frightened hands and impelled by the weight of so many men, the sail slowly came down to the deck. The Lady lost her dangerous sternway. The quick peril was over.

The master sent Jacques of Bourges and another good man aloft to see, in the failing light, whether the mast had split. It was sound enough at the deck line.

The captain disappeared into his cabin. Pierre went back to thank him for his supper. If Justin had been terrified like everybody else, he did not show it.

"Finish your wine, Pierre," he said. "I saw you help with the sail. If the minister ever dispenses with your mathematical services, come ask me for a berth on the Lady."

"Thank you, Sir John."

"If you did not know it, we were in monstrous danger there for a few moments." They felt the ship heel over and grow steady as the sail went up on a new tack. John Justin smiled, but there was no joke in his face. "You should be able to count slowly to about ten, I should say, before there will be a loud knock on my door."

It did not take that long.

"Come in, Dumont!" he called.

The sailing master entered the cabin. His face was flushed and angry. On his heels came the page with the captain's large lantern that he had lighted at the cook's fire and brought aft to hang up in the great cabin as he always did in the evening. Tristan waited, chewing his lip and twisting his feet, until the page, who felt the tension in the air, scampered out. Then he exploded.

"I am furiously ashamed of myself, Sir John! Such a thing never happened to me before. I want your permission to flog the man! I'll do it myself, tonight! We might have lost the ship. It's a wonder we aren't all in purgatory this minute! I implore your forgiveness. May I beat the wretch, sir?"

"Softly, softly, Tristan. Whom do you want to beat? Pierre here? And have the pilot fees go up? The page? Me? Compose yourself, my friend. Take a cup of wine, and tell me slowly and distinctly that you want the helmsman flogged for his blunder, which I shall not permit. Rather, thank God that we are alive. Maybe the wind changed. It looked shifty from here. Who was at the tiller, Master Tristan?"

"Pedro Dineo, sir."

"Pedro usually steers better than that."

"He is in one of his silly moods, Sir John. I warned him several times he was steering too close. He said 'Yes, sir,' and laughed, but he did it again and again, as if he were playing a game."

"A very foolish game," observed Sir John.

"I was thinking of relieving him and then he suddenly put the helm hard over—I know he did; I felt it in my feet—and then you know what happened. The wind was perfectly steady at that moment."

The captain thought for a few seconds and then he said: "Pedro is mourning his poor brother, I'm afraid, in his own peculiar way. Did you know that he has scarcely eaten a bite of food since we left Montpellier?"

"Nay, Sir John, I did not."

"Perhaps he has taken a fasting vow. Sometimes I think he blames me for not stopping the ship for Antony. As if I could have! Ah, well." He reached over and pulled a cord that set a bell to ringing down in the hold where the page slept. "I'm sorry for Pedro, but he obviously isn't dependable any more. Who is at the tiller, now?"

"Jacques of Bourges, sir."

Almost immediately the door opened. The page stuck in his head and said, "Yes, Sir John?"

The captain eyed him coldly.

"Did you fly through the air, Henri, like an angel, without traversing the intervening space? That was a marvelous quick trip!"

"I heard the bell, Sir John. I was on deck. I thought you rang smartly, and I hurried, sir."

"That you were on deck, I believe. Next time walk a little distance away from the door you are listening at, and then make a noise with your feet coming back. It sounds more convincing. If you plan to spend your life peeking through keyholes and listening at doors, learn to do it well. Pins sometimes stick suddenly through them, however. Watch lest you lose an eye or get your ear punctured."

"Yes, Sir John," said the page in hopeless confusion.

"Go to Pedro Dineo, boy. Tell him that the captain orders him relieved of his helmsman's duties and reduced to ordinary seaman's rank and pay for the rest of the voyage. He shall receive no other punishment. And if you make fun of him, I'll have you caned. D'ye hear?"

"No, Sir John. I mean I do hear, Sir John!" The youth stumbled over his feet in his hurry to get away. They heard him running down the deck.

"That's a good lad," said the captain, "but he's developed snoopy habits lately. Maybe I don't keep him busy enough."

Dumont said in a very tired voice: "Sir John, I am shamefully aware that you have not said a single reproachful word to me for my part in the accident. The responsibility was mine, of course. I shall be more careful in the future. It is things like this that make your men love you, sir."

"Go get some sleep, you old goat."

Dumont was ten years younger than the captain, but he had a short grizzly beard that he clipped himself with scissors because he was afraid of Master Crispin's razor.

"And inform my landsman's ears," Sir John added, "whether I heard the mainsail hoisted just now, will you?"

Dumont did not have to look. He could feel the steadier deck, the sharper list underfoot. The ship pitched less rapidly, climbing the swells that had lost their choppy surface and grown big and wide and smooth. The Lady stuck her nose almost noiselessly into the huge black masses of moving water and rode lightly up them, as if she were taking a deep breath. Then the seas rushed aft—it was always the water that seemed to move, never the ship; the illusion was puzzling and beautiful—leaving a great turbulent wake behind the stern, and then the ship rushed down the other side, throwing a curtain of white spray away from her bow like two big, white, momentary wings, full of sparkling points of phosphorescent light. Sometimes in daytime the sun made rainbows under the bow when the ship sailed like this. Sometimes at night the moon conjured back their ghosts. A lunar rainbow is a chaste and wonderful thing.

"The sail is up, Sir John. I think the wind is blowing from the northwest now. And unless the moon yonder," he nodded toward the window, "has taken to rising out of Europe, we are headed straight for Chios."

# CHAPTER

## ✤ 19 ✤

PIERRE in his narrow bunk in his cabin could not sleep. He had shut the door to keep out the brilliant moonlight. But the cabin grew stuffy and he opened the door again. The wind had lessened, and all the Lady's sails were up. In daytime they were the warm yellow of unbleached linen canvas. But at night, taut and swaying rhythmically against the black sky full of bright stars in the light of a full moon, they shone like cloth of silver. The illusory immobility of the ship caused the stars, not the sails, to appear to swing back and forth when the ship moved. The fresh air smelled good.

Pierre was wide awake. His mind was full of the snoopy page, the shrewd captain, the helmsman's blunder, his mission, and the memory of Claire, back in Europe, four broad seas away. He wondered who, among the minister's servants he had met so far, might be implicated in the smuggling. He wondered how he was going to accomplish the reduction of the Constantinople pilot fees, which he had firmly decided to do if he could. He wondered if Claire would really have waited behind the curtains. He imagined himself a rich nobleman, full of blue blood, asking for her. If the blood were blue enough, or if he were rich enough (and it was as easy to imagine the one as the other), he would not, of course, have to plead. More likely they would be haggling over the terms of her dowry. La Salle had taught him how that was done, too. *"Peste!* I cannot think of it!" He stepped out of his cabin and climbed the short ladder up to the poop deck atop the sterncastle. The wind was warm and fresh on his naked chest and full of the piny smell of the black Cyclades scattered around the horizon. One of them was quite close, and the bare stone cliffs shone in the moonlight.

The watch officer was a young German named Brandt, who had tired of the cold, stormy Baltic and the venerable Hanseatic service, where promotion was slow, and come south to France for a year or a lifetime, if men could rise as fast as the rumors said they could. He was a chunky pompous man. He wore his hat as if it were Sunday in Hamburg instead of midnight in the Aegean, and he paced back and forth across the deck as if there were an engine in his legs, stopping each time to bend over and look at the compass card shining in the light of the binnacle. Since the moon was so bright, Brandt had turned the lamp low to save oil. He was astonished to see Pierre suddenly appear on the deck in his bare feet, wearing nothing but a pair of drawers.

Pierre waved him a greeting. Brandt stolidly completed one of his interminable excursions to the rail. Perhaps he was counting them. He returned, looked at the card, acknowledged Pierre's existence by bowing silently and formally to him, and took up his walk again. Pierre sat down on the deck. It was gritty with the salt that had dried out of the spray thrown up during the stormy afternoon.

There was another man standing still and black against the sky at the opposite rail. The moon was in Pierre's eyes, but he assumed it was the captain, since only he and the watch officer had any right to be on the poop deck. Sailors went there when their duty required them to clean it, using heavy stones, sand, and salt water, or to attend the line that held down the corner of the aftersail, when a change in the wind or the ship's course made it necessary to lengthen or shorten it. Pierre, of course, had the run of the ship. But he was content to be alone with his own troubled thoughts on so fine a night, remembering the last time the moon was full.

For a minute or two he stared full in the face of the silver, hypnotic planet; the light hurt his eyes and blacked everything else out of the universe. He had to look away, and when he did, the details of the ship slowly emerged again out of the blackness, hazy and vibrating with cold colors, moving uncertainly, as the mechanism of his eyes accommodated itself to the change: the line of the rail, the captain's motionless figure, and, finally, the black tarpaulin that covered a coil of rope in the dark shadow of the rail near where the captain stood.

But when everything else was optically stable again, the tarpaulin continued to move, or appeared to, ever so slightly. Pierre shook his head and blinked the moonlight out of his eyes, and the tarpaulin stopped. He put it down to a trick of his eyes and glanced back to

Brandt, who, at that moment, was bending very low over the compass. The dim binnacle lamp cast up a dull yellow cone of light and illuminated his face, which wore a look of tense and serious concentration. Pierre knew from the stars, which always show quicker than the compass card when a ship veers off her course, that the Lady was being steered with unerring precision. What the German was worried about he could not imagine and did not bother to wonder.

Actually Brandt was suffering acutely from a fullness of the bladder, which he could not politely relieve from the captain's deck in the captain's presence. Nor, after the accident of the afternoon, did he wish to desert his post even for an instant. He struggled with his conscience and the pressure within him, which became more imperious with every passing minute. Something had to give.

He stopped studying the card, which had not moved a hair's breadth, and incontinently rushed down the ladder, as quietly as he was able, so as not to inform the captain; and in a moment there drifted up from the lee rail in the waist of the ship below such a deep and happy sigh of unalloyed relief that Pierre, who now realized what had troubled the conscientious officer, could hardly keep from laughing.

Then the tarpaulin undoubtedly moved, and a black shadow began to emerge out of its substance like a head cautiously coming out of the body of a tortoise. Pierre stared fascinated for an instant. Then the shadows separated, the figure of a man suddenly stood erect and darted for the captain, silently, on his bare feet. His arm came up to a striking position, high and crooked over his head, outlined against the sky while he ran. Steel flashed in his hand.

"Look out!" Pierre yelled.

Justin swung round at the cry, astonished and instantly alert. He saw the man running at him and ducked, but the knife came down and he grunted in pain, while Pierre leaped to his feet and ran toward him across the deck. The captain crooked one arm around the rail. He could not move the other. The assassin leaned down and passed his arms around the wounded captain's legs as if he meant to heave him over the side. Justin raised his knee frantically to kick the man off. The man sank his teeth into Justin's thigh, growling and snorting like a beast, and lifted him bodily off the deck with a terrific heave.

Then Pierre fell upon him with his whole weight and threw him and the captain both away from the rail. For a moment he, the assailant, and John Justin were inextricably tangled on the deck.

Pierre got his arm around the man's shoulders and tried to pull him off, and with the other hand he caught the wild, strong arm that continued to brandish the knife. He braced his knees against the captain's body and wrenched with all his might, but the fellow stuck like a wildcat, screaming and swearing foully in Italian. Pierre had temporarily immobilized the knife, though the man still clutched it.

Pierre pinned his wrist and the murderous weapon against the deck with his knee. That freed his right arm, which he hooked round the man's neck, and he grabbed with his left at the man's leg and tried again to pull him away from the captain. But the man locked his legs around Justin with frantic strength, and the captain began to gasp for breath. Pierre did not dare to push the wounded captain again with his knees in another effort to pull the man away. Moreover he was suddenly busy with the knife again, for the man wrenched it free of his knee and jabbed quickly back at Pierre.

His blow struck Pierre in the hip. Pierre had by no means attempted to be gentle, but the sudden bite of the steel in his flesh infuriated him, and he caught the man's arm and wrenched it back till the shoulder bone tore out of its socket, and the bloody knife fell to the bloody deck. Unaccountably the man, who must have been in terrible pain, began to laugh wildly. Justin panted, "His legs are bursting my belly!" Pierre moved slightly away from the man, heedless that his hand was free and had begun to claw and tear at Pierre's naked chest. He closed one of his big hands over the man's face, and with all his weight and strength threw him down against the deck. His head hit the deck with a terrifying crack; the man lay still, and Pierre saw that it was Pedro Dineo. There was bloody foam about his mouth; his eyes were open, and he looked quite dead.

Brandt, at the rail, heard the noise and rushed back up the ladder, his meticulous garb in astonishing disarray. He saw the blood and the men on the deck in the moonlight, and shouted loudly for the watch, Master Crispin, and St. Hildegard of Böckelheim, who, in her blessed lifetime, wrote medical treatises; and then he lent a hand himself, which was sorely needed.

He and Pierre carried the captain down the steep ladder. Justin was conscious and in great pain. The blood from his wound had run down under his jacket and soaked it through from the shoulder to the navel. Crispin appeared with his brazier, blowing with his mouth against the coals to kindle them to a higher heat. The watch had tumbled aft, and was standing with frightened faces around the door of the great cabin.

"Send the men away!" Justin ordered. The pain of the cut in his shoulder made him bite his lip. He knew what was in store for him, and he was too proud a man to tolerate curious, sympathetic eyes that might see him wince away from the cautery.

They laid him on his bunk and the page turned up the lamp. Brandt and Pierre supported him while the chirurgeon took off his jacket, roughly and quickly, with a certain kind of brutal efficiency. There were strands of the fabric of his slashed tunic within the cut. It hurt to have them yanked out.

"Oh, you bloody demon!" he growled in florid Italian. "Be careful of me, can't you?"

"Steady, *padrone!* Steady, *capitano mio!* It will be over in a minute or two. The chirurgeon works fast." Pierre had lapsed into the armorer's Italian without thinking.

"It is absolutely necessary, Sir John," Crispin said. He was dismayed at the length of the cut, and he noted the bitten thigh, bleeding profusely.

"You go away, too, Pierre," ordered the captain.

Pierre did, holding his hand over his punctured hip. But Crispin saw the blood running down his leg.

"I'll attend to you in a moment, Master Pierre," he called.

The page closed the door of the great cabin and stood in front of it, his arms folded. There was not a sound from within. The men gathered below on the hatch in little groups and talked in subdued voices among themselves.

Pierre limped to his cabin and tried to examine his own wound, but it was out of his line of vision. He took a handkerchief and held it against the cut, thinking the bleeding perhaps would stop, but it did not. Someone had thought to light his own cabin lamp, which he seldom used, and he turned it up and looked at the handkerchief, which had become a soggy crimson lump in his hand.

Just then there was a quick step on the ladder, and Brandt appeared at the door.

"Worthy-Master-Official-Pierre," he pronounced in an excited transliteration of something respectful in German, "I am not deserting my post. The sailing master himself has taken over."

"That is excellent, Brandt. How is the captain?"

"We do not know yet, sir. The chirurgeon is still attending him. I came down to report to you that Pedro Dineo is gone."

"I know," Pierre said. "I had to do it, or he'd have killed the captain. God rest his wicked soul."

"I do not mean that, sir. I mean he is gone. He is not on the ship. He is over the side."

208

"That was a savage thing to do, Brandt. Did Dumont order the body thrown overboard without a prayer? I personally do not blame him, but the captain may, if he recovers."

"Nay, you did not kill the man, sir. He destroyed himself. There is a path of blood to the scuppers and the print of his hand as plain as day on the rail. You can see where he dragged himself up and precipitated himself into the sea. Is your own wound serious? We all heard Master Crispin say he would attend you as soon as he had finished with the captain. I can see no cut, sir."

"A man is possessed who destroys himself," said Pierre. "As for my own cut, Worthy-Second-Sailing-Officer-Brandt, I cannot see it either. Would you be kind enough to examine it?" He removed the handkerchief and turned around, and the careful German answered:

"The cut is two fingers long with no width whatsoever; it is a stab, how deep I do not know. It bleeds from the lower extremity of itself in intermittent spurts. That is not good."

"Nay, I know it is not. Stuff the handkerchief into it, will you?"

"It will hurt, sir."

"No doubt. I do not pretend to be anxious to have you do it. But it will stop the bleeding."

"Very well, sir." He began to pack the end of the linen into the wound. "I am sure the chirurgeon," he said as Pierre clenched his teeth and held his breath, "could do this better than I, but it is wise to stop the bleeding."

In a little while Master Crispin came from the great cabin, where he reported the captain sleeping peacefully under the influence of a drug. He closed Pierre's wound and stopped the arterial haemorrhage in the only way that he or any other chirurgeon knew how to do, and gave him a little liquid at the bottom of a cup to drink.

Crispin's medical theories were elaborate. Analogy played an important part in the compounding of his medicines. The captain's wound was shallow and long: therefore the chirurgeon prepared a great draught of watered wine with a minute quantity of opium in it. He reasoned that much substance and a little of the active principle was required to deaden the pain of such a slash. But Pierre's wound was narrow and deep: therefore Crispin had him drink a small, intensely concentrated dose of the drug, which, by the same logic, was required to penetrate and neutralize the pain of the stab. So the captain was cruelly underdosed and Pierre was massively overdosed, but since neither's wounds were to kill them, Crispin's skill came to be much admired.

Justin woke next day with a terrible thirst and asked for Pierre.

He was told that Pierre was asleep. Nothing could have been truer. Pierre slept three days.

They propped the captain up on soft crumpled lengths of woolen goods cut from the bolts in the cargo, for there was nothing so luxurious as a cushion aboard the Lady. Master Crispin raised no objection when Justin suggested that his bandages be doused with sea water, which served to soften the seared flesh and added greatly to his comfort.

Justin was far from well when Pierre came out of his stupor, but he was sufficiently recovered to know that he would not die, and he expected no serious complication in the ordinary course of events that attended the healing of a well cared for wound: swelling, pus, opening, drainage, closing, and, in a month or six weeks, one could forget about it.

He set a watch over Pierre night and day with instructions to report to him the minute the young man opened his eyes, which Pierre did, very languidly, after what seemed to his drugged senses an eternity in a cloudy land where time did not exist, where all was quiet, and the face of Claire very close.

It was distressing to wake up on a ship, to an intimate pain, and watch the etherial countenance fade away and be replaced by the honest, stubbly, sympathetic face of Jacques of Bourges.

"Are ye awake, Master Pierre?" The voice sounded like the roar of an earthquake to Pierre. Actually Jacques was speaking softly, as one instinctively does to a sick person. "Then I must leave you for a moment and tell the captain."

Pierre muttered, "Pray do!" and he drifted off again into unconsciousness. But the cloudy land was gone, and the dream would not receive him. Instantly, he thought, Jacques was back again, with the captain, and then came Master Crispin, beaming like the sun. The chirurgeon was secretly congratulating himself that Pierre had not succumbed. Then came the cook, with a bowl of soup, and Jacques of Bourges fed Pierre with a wooden spoon; then he went off again into a deep, dreamless, healthy sleep.

Crispin examined the wound next day and expressed concern that there was no swelling nor any of the usual signs of the development of healing pus.

"I cannot understand it," he said, shaking his head. "I have rarely witnessed such a thing before. Now you ought to see the captain! Flowing like a scupper, upon my word; perfectly normal and proper. Perhaps I did not burn deep enough."

"I thought you did very nicely, Master Crispin. But I do not understand it either." Pierre was also concerned, for everybody knew how wounds ought to heal.

"Well, sir, there's nothing to be done now. Another application of the cautery sometimes helps these stubborn cases, but there is no telling how one of Villanova's patients will react. You are still, perhaps, under the influence of his slow medication. I notice that your old leg sores have finally disappeared."

"Yes, quite, Master Crispin."

"I am inclined to delay further treatment of your wound. Perhaps it will heal without the usual healthy signs."

"I confess that I hope it does, good doctor. Nobody likes your cauteries."

"Saints, man! What else is there to do?"

No one in Christendom could have answered him.

The captain's perfectly normal and proper recovery brought him a high fever, which his sturdy constitution took several days to throw off. The ship drew close to Chios. Pierre returned the visit which he could not remember the captain's paying him.

The page put a chair close to the bunk. Justin, pale, weak, and convalescent on his improvised pillows, invited Pierre to sit down.

"I have already publicly expressed my gratitude to you, Pierre. Let me thank you again, now that you can hear. All the sailors know that I praised you to your face, but you were unconscious. Jacques of Bourges says you ate very heartily of the cook's soup, however. This Jacques has conceived a great fondness for you. It is good when men like you, Pierre. I again ask your pardon for what I said about you and the ladies. He refused to let anyone else attend you, though I had ordered a change of watch. Sit down, my friend. Must I crane my neck up at your great height and run the risk of opening my wound?"

"I trust your wound is better, Sir John. My own small one," he said grinning, "prevents my accepting your generous offer to sit."

"Nay, does it, Pierre? Stand then, if you must. The chirurgeon said you had got deeply stuck. I am glad to see you able to smile at it. My wound improves every day, thank God, though I was afraid at first the arm was paralyzed. It is not. Maybe old Sizzle-Irons is a better chirurgeon than I thought. What blessed angel prompted you to come up on my deck, young man, and save my life?"

Pierre could have named the angel, but he said, "The moon kept me awake, Sir John."

"Now that moon is a puzzling thing, Pierre. Of all the ridiculous times to try to kill a man. Dineo was an Italian. He ought to have known better. The man must have been possessed. He fought like a devil, didn't he?"

"He did indeed, Sir John. And then he threw himself into the sea. I wonder why he did that."

"Maybe he still had sense enough in his head—what a crack you gave him, Pierre!—maybe when he regained consciousness he realized he'd be hanged next day. Or maybe the Devil threw him in; I'm sure I don't know."

"Could he have been brooding over your mild punishment for his awkward seamanship, Sir John, as well as the loss of his brother?"

"The punishment was light for the very reason that I knew he was brooding. But you have probably hit upon exactly the reason why he wanted to kill me. He could have easily hidden on the poop during the excitement of the afternoon. Did you happen to observe where he secreted himself?"

"Under the tarpaulin over the ropes right close to where you were standing."

"He couldn't have chosen a better spot. I often stand there."

"Then perhaps he heard Brandt go below for a moment. Brandt and I had not spoken. I was barefooted; he could not have heard me. He must have believed you were alone on the deck, Sir John."

"Undoubtedly. Watch officers seldom leave the poop. Brandt will be reminded of his duty when he collects his pay. What a sailor! No wife, no children, and still he loves money! I think he spends it all on himself and those lovely velvet hats. Nay, though, perhaps I shall deal softly with him." He laughed. "Brandt took half an hour by the glass apologizing and explaining the circumstances. I was so affected that I had to have Henri bring me the pot. I was confined to my cabin at the time with a fever. Master Crispin says that a fever is the best possible symptom."

"I have not suffered from one yet, Sir John."

"Well, I hope you do not. I've seen many wounds heal without fevers or healing pus either. The bright moonlight still puzzles me, Pierre."

"Dineo was frothing at the mouth when I quieted him."

"Nay, was he? Then he was surely possessed. Who knows how men think when the Devil drives them mad?"

"Was the moon full, Sir John, when his brother was lost?"

"I do not remember." He puzzled a moment. "Pierre, that is a remarkable thought. I shall have it looked up in the log."

Next morning, at dawn, the lookout in the roundtop sighted Cape Mastica. Pierre's hip had given him a restless night. He heard the welcome shout and got up early and had a big breakfast. Shortly afterward he met the captain on the deck. Except for the sling around his arm and a certain whiteness in his face, Justin looked almost well again. The tube of manifests, which he had unstrapped for a few days and kept in his bunk with him, Pierre now saw fastened again around his wrist, almost concealed in the sling. He greeted Pierre affectionately.

"I have developed a great deal of admiration for that head of yours, young man. Are you sure there is no Italian blood in you? Nay, you're the wrong color. The moon was full, Pierre, on the stormy night that we lost poor Antony off Sardinia. Naturally that, coupled with my punishment, is what crazed Pedro. How did you happen to think of it?"

"The moon reminded me of a beloved lady, Sir John. I suspected it might have reminded Pedro of his brother, if he loved him."

"He did, poor creature. Yonder is Chios, my friend. You should get your first pilot today, about noon, I should think. Can I be of any help to you in the accomplishment of your mission? Don't ask me what the Greeks love—they love money, women, and wine, in that order, and they are surrounded by plenty of everything but money from the day of their birth. When you haggle with the pilot, you will touch on the first love of his life. I think you ought to know."

"I shall certainly not haggle with the pilot."

"You shall certainly have to if you expect to succeed. Listen." He took Pierre over to the rail and looked carefully around him as if he were a conspirator on his own ship. "I have a little plan that may help you. The minister has sent you on a hopeless mission. The fees are established by law. But it so happens, I am ashamed to tell you, that the ship's accounts are not, well, not quite exactly in order."

"Sir John, you astonish me."

The blood rushed to the captain's face and gave him a healthier appearance than he had displayed since Dineo attacked him.

"The pilot fees are generous, as you know. But the Greeks are insatiable. I have sometimes—quite often, in fact—connived at the steward's payment of double the usual fees. You must realize that that amounts to £20 for the Bosporus instead of £10. It ought to be less in Trebizond, because the sailing is simpler there. But the Trapezuntians—" He made an Italian gesture of hopelessness that Pierre had seen all his life. "I may as well tell you that it is £20 there, too. Naturally the pilots fight for the privilege of bringing the Lady in. They deliver the legal fee to their superiors, pocket my bribe of £10, and exert all their skill to pilot me well. It is corrupt, perhaps, but I get the best pilots in the East that way."

"Where does the money come from?" Pierre asked. "Do not tell me that it comes out of your own purse."

"I should never be so naïve. Besides, I couldn't afford it. There is another fund for new sails, new lines, anchors, and other gear that we sometimes have to purchase en route. That fund is invariably exhausted at the end of a voyage. Actually, the Lady sails cheaper and smarter than any other ship in the minister's fleet." Sir John looked very shamefaced. "But the records show that her sails blow away and we lose her expensive anchors at a terrific rate. I must have a dreadful name as a captain. Now it has occurred to me that we might suddenly learn to conserve most of our gear. You can inform the pilots, and I shall back you up, that these fancy extra fees are to cease forthwith. It will take some management on my part, for it is hard to stop bribery once it is started, but I shall see that the new practice is adhered to, and the saving will be considerable. The legal fee will have to be paid, of course. But we shall continue to lose our sails. The fund for extra gear will continue to be exhausted when a trip ends. That will give us another substantial saving. And with that money, Pierre—it is only a matter of bookkeeping—we can reduce the fees as they appear in the ship's records to £5! Pierre, we can cut them in half!"

Pierre stared at John Justin in frank admiration.

He ran a red line through the sturdy captain's name in his mental tablet of potential opium smugglers.

"Sir John, you have just informed me, at some danger to yourself, since I might pretend to accept your offer and then simply report you to the minister, of a piece of the noblest chicanery I have ever listened to. By all means continue to bribe the pilots, if that is the way to get the best ones. Your own confessor would not forget such a sin, if it is a sin to keep your men from drowning, quicker than I shall. A man who takes a pound or two from a liberal fund for such a good cause, does not—"

Pierre bit the words off short. The captain's intelligent eyes narrowed.

"Does not what, Pierre?"

"Does not have to worry," Pierre quickly improvised, "that he has confided in me such a generous offer to help me."

"That is all I meant to do. It never occurred to me that you might tell the minister."

"You are trusting for an Italian, Sir John. I was reared by one."

"Were you, Pierre? Nay, I remember now. You spoke a few words of my beautiful language."

"I have another plan, Sir John." Pierre had not meant to divulge it so soon. "Have you a few moments to talk to me alone in your cabin?"

"Certainly I have."

"Then tell me, if you will, everything you know about Michael Cantacuzene, the factor in Constantinople. To me he is only a name on a manifest, in gorgeous hyacinth ink. He is the man I want to talk to about the pilot fees. You recall, of course, that not an ounce of cargo is consigned to him."

"Saints! That is true! For all the profit this voyage will mean to him we could sail right past Constantinople! He is the neediest, greediest Greek in the East. Highly connected. Extravagant tastes. I begin to see what you are up to. Pierre, you make me proud of my countryman who reared you. Come into my cabin and let me talk to you in Italian. I shall teach you to confound the 'Proktor of the Port'—one of his duties, Pierre. You must call him 'Illustrious'—one of his many titles. Ah, but this is a pleasure!"

# CHAPTER

## ✳ 20 ✳

BY A SINGULAR PROVIDENCE, no man, not even a deathly sick man, knows the hour of his death. Neither could the Greek population of Constantinople, capital of the venerable Roman Empire of the East, foresee on August 1, 1444, when a capable pilot brought the Lady through the Turkish straits of Gallipoli and into the narrow waters of the Bosporus, the dreadful fate that nine years hence would be their lot at the hands of the Turk, sitting in his castles in Asia, in plain sight and almost within bowshot.

Everyone thought Constantinople impregnable. A few years before it had proven so, when the Ottoman sultan attempted a short siege of the city. But one night the Virgin herself, in a blue robe, was seen to walk upon the walls, sanctifying them and their hundred and fifty-three towers, which, heightened and strengthened by generation after generation, had protected the city for eleven hundred years.

The sultan, influenced perhaps by his beautiful Christian wife, sent his armies of formidable Janizaries through Thessalonica to fight less well protected Christians in the mountains of Albania, and never again in his lifetime disturbed Constantinople.

To the north of the ancient city was the fierce, half-Christianized nation of the Bulgars. Far to the south, from Cairo to Tangier and west to the cold, unknown Atlantic was a series of Egyptian, Arab, and Moorish sultanates, fighting often among themselves, but united in the fierce and warlike faith of Islam. Across the narrow Bosporus, where a strong man could swim from Europe to Asia, were the terrible Turks themselves.

The Western nations were far away and preoccupied with their own wars. No European prince concerned himself with the shrinking frontiers of the Eastern Empire, which every year contracted closer and closer to the ornate and fabulously wealthy capital.

The Holy Father in Rome and the Patriarch of the East had indeed foreseen the peril to Christendom. A thin and futile union of the two great Christian Churches had been accomplished. But the celibate priests of the West believed that the Greek priests married and bred like rabbits. The orthodox clergy of the East were convinced that the European barbarians said a hypocritical Mass with gloves on their hands and rings on their gloves. Neither the clergy nor the people were willing to forget their prejudices and unite in a common effort against the common enemy of their faith.

Except for Trebizond, far to the East on the Euxine Sea, Constantinople stood alone, in flamboyant decrepitude, without a friend, an island of Christianity slowly drowning in a heathen tide.

The rich old empire, like a rich old man, fondly remembered its youth, when it was poor, strong, and venturesome. This archaic nostalgia was apparent in the imperial court, where elaborate ceremonial and magnificent costumes consciously copied the elegance of ancient Byzantium, and, to some extent, set the style in dress for the better class of citizens.

No one believed that a city that had stood for more than a thousand years would ever actually fall. But in their weakness, the Greeks of Constantinople, like the Greeks of Trebizond, had long had to live by their wits.

Michael Cantacuzene, sitting on a brocaded cushion on a marble bench in the pleasant garden behind his white villa in the heart of the city, listening to his strapping son read to him, did not look like the needy, greedy Greek the captain had so excitedly and inadequately described.

A servant stood in the shadow under the sculptured portico to attend him if he should clap his hands or call for a cooling drink of fruit juice. The factor wore a long, loose tunic of cool cotton fabric, which the Eastern Greeks alone among Christians knew how to spin and weave to a silklike texture; it was exquisitely soft and easier on the skin than either silk or wool, especially in summertime. There were blue, open sandals on his feet, buckled with mother-of-pearl, wholly unlike the long, pointed, leather shoes of the Westerners. Around his lean middle was a cincture of pliable Russia leather, with eyelets for the thongs that might hold a sword. But Greek gentlemen did not march through the streets of their impregnable capital rattling their swords. His thin face was clean-shaven and his hair was cut short.

One of the hundreds of golden domes that dotted the city, to the despair of Western architects, who saw, counted, and could not duplicate them in Europe, reflected a glory of aureate light into an ancient fountain in the garden wall. In such a light the bronze head of the angry, horned satyr, green with the patina of ages, spat a stream of liquid gold into the porphyry basin beneath, full of dancing white aquatic flowers and flashing with golden fishes.

Much of his wealth and some of his titles Cantacuzene owed to a fortunate meeting with Jacques Coeur some years before. He had been heavily in debt when the ambitious young French merchant made his acquaintance and promised to consign to him cargoes of certain ships that he planned to send to the East on his return to France, in daring and direct competition with the Genoese and Venetians, who had monopolized the trade since the crusades. Coeur had kept his promise, and Cantacuzene had disposed of the shipments promptly and profitably. More and more cargoes had followed.

It was no disgrace for a Greek nobleman to engage in trade. In fact, Cantacuzene would have been hard put to it to name anything that was considered a disgrace among his unprejudiced countrymen, from the spurious fabrication of relics of the saints to the lucrative traffic in attractive young Turkish girls, so long as the injunction of blessed Paul to the Corinthians was observed and all things were done decently and in order.

He had cleared himself of debt, and purchased, at an enormous price, the office and title of Proktor of the Port, and through his busy countinghouses passed all the tax money levied by law on the heavy marine traffic of the Bosporus. George Phranza himself, the great logothete, or imperial chancellor, had praised his honesty. Never, he said, in his chancellorship, had the taxes suffered so inconsequential a diminution in the hands of any collector. Cantacuzene had bought his son a string of polo ponies and often proudly watched the boy display his skill in the vigorous, intricate sport that had come all the way from India. The Turks played polo and the Greeks had learned it from them. It was pleasanter to play polo with the Turks than to fight them.

Michael Cantacuzene was at peace with the world and his conscience. He managed his numerous affairs with a vigor that was astonishing, for a Greek, and succeeded so well that some jealous people suspected his shrewdness came from the Devil. But the Proktor of the

Port maintained that his success was due to his ability to guess the other fellow's secrets. It was a knowledge of human nature, he said, an intuitive ability to yield gracefully when occasion demanded, or to strike quickly and secretly, in the dark, if necessary; and, of course, it was easily understood how that could be.

His son would rather have been batting a ball around the hippodrome than puzzling through the involved dialectical argumentation of Zeno of Elea, an excessively cerebral Greek who wrote in the fifth century B.C. He intimated as much, very politely, to his father.

"Alexius," his father replied, "I want you to be subtle as a serpent, as St. Matthew says, for I want you to succeed in the world. You will never get rich, nay, if I am fortunate enough to leave you what little we already possess, you will never be able to conserve and augment it, if you spend your time on the back of a horse, getting all sweaty in the sun and wearing callouses into the flesh of your backside. Learn to use the other end of your spine, my boy.

"Now read me the paradox of Zeno again. Do not slur over the vowels and make them all sound like the omega the way the peasants do. Then tell me in your own words what the paradox says, why it appears to be true, and why, if you can guess, it is not true."

Alexius pronounced the ancient Greek words as well as he could, from a thin, almost transparent scroll, the parchment of which, his father once told him, had been made from the intestines of a sea serpent fifty feet long. It was very old and valuable.

"Little Father," the youth said, "Zeno of Elea states that if a tortoise has the start on Achilles in a footrace, then, though Achilles run with all his might, he can never overtake the cumbersome reptile. For when Achilles has traversed the distance that originally separated the two, the tortoise will also have advanced a certain distance. They continue to run, and when Achilles has traversed this distance, he still has not overtaken the tortoise because, while he was running, the tortoise advanced a certain further distance. It is still ahead of him. Thus Achilles can never win the race, no matter how long they run. That is what Zeno of Elea says."

"Well, Alexius?"

"But this paradox is simply elegant nonsense, Little Father. Anybody can run faster than a tortoise."

"It is elegant, Alexius, but it is not nonsense. It is merely fallacious. It will sharpen your wits to spot the fallacy. Can you do that, my boy?"

The youth mumbled the words to himself again and looked up, thoroughly puzzled.

"Nay, the more I read the silly words, the more plausible they seem."

"You see, Alexius? There is always a deeper truth than appears on the surface of things. Now, the fallacy is simple—"

But the lesson ended suddenly. Alexius went back to his polo before the fallacy was explained. For a servant appeared with the news that John Justin, captain of the *Sainte-Eulalie,* and another Frank official with an unpronounceable name, were awaiting the pleasure of the Illustrious, the Proktor of the Port. "And, Illustrious Cantacuzene, it is whispered on the docks that there is no cargo for you!"

"That is also nonsense," Cantacuzene replied. "But always catch these rumors, Theotocopoulos. Let the men come into the garden."

The factor was well acquainted with Europeans and their abrupt barbarian manners. There would be a jerky bow, and then they would instantly talk business in Latin, with a bad accent. Well, he knew how to do that, too.

"Sir John," he said, as his visitors approached, "I am delighted to see you again. Had I been apprised of your coming, I should have prepared suitable refreshment and entertainment for you."

"There was no time, Illustrious Cantacuzene," said the captain. "I am making a very fast trip at the minister's special behest, to acquaint Master Pierre here, the auditor-general, with the handling of cargo en route and the various shore activities that take place during a voyage."

The factor bowed to Pierre, but could not say his name.

Pierre said: "It is always valuable for a landsman to see a cargo loaded, Illustrious Cantacuzene; to see it impounded, housed, taxed, released, and prepared for sale. These details are probably so familiar to you that you cannot realize how much more meaningful the masses of impersonal white documents become when one has actually witnessed where all the figures originate."

"My friend Coeur," said the factor, "is displaying the thorough, systematic management which has made him famous. I quite understand how much more authoritatively you can audit the books and instruct your subordinates, having actually made a long voyage." And, turning to Sir John: "You appear to have suffered an accident to your arm, captain. I trust it is nothing serious. Nay," he added, "from the speed of your trip and your sudden unannounced appearance, I am inclined to suspect it is a fictitious hurt, so that you can better conceal the tube of manifests, which I spy, however, in your sling. Perhaps you have an unusually valuable cargo for me, Sir John?"

"Nay, Illustrious Cantacuzene, the cargo is all consigned to Baltha Ogli in Trebizond."

Cantacuzene instantly talked about something else.

But the mental picture of the *Sainte-Eulalie*, tied up at the dock, heavy with tons of profitable goods consigned to the Trapezuntian, made him physically ill. He wondered what deep reason was behind such an extraordinary oversight.

"We are sailing tonight," Justin continued, "but Auditor Pierre and I should never have considered passing Constantinople without paying our respects to you. It gives the men a day ashore, too. Naturally they always look forward to the stop at Constantinople."

Cantacuzene turned to Pierre. His French name utterly eluded the precise enunciation of the factor. "Pee-airay" he could say, but he knew that was foolish. Nor would the Greek take the simple way out, and address him as Petros, which was Greek and perfectly understandable. So he called him Peter, which was English, the very spirit of compromise and easy to say.

"Is this your first trip, Auditor Peter?"

"My first long one, Illustrious Cantacuzene. I have never seen so beautiful a city as Constantinople."

"New Rome is indeed lovely. Even the Turks are impressed with its magnificence. Too impressed, I sometimes think. They have some beautiful cities themselves, but to them Constantinople is The City. In fact, they call it Istambul, which is as near as they can come to the Greek words that mean 'The City.' Tell me some of your impressions during the voyage, Auditor Peter. What commercial activities have you particularly observed that will be helpful to you and your staff when you return to France?"

"Why, it has all been immensely valuable, Illustrious Cantacuzene. There has been little handling of cargo as yet, of course, but I have learned a great deal. I have had the opportunity to witness how justifiable are the somewhat costly pilot fees, for example. Back in France, whenever I looked over a sheet that listed the expenses of a ship's voyage, it always seemed incredible to me that it should be necessary to pay a pilot £10 to bring a ship from Chios the little distance to Constantinople. I realize now, of course, having seen the dangerous straits of Gallipoli and the Sea of Marmora, to say nothing of the Bosporus, that a good native pilot is necessary in these waters."

"Indeed, indeed," the factor murmured, thinking very hard. "Perhaps the pilot fees do seem extravagant to the officials in Montpellier. It never occurred to me. All nations pay the same rates, of course. Oh, perhaps the English pay a little more, because they have so few ships. Perhaps the Venetians pay a little less, because they have so many. I know very little about the details, though one of my protospathars collects the fees. Did you know that, Auditor Peter?"

"Nay, I did not, Illustrious Cantacuzene."

"Perhaps Jacques Coeur does not either, though I have had some small authority over the marine moneys for several years now. Nay, surely he must know."

"The minister is usually well informed," Pierre observed.

So the minister was usually well informed! Michael Cantacuzene congratulated himself that he had so quickly found the deeper truth that always lies under the surface of things.

"Coeur did me a great favor years ago when I badly needed it," he said. "Although I sell his cargoes as profitably as anyone could and remit great sums to him, I have always wondered whether it might not be possible for me to express my personal gratitude by some graceful gesture or other. I have never until this moment thought of anything that would be acceptable to his stern and upright sense of propriety. But your inadvertent mention of the pilot fees just now, Auditor Peter, has given me an idea."

Justin thought Pierre was doing nicely. Cantacuzene, though he was at peace with his conscience, was relieved that Coeur's failure to consign a cargo to himself was due to nothing more serious than the pilot fees. He began almost to enjoy the interview. And then Justin was dismayed to hear Pierre, who had already accomplished so much, endanger it all by adding: "I was also impressed with the polite manners of the officer who collected the head tax. I believe it was £51 on the ship's company. I was so unacquainted with your customs here that I foolishly asked him whether there would be time to engross an instrument of credit to rebate them when the ship sailed tonight or whether the specie itself would be returned. He told me that nothing is ever returned. I felt very ashamed of my ignorance."

The Proktor of the Port groaned in his secret heart. Decidedly the young Frank official was a man to deal with.

"But they are always returned, Auditor Peter! Or at least I think they are. Perhaps you misunderstood the man's inadequate Latin. Say no more about it. I shall look into the matter myself. Why, the law requires the head taxes to be returned! I never heard of such a thing! Of course," he continued with a sly smile, "the law also fixes the pilot fees. But here, perhaps, my position as Proktor of the Port will enable me to make the small gesture of gratitude I mentioned just now. The law cannot be changed, of course. But I see no reason at all why the fees should not be collected on a fifty-year basis. The imperial treasury will not lose a penny. The great logothete will never know. I have, shall we say, a set of private records, which shows a very comfortable balance in regard to these very pilot fees. You cannot believe me when I tell you, Sir John, but some ships' captains pay a great deal more than the legal fees in order to obtain certain especially good pilots. Naturally, a good pilot, when he comes to renew his license, pays a little more for it than a poor one. The popular ones make a great deal of money, and wish to remain on the rolls. As I remember, that is the source of the balance. I do not know how big it is, but there is surely enough to cover this little gift to my old friend. I shall immediately write your master that, as far as his ships are concerned, the pilot fees will be collected fifty years from now. He need not give them another thought for half a century. Who knows? Maybe in fifty years, if anybody finds my books, which I doubt, someone in Constantinople will actually try to collect an enormous sum of money!"

"That is extraordinarily thoughtful of you, Illustrious Cantacuzene," said Pierre. "I know the minister will be delighted to hear that you have been appointed Proktor of the Port, if he does not already know."

The factor clapped his hands to summon a servant, and asked for writing materials. "When you get back to France," said Michael Cantacuzene cautiously and almost apologetically to Pierre, "I should count it a favor if you would mention to the minister how highly I value his patronage and what a pleasure it is to serve him here in the East."

That was as close as the subtle Greek came to mentioning the Lady and the cargo that was all consigned to Baltha Ogli.

Constantinople was honeycombed by a vast underground region almost as populous and busy as the surface city. The ancient emperors had dug a mighty system of reservoirs under their capital, so that if an enemy ruptured an arch of the slender, beautiful aqueducts that conveyed the vital water supply from the hills beyond the walls, the people would not perish of thirst during a siege. But through the ages thoughtless rulers had partially filled a great many of the cisterns, big and small alike, with earth, rubble, and stones, the result of excavations for foundations of new buildings. It was easier to fling the debris into the reservoirs than cart it beyond the walls. Often the roofs were supported by venerable marble columns, reared and exquisitely carved with infinite skill and patience by the old builders.

It was inevitable in the overpopulated city that these cool, dark, subterranean areas should be converted into habitations and eagerly sought as dwellings by people too poor to afford a brighter home, or for commercial houses whose wares were just as attractive by lamplight as by daylight, and often much more so.

Untroubled by numerous police officials, who knew all about them, and who, for a price, ignored them, an enormous number of unlicensed, unauthorized, untaxed brothels, some of them very unusual and elegant, maintained a dim, quiet, flourishing existence.

Most of the European clients were illiterate, and it was not possible, of course, to hang out a sign sufficiently graphic to portray the character of such an establishment. But an enterprising body of well dressed, sophisticated representatives, speaking every known tongue, made it their business to accost every lonesome stranger, from the wharves of the Golden Horn to the Church of the Holy Wisdom, and acquaint him with the fact that Constantinople was a friendly place and someone would be uncommonly glad to see him. There were so many houses that the trade was specialized by colors, by nationalities, or by different rates for different services, and they all had names, so that a lusty client who wished suddenly to return might ask the way back even if he were too drunk to remember the location.

The *Saint-Eulalie* had been more than forty days at sea. The men had collected their pay. Home was far away; Trebizond was two weeks to the east. When the captain told Cantacuzene that the Lady would sail that night, he thought he was telling the truth; but a ship cannot sail without her crew, and John Justin had no magic to conjure back through the air Jacques of Bourges from the Fille Parisienne, Second Officer Brandt from the Valkyrie, or even the respectable English steward from a beery little dive that a fallen countrywoman of his had named The Great Boar to honor the hunting prowess of the men of her native island. Nor were these the only ones. When Pierre and the captain went back aboard the ship, they found her virtually deserted. Master Crispin himself, who of all men should have known better, was among the missing.

Sir John surveyed the lifeless decks and said: "It appears that I demanded too much of the men, Pierre. Or should I call you Peter now? We'll be lucky if we get out of here by noon tomorrow, from the looks of things. I cannot punish them all, of course, and indeed I am in a mood to overlook the whole mutinous desertion. It has been a fast, hard trip, and I am elated at your success with the factor."

"Nay, it was you who accomplished it, Sir John. Your lucid description of the man's oversubtle character. I'd never have known how to talk to him without it."

"It was a pleasure to hear him talk himself out of the pilot fees. Not a sou for the next fifty years! What a country! I nearly sank through the deck, however, when you brought up the head taxes. To have those remitted goes even beyond your instructions, does it not?"

"Actually it does, Sir John. But I don't think Cantacuzene will miss them. His bookkeeping seems to cover everything. Even the poor pilots have to split their bribes with him one way or another. That astonished me."

"Me too. He looked squarely at me, as if I had never heard of the practice. Never fluttered an eyelid."

Pierre had noticed that the brilliant blue ink in which Cantacuzene wrote his familiar signature, when fresh, was actually fragrant like a flower. The factor had rolled the letter and put it into a beautifully carved ivory tube and given it to him unsealed, never doubting for an instant that Auditor Peter would appropriate the costly container. Pierre sealed it with some of the captain's wax and hid it at the bottom of one of his sea chests in the point of a shoe he had worn when he rode with Claire.

225

# CHAPTER

## ✤ 21 ✤

THE GREATNESS of the Empire of Trebizond dated from the shameful Fourth Crusade. Two and a half centuries before, a group of cynical, debt-ridden European princes and their hungry horde of knights and soldiers had arrived, quarreling and exhausted, under the walls of Constantinople on their way to the Holy Land to rescue the Sepulcher of Christ. The success of the expedition would win them, they believed, peace in the world to come, and, if they could capture and hold to ransom a large enough number of infidels, a comfortable fortune in this world also.

Constantinople hospitably opened her gates and refreshed the weary travelers for a whole year. But the sight of the soft manners of their Eastern brethren in the rich Christian city, the uninviting deserts of the still remote Holy Land, and the obstinate bravery of the Turk wrought a wonderful change in the plans of the crusaders. With a cynicism that dismayed the Holy Father and delighted the Turk, the Westerners forgot the barren tomb of the Lord. They fell upon Constantinople with their swords, which had been blessed in a different cause. They slaughtered the men and ravished the women. They deposed the emperor and sacked the imperial palace and despoiled the churches where the Greeks recited a creed that differed by a word or two from their own. They loaded the Venetian galleys, the rent on which they could now afford to pay, with a vaster quantity of gold and silver loot than ever had or ever would come out of the Holy Land, and despatched them back to Europe with the news that Christendom was now united and the emancipation of the Holy Sepulcher would have to await a more propitious moment. Their conquest was not to last long, and the Greeks soon drove the Europeans out of their capital, but for some years Constantinople was ruled by Western emperors.

Not all the Greeks submitted. One hardy adventurer, with ancient imperial blood in his veins, Alexius Comnenus, fled with a small stubborn army round the elbow of the Black Sea and discovered on its southern shores the city of Trebizond, in the center of a district which, if God had turned castle builder, could not have been designed more like a fortress. The Greek-speaking populace, remnants of a forgotten colony planted by the ancient Hellenes, welcomed the fugitive, and, since he had ten thousand men with him, willingly accepted him as their ruler. Subsequent generations of the Comnenus family pushed the frontiers east and west along the Euxine and back to the mountains, and assumed the ever more sonorous titles of King, Despot, and, finally, Emperor of the Faithful Romans, Autocrat of all the East, the Iberians, and the Transmarine Provinces.

Trebizond, when Pierre first saw it from the deck of the *Sainte-Eulalie*, rounding the cape of Sinope, was an empire of no mean dimensions. It stretched nine days by caravan along the inhospitable southern shores of the tideless sea and two days across a mighty tableland that rose higher and higher till it terminated in the long chain of the snowy Caucasus to the south. That was more land than the kingdom of Navarre or the duchy of Milan or the powerful Venetian Republic, and almost as much as the shrunken domain of the Eastern Empire itself. The rugged, dangerous mountains were virtually impenetrable to man and so high that not a trickle of water ran through them from the interior of Asia Minor, though Trebizond was watered by many small rapid streams, rising in the mountain barrier and rushing north to the Euxine through luxuriant plains, green hills covered with fertile productive vineyards, vast pasture lands full of fat sheep and majestic primeval forests full of wild game.

But John Comnenus, the nineteenth emperor of his proud, capable dynasty, did not have to depend on the taxes from his own people to support his luxurious court. Trebizond was the marine terminus of the busy, rich caravan route across the Armenian plateau from Persia and the depths of Central Asia.

A huge valley beyond the capital city split into two precipitous gorges that ran parallel at no great distance from each other to the sea. This triangle of unapproachable ground, surrounded by a deep, natural, rocky moat, had been further strengthened by thick, high, crenelated walls. Two massive stone bridges spanned the ravines on either side of the city. Double portcullises could be dropped where they pierced the walls; strong towers rose over them, and on the farther banks of the ravines were additional fortifications and gates. South of the city an enormous keep guarded the high apex of the triangle. To the north a strong wall had been raised along the sea faced with flanking towers and two castles belonging nominally to the Venetians and the Genoese, but garrisoned mainly by Greeks. Behind this was a second wall, actually a string of castles belonging to the emperor and some of the higher Trapezuntian nobility. Between the two walls was a noisy, crowded commercial district full of Eastern merchants, Western sailors, customs officials, street vendors selling the sweets of Europe and Asia, great trading establishments, bulging warehouses, busy taverns, inns, and a variety of places of refreshment and entertainment.

In the heart of the city within the inner walls was the imperial palace, residence of the Emperor John and David, his son, who shared with him the style of Great Comnenus, proudest of all the titles of the imperial family, and the right to wear a purple robe and the red, imperial shoes.

It was not entirely family affection that originated the custom of crowning the son as well as the father. For two and a half centuries Trebizond had maintained its independence against Genoa, Constantinople, the Arabs, the Persians, and the Turks by a series of desperately fought wars, cheerfully paid tributes, and wily treaties. Offensive and defensive alliances were continually negotiated in the throne room and magnificent antechambers of the palace with infidel and Christian nations alike, often sealed by the marriage of one of the Trapezuntian noblewomen, whose disturbing beauty was a warm and wonderful asset to the foreign policy of the state. The emperor's own aunt was the wife of Djihan Shah, chief of a nation of powerful neighboring Turkomans.

There had been nineteen emperors in two hundred and forty years. Some of them lived to a venerable old age, but most of them died young, naturally in battle or unnaturally in bed. Eastern poisons were subtle, legion, and deadly. Parricide was a constant temptation in a family where it was unthinkable that any one but a Comnenus should rule. To guard against death at the hands of their own sons, the emperors of Trebizond had them crowned and, as the ceremonial termed it, adored, as soon as their young heads could bear the weight of the gold and the strings of pearls in the heavy imperial crown.

John loved his son, the heir to his throne, like many a Comnenus father and emperor before him. But there were whispers—for even in Trebizond public opinion could be scandalized—that John himself was not quite entirely free of the suspicion of parricide. David was a venturesome young man, full of the courage of his race, given to harmless scalawag escapades in the unsavory waterfront district between the walls. The emperor was glad David was already a Great Comnenus, like himself, and showered honors upon him. If the emperor's conscience had been a shade whiter, he would have remembered that the sins of a father usually skip a generation before they duplicate themselves in his grandsons. John was safer from murder by the trivial David than by some of his powerful conspiring nobles.

The Church of the Golden-Haired Virgin was only a hundred paces from the gate of the palace. When, on great occasions, the emperor went there to pray, a seamless red carpet was unrolled upon the street and strewn with flowers. A young knight named Horchi carried his silver bow before him. A closed line of guards with drawn swords stood with their faces toward the people, their backs to the emperor. A white Arabian steed bore his sacred, glittering person to the steps of the church. The crowd cheered and prostrated themselves to the ground when he passed, and if the cheering faltered, a band of music struck up a hymn of praise to him, for nothing was left to chance. Following the emperor on foot came the greatest nobles and officers of the empire: Nicetas, the great logothete, or imperial chancellor; Alexius, the grand duke and great domestic of the palace, who was a eunuch and immensely powerful; Leon Maizomates, commander in chief of the armies; Gregory Doranites, grand drungar of the fleet; and Baltha Ogli, whose kinswoman was the wife of Murad II, sultan of the Osmanlis, the fearful, powerful Turks who completely surrounded the empire. The presence of this Bulgarian prince was considered a safeguard against the Turk, and he ranked high among the Trapezuntian nobility. At the steps of the cathedral the Metropolitan of Trebizond met the emperor and greeted him with the ancient Christian kiss of peace, and the monarch entered and knelt to the triune God like the humblest of his subjects.

But such occasions for public rejoicings and holidays were rare; the emperor lived largely in the seclusion of the palace. David, on the other hand, was notorious for his frequent absences both from church and the numerous elaborate court functions that bemused the Western ambassadors and impressed even the Turks, who were used to such things, with the power and glory of Trebizond.

Near the palace were the residences of the great nobles. Baltha Ogli's was one of the newest, the best built, and the stateliest, full of many Eastern conveniences that the rich factor had copied from the Turks. As soon as the Lady was securely tied up at the dock, the page was dispatched with the news of the ship's arrival and a request from the captain that Ogli Pasha name the hour that would be most convenient to receive him and Peter, the auditor-general, who was making his first trip to the East and desirous of paying his respects to the Trapezuntian lord.

Henri returned with the message that the factor was indisposed and could not see them till afternoon. The page brought with him two high-blooded Arabian horses, so that no one might have to approach on foot the residence of Baltha Ogli.

"His courtesy honors himself as well as us," the captain observed. They passed the Greek guards at the gates of the inner wall without challenge. Everyone knew the *Sainte-Eulalie,* and Justin himself was vaguely familiar to the guards after his many voyages. Had they been complete strangers, however, Ogli's horses were a sure passport through any gate of the city. "Baltha Ogli loves display. It would shame him to have the Europeans who symbolize his Western commercial activities walk to the front door of his castle."

"I am just as well pleased," said Pierre, who had on his long furred blue mantle and De Coucy's sword. "It is very hot."

Sir John was a knight of the Italian Order of the *Collare*. He wore the white tunic of satin embroidered with silk and the silver collar with fifteen love knots and roses; but he could not wear in Trebizond the purple velvet cloak, covered with roses and embroidery. Shorn of half his chivalric insignia, he was much more comfortable than Pierre.

The streets of Trebizond were paved with flat stones, smoother than the streets in most Western cities. They were narrow, like city streets everywhere. Wheeled vehicles were uncommon, uncomfortable, and unfashionable. The great age of the carriage was still to come, all over the world. Even in Europe the upper stories of houses often projected over the streets. But in Trebizond it was not uncommon to have them actually touch each other like a long series of bridges over the thoroughfares, especially before one mounted toward the higher ground around the palace in the exclusive center of town. Thus, many streets were actually covered arcades, which at night would have been pitch black except for the lanterns of the numerous guards and watchmen and the torches that anyone who could afford a servant always had carried before him.

Pierre and Sir John, who knew the way, rode the factor's fine horses up one long, tunnel-like street that was so steep there were steps in it every few paces and gloomy even in the daytime. Then they emerged onto a brilliant, sunlit, open plaza in full view of the massive, squat pile of the Church of the Golden-Haired Virgin, the turreted imperial palace, with water lilies and white swans in the moat, and, a little beyond it, the pink, stone house of Baltha Ogli. There was not a pane of window glass in Trebizond except in the churches and the chapel of the imperial palace. Ogli's house was perhaps more beautiful for its absence, for he had built into the walls dozens of picturesque projecting windows. They were screened in the Eastern fashion with intricately turned grillwork of dense, black, polished wood, so that light and air were freely admitted and privacy simultaneously assured.

A gigantic old plane tree threw a mottle of shadow across the high, cool, triple arches of the portico. An airy balcony supported by pale-green columns of polished serpentine lent an air of lightness to the upper story. A short, wide flight of red marble steps led up to the door. Their blue and crystal veining was artfully matched and produced a curious illusion of little streamlets of water running down over them.

There was a low stone wall along the street that a man on horseback could easily see over. Its function was not to keep the people out, who would not have dared trespass on Baltha Ogli's gardens, but to keep in the swans that sailed in the fountains and the peacocks that strutted and spread their tails under the rose- and rare white-flowered oleanders.

A porter with a Turkish face and a high, green turban carried his hand to his heart and his mouth in a salutation, and threw open the gates, that were formed of strips of iron woven into a design like two great flowers. A groom took their horses round to the stables in the rear on a trim little path of hard, crunching, blue volcanic stone. Then the heavy doors of the house opened, and a tall, corpulent person in a long saffron tunic, with no covering at all on his completely bald, pink head, walked in white sandals down the steps and advanced to meet them. There was a broad welcoming smile on his big face. He had deep-set, little blue eyes.

"It is Basil," whispered the captain. "He is the factor's chief domestic, or major-domo, and secretary. He is a eunuch, but not a slave. Call him by his Christian name."

Basil advanced to meet the men, and bowed as low as his ample figure would permit, so that for a moment the thin golden hem of his tunic buried itself in the green, well trimmed grass of the garden. Righting himself he said in excellent Latin:

"The master greets you, Sir John, and you, Auditor Peter. He is in the bath, diffusing a monstrous fluxion of vapors that has afflicted his poor head since last night, when he tasted too conscientiously of the new crop of several of his vineyards. At first I was horribly frightened that he might have been poisoned. He regrets not having been able to receive you sooner and has instructed me to bring you to him at once."

"Had we not better wait till he has finished with his bath, Basil?" the captain asked.

"Not at all, Sir John," replied the eunuch. "The mistress, the wife of Ogli Pasha, is spending a fortnight in a retreat in the Convent of Saint Eugenios. His son is in Magnesia on an urgent mission to the sultan. He is dying of boredom with nobody but the servants and slaves in the house. I am sure your visit, and the visit of the auditor-general will lift his spirits." Here Basil favored Pierre with such a searching, instantaneous look as Pierre had never before had to withstand. It was like the spark that leaps out of the fur of a cat.

"Then we shall go in to him at once," Justin said, and Basil led the way.

A noble staircase with a carved and guilded balustrade swept crescentwise from the entrance hall to the apartments above. The floor was of mosaics in porphyry and multicolored marbles, or at least what was visible was; most of it was hidden by a cream-colored Turkish carpet, elaborately worked into a pattern of white flowers, green leaves, golden elephants, and red peacocks, confounded in a vast ornamental jungle under their feet. They passed through a living apartment luxuriously supplied with divans and sofas, covered with cut velvet or embroidered satin, where nothing was Greek but a large fireplace; through flat, painted Turkish arches hung with green brocaded damask, and into a sizable room surrounded on three sides by windows. A cool breeze swept through the ornamental grillwork, and Pierre thanked God for it. The room would have been stifling otherwise.

Baltha Ogli sat up to his waist in steaming hot water in a large, oval, porphyry basin sunk into the marble of the floor. He was a big man, with huge, hairy arms. He had a short, intensely black beard, and his long black hair was carelessly tied up in the folds of a thick, white, absorbent towel, wrapped round his head like the turbans he habitually wore. His nakedness was covered, modestly, Pierre thought, from the slave girl who attended him, by a circular cape of thin silk that clung to his power-ful wet shoulders and stuck to the wiry black hair of his perspiring chest, and then floated round him on the surface of the bath like a grotesque yellow lily pad.

The air was laden with a pleasant, penetrating, aromatic scent that came from a black liquid bubbling in a silver bowl over a glowing brazier set in a corner between the windows. At the appearance of the visitors, the slave girl, without seeming to notice them, set down the alabaster pitcher of boiling water she had been pouring into the bath and quietly went over to the brazier and stirred the liquid with a long silver spoon. She seemed perfectly at ease. Justin's quick Italian eye noted that she was almost as coolly dressed as the factor in his tub. Basil announced them in the savage, gnashing consonants of the wild, unknown Bulgarian tongue; the factor answered in Greek, and the eunuch translated into Latin: "The master says that he is delighted to see you and regrets that though he speaks Bulgarian, Greek, Turkish, Arabian, and Persian, he has never had the leisure from his numerous state affairs to learn either French or Latin." Then he took a position behind them; Pierre and the captain stepped to the brink of the bath and bowed.

The movement startled a silly, chattering pet monkey who had been cowering in a corner. He shrieked like a frightened woman and ran across the damp, sweating marble floor and leaped to Ogli's shoulder, wrapping his prehensile tail around his master's thick neck and holding on with his paws to a hank of black hair that hung out of the towel. He worked his gray little old man's face in rage and perplexity.

"Hush, Lala; quiet, Lala Bey; the Franks are friends," said Ogli in Turkish, patting the excited monkey affectionately. It stopped snarling but maintained its perch on the factor's shoulder as if it felt safer there, glaring at the Franks malevolently. Without looking toward his slave, Baltha Ogli held out a large, half-opened hand to her, and she instantly glided over the floor, without seeming to touch it or making a sound on her bare feet, and placed a minute, porcelain cup full of the scalding liquid in his fingers. Ogli inhaled the fragrant steam and tasted it, sigh-ing appreciatively between the little sips.

"Basil, inquire of my guests whether they take coffee. You may men-tion that I recommend it. Chadaze, more hot water."

Basil translated the courteous invitation, explaining particularly to Pierre, who was new to the East, that the drink was a harmless stimulant that even the abstemious Turks drank with pleasure; it was bitter if

233

gulped like wine, but delicious if sipped slowly as the factor was doing. While he was speaking, the slave girl picked up the pitcher again and poured it into the bath. But the stream of hot water came a little too close to the body of her master. Ogli roared a torrent of vile Turkish abuse at her, ending with: "I shall strip you naked and whip your ugly, useless behind if you cannot be more dexterous." Basil did not, of course, translate this.

Justin, if he had ever learned Turkish, would have disagreed with the description. Pierre slowly colored up to the roots of his hair.

"Do not shame me, master," the girl pleaded. "Look at the young Frank's face. I think your words are understood."

"Eh?" Ogli grunted in astonishment. "The Franks never talk anything but Latin, and their own dreadful dialect through their noses." He looked up at Pierre shrewdly over the little pool of black coffee in the tiny blue cup just under his nose. His coal-black eyes were still a little bloodshot from conscientiously tasting the products of his vineyards the night before. Pierre grew redder and redder under the intense, level scrutiny. "Saints!" Ogli gasped, "I think you are right, Chadaze."

"I was taught a smattering of it, my lord," Pierre said quickly. "The French minister intimated that Ogli Pasha might prefer to speak Turkish. But the old man who taught me spent many years of his life in Isfahan, and perhaps his Turkish is tainted with Persian, or perhaps I learned it all backwards, for, a minute ago, I thought I heard you call your pet a name that meant 'My Lord Preceptor,' and now I seem to have heard you call your beautiful slave, who, like everyone else I have seen in your house does such honor to your elegant tastes, ugly and useless. Surely my Turkish is a poor thing."

Justin had to turn his head to see who was speaking. Baltha Ogli showed all his strong, even teeth, startlingly white against the black of the beard around his mouth, in a great, pleased smile.

"This is a rare courtesy on the minister's part, Peter. Never before has he sent me an official to whom I could speak directly without the intermediary offices of my dragoman. I love to talk, and I love to eat: I like to do both at first hand. I shall write your master how pleased I am. Your Turkish is perfectly understandable, though a bit stilted. Did you learn it from a stuffy old scholar? Some old heathen priest?"

"Nay, my lord, he was old, but he was neither an imam nor a scholar. He was an old swordmaker, who could not write a word of his own language."

"You should have learned to write it too, Peter. Do not worry about

234

the name of my monkey. He deserves his title, which you correctly understood. He is wiser than most of the men I meet. As for the girl, she is a clumsy wench. I do really plan to sell her. Perhaps we can do business together, Auditor Peter."

The eunuch rapidly translated this into the incredulous ear of the captain.

"I could never afford her, my lord."

"Couldn't you? Well, I value my skin, and I do not propose to have it scalded on my body. Perhaps I shall make you a present of her." Pierre knew that to be given away was a terrible insult to a slave. Justin, to whom the information came tardily in Latin, did not think the girl looked unduly alarmed. Perhaps Ogli was joking, or perhaps she would have welcomed the change.

"I should never know what to do with her, my lord," Pierre said.

The factor snorted and sent a little ripple of water over the surface of his bath. It bounced off the wall of the tub and came back again like a returning tide and spent itself against his round, protruding belly under the floating yellow silk. He drained his cup and held it out to the girl.

"The swordmaker must have been ancient indeed," Ogli observed. "Give Peter Effendi a cup of coffee, Chadaze. Anyone who speaks Turkish, Peter, should also learn to drink coffee."

"I have brought the manifests with me," Justin said; "I shall be glad to deliver them as soon as Ogli Pasha can look at them." He accepted a cup of coffee from Chadaze, and so did Pierre, who, when Basil had translated the captain's remark to the factor, added:

"The cargo is all consigned to you, my lord."

"Is it?" said Ogli. "Nay, the minister is more courteous than ever. But what did Michael in Constantinople have to say about that?"

"Cantacuzene was distressed, but he understood that the ship was making a fast trip to avoid the autumnal storms." Pierre repeated this in Latin to Justin, who nodded. Basil nodded, also. Everyone knew about the fierce, late-season storms on the Eastern seas.

"I can always use a good cargo," Ogli said. "The Turkish tribute gets more and more burdensome. My son is even now in Magnesia, pleading with my kinswoman, who, as perhaps you know, is Mara the sultana, *première* wife of the sultan Murad, mother of his son, Mohammed, who, when Murad dies, will be the next sultan. It is a great honor to my family, of course, though it will be an anomaly to be cousin to the great threat to Christendom. Perhaps my son's mission will succeed and bring about a reduction of the tribute. My dear wife has been praying for him for a week now, and has, if I remember correctly, a week more to pray. Is it not a week, Basil?"

"It is a week, my lord, and two days," replied the eunuch.

"All of us," Ogli continued, "from the Great Comneni down to the humblest street vendor, must bear our share of the tribute. So do not think me unappreciative of the importance of the cargo, Sir John, but my head still hurts and I shall do no business till after dinner."

Basil told Justin that the master was still slightly indisposed and could not look at the ship's documents till later. The captain's own head was a bit light from the effects of the coffee, which he did not like and drank only out of politeness. Pierre did not like it either, and had drunk it too hurriedly. He was suffering from a sudden, mild, alert sort of intoxication from the bitter unaccustomed stimulant, which Chadaze brewed very thick and strong after the Turkish fashion.

"Basil," said Ogli in Greek, "the Franks are drunk on coffee, as usual, and the old one is very offensive to the nose, like a goat."

"May I suggest to my lord," Basil quickly interrupted, "that the unusual young one may perhaps understand Greek?"

"By the holy, flying coffin! Perhaps he does!" Ogli continued cautiously in Bulgarian. "Bid my guests refresh themselves, Basil. They will want to wash the salt off themselves after so long a voyage. Let Chadaze attend the young man; let her give him no more coffee. Unless she actually wants to be given away, her intelligence and a hint from you will instruct her what else to do. And do thou," he said in Turkish for Pierre's benefit, "after the wants of my guests have been satisfied, have a good dinner prepared for Sir John and the auditor-general. It will please me, Basil, if you would do that foolish juggling trick of yours with the long bamboo pole."

Despite the mature intelligence which Pierre had already divined in Basil, the eunuch was childishly proud of his enormous strength and inordinately fond of displaying it in skillful feats of juggling and mummery.

"The master's commands are branded in my useless heart in letters of fire," Basil answered, carrying his hand to his heart and bowing.

Ogli inclined his head courteously, to signify to the Franks that the audience was at an end. The Trapezuntian nobleman in his tub with a monkey on his shoulder somehow contrived to give the gesture a sort of barbaric majesty. Pierre was astonished at its crushing, powerful effect, and put it down to the subtle action of the coffee which, in his hungry stomach, gave every improbable thing an aura of happy plausibility. He was sweating profusely under his velvet mantle. The sudden suspicion of poison crossed his mind, but Ogli had no reason to poison him. The eunuch looked capable of almost anything, but Basil would not poison him without instructions from his master. Pierre suddenly reined in his galloping imagination and set his jaw. Decidedly coffee was a drug to beware of in the future.

Basil bowed Pierre into a spacious room with a canopied divan covered with cushions. There was a room beyond, very like the bath he had just come from, but smaller and less richly furnished.

"Should the auditor-general care to refresh himself, there is plenty of time before dinner," Basil suggested. "If I may say so, sir, the coffee has perhaps heated your blood. Your forehead is all aglow. Coffee sometimes does that to people who are not used to it, but the effects pass off very quickly. Should you try the bath and find it too cold, you have only to clap your hands, and hot water will be brought you."

"Thank you, Basil. I hope there is ice in it!" Pierre said, laughing.

Basil felt that the auditor-general would try the bath, which Pierre instantly did, but he anticipated more difficulty with the captain. He bowed himself out of the room, and Pierre heard him speaking earnestly to Sir John about the pleasure of the tub as he piloted him into another apartment.

The water felt good. It was exactly room temperature and it washed the coffee fumes out of his mind.

Suddenly there was a scratching at the doorpost. Pierre, up to his neck in the cool, refreshing water, bade him enter, whoever it was, and he was astonished to behold a Turkish servant with a wooden bucket on his shoulder. There was sawdust clinging to its outside.

"Am I permitted?" the man asked, averting his eyes, for the fastidious Turks did not like to see naked bodies.

"Certainly," answered Pierre, not quite sure what he was permitting.

The man emptied a bucket of snow into the water, raised his hand to his heart and his mouth, and shook his head in perplexity. Then, frightened and ashamed of the bad manners his wonderment had betrayed him into exhibiting, he left the Frank to turn blue or congeal, if that were his pleasure, in the icy bath he had ordered.

Pierre was more astounded than the Turk, not only to see snow in summertime, but to be so quickly taken at his word. The snow obviously came from the distant mountains. But the effort of running it into the city on horses or mules or however it was done seemed overwhelming and must have been extremely costly. Pierre surmised that it was not only

237

the Turkish tribute that made Ogli glad to engage in commerce. He wondered how much it cost to run a household that could command hot water or snow at a moment's notice. He was cool and calm again and about to get out of the tub when there was another scratching at the doorpost. He again bade the man enter, but he had firmly decided that if it was more snow, he would send it back to the cellars, regardless of how costly the stuff was.

But it was Chadaze, with a silver cup in her hand and a yellow cape on her arm.

Pierre frantically seeking the bottom of the tub, almost drowned himself.

"The master himself commanded me to attend you, sir," she said. She displayed much less reserve than the man who brought the snow, and looked directly into his face, smiling prettily.

"Maybe she is used to this," Pierre thought, "but I am not." What of his flesh was visible above the surface of the bath grew redder than when the factor cursed her. She saw his confusion and tried to put him at his ease.

"I did not realize you would unvest so rapidly," she said, "or I should have been here sooner with the cloak, Peter Effendi. The Trape-zuntian lords take much longer."

"Give me the cloak, in God's name!"

She set the cup of wine on a little taboret of sandalwood inlaid with ivory, and cast the cloak around his shoulders with a hand that, for all her youth, bespoke years of long practice. Pierre found himself sitting in the center of a golden lily pad like the factor, without a shred of the factor's dignity.

"You need only a little more flesh on your body, Peter Effendi, and Lala Bey here," she patted his shoulder, "to look like the prince himself. Do not be afraid of me, sir. The slave is the slave of her master's honored guest. You are by no means the first man I have attended at his bath. It is common among the Osmanli slaves, and Trebizond is almost like home. Only at home, of course, the slaves are all Christian. Every country has its own customs."

"Indeed they do, Chadaze, but this is one that I confess I have never experienced before." He felt a little more at ease now that he was no longer entirely naked in front of the pleasant, pretty girl.

"I was terribly ashamed when Ogli Pasha reviled me in your presence. I think I was awkward with the water because I was trying to look out of the corner of my eye to see whether you had noticed me."

"It would be extremely difficult for a man not to notice you Chadaze."

Outside the curtain a shell-pink ear on a fat bald head bent close to listen, and a contented smile spread over Basil's face. The interview had started very nicely, he thought.

"It is no treason to my noble master," Chadaze said, "when I admit that every little Turkish slave girl dreams of being bought by a handsome, long-limbed Frank. For a moment I thought my master was so angry he was going to give me to you. Would you take me, Peter Effendi? Won't you sip the wine? Coffee is bad for the stomach before dinner, I think."

"I found it so. I should like the wine, Chadaze."

She gave him the cup and he tasted it carefully. It was good French wine, and he took a deep, grateful draught of it.

"Muscadine in Trebizond is a delicate attention to a Frenchman," he observed.

"Perhaps Peter Effendi does not like his slave," the girl said pouting; "I asked a question, and it has not been answered. What golden hair you have, my master-perhaps-to-be. I have never seen anything like it except on a statue in the big church here. There are no statues in mosques, and I think they are so pretty. May I put a scent in it?"

"I don't care," Pierre said. "Is that also a custom?"

"Oh, indeed it is. You ought to smell the master when I am through with him. All sandalwood, aloes, Indian myrtle and jasmine! It is wonderful!"

Pierre laughed. "I can imagine. I know sandalwood, Chadaze. Try some of that."

The slave had a tiny gold box, and when she opened the lid a sweet fragrance seemed instantly to permeate the apartment. She put a minute dab of ointment on her finger and ran it through his hair. This was the first time she had touched him, except for the pat on his silk-clad shoulder. Pierre was astonished that a woman's fingertips could so mysteriously convey the idea of a caress, and he shut his eyes for a moment and leaned his head back on the marble.

Chadaze spoke very softly. Pierre had always loved the sibilant sounds of the Turkish tongue. On her lips it was music. "A Turkish woman seldom sees a man's hair, Effendi," she said. "Especially golden curly hair. Many a girl I know would be jealous of me this minute." Then, without altering the tone of her voice, she said in the Greek language these astonishing words: "Your mother must have been a whoring bitch to have had so ugly a son."

"What did you say, Chadaze?" he asked, opening his eyes. She scrutinized his face closely. There was not a flicker of understanding or resentment.

"I think I spoke Greek for a moment. I often slip from one language to another in this polyglot house. Do you not speak Greek, Peter Effendi?"

"Not a word, Chadaze."

Basil, behind the curtains, believed what he heard. So much, at least, he had found out about the mysterious auditor-general. He hurried off to tell his master. Chadaze heard him go.

"What did you say in Greek?" Pierre asked.

"Nay, I shall not tell you. Even a slave girl is not expected to bare her true heart. A moment ago I could not get an answer from you when I asked if you would take me as a gift. Now we are quits, Peter Effendi."

Pierre prepared to explain how impossible it was to keep beautiful Turkish slave girls in France, but Chadaze suddenly pressed her hand hard upon his mouth and whispered fiercely in his ear:

"We are alone only for a moment, you careless Frank. I know nothing of what is afoot against you, but you are being closely spied upon. You are not to be poisoned or you would be dead already. Do not betray me, Peter. Now say what you were going to say."

Pierre gulped hard. He had been chilly enough in his cold bath before Chadaze came and made him forget it for a moment. He was quite awake to its chill again. Obviously he could not immediately get out after such a revelation. Whoever was spying would be instantly suspicious of any sudden termination of a conversation that he now realized had been distinctly amorous, at least on her part. His teeth could easily have chattered with cold, but he found himself ashamed to be taken for a coward by the slave, who might, for all he knew, be an exceptionally brave woman. He was very confused for a moment.

"Give me another sip of the wine of my own country," he said quickly, as soon as he could control his voice.

Basil was back at the curtain. He smiled again to hear the auditor-general asking for more wine.

She gave him the cup and he swallowed a bit. It was sweet and pure, but it went down hard.

"This French wine serves to remind me how awkward it would be if I tried to accept Ogli Pasha's generous gift," he said, "which I am sure he did not mean seriously anyway. In France, Chadaze, men marry only one wife, of course, and the wives are always jealous. I have

240

already picked my own love, Chadaze. I can imagine how your presence would disturb her."

"Does she look like me, Peter Effendi? Give me a sip of the French wine. Maybe I will look like her."

Pierre held the goblet to her lips and she placed her hand on his while she drank.

"Saints! How cold your hands are!" She touched the water. "What in the name of the Prophet has happened to your bath?"

"Why, the man threw snow into it. I jokingly asked Basil for some ice, and he sent a man with a bucket of snow right away. It was a courteous thing to do, since I asked for it, but I was surprised to see it."

"Is it the custom in France to take ice-cold baths, Peter Effendi? I had heard that France was a country of love and romance! I cannot understand how a man can freeze his limbs in water and then embrace a woman!"

Basil saw his terrible error. He went to Baltha Ogli's apartments wringing his hands in an agony of self-accusation. Another slave was dressing the master's hair. Ogli had decided not to wear a turban, in honor of his fellow Christian guests. Basil prostrated himself like a slave, and Ogli instantly sent the hairdresser away.

"What is the matter, Basil?"

"I am a fool, my lord, an unnatural miserable fool!"

"You are not always a fool, Basil. What have you done?"

"Master, you should beat me like a slave. Oh, that snow!"

"Stop blubbering and get up off the floor. What snow? What are you talking about?"

"Both Franks are bathed, my lord, and one of them has the odor of sandalwood in his hair. But the sweet one, the Auditor General, that I set the subtle Chadaze to beguile—he speaks no Greek, as I told you— but that is all I know about him. Chadaze made wonderful love, or at least I thought it was. But Auditor Peter asked for ice in his bath, and I had a little put into it. Of course, he was cold as a fish all the time, even with Chadaze in the room."

"You are a stupid fool, Basil. Only a eunuch could be stupid. Did you learn nothing more at all?"

"Nothing, my lord. I cannot help my affliction. I did not choose it."

Ogli grunted contemptuously, "Oh, maybe he's as innocent as he looks. But continue to watch him carefully. I am very curious to know why the Auditor General is in Trebizond."

# CHAPTER

## ❋ 22 ❋

I N THE ABSENCE of his wife and son, Baltha Ogli had dinner
spread for his two Western visitors not in the great hall, which
could easily have accommodated a hundred guests, but in one of the
spacious living rooms of his own apartments.

He wore a Western jacket, and his long, black hair had been cunningly arranged to give the appearance of the ear-length hairdress
common among north European knights and noblemen. There was a good
deal of hair to be kept in place, however, and Ogli wore around his
head a narrow circlet of gold to confine it, set with pearls and a flashing,
magnificent sapphire, blue and big as a robin's egg, on his forehead.
Pierre tried to imagine it on the sunburned brow of the honest captain,
and could not. But Ogli wore it like a crown.

A Turkish servant was stationed behind each chair, to fill their
goblets, or change the Chinese porcelain dishes after each course, or
wipe their mouths and fingers on a white linen napkin which they held
ready for the purpose. Napkins were not used in Europe. It seemed to
Pierre that if one were rich enough and lazy enough, he might pass his
entire life in the East without lifting a hand to supply even the simplest
of his bodily wants; there was always a servant or a slave ready and
trained to do it for one.

In the center of the table, activated by a silent, mysterious mechanism, there was a dainty fountain, a little larger than a man's hand,
formed of translucent alabaster carved into a cluster of feathers. Red
wine spouted from a hidden nozzle and ran down the feathers, dripping
from their points, that seemed to bend under the weight of the liquid,
into a shallow basin of clear rock crystal beneath.

Pierre had no idea what fish, foul, and game had been killed and admixed into the series of spicy dishes he ate. Only the sweet course retained any of its original appearance. That was a small cone of green, frozen sherbet, acid with the juice of lemon and lime, with a large, red rose, crusted with crystallized sugar and sprinkled, he thought, with cinnamon, pressed into the apex. He ate the petals, as Ogli did.

Just before this fragile, pretty sweet was placed before them, a Turk, whom Ogli addressed as Mousa and who had poured their successively smaller cups of successively sweeter wines, replaced the gold and silver goblets with a tiny, tapering one of clear Venetian glass. This was to hold a minty, fiery, sweet green cordial. Mousa was elderly, and had a thin, ascetic face. He was afflicted perhaps, with a palsy, or perhaps he was nervous or careless. He filled Ogli's glass first, as was usual, and Ogli tasted a sip; but when he filled Pierre's, he spilled a drop or two over the lip of the glass. It ran down the stem and over the foot and spread in a bright green stain on the tablecloth. Ogli scowled and Basil rushed forward, mumbling an apology, and snatched the little pitcher out of Mousa's hand. Basil himself filled Justin's glass and Mousa retired, pale and quaking, to the wall.

"The servants are all clumsy today," Ogli said in a low rumbling voice. "What has happened to your staff, Basil?"

"My lord, I am desolate! Mousa didn't watch what he was doing. I saw him out of the corner of my eye. He is to be punished, is he not, my lord?"

"Naturally," said Ogli.

"May I see to it myself, my master?"

"If you care to. But do not be too long. We are ready for your entertainment. And punish not too severely the hand that wavered: I want him to be able to pour again. You are sometimes overindustrious with your whippings and brandings. Remember, Basil, my discipline is designed to maintain a high standard of service, not to afford you amusement."

"Nay, my lord, I shall not even leave a scar. But Mousa shall howl! Mousa shall sweat!" Basil's nostrils dilated a little. Pierre was suddenly sickened with the conviction that Basil would relish disciplining the unfortunate slave.

Pierre protested: "I think I moved the glass a little, my lord; it was not the fault of the slave."

"If that were true, Auditor Peter," Ogli replied haughtily, "Mousa was even more at fault for not exercising the considerable skill that I know he possesses. My chief domestic displays a cheerful aptitude in punishing the slaves. I think he enjoys it even more than the secretarial duties that he discharges so well for me. I seldom have to think about either business details or the management of the house. It is surely not your intention to instruct me how to maintain decent order in my own castle, Auditor Peter."

Pierre smarted under the factor's rebuke and ate his frozen sherbet in silence. Ogli watched him closely for a moment and then glanced at Sir John, who had not understood a word of the Turkish conversation.

Ogli said: "The good Sir John observes your angry countenance, Auditor Peter. You may tell him that I have said nothing discourteous. As a sea captain he will understand better than yourself the importance of ready, skillful obedience among one's servants."

Pierre rapidly informed Justin that Ogli Pasha had sent the eunuch off to brand or whip poor Mousa's hand because he had spilled a drop of cordial with it. Sir John nodded his head and kept his face perfectly blank.

"Do not anger the factor, Pierre," was all he said.

Whatever Basil did, did not take him long. Another slave instantly replaced Mousa behind the master's thronelike chair. In a little while the curtains parted and Basil reappeared, clad in a strange orange costume that was a theatrical travesty on the garb worn by the sacred Moslem whirling dervishes: the tall, conical cap, the long, loose sleeves, a belt around his ample girth, and an enormous circular skirt embroidered with silver and gold in cabalistic symbols that were, of course, no part of a dervish's costume. The hem was weighted with hundreds of tinkling little brass bells. Basil slowly turned on his own axis and the skirt billowed out around him like a huge, hanging flower of the trumpet tree. He carried a bamboo pole twice as high as himself; there was a short crosspiece fixed near its upper extremity, and from this horizontal bar hung small loops of rope, wrapped in cloth of silver. Basil's belt was stuck full of daggers, and as he whirled closer to the table, there could be seen under his flying skirt three pairs of legs, which by no stretch of the imagination could all be his own.

Arriving at a position opposite the table and near the center of the room, Basil ceased his forward progress and whirled faster and faster in one spot till his circular skirt stood straight out from his body. Two of the tiniest human beings Pierre had ever seen darted out from under it. Basil suddenly stopped whirling; the momentum of the skirt wrapped it round his legs with an incredible jangling of the little bells, and the two dwarfs scampered up the pole. Their sex was a mystery to Pierre, for, while they were otherwise entirely naked, they were cinctured with close and seemingly elastic silver cloth. Their heads were shaved and their bodies painted with dazzling gold paint. There was no misshapen head, no stunted limb, no ungainliness so commonly associated with dwarfism. Except for the maturity of their faces and the ropelike muscles flexing under their metallic skins, they might have been children.

"I bought them in Brousa," Ogli observed. "They were twin brothers. I had them made eunuchs so that their beards would not grow and spoil the effect of the paint on their faces."

Basil inserted the lower end of the pole into a sconce in his belt similar to the holder that a squire carried his master's lance in. Basil's arms were now free, and he extended them from the shoulders and began to whirl again, balancing the pole dexterously, while the dwarfs performed on top, hanging from the rope loops or somersaulting over each other.

It was a part of the trick for Basil to affect complete indifference to the two golden little creatures tumbling and cavorting on top of his pole. Light as they were, their combined weights would have been difficult for an ordinary man to manage.

Basil drew first one, then another, then all five of the daggers from his belt, and juggled them in the air, throwing them higher and higher. The dwarves caught them when they came into reach and tossed them back and forth to each other. Basil affected consternation, in excellent pantomine, that his weapons had disappeared into the air. After a few moments one fell flashing in front of his face; Basil caught it with an exaggerated gesture of clumsy fright, and almost instantly the four others rained in a sharp, dangerous shower around his face and shoulders. He caught them all, looked up, feigned astonishment at the little men above him, and threw the daggers back as if he were angry and trying to stick them. They danced and dodged and caught the daggers skillfully. The trick reached a flashing climax with Basil whirling rapidly round again, slowly moving out of the room through the curtains of an arch that two slaves held apart to let him pass, the daggers flying in a great glittering circle of light, whose circumference was full of busy hands, moving so fast they were hardly visible.

"A man with so keen an eye would make a wonderful pilot," Sir John observed. Pierre agreed, and told the factor what the captain had said.

Ogli enjoyed the performance. He had forgotten all about the headache that had afflicted him during the day. The green cordial had lifted his spirits wonderfully.

"Have I not heard somewhere that the *Sainte-Eulalie* is already equipped with an able Turkish pilot?" he asked pleasantly.

"Ilderim unfortunately died, my lord," Pierre answered.

"Did he, Auditor Peter? I think I had heard he was a strong, active man in the prime of life. What sickness killed him, if you know?"

"The chirurgeon stated that he could not be sure," Pierre said. "There was some talk among the men that his spleen had burst."

"That is too bad," said Ogli. "Inform Sir John, when you have the leisure, that I happen to know of another who is reputed to be almost as dexterous as the one you have called Ilderim." Ogli seemed thoughtful. "I should like to look at the ship's manifests now, if you gentlemen will attend me in the next room. Undoubtedly the captain will be pleased to be quit of his chafing leather manacle." He stood up and Pierre and Sir John followed him. Silent servants moved their heavy chairs, not dragging them over the carpet but lifting them bodily and quickly out of their way.

Two of the slaves held aside the curtain under another arch, revealing a narrow door. It was the only door Pierre had seen in the interior of Baltha Ogli's house. It was not pierced or grilled in the Eastern fashion, but solid and European in appearance, and beyond it was a private room with no windows. Panels of decoratively inlaid woods covered the walls, which were smooth and otherwise devoid of ornament. There was a niche like a Turkish mihrab in one of them, but instead of being empty, as it would have been in a mosque, it held an ancient Byzantine statue of the Virgin, whose eyes were so lifelike that Pierre had the uncomfortable feeling that they could see. A votive light in a blue glass cup burned at its feet. The only other source of illumination came from two high silver candelabra on a massive Chinese teakwood table at which Ogli seated himself. The tall wax candles threw a flood of clear, golden light on the factor's face. He sat perfectly still and silent for a few seconds, absorbed in thought, his face absolutely expressionless, the candlelight in the jeweled circlet of gold around his forehead, like a heathen idol competing successfully for the light with the statue of the Virgin. If this were the setting in which the factor habitually transacted his business, Pierre could imagine the overwhelming impression of power he created on his clients. Justin, however, had seen the imperial court and was more familiar with the studied attention the Easterners gave to the backgrounds before which they appeared. Since he could not speak Turkish, he seated himself across the room near the mihrab. Ogli tapped a small bronze bowl, the inside of which was dusty with ashes of incense that had been burned in it, with a felt-covered ivory wand. The slave who took Mousa's place entered with coffee and more of the mint cordial.

"Basil will be here presently," Ogli said, "to read me the manifests. Would you care to taste my coffee again, Auditor Peter? I know Sir John will not."

Pierre's mouth was sticky with the sweet wines. The idea of the bitter drink appealed to him.

"Indeed I should, Ogli Pasha. Though I shall drink it slower this time."

"You would make a good Trapezuntian, Auditor Peter. You speak Turkish and you are learning to like coffee. Of course, you have one curious trait. Your passion for ice-cold baths, I am informed, is quite as incomprehensible to my heathen servitors as the Resurrection itself. Pray, how did you acquire such an uncomfortable habit?"

"Nay, my lord, it is not a habit. I never had an ice-cold bath before, except once, perhaps, when a priest recommended the chilly Seine for a swim. I was warm and I told Basil I hoped there would be ice in the water. I had no idea it would be procured. Actually I was a little too cold in it." Pierre sipped his coffee. Justin took more of the cordial.

"Basil must have suffered the loss of his sense of humor along with certain other of his appendages," Ogli said. "He is returning, if my ears do not deceive me. Please ask Sir John for the manifests."

Pierre had heard no footsteps, but Basil slid into the room, dressed in his tunic again, cool, composed, and dignified, as if he had never performed the dizzy, athletic juggling trick. Lala Bey followed him. The door closed without a sound.

Sir John unstrapped the tube, rubbed his chafed, white wrist, delivered the tube to Basil, and retired again to his seat under the statue. Basil broke the seals and started to read the manifests. There were a great many of the parchment sheets. He read slowly and carefully. Justin had witnessed this little ceremony on many other voyages. But there had seldom been so many documents. It was partly caused by Ogli's having all the cargo this time. And seldom, he thought, had Ogli himself paid such attention. The factor nodded his head a number of times and expressed his satisfaction, especially when Basil came to a sheet which stated that Coeur had received a special license from the king to export a certain quantity of minted gold.

247

"Now that is wonderful, Auditor Peter! How Coeur managed to get around the law I cannot imagine! His solid, honest gold pieces circulate here in the East with less question than anything since the old imperial bezants. I can never get enough of them. It is not even necessary to assay them. Should Coeur ever decide to debase the coinage, it would take months to discover, so trusted is the Frank money. He would not care to make a fortune that way, of course."

"Naturally not, my lord. And as the manifest states, this gold is exported by special license, not in defiance of the law."

"Oh, of course, of course," Ogli replied. Basil continued the reading. Ships' documents had not attained the standardization they were later to acquire. Some of the sheets were large and others small. Basil suddenly stopped his reading and bent his head to decipher the minute handwriting on one of a number of the smaller ones.

"This is a little note of instruction to the steward dealing with the ship's provisions. It does not list cargo and was probably included by mistake among the manifests." He slipped it to the bottom of the pile of documents he held and began to read the next large sheet.

"Perhaps Sir John should take the steward's note now, before it is forgotten," Pierre suggested. Lala Bey, bored by the motionless men and the singsong monotonous voice of the eunuch, leaped onto the table and began to play with the empty container, reaching his long furry arm into its depth as if something wonderful to a monkey were hidden at the bottom.

"There is plenty of time," Ogli said. "The cargo is a rich one and I am anxious to hear all of it."

Finding nothing in the tube, Lala Bey vaulted up to Basil's shoulder, in a friendly way, and began to pull at the eunuch's pink ear. But the affectionate little animal seemed to irritate the eunuch, who pushed him petulantly off his shoulder. Lala Bey was used to more courteous treatment. Ogli half arose from his seat, astonished at his chief domestic's unkind behavior to the pet. Lala Bey fell, screeching with fright, flailing out his long arms and legs and tail, instinctively seeking a forest branch to check his fall. He happened to grasp the manifests, wrenching them out of Basil's hand and scattering them over the factor, the table, Pierre, and the floor, which was white with them almost halfway to the mihrab. Lala Bey rushed for the door, but it was closed, and so he leaped onto Ogli's shoulder. Ogli patted and soothed him.

"Whatever you did to Mousa shall be done to your own hand, Basil. You know better than to strike Lala Bey."

Basil, for reasons of his own, did not reply. He unceremoniously went down on his hands and knees, a great indignity for him, and began to pick up the manifests. Pierre courteously helped. Ogli glared at his servant and stroked the monkey.

In the dim light beyond the illuminated area immediately around the table where most of the sheets had fallen, Pierre saw several of the smaller ones, which he reached over to pick up. One of them, the one which he instantly realized had caused the eunuch to hesitate in his reading, bore his name. It was too dark to read, and he did not want to appear curious or prying, but he distinctly saw the words: "Beware of the so-called 'auditor-general.' " It was in De Coucy's well known handwriting. Pierre knelt, his back to the light, and furtively secreted the note in the neck of his mantle, shielding the gesture with his body. He felt it fall down to his belt, which held it from falling farther. The incredible document would bear reading at the earliest possible moment. He amassed the other sheets and turned toward the light again, pretending to feel even in the dim areas near the wall, so that he might appear anxious to miss none of them. Then he stood up and gave them to Basil, who had begun to sweat and breathe heavily. Basil said something in Bulgarian to his master, and Ogli instantly rose and said: "The clumsy chief of my clumsy servants has so mixed up the manifests that it will not be possible to finish the reading of them tonight. I must ask you to attend me again tomorrow, gentlemen. Especially you, Auditor Peter. Basil says he may need help with one or two of the complicated listings. I myself am not familiar with all the details."

The note was burning a hole into Pierre's flesh. He was desperately concerned that Basil might miss it. Basil, of course, had read it through, but though he had perhaps intimated something of what it contained when he spoke to the factor in Bulgarian, Pierre reasoned that he might not yet have said anything unduly alarming. The prospect of Ogli's giving him and the captain a means of escape from his house, that suddenly oppressed him like a dark and dangerous prison, came like a breath of fresh air into the closed room.

"I have personally prepared many ship's manifests, Ogli Pasha," he said, "and I know that they read better when arranged in logical order. Sir John and I shall wait upon you at any hour you care to fix tomorrow."

"About noon, perhaps, Auditor Peter. Such a young man as yourself will probably want to visit some, shall we say, of our interesting old churches." He managed to smile a little while Basil arranged, with a

249

shaking hand, the mass of manifests in as neat a pile as he could manage on the table. "The captain knows Trebizond well," Ogli continued. "He will make a wonderful guide. There is a stable near the docks, if you care to keep the horses overnight. Men in your position should not walk in Trebizond. You Franks are sometimes careless."

"You are very kind, my lord. We shall be here at noon." It was the second time Pierre had been called a careless Frank that day.

Pierre did not speak to the captain, and Sir John himself was curiously silent until they passed, at a decorous pace, the bands of soldiers with lighted torches marching up and down before the imperial palace. At the entrance to the long, dark tunnel of a street that separated the plaza from the lower part of town, Pierre nudged his horse with his heels and the well trained animal broke into a trot.

"Are you in a hurry, Pierre?" Sir John asked. He loosened his sword in its scabbard.

"I certainly am."

"I think you ought to be, Pierre." The captain was wearing spurs, and he pricked his horse into a gallop, and Pierre followed him into the tunnel. They galloped furiously down the dark, steep narrow street and out into the twisting little alleys of the lower part of town. The gates of the inner wall were open, blazing with light and full of guards. The Greeks saw the galloping Franks on the well known horses and let them pass, with a superior smirk at the foolish Westerners, apparently drunk and racing their horses to the waterfront.

The crowded district between the inner and outer sea walls was almost as busy at night as in the daytime, though far darker. They reined in their horses so as not to trample on the people, and Justin said in a whisper: "If it is not impertinent, Auditor Peter, would you deign to explain to my guileless Italian mind why you save my life one day only to put it in terrible jeopardy the next by stealing the ship's papers from under the very eyes of Ogli Pasha and his horrible eunuch? Do you realize what would have happened to us if you had been caught? I am tempted to sail for France tonight! You do not know Trebizond, Pierre!"

Pierre put his hand on the captain's arm. "My noble friend," he answered cautiously, "look at what we are surrounded by. French is no protection against the ears of this mob. Who knows who they are and what languages they speak?"

The warehouses and commercial buildings were all closed and heavily guarded by men-at-arms with pikes, swords, and arbalests;

most of them carried lanterns. But many taverns were open and doing a flourishing business. Western sailors, their day's work done, well armed and wide awake, walked up and down the cosmopolitan thoroughfare, debating which taverns might have the cheapest wines or the prettiest attendants. Armenian pedlars in long Eastern tunics hawked their laces, their shawls, and their sweetmeats to the Europeans, who often mistook their Christian brethren for heathen Turks. Which was not to be wondered at, for the area was full of Turks, some of them prosperous merchants, some of them well paid guides hired by the Persians, who also thronged the place, to conduct their caravans through the mountains and over the plains to the city of Trebizond. The neighboring Turks knew every mule path in the empire, a fact that often troubled the Emperor John, though the other Great Comnenus, David, never worried his head about it.

From the Genoese castle at one end of the waterfront to the Venetian castle at the other, the place was alive with the babble of dozens of Christian and heathen tongues, spoken by hundreds of men, mostly good-natured, largely young, with time on their hands in a foreign capital. Some of them had drunk too much wine. Many a Frank, as the Easterners called anyone who came from Europe, far from home and ashore for the first time in weeks, eagerly pressed on from one tavern to another, hoping that the next house would miraculously present him with a fortune at dice or one of the beautiful slave girls that were constantly offered as prizes in dishonest games of chance. Nobody ever got the girls, but for the appearance of things a Greek or a Frank would sometimes hold up a winning ticket, receive the blushing creature into his arms, hustle her away through the enviously cheering crowd, only to bring her round again to the back door to be won again the next night in another game, and receive the price of his services.

A peddler speaking a dialect strikingly similar to Ogli's Bulgarian held up a bowlful of sour confection of goat's milk, inquiring, probably, if Sir John would care to buy it, pronouncing, as he did so, a word that sounded like "youghurt," which may have been the name of the stuff. Justin held the man off with the scabbard of his sword. The odor was frightful.

"What you say is true, Pierre."

Pierre whispered again: "I am going to the Lady, Sir John. But I do not wish to be seen aboard her. I plan to stay there only a moment or two. I want to read this note, which may be too dangerous to carry around. Then I have a great deal to tell you, sir."

"That I believe, young man."

"It is possible that we shall be followed, Sir John."

"I do not doubt it for a moment. I am anxious to talk with you so that I may better be able to help you. I confess that I am mystified by your action. There is a quiet inn near the ship called in Greek the Fair Haven. I could meet you there."

"If you were a careless Frank with a stolen letter, would you not go first to just such a quiet respectable place, Sir John?"

"Nay, of course I would. I shall meet you at the Eastern Star, Pierre. It's the biggest, busiest, wickedest tavern in town." He laughed shortly. "There are some small tables near a platform where very exotic dances are sometimes performed. If one wishes privacy, he may pay for as many guests as could possibly squeeze up to the table, which brings the cost of a cup of wine to about a pound. I may need some money, Pierre. Here is the key to my strong box. You had better come well supplied."

"It is not necessary to spend your money. I have," here he laughed in his turn, "quite a fund of my own, Sir John, that the minister gave me to cover my dealings with the pilots. I am sure I could not spend some of it better than at the Eastern Star."

"Have you, Pierre? You cannot surprise me any more. Hurry back then, and meet me there."

Pierre left the captain and urged his horse as fast as he safely could through the crowded street, and passed the gates in the outer wall. The Lady lay quietly at her wharf some distance beyond the public stables. Pierre left his horse, and inquired of the groom whether there were a tavern in the direction he was going, and gave the man a gold coin. The groom said there were taverns in every direction and mentioned one that he believed would afford a noble Frank with gold in his purse everything a man could ask for. Pierre pretended to be a little drunk, and stumbled off toward the place, bracing himself from time to time against the cold salt-crusted stones of the wall. When he was sure he was out of sight, he ran as if the Devil were at his heels.

Jacques of Bourges was standing watch on the dock.

"Shield your lantern, Jacques," Pierre called in a low voice; "it is Pierre. I want to go aboard the Lady. I do not wish to be observed."

With wonderful presence of mind, Jacques pretended to examine a crack in the planks under his feet, kneeling close to the lantern so that his cloak almost smothered it. "God speed you, sir," he whispered as Pierre flew through the grateful shadow like the wind and leaped aboard the Lady.

There was no light in his own cabin, but the captain's lamp was burning low, to conserve oil, since Justin was known to be ashore. Pierre opened the door of the great cabin and was inside in an instant. He fished out the note and held it up to the lamp, and then he knew why he had come to Trebizond. The missive was terse and unequivocal. It read:

BERNARD DE COUCY, TO OGLI PASHA—Greeting, Good Health, and Long Life:

Ilderim is dead of the drug. I take this only desperate means of informing Your Excellency, praying always that my words meet no eye but your own, that the last box never reached the Friar. Dispatch no more till this dreadful mischance is rectified. Beware of the so-called "auditor-general," Pierre, whose unaccountable knowledge of Turkish discovered our secret to the minister. He is sent to spy on you. You will know how to deal with him.

Pierre stifled a whistle of amazement. De Coucy himself! he thought. That fat, pompous, ineffectual snob! Under all his cloak of petty maliciousness, the genuine unalloyed evil the minister spoke of and could not recognize! The Devil knows how to disguise himself as a peevish imp!

It was not so hard to think evil of Ogli and his eunuch. That that precious pair should smuggle jewelry and trade illicitly in opium seemed the most likely thing in the world.

There remained the note to dispose of, which he did not wish to destroy and could not safely carry on his person. He opened the door a crack. The decks of the Lady were dark and quiet. He quickly left the great cabin, closing the door softly behind him, and tiptoed into his own dark little room where he threw off the heavy mantle that had oppressed him all day and put on the lightest jacket he owned. He hid the note in the point of the shoe he had worn when he rode with Claire, along with the ivory tube containing the letter which the factor in Constantinople had written.

Then he buckled on his money belt under his jacket, his purse, De Coucy's sword, and Abdul's dagger. He was aware that his weapons were too ornamental for the plain garb he now wore, but he could not help that. He vaulted over the rail to the dock again, and Jacques of Bourges, who heard his light running steps on the wharf, again examined the green waves of the Black Sea through the crack in the planks. He noticed Pierre's considerable armament flashing in the dark. "Don't get stuck again, Pierre!" he cautioned.

Pierre paused only a moment: "I shall perhaps be looked for,

Jacques," he said. "If my guess is correct, they will be pleasant men with good manners, speaking French. They will be Greeks, however, my friend, and wonderfully anxious to murder me."

"Saints!" muttered Jacques, "I shall call the ship's company and we'll throw them into the sea."

"You dare not. They will be sent by a great Trapezuntian lord."

"Then I shall not know you, Pierre. I never heard of you."

"No, just say I am at the inn—say you think I may be at the inn called the 'Fair Haven.' Adieu, Jacques!"

"Au revoir," the sailor replied, too cautiously for him to hear. "St. Michael-of-Peril go with you, Pierre."

Pierre had some difficulty convincing the guards at the gate of the inner wall that he was the same Frank official who, in a long furred mantle of blue velvet, had ridden Baltha Ogli's well known horse to the stables so short a time before. But a Turkish-speaking sergeant, for a heavy French gold piece, instantly recognized him, and courteously directed him to the tavern of the Eastern Star, which was big, near by, and unmistakable.

A courteous Greek at the door, whose duty in life was to see through the clothes and into the purses of the patrons who sought to enter Trebizond's gaudiest tavern, had some trouble classifying the hatless Frank. But Pierre took a gold piece from his purse and slipped it into the man's hand, which simultaneously closed on the gold and motioned an attendant to open both the doors. Pierre addressed the man he had bribed in Turkish: "I hope there is a table near the platform. I shall want it for myself and a guest; he may be here already."

At the sound of the pure Turkish from the lips of so obvious a Westerner and the sight of the jeweled weapons, the man instantly assumed that Pierre was some European ambassador, whose youth and important station in life were amply sufficient cause for him to visit the Eastern Star and to visit it incognito. He offered to conduct Pierre to just such a table, which he insisted had been reserved for just such a guest. But Pierre preferred to be less conspicuous. "A waiter will do very well, thank you," he said.

The man replied, "I quite understand, my lord."

But it would have been hard to be conspicuous among the Greek, European, and Asiatic clientele of the Eastern Star. Pierre saw a Chinaman in a yellow robe sitting alone at a table. He wore a curious golden hat with a stiff, flat, upright projection on top that was perhaps a mark of his rank. A servant fanned him with a small feather fan, and perhaps he was on fire internally, for there was a thin wisp of blue smoke coming out of his nostrils. And then Pierre noticed that he was eating the smoke out of a long, bamboo tube with a little bowl of fire at the end. There were groups of Europeans at other tables, some of them wearing their cuirasses. A prudent precaution, Pierre thought, and he wished he had had the time to put on his own. There were a few Persians in their long, loose, baggy trousers that looked so exactly like skirts, but that could part for easier riding. Turkish trousers were a little tighter, and the Indians wore tighter ones still. None of the Eastern clothes allowed so much freedom, of course, as the skintight hose of the Europeans.

But in all the colorful, crowded room nobody wore anything like the white and gold tunic of a Knight of the Collar, and since it was not visible, Pierre assumed that the captain had purposely delayed his arrival for some reason of his own. That Basil already missed the note from De Coucy, Pierre was sure. But he had no fear that the captain would be set upon, because he was far across the room when Lala Bey threw the manifests around; he could not possibly have taken the note. But it was hard to be sure, and he would have given a good many broad gold pieces for a glimpse of Justin's honest face.

The waiter took him to an inconspicuous table near the wall. Pierre ordered a bottle of French wine and paid for it. He also paid for the privacy of the table and the attentions of the waiter, and then he furtively weighed his purse under the table. It was very light. He wished he had had the wit to transfer some of the gold from his money belt while he had been aboard the ship, but there had been no time. He managed to reach under his jacket and extract a small handful of coins from one of the pockets of the belt. He slipped them as unobtrusively as he could into his purse, and slid his closed fingers down its long, velvet body so that the coins would not make a noise. He thought: A few more days of this city and I'll turn into a juggler, like the eunuch.

But nobody was looking at him, because the entertainment had begun. Glancing at the platform where two men and a girl had begun to dance, Pierre could understand why no one was looking at him. One of the men had on a costume of cloth of silver, cunningly marked in chalk to look like a suit of plate mail. The girl was dressed in a bit of seaweed and glistening with an oil that looked like water but did not dry. She had obviously been shipwrecked, for the purpose of the dance, with one survivor on an alien, lustful shore, for the other dancer was dressed in a satyr's costume consisting mostly of fur from the waist down. Pierre assumed that there was only one way for such a dance to end, which it did, after a protracted, exciting while, with the death of the knight and the dreadful, but not quite visible, fate of the maiden.

At the climax of the dance, with the Europeans clapping their hands, beating their cups against the tables and shouting for more, and the politer, more orderly Easterners murmuring their approval in singsong hums, a courteous young Turk paused at Pierre's table and requested permission to sit. Pierre had attempted to keep his eye open for the captain, but, like everyone else, he had become absorbed in the dance. Now he saw that not a single seat remained in the tavern. Even the Chinaman was no longer alone: his own servant had sat down beside him to keep other guests from disturbing his Celestial master. Justin was nowhere in sight. Servants and sailors, who could not afford the tables, stood three deep around the entrance of the Eastern Star. Presumably they paid something for their standing room.

"Certainly," Pierre said. "I am expecting a guest, however, who seems temporarily to have lost himself on the waterfront. I shall not, perhaps, enjoy your company long."

"I shall leave at once if he arrives," the Turk replied.

"I did not mean that, Effendi. The tavern is getting too crowded for the quiet talk I planned with my friend. It is I who shall leave."

"While you remain, I beg you to be my guest," the Turk said. "I never heard a Frank speak my language so well."

Pierre thought he had never heard a Turk speak it so badly. The young man did not look Turkish, and his hands appeared a shade lighter than his face.

"I am Abou Ayub."

The problematical Turk volunteered the information as if he were anxious to establish his identity. "I have just guided a Persian caravan from a great distance. I heard that Irene was dancing tonight, and naturally I wanted to witness her performance."

Pierre wondered if Abou Ayub wore gloves, on the back of his camel, in the desert, but he said: "So does everyone, noble Abou Ayub. Listen to them roar! But I am afraid you have missed the dance. My own name is Pierre and I come from France."

A Turk should have been able to say Pierre, but Abou Ayub avoided his name.

"Of course, I am called Peter, in Trebizond," Pierre said, and immediately Abou Ayub called him Peter Effendi.

Pierre was certain the man was Greek, and he loosened Abdul's dagger slightly in its scabbard. But if the man was sent from Ogli, he was singularly careless of his mission, whatever it was. He ordered a bottle of very expensive wine and kept looking toward the empty platform.

"Perhaps Irene will dance again," he said.

"I hope so myself," said Pierre, so earnestly that Abou Ayub smiled, mistaking him completely. Pierre was thinking how convenient it would be to get out of the Eastern Star when everybody was looking at the dance. Pierre did not think a murderer, bent on his destruction, would be so guileless as to imagine him really interested in the dance, and a little of his suspicion of the pseudo-Turk disappeared.

The noisy Europeans continued their shouting for more entertainment. The quiet Chinese, who had not appeared to look at the dance, drew a long, silken purse with a yellow tassel from his lap and said something to his servant. The man drew out a handful of round, Ming gold pieces with square holes punched through their centers and threw them upon the stage. Instantly the air was full of the coinage of Europe and Asia: gold from the side tables, silver from the center tables, and a vast shower of copper and brass and bronze from the standing commoners around the entrance. A man with a broom swept up the coins into a little pile and another man carried them off the stage to a safe place. Irene was wrecked in her seaweed again, the silver-clad knight was killed again, and Irene was about to suffer her fate again, when three very obvious Greeks, dressed up in jackets and hose and pointed shoes like Frenchmen, pushed their way to Pierre's table and requested, in very bad French, the impossible privilege of sitting down with him. The table was much too small. If Abou Ayub were a false Turk, these were falser Franks. Pierre was glad his companion was armed.

"Beware of these men, good Abou Ayub, or whatever your name is. They are no countrymen of mine, and I think they mean me no good."

Abou Ayub suddenly found his Greek tongue and ordered the men out of the place with an astonishingly imperious gesture which was perfectly understandable to Pierre, though his words were not. It ill became a Turk, no matter how proficient in Greek, to spoil the entertainment of the entire clientele of the Eastern Star. Men shouted angrily at him from every part of the room.

Abou Ayub foolishly drew his sword.

That was just what Ogli's men wanted. A fight with all the witnesses on their side! Nothing could have been more welcome. All their swords leaped out of their scabbards at once, and Abou Ayub fell to the floor

257

from a stroke that slit his turban clean through, like a knife going through butter.

Pierre drew De Coucy's sword and Abdul's dagger as well, and kicked the table over Abou Ayub's recumbent body, hitting one of the assailants a crashing blow in the shins. He straddled the Turk, though he did not think he could protect him long against three men, or perhaps himself, for that matter, and parried the swords that leaped at him from all directions.

The dancing stopped. Patrons drew away from the fighting men. The cumbersome machinery of the tavern, designed to stop such things, slowly got under way. A few of the Europeans forgot the dance and realized that the three disguised Greeks had murdered the Turk and were about to slay a Western countryman before their eyes.

Pierre thrust quickly at one of his attackers and ran the man's sword arm through and withdrew the bloody blade to parry a flashing slash from another man.

He caught the blow fair and square near the hilt of the sword, but the miserable blade of De Coucy's ornamental weapon broke off at the pommel and left him holding the jeweled hilt. He glanced down, hoping he could pick up the blade and use it as a pike. And saw an astonishing thing:

The young Turk was alive and moving slightly. Under his split and displaced turban there was a bright, steel skullcap, which had turned the blow, and around its rim was graven a circlet of hearts! And he thought he saw under the canvas desert shoes the glint of a pearl and the flash of a red buskin, but he could not be sure and there was no time to look. The blade was too far away to reach.

He hurled the jeweled sword hilt into the face of one of the men who had aimed a terrific blow at his head. The other man's sword slashed at his neck and he could not parry it efficiently with his dagger. Pierre felt a sudden fiery cut in his chest. He saw the jeweled hilt land squarely in the face of the man whose sword was that instant coming down. It was, he was sure, the last thing he would see in this world.

It was actually the last thing he was to see in the Eastern Star. The hilt was full of points where a good many of the carelessly set jewels had fallen out of their settings the minute the useless weapon went into action. It cut like an animal's claw when it hit, and the man winced. His sword turned in his hand, and Pierre went down unconscious under a blow from the flat of the blade, falling over the body of Abou Ayub.

One of Ogli's men had a punctured sword arm. Another had a bloody, mangled face. The other, who was unharmed, was a sergeant, and in charge of the mission, which was to take Pierre alive, if it could be conveniently done. The Turk did not matter, of course. He had attacked them first. The sergeant told the men to take Pierre out of the tavern, but they suddenly had to defend themselves against a determined little group of armed and angry Europeans who had come, they thought, too late to prevent, but not too late to avenge, the death of the Westerner.

But these men were roughly pushed aside by a great many of the commoners who had stood around the door. The instant Abou Ayub had drawn his sword they had rushed to his assistance. He had gone down before they could reach him. Pierre had fallen only a second later. There were so many of them that the Westerners were hopelessly outnumbered. They were thrust aside by the sheer weight of the bodies of running men. One or two attempted to fight their way through to Ogli's assassins, but they were instantly disarmed, thrown to the floor and sat upon. Some tables overturned, and for a time the tavern was in an indescribable uproar. The commoners picked Abou Ayub off the floor and carried him out to the street. They were not in the least concerned with Pierre. In the confusion Ogli's men, who were desperately concerned with Pierre, had a chance to carry him out of the tavern also, bleeding and unconscious.

The efficient Trapezuntian police, summoned by the management, appeared, but there was nothing to do. The Westerners put up their swords. Almost no men were standing about the door now.

It was not particularly late in the evening. The servant who had swept up the coins threw sand on the bloody floor so that no one might slip and hurt himself. In a little while the table Pierre and Abou Ayub had occupied was reoccupied by two new patrons of the establishment. Someone called for Irene again, and the management decided that the incident could be most quickly forgotten if the popular dancer should be shipwrecked for the third time that night in her seaweed costume.

# CHAPTER

## ❊ 23 ❊

THE SLY, AMBITIOUS TRIO of men that Ogli sent to seek out and rob the auditor-general of the monstrously incriminating note were not fools. Since they had not already killed Pierre, they could not now immediately do so, because it was too early in the evening, there were too many people around, and even in Trebizond a bleeding, unconscious man could neither be searched nor murdered without endless embarrassing questions by the watchmen and police. Therefore the sergeant bade his men make themselves as presentable as possible. The one bound up his sword arm with a tight bandage that he tore from the lining of his jacket. The other held a handkerchief up to the cuts in his face and wiped off some of the blood. Pierre was breathing and beginning to moan. The cut on his chest was not visible, but his jacket was wet with blood. The sergeant and the man who was not hurt threw Pierre across a horse. The sergeant mounted behind him and kept him from falling to the street, and they galloped over a wooden bridge beyond the walls, spanning the great ravine to the west of the city.

This wooden bridge had been built to accommodate the commercial caravan traffic. It paralleled the stone bridge, which was for military purposes and actually a part of the fortifications. It was lightly built and made to be burned, if the city were ever besieged. For many peaceful years, however, it had served to keep the caravans and their hundreds of followers, who might at any time have been hostile soldiers disguised as merchants, safely out of the heart of the city, confined within the double sea walls. This bridge, over which so many foreigners passed, was heavily guarded. But the guards were always polite and obliging, as was fitting to a corps of men that dealt largely with Oriental travelers.

It was known that the Grand Duke Alexius chose the guards for their good manners and their knowledge of the Eastern tongues. But not even Baltha Ogli's usually well informed household knew the reason for their chatty inquisitiveness.

The captain on the bridge was acquainted with Ogli's sergeant and he questioned him courteously.

"You have a bloody bundle on your horse tonight, friend Leo. What happened to the poor Frank? Where are you taking him?"

"Alas, Gregory Captain, the sailor is possessed. He and a heathen Turk drew their swords on us while we were watching a dance at the Eastern Star."

"Who do you suppose he is, friend Leo?"

"I have no idea. But he nearly killed us. We are taking him to the Church of the Hagia Sophia, where a priest, no doubt, will be able to exorcise the demon out of him."

It was no part of the bridge captain's duty to observe that there were closer churches, and that the Frank was bleeding badly.

"Shall I send a torch man with you, Leo? The way is a little dark."

"My master will be delighted with your courtesy. I shall make it my business to tell him of it, captain. But we are riding fast, and an unmounted man could not keep up with us. A lantern would be greatly appreciated, however!"

The captain ordered a lantern given the sergeant. Leo and his two soldiers rode rapidly off in the direction of the church.

Perhaps fifty seconds after the sound of their footsteps died away on the wide, well trodden route, a messenger spurred furiously across the bridge toward the city, with a good description of Pierre in his head, a verbatim report of the conversation on his tongue, and a mental note to inform the chief of police in the palace that Ogli's men were disguised as Franks. If the chief of police, whose business it was to know what went on in Trebizond and to whom a number of breathless officials had already reported that night, considered the incident sufficiently important, the Grand Duke Alexius himself might well hear of it next morning in his bath.

Pierre slowly regained consciousness, not to behold the fires of purgatory, but the smoky flame of a watchman's lamp. The wire frame that protected its yellow shade of greased goatskin swung repeatedly against his head as the horse galloped. His head was hanging down toward the road, which he saw flying beneath the horse's hoofs, and he saw very close to his face, which was streaked with drying blood that

261

had run out of the wound in his chest, a hose-clad leg ending in a long Western shoe set in a stirrup that had never come from Europe.

He heard the men talking Greek, but, of course, he did not know what they were saying. He remembered Abou Ayub and the Eastern Star, but they seemed far away and unimportant. He was very dizzy; his chest pain was minor compared with the dreadful ache in his head where the sword had hit him, and even that was less distressing than the nausea which the blow, his cut, and the motion of the horse caused almost to overwhelm him. He grew wider awake all the time and fought back the need to vomit.

Leo and his men came to a bend in the road around a little promontory that jutted into a deep, narrow, boulder-strewn gorge, midway between the city and the church that was supposed to be their destination. They reined in their horses and the sergeant said, "This will do."

At that moment Pierre retched over the sergeant's leg and shoe.

"Pig!" cried the sergeant angrily, "You shall die a little slower for that!"

Then he threw Pierre from the horse, and they searched him.

There was a young crescent moon setting over the Turkish slope of the distant Caucasus mountains on the horizon. It gave almost no light whatsoever, and the thousand stars overhead served only to increase the darkness. This region was lonely, infertile, and desolate. They heard the melancholy bell of an ox, grazing sleepily in a stubbly pasture beyond the ravine, and the faint splashing of an almost dried up little stream at the bottom of the gorge; but the night was otherwise absolutely quiet.

The fall from the horse had stunned Pierre into momentary insensibility again. Not finding the note, they stripped off his clothes and examined them inside and out, including his shoes, running their fingers into the long points, but of course there was nothing.

Pierre was stripped now of all but his drawers. His stomach had emptied itself, and the strong, cool wind, blowing on his body, revived him completely. His senses returned with a rush, and gave him the wit to lie quiet and pretend to be still unconscious. He saw his dagger lying near his money belt and the clothes they were examining in the light of the lantern.

When it was apparent that the note was not in his clothing, the sergeant emptied the contents of his money belt into the road and felt in the pockets. The note was not there. The coins, all gold, in a pile close to the lantern, made the sergeant's eyes stare.

"The Frank is rich," he observed. "Now I shall question him."

They dragged Pierre to the side of the road and sat him against a low boulder, throwing his arm over the top, which happened to be rather flat, to help support him. One man sat on his legs, another held the lantern close to his face. Pierre opened his eyes as if he were just coming to. He moaned a little, which he did not have to force to make sound convincing, and lifted his head. He saw that their swords were all unsheathed, and that Abdul's dagger was just beyond his feet.

"Tell us where you hid the note," the sergeant commanded in bad, but comprehensible French.

Pierre shook his head, and muttered weakly that he could not understand what was said. The sergeant repeated the command in Turkish.

"I heard you speak Turkish to the Turk in the Eastern Star," he said. "Perhaps you prefer that heathen tongue. If you do, that is perfectly all right with me. I have all night to converse with you if necessary. Now, perhaps, if you tell me quickly and courteously where you hid the note, I shall forget about how you befouled my clothes and let you live."

"It's in the palace," Pierre said, as if he could hardly gasp out the words. "It is in safe hands." Much too late, he wished he had actually taken it there.

His reply made the sergeant think a moment. Then he said: "You are lying. You were observed to pass the palace and go to the waterfront. It is foolish to try to lie." Then he addressed the man who had been hit in the face with the hilt of De Coucy's sword. "Give me that stone, Manuel," he said. He pointed to a stone a little larger than a man's two fists, lying within the light cast by the lantern.

The man reached over to get it. He had a notion of what the sergeant was thinking. "Would it not be better to stick the Frank a little with his pretty dagger, sir?"

"He'd probably faint again. He must have lost a good deal of blood already." The sergeant took the stone and leaped to the top of the flat boulder that Pierre was leaning against. He knelt with both knees on Pierre's arm. Pierre's hand was lying open on the boulder.

"Where did you hide the note?" the sergeant asked, menacing Pierre with the stone.

Pierre tensed his body and prepared to dodge. The sergeant had raised the stone as if to strike Pierre on the head.

"The note is in the palace," Pierre repeated slowly.

The sergeant struck him with the stone and ground it into his flesh, not on the head, which might have rendered him unconscious, but on his open hand. The blow was shrewd and unexpected and terribly painful.

But as a torture designed to elicit information it was stupid, too quick and brutal to result in anything but eventual failure. Basil would have known how to do it better. For a hand grows quickly numb after such a blow, even if one sits quietly and thinks about it, which Pierre did not do.

His gasp of pain was so loud that the men were astonished there was so much breath still left in him. He snatched his arm from under the sergeant's knees and struggled to his feet. The sergeant leapt to Pierre's back like a cat and caught him round the neck, trying frantically to throw him off balance to the ground again. But such a hold was not impossible for anyone tutored by the Chevalier de la Salle to break.

Pierre kicked his knee with terrific force into the face of the man who was still clinging to his legs, throwing him to the ground for an instant. Then he reached back with his good hand, caught the sergeant's neck and hurled the man over his head and fell upon him with every intention of killing him instantly if he could. Both of the other men drew their swords, though one of them did so very awkwardly with his left hand. Pierre and the sergeant, wrestling on the ground, rolled over and away from the lantern. Neither of the standing men dared strike for fear of killing their sergeant. The one who was wounded dropped his sword and ran back to get the light, and when he came up with it, both men shouted a loud warning to the sergeant, because the edge of the chasm was perilously close. One of them desperately raised his sword, heedless of which man it might strike. But before the blow fell, the struggling men disappeared over the edge of the chasm. The man with the wounded arm held up the lantern and they both looked down, but they could see nothing. For when Pierre and the sergeant fell, they knocked a great many stones out of the sloping, dirt wall of the gorge. The stones and dirt fell with them, and the wind caught the dust and blew it in a cloud up over the lip of the gorge into the men's faces. The man Pierre had kicked in the nose was now bleeding profusely. He held up his sleeve to it, but it was painful to touch and felt pulpy, as if it were broken. His face looked more battered than his comrade's, which the hilt of De Coucy's sword had ripped open in several places.

The little avalanche of rocks and rubble spent itself quickly. Most of the debris lodged against the multitude of outcropping boulders. A few of the heaviest stones thumped all the way to the bottom. There was a splash or two, and then the night was perfectly still again.

The disappearance and probable death of both Pierre and the sergeant had happened very quickly. The two men at the edge of the ravine looked at each other's bloody faces in the lantern light. They were both thinking the same thing and reluctant to talk about it.

Quite unexpectedly, they heard the light, leisurely noises that mules make when they walk. Whatever strangers were approaching were still some distance around the bend in the road.

The man holding the lantern lowered it as far as he could down the face of the slope. Both Pierre and the sergeant were visible, motionless, lodged, like the stuff of the landslide, against the big, round boulders.

"I think I might be able to climb down to the Frank if I had the use of my other arm," the wounded man said, "but I could never reach poor Leo."

"They are undoubtedly both dead," said the other.

"That is exactly what I think, Manuel."

They looked at each other again; they had known each other for a long time.

"Ogli Pasha will be furious," said the man who had been addressed as Manuel.

"I am terrified at the prospect of facing the eunuch," said the other.

One of the men below in the gorge moaned, weakly, but audibly.

"No one could survive such a fall," Manuel said positively.

"Certainly not. They are both dead. And we dare not go back and admit how miserably we bungled this business, do we, Manuel?"

"I, for one, certainly, dare not."

"I have heard that the Turks often deal courteously with the Trapezuntians, who sometimes settle among them, Manuel."

"The same thought has occurred to me. The dead Frank had a fortune in gold on him."

"Ogli Pasha will never miss it. Let us admit, good Manuel, like honest men, that we have failed our master and we face a terrible punishment at the hands of the eunuch, who loves to hurt people. Is it not wiser and more profitable to divide the Frank's gold and fly over the mountains to the Turks?"

"You are keen and logical, my friend. You are absolutely right. But let us hurry, for I hear someone coming."

They rushed back to the pile of gold in the road and hurriedly filled their slender purses, which were much too small to hold all of it. With Abdul's dagger they slit Pierre's jacket in two and hastily divided the rest into remarkably equal piles, considering the frantic speed at which they worked.

"I shall not mind marrying a wife or two in Turkey," Manuel whispered, glancing over his shoulder. Their hands flew and a good deal of the dust of the road, some of it bloody, got mixed up with the gold in their clutching fingers. "Do not take more than your share, my friend. Observe that I have the use of only one arm."

"Nay, Manuel, we will divide it again as soon as we are out of danger. Like good old friends, Manuel."

"Of course."

The mules sounded very close now. The pile of gold was gone and wrapped in the remnants of Pierre's jacket. Manuel kicked the lantern into the ravine. They leaped onto their horses and galloped like the wind.

"With good luck we can reach the frontier by this time tomorrow," Manuel called to his companion. "My horse is fresh, and I can move my sword arm a little now."

He could not move his sword arm.

"Mine is just as fresh as yours, friend Manuel. And my nose has stopped bleeding. I never felt better, I think, in my life."

His nose had not stopped bleeding, and he felt dreadful.

"We will stick closely together, like good friends," Manuel said. "We must both tell the same story at the border."

"Naturally we must."

Each man was weighing his chances of getting there alive. Neither thought the other would quite make it.

Back in the ravine the goatskin shade of the lantern took fire and blazed smokily up like a beacon light on Pierre, who had started to struggle painfully back up the slope to the road.

S HORTLY AFTER MANUEL and his companion fled into the dark, laden with stolen money and protesting friendship for each other, a man on foot bearing a lighted torch appeared round the bend of the road. He wore the light, tight woolen leggings of a peasant, wrapped around his legs to the knee. A baggy pair of trousers was tucked into them. His jacket was a sleeveless sort of vest over a rough woolen shirt. He walked fast and easily, as if he were used to it.

He was followed by two men on horseback, armed with swords and wearing cuirasses over their knee-length tunics, and cloaks around their shoulders against the wind. Behind these leaders rode half a dozen men-at-arms armed with pikes, swords, and arbalests. Some of them carried small lanterns. The arbalests would have marked them as Greek, if their garb had not, for the Oriental nations never generally adopted the mechanical, slow-firing, but terribly effective crossbow. The last two men led sumpter mules by rope halters. Slung over their backs were colorful camel bags of rich Eastern manufacture, the convenient carryalls that were common among Christian and Moslem travelers alike. The bags were lightly loaded. It was not unusual to travel at night on that wide, well known way, and the scanty burden of the pack animals indicated a short journey.

The oil had leaked out of the lantern tank and saturated what was left of the shade, which now burned like a wick and stank in the wind. The torch man ran to the side of the road and thrust his head over the edge of the ravine to see what was burning. He saw the flaming, battered lantern and the body of the sergeant far below it, hanging grotesquely over a dry, dead, projecting root. The bush or tree it had once supported and fed had long since washed out of the bank and fallen into the gorge. The body bent sharply in the middle and hung like two ends of a wet rag. His back was obviously broken.

Another man, almost naked, appeared not to have fallen so far, for he lay, just out of reach, on a little ledge below the edge of the chasm.

Pierre had climbed back that far and lain down on the safe ledge to rest, and immediately fainted, exhausted by his struggle and weak with the loss of blood.

One of the men-at-arms discovered Pierre's Western shoes and hose. The torch man turned and reported what he had observed.

"I am not anxious to play the Good Samaritan to drunken Franks who fall into St. Sumelas' river," said one of the men on horseback. "Maybe they tried to go swimming. It is no business of mine." The other man saw the jewels of Abdul's dagger flashing in the road. He instantly dismounted and picked it up. Lying close to it in the dust were a couple of gold pieces that Manuel and his companion had half buried in their excitement. He picked them up, also. One of them was sticky in his fingers.

"Bring your torch here, John," he called excitedly. In the bright light he held the ancient Turkish weapon and the coins up to the man who had first spoken.

"Look what the Franks left us in the road, sir," he said.

The leader looked, very critically, turning the dagger over in his hands and running his finger over the face of the freshly struck coin. "You've a good eye, Sylvester," he said. "It is more of the new French gold. It circulates quickly, doesn't it? And it has blood on it already. The dagger dates back at least three centuries. It would fetch £1,000 anywhere. A sultan would be proud to wear it." He drew it out of its scabbard. The delicate, curved, blue blade flashed in the torchlight. "No Turkish robber ever wore a dagger like this one."

"If he wore it, he wouldn't lose it," Sylvester observed.

"And if he lost it, it would be bloody," the leader added, "which this one is not. Besides, whoever heard of Turkish robbers so close to the city. Let me see his clothes."

Sylvester handed up to him Pierre's shoes and hose, which were all that could be found. The leader bent his thin, tanned face over them in the torchlight and felt the material with a knowledgeable hand, for all the world like a shrewd, young pawnbroker in a shop, pleased with a pledge and willing to advance a substantial amount on it.

"Whoever wore these was no sailor," he said. "It is pure Flanders wool, and the dye is fast. It may be worth while to stop for a few moments and look further into this interesting matter. The dagger, of course, is puzzling. See if the men can fish the Franks out of the gully, Sylvester. Perhaps St. Eugenius has sent me to play the Good Samaritan after all."

"Sir Theodore," the other said, in a friendly familiar way, "you are very confident of the Blessed Patron's favor, are you not?"

The mounted leader laughed again. He was in an excellent humor. "Confess that some one of the blessed hagiarchy up there," he cocked up his eye and grinned at the star-studded heavens, "has been wonderfully thoughtful of us tonight."

Sylvester went over to the edge of the ravine. The men had taken several lengths of rope, that were used to hobble the mules, out of the camel bags and knotted them together. One of them let himself down to the ledge where Pierre was lying. The light of the torches and lantern shone down on them, and the man bent over Pierre.

"He's alive!" he shouted. "Now grab his shoulders quickly when I pass him up to you. I don't like it down here!" He thought the rock that formed the ledge gave a little under their combined weights. "Ugh, but the Frank is heavy!"

To Pierre, half conscious again for an instant, it seemed that he was floating through the air, up to the starry sky, with a great light in his face. He held up his arms, and he felt them firmly grasped. The man climbed back up the knots in the rope, and the ledge tilted and fell thundering to the bottom of the gorge, starting a landslide that rattled and roared for several minutes. When the dust cleared away, the dead body of sergeant Leo and the dead root that had supported it had disappeared. Pierre lay on the road again and the man who had rescued him sat down on a rock and crossed himself, pale and shaking.

"I'll save no more Franks tonight for all the gold in Christendom!" he said.

"You'll not have to," the leader remarked, "you nor anyone else. You've made a sizable dam in St. Sumelas' brook with your avalanche, and I dare say the other Frank is at the bottom of it. Give this one a mouthful of brandy and take a nip for yourself. You could use it, friend."

But the man was too frightened to move for a moment, and one of the other men took an earthen bottle out of the camel bag and gave him a long pull at it. Then he poured some into Pierre's mouth.

Pierre heard the Greek spoken on all sides of him and felt the brandy in his throat. For the second time that night he awoke to the comparative comfort of the knowledge that he was neither in purgatory nor paradise.

"Thank you, Effendi," he muttered.

The leader raised his eyebrows. Turkish-speaking Franks were rare.

"You appear to have suffered an accident," he said. "What happened to you, pray?"

Pierre shook his head. His chest wound was slowly oozing blood. His right hand throbbed; it looked crushed. His whole body was bruised and badly scratched from his fall and bleeding in a dozen places.

One of the men unrolled his long leggings and wound one of them tightly around Pierre's chest to stop the bleeding. He bound up Pierre's hand, also, and examined the other cuts as if he were familiar with such things.

"The Frank won't die of the crushed hand," he said; "no bones stick through the skin. Since he hasn't already died of the cut in his chest, which must have closed once from the looks of it, he probably never will. The others look bad, but they are not deep. I think what he needs is another mouthful of brandy."

He held the bottle to Pierre's mouth, and Pierre swallowed some. It was sweeter than any spirit he had ever tasted, and it sent a flood of warmth through his body and gave him the strength to shiver so that he appeared suddenly seized with chill. One of the men threw a blanket around him.

The leader held up Abdul's dagger and said courteously, but without a trace of friendliness, "Where did you get this, Effendi?"

"I've always had it. I brought it from France."

"Where did you get the gold?"

"From France, too."

"I believe that, at least. How do you come to be so wounded?"

"Some men attacked me in the Eastern Star. They brought me here." Pierre thought swiftly. Never on a man so young, he thought, had he seen such a hard and calculating face. "They robbed me," he continued, "and decided to kill me. But I fought back, and one of the men and I fell off the road. I do not know what happened to them."

"How many were there?"

"Three, I think."

"What is your name?"

"Peter."

"Do you always carry gold on you?"

"As a rule."

"Why did your countrymen want to kill you?"

"Because they had robbed me, I suppose."

"Do you know who they were?"

"No."

Sylvester said in Greek that Trebizond was always full of Franks. "It could easily happen that a careless nobleman might fall victim to his own unscrupulous countrymen. But the Frank isn't very talkative, is he, Sir Theodore? Perhaps he is still faint."

"Observe his color," the leader continued. "I don't think he's as badly wounded as he pretends to be. He is just more cautious than most of the Westerners." Then he continued in Turkish: "You are severely wounded, Effendi. I don't think you could stand the ride back to the city alone."

"I think perhaps I could."

"Nay, I should hate to have your death on my conscience. Perhaps your assailants are still in the vicinity. Your wounds need attention. In a day or two, when you feel better, I shall send you back. In the meantime, whom do you wish me to send word to in Trebizond that you are safe, and in safe hands?"

"Tell John Justin, if you will, captain of the French king's ship, *Sainte-Eulalie*. He is probably now at the Eastern Star, waiting for me. Anybody could recognize him; he is wearing the white tunic and the silver collar of his order."

"Indeed," the leader remarked thoughtfully. "I shall bear the name in mind."

But nobody left the little band to carry a message to Sir John.

If, as he professed, the leader was concerned with Pierre's health, he showed it in an odd way. Pierre was forced to ride till dawn on the back of one of the sumpter mules, straddling a half-filled camel bag, completely surrounded by the men-at-arms, whose watchfulness prevented him from falling off his mount, and also from returning to Trebizond, if he had tried to.

They turned aside from the caravan route and followed a little used mule path through a wild, eroded terrain. Pierre was stupefied with fatigue. Periodically one of the men put the brandy to his lips. It numbed his pain and befuddled his mind. Under him, it seemed, a jolting mule had walked since the world began, and would walk, he knew, till it ended; and then perhaps his body would stop throbbing. In a tiny, rational fragment of his brain, Pierre realized that his senses were all askew.

With the coming of a little gray morning light he thought he saw

271

a mountain with an absolutely smooth perpendicular face rising in front of him, black against the sky. Incredibly high above the path that led round its base there was a mighty, gaping, square hole in the cliff, with white buildings in it, and men living in the buildings, for a chorus of chanting voices floated down into the valley out of the mountain. Such a thing could not be real.

Oddly, it was real. The monks of St. Sumelas' Monastery were chanting the prayers of Matins at the beginning of their religious day. The chorus came from the chapel of their cloistered buildings perched in a great natural cave in the rocky face of the mountain, accessible only by thousands and thousands of steps in a wooden scaffolding set against the precipitous cliff. Travelers more sober than Pierre had doubted their eyes at the prodigy.

In a direction and at a distance from the monastery which Pierre could only faintly surmise, the land in the growing light took on a happier, more fruitful look. The mule path emerged from the wild rocks and ravines and entered upon a broad plain, dotted with trees, beyond which rose the interminable chain of the Caucasus. Near them, on a little elevation, close to a road that stretched into invisibility to the south, stood a small, old castle with a newer structure like an Eastern caravansary at no great distance. A spring between the castle and the stone shelter had been walled to conserve its water, and the overflow formed a little stony brook that fed the castle moat.

Some of the battlements were in ruins, and in the outer walls there were numerous cracks, the result of long neglect and the frequent Trapezuntian earthquakes. Vegetation had sprouted in them and starved, staining the stones with decay.

The castle was dark and the bridge over the moat was up. Philelphus, Count of Mesembria, lord of the castle, had sharper ears than any of his small staff of servants. He always rose at dawn to assure himself that he could still see the sun. The world was a gloomy gray to the half-blind, aging man, full of shifting, colorless, ill defined shapes, and his hearing had grown more acute as a result of his affliction. When, as today, he found the light still there at dawn, he knelt and thanked God for it.

He called his steward with the words, "My son is here," and sent him to the castle gate to have the guards let down the bridge. The count had always been a slight man, like many of the old Pontic aristocrats, but his near blindness forced him to be inactive. He had kept much to his castle in recent years and his body was now heavy.

His hair, confined in a Phrygian cap, he let go untrimmed for months at a time. His beard was long and streaked with gray. Patience and self-discipline had imparted a placid expression to his countenance, which twenty years before had been noted for its fiery mobility. There was nothing now in his benign and patriarchal aspect to remind one that his courageous, and very unfortunate, exploits had almost restored the wealth of the ancient counts of Mesembria. He waited impatiently for his son.

Since there was no chirurgeon closer than the monastery, and he was never called to the castle unless a man was so sick as to need his spiritual as well as physical offices, Pierre's wounds were not cauterized. He was wrapped in blankets and put into a clean bed to shiver with a chill and babble in a delirious fever and get well if he could. The rough-and-ready man-at-arms, who had first examined him and pronounced that he would live, recognized two cardinal rules for the sick. Wounds were washed in water, diluted with brandy, and bound up to heal. Fevers were starved, and water was poured into the sufferer's mouth at frequent intervals. It was seldom necessary to summon the chirurgeon-priest and always more convenient not to have to.

With Pierre made as comfortable as possible and a man set over him to attend his wants, if he should voice any, and see that he did not fly out of the window, Theodore went to the count's rooms. In the presence of his father all the hardness that Pierre had observed went out of his face.

"Little Father," he said, "the news is all good. We have been paid, all in new French gold, for the rent of our storehouse."

"Has our own rent been paid?"

"Every penny. And there is a comfortable balance."

"I am glad, son. I am always glad when our miserable khan is empty. Did you behave yourself?"

"I did, sir. Better than usual. Wait till I tell you!"

"Did the men behave?"

"All but John. The silver collar of an oddly dressed Western knight caught his eye. He stole it in the city."

"That was foolish. Did he kill the man?"

"No, sir. He tapped him ever so lightly on the head. The man was big and powerful. He got up bellowing like a bull, waving his sword, and we all ran. Fortunately there was a scuffle of some sort at the Eastern Star and we succeeded in losing ourselves."

"I hope you disciplined the man."

273

"He had to carry a torch all the way home. When it burned out, I made him walk anyway. We killed no one, sir. In fact, we saved a man's life."

"That is the best news I have ever heard from your lips. I hope you always save lives instead of taking them. It has often occurred to me in my meditations, Theodore, that if every son could profit by his father's mistakes, heaven itself could scarcely be sweeter than this earth in the space of a few generations. Let me see your face, son."

Theodore bent his head close to his father's hand. The count touched his face and smoothed out with his fingers the furious scowl that suddenly contorted the young man's brow.

"I knew you had that wicked thought in your mind, son. Stop it. I have forbidden revenge. Tell me, did I hear a strange voice in the house?"

Theodore stood up again and smiled.

"That is the man we saved, Little Father. He is naked and wounded, apparently the victim of robbers. But he seems to have had a sum of the new French gold on him, as well as a valuable, curious old Turkish dagger. He is very sick and taciturn right now. But I am confident that he is someone of importance. When he is well again he will undoubtedly be grateful for our hospitality."

"And offer a substantial sum to bring it to an end. Do I understand you, Theodore?"

"Certainly, Father."

"It is no disgrace for a Pontic gentleman to hold a rich Frank to ransom. But for the Franks, some generations ago, we ourselves would be the lords of Trebizond, and the name of Comnenus would never have been heard in the land. Ah, well. Treat him courteously, of course, but delay his return until he is willing to pay handsomely for it."

"I was sure you would approve, sir."

"Naturally, I do."

# CHAPTER

# * 25 *

PIERRE SLEPT a shallow sleep all during the first and second day, hag-ridden with nightmares of desperate fights, all of which he lost, on the Lady, in the Eastern Star, and on lonely Trapezuntian mule paths. Actually, there were real people in the room from time to time, solicitously wondering whether he would live or die, but their voices came to him like a chorus of men out of a cave in a monstrous mountain, and once he thought he heard the sweet whisper of Chadaze, warning him that he was not alone and had better be wary.

It was dark outside the castle when he woke up, hungry, thirsty, and rational, on the evening of the second day. A man-at-arms was dozing on a rickety stool, leaning his tired back against a rich Persian tapestry against the wall. He heard Pierre move and instantly turned up the flame of a large, brass, Eastern lamp such as wealthy Arab sheiks had in their desert tents. He held out to Pierre a silver goblet of water. Pierre half sat up in bed and took it in his hand and drank it all. "More," he said, and the man filled it from a pitcher and gave it to him.

"I am hungry," Pierre said, but the man shook his head. Pierre thought perhaps the man did not understand him. "I am hungry," he repeated in Latin, French, Italian, and English, exhausting his not inconsiderable store of languages.

"It is better for you to starve yourself for a while," the man said in Turkish. "You will get well quicker that way."

"I feel pretty well now," Pierre answered. "Nobody can live on a diet of water."

"I am sorry, sir. I have my orders, and water is all you get. Of course, you may have any amount of water you desire. In fact, if you do not ask for enough of it, I shall be forced to pour it down your throat. Those are my orders."

"Who gave you such foolish orders?"

"That does not concern you, sir. Go to sleep again," and he turned down the lamp and went back to his stool. Pierre looked at his little cell-like room. The window was high. The table and chairs were incredibly poor, old, and battered. Yet his blankets were softer than any he had ever felt, the tapestry was extremely rich, and the lamp was patently rare and valuable. Everything little and movable was Eastern and costly; everything big and stationary was drab and mean. The contrast struck him, but he was too hungry to think much about it. *"Peste!"* he swore in good French, and turned over to obey the man's orders and forget his hunger. His guardian nurse sleepily opened his eyes and made a mental note to report to Sir Theodore that the Frank was reacting nicely.

He slept all the next day, and in the evening Sir Theodore visited him. Pierre was wide awake when he came. The young man drew up the stool, felt Pierre's head for a fever, and said: "I am glad you are more at ease, Sir Peter. Probably you can get up tomorrow. One of my men, who is almost a doctor, dressed your wound yesterday while you were asleep. It is not deep and it has closed. He says you will recover."

"I am very glad, sir."

"I am just as glad, though my reason is different. I am Theodore, son of the Count Philelphus of Mesembria. How does your hand feel, Sir Peter?"

"It hurts."

"That is to be expected. There is hardly any skin left on it. Can you move it?"

Pierre tried. "Yes, Sir Theodore. It feels better when I do not, however."

"That is not to be wondered at. Probably a rock struck it when you fell."

"I remember a rock. Your man refused me food. Am I a guest or a prisoner, and if I am a prisoner, is it your plan to starve me to death?"

"You will not be starved, Sir Peter. Your continued existence in this world is almost as precious to me as it is to yourself. But no chirurgeon is available to care for you and we must, perforce, nurse you back to health the way we do ourselves when, sometimes, we meet with an accident. You will be fed tomorrow."

Pierre said nothing.

"As soon as you can ride again, you will be given a horse and a sword, since you appear to have lost your own, and put upon the way to the city. You could not walk so far and, of course, you should go armed. You will also need a few articles of clothing, since all we could find of yours were a pair of hose and shoes. Naturally, you cannot ride naked back to Trebizond."

"Naturally not," Pierre said. He suspected what the polite Greek was driving at.

"Horses and swords are costly, of course," Sir Theodore continued, "and you will want no peasant's garb. It has occurred to me that your knowledge of the value of such things, to say nothing of the gratitude that you feel toward us for plucking you out of the ravine where you would surely have died, might express itself in a substantial gift to the count, my father. We are not rich, and I am sure he would accept it."

Pierre's premonition was confirmed. "What is my ransom to amount to? And am I to be tortured with hunger until I agree to a larger sum?"

Pierre was not prepared for the violent reaction his words caused. His young captor flushed dark as a Turk under his tan and glared fiercely at him.

"Torture is never mentioned here," he answered, controlling his voice with difficulty. "Should it be necessary to kill you, you will not feel a thing. Believe me, I know exactly how to do it painlessly."

"That is a comfort, in a small way," Pierre said. He almost liked the man. "I think I should beg your pardon for inadvertently offending you."

"It is granted. I might add, Sir Peter, that you look to me well on the way to recovery already. You will soon find out, if you have not already observed, that my force is small. It would simplify matters greatly if you would give me your knightly word not to try to escape till your ransom is paid."

"That I cannot do, Sir Theodore. I am sorry."

"Very well; though it is customary."

"I know it is."

"You will simply be guarded a little more closely."

"I cannot help that. May I touch again on the subject of food, Sir Theodore?"

The man thought for a moment. "Truly, I dare not," he said. "But you will be fed in the morning. My father is anxious to see you and arrange the terms of your ransom."

"I shall look forward to meeting your noble father. In the meantime—I do not wish to offend you again—I shall probably spend the night fasting like a monk and meditating on a juicy joint of meat."

"Perhaps the monks do that too. But you will not spend the night in uneasy vigil. The lady Stephanie, my sister, who is adept at such things, has brewed you a draught of Persian herbs that will cleanse your organs and put you to sleep. You may drink it without fear."

"I am not afraid you will poison me, Sir Theodore, not if you intend to hold me for ransom. Though I warn you, I am a poor man and already robbed of everything I brought with me from France."

"I shall not haggle with you tonight. My father will fix your ransom in the morning. Do not try to overpower your guard, Sir Peter. Promise me so much, at least."

Pierre held up his bandaged right hand. "Do you think I could accomplish much with this?" he asked. "I confess that it throbs exceedingly and I am in no mood to fight with the man who sits under the pretty tapestry and threatens to drown me with water every five minutes. Nay, so much I can promise you with all my heart."

"Very well, I shall caution him not to overburden you with his spring water."

He left Pierre, who noticed that he had knighted him, either out of conviction that his unwilling guest was a nobleman or through some quirk of the Turkish tongue. He spoke it with a totally different accent from Pierre's.

Shortly there arrived, walking softly in a pair of pointed Eastern slippers, a lady who must have been his sister, for she had a little bowl of liquid in her hand, and she did not look like a servant.

Stephanie had already seen the captive Frank. In the widowed household of the Count of Mesembria, alone among so many men, with no women but a few of the soldiers' wives and some ancient female servants, her position was an anomalous one. She was younger than her brother, but ever since she could remember, she had had to discharge the duties of mistress of the castle, entertaining the count's infrequent visitors, keeping order in the kitchens and directing the superannuated cleaning women like any chatelaine. When her brother and his men were absent, which they frequently were, it was her sharp, young eyes that kept watch from the walls over the surrounding countryside, every path of which she had known from girlhood, waiting their return. She could ride like a man. Theodore suspected she might be able to fight like one, too, if it were necessary, for she had the fiery, obstinate temper that ran in the family. The need of a woman to run the household and care for her father was so great and so constant that she almost never left the castle except to ride her horse furiously once in a while for the sheer physical joy that the exhaustion gave her.

She was slight, like her brother, and as their father had been before his blindness. Her hair was intensely black and luxuriantly long when she let it grow. Usually she cut it short at her shoulders because she liked the free feel of it that way. Often she wore no headdress at all, especially during those long periods when nobody visited the castle, though all civilized, Christian women wore some sort of covering over their heads. Stephanie's habit of going bareheaded was a reproach to her brother, who constantly admonished her to cover it in a more seemly fashion. When he did, her black eyes were likely to flash at him, she was likely to swear like a man and say: "Who cares, you night-riding, miscreant, half-noble thieving knight of a brother? Who sees me anyway?" Then he would pat her shoulder and say:

"Never mind, dear Stephanie. You'll be proud to invite me to dinner when I'm rich and you're married to a great lord in Trebizond."

How that might be accomplished was often the subject of the meditations of the count, her father. For the Pontic aristocrats, descendants of the Hellenes who had been in the empire before the first Comnenus and the ten thousand Byzantines took it over, seldom married among the rich nobles of the city. They occupied a position in the social scale midway between the merchants and the higher nobility of the capital. Seldom, except in England after the Norman conquest, had the distinction between the old and the new owners of the land been so sharp and persisted so long.

Pierre watched her, and then looked quickly away when he noticed that she, too, was looking at him. It was not the frank, level look of the Turkish slave girl, with nothing to lose and favor to be gained if she pleased; neither was it the proud glance of a Western woman, modest but conscious of her value, such as it was, in the world. Stephanie's covert glance at Pierre was partly a shrewd appraisal of his mood: whether he would or would not accept the medicine from her hand without the help of the guard. If he looked belligerent, she was prepared to summon the guard, order the Frank held flat on his back and pour the potion down his throat. But she was also timidly curious to determine whether Pierre was as handsome awake as he had been asleep.

Her Turkish was almost unintelligible, but Pierre thought she said: "Drink this, Peter Effendi. It will ease the pain in your wounded hand and put you to sleep."

Pierre nodded, thanked her, took a sip of the stuff and scalded his tongue.

"It is too hot," he said, sputtering a little.

She took a sip herself, which reassured Pierre, though he had not actually suspected the drink.

"I am sorry, sir. It ought to be hot, but I did not mean to burn you." She put the bowl aside. "It will cool in a moment," she said. Her quick mind instantly decided that the Frank was even more handsome awake, with eyes, her fertile imagination assured her, like deep, blue sapphires. Pierre, for his part, wondered how so hard-faced a brother could possibly have a sister with so gentle a countenance, and put it down to some mystical reciprocity of nature, which produces hard stones that crush the flesh of one's hand, and also beautiful flowers that delight the sense of one's eyes.

"When Sir Theodore informed me that his sister was brewing me a draught," he said pleasantly, "I confess that I saw in my mind's eye an old mountain witch with a kettle on the fire, stirring it with a broom. I cheerfully dedicate the little aches in my hand as a self-imposed penance for so false a thought."

Stephanie blushed, though Pierre was only trying to be polite, and suppressed a remark that leaped, out of her loneliness to her lips: "Oh, how I wish other men would talk to me like that once in a while!" What she said aloud was:

"Does it pain you sorely?"

"No wound is comfortable," Pierre said practically, "and a crush hurts worse than a cut. I am not affecting a show of courage, however, when I tell you that it hurts a good deal less than I thought it would. I hate to hurt, and I admit it frankly."

"Only a proud man from Europe would feel ashamed to confess pain, Peter Effendi. We Greeks, and all the Eastern nations around us, know that pain is a terrible thing. That is why we have so many drugs to cure it, when it ought to be cured, and know so many ways of causing it, when wicked people have to be punished. Your hand feels better because we soaked it yesterday in cold water from the spring. I am glad the pain is less." She tried another sip of the drink again. "I think it is I who shall have the good night's sleep if I keep on tasting your medicine," she said smiling. "It is still too hot." Pierre saw no steam. "Do you like it here in Trebizond?"

"It's an extraordinary country," Pierre answered truthfully; "I have seen very little of it. Most of the time," he said, laughing, "I have been unconscious or terribly hungry."

"Are you hungry now?"

"I certainly am."

"I'll get you something to eat."

"Perhaps you had better not. Your brother, or somebody, has a theory that starvation is a wonderful cure for a fever. But," he said hopefully, "I do not believe that I have a fever."

She felt his head. The relative difference in temperature that makes a fever apparent to a solicitous hand told her that Pierre's brow was cool; it seemed to Pierre that her touch was soft and warm. He was sure he had no fever.

"I don't think you have either," she said. "Do not drink the potion till I return. It works quickly."

Pierre promised not to, and she left the room. The guard squatted sleepily on the floor outside the door.

"The Frank needs more medicine," she said shortly. "Do not disturb him."

"I shall not, Lady Stephanie," he said, rising halfway to his feet and immediately sitting down again. In his dream there was a rich, weak nobleman in the woods with a beautiful daughter and a bag full of gold, all alone. He savagely fell upon them again, and spent the money riotously in the Eastern Star for days and days. Stephanie came back with another bowl, exactly like the first except that there was a spoon in it. She smiled at the snoring guard and stepped lightly over his legs. She had no idea that his dream had now shod them in the purple imperial buskins of the Great Comnenus.

The lady Stephanie and the bowl of hot, meaty soup filled the little room with the odor of musk and mutton. Pierre awkwardly ate with his left hand.

"If you aren't more careful, you'll spill the broth on the blanket." she said, "and betray my little treason. Here, let me help you." She fed him with the spoon, and Pierre had nothing to do but look at her face and her long, black, uncovered hair. Pierre thought this part of his captivity quite tolerable.

Then she gave him his medicine, which was stone cold, and he instantly went to sleep. Stephanie nested the bowls into each other and looked at the sleeping Frank. Then she took the bowls to the kitchens and washed the soupy one and went to her own apartment, and, when she said her prayers, she asked St. Eugenius, if he deemed it wise, to delay for a little while the payment of Sir Peter's ransom.

The pleasant interlude of Stephanie's medication ended in a puzzling fashion. Pierre awoke next morning to see a brazier burning in the room and to hear the flap, flap, flap of a sharp steel instrument in the hands of a wild-faced man with a bushy beard sharpening it on a strip of leather. Sir Theodore was there, probably to witness whatever was going to happen. Pierre sat up in bed, confused and a little alarmed.

"I am glad you are finally awake, Sir Peter," Theodore said courteously. "My sister must have drugged you severely. There will be coffee for you in a moment, if you can drink it."

"I have had it before," Pierre said.

"There is nothing like coffee to counteract a sedative. Then you must be shaved."

"Oh," said Pierre. "Perhaps it is one of your customs."

"My father requests it," Theodore explained. "The count is nearly blind. He sees with his fingers. He always wishes to know what a man looks like when he talks to him. Once he touches your face he can see you. He was not always blind, of course. He says that the world is lonely, full of voices with no faces. I hope you will not mind." His voice was apologetic.

"Certainly not," Pierre said. He understood Theodore, however, for he knew that neither the Greeks nor the Turks liked to have their bodies touched by strangers. It was a peculiar Eastern fastidiousness totally foreign to the hardier temperament of a European. "I feel very sorry for your poor father. Did he meet with an accident?"

The man stopped stropping the razor. Stephanie, stirring the coffee over the brazier, held her fingers to her lips with a shocked expression. Theodore's face set and he said: "I must caution you at once, Sir Peter, never to mention my father's affliction either to him or to anyone else in the house. We do not talk about it."

The bushy-faced man was the count's own steward. He shaved Pierre lightly and delicately. Pierre noticed that his swift, sure hand was almost as slender as a woman's. Then the steward went to get his hose, which had been washed clean and dried, and his shoes, which a man had whisked with a stiff little broom for an hour. Theodore went to the count's apartment. A woman came from the kitchens with a tray full of hot breakfast. Stephanie helped him drink a tiny silver cup of hot coffee: the inside of the cup was marvelously plated with shining gold. Pierre wondered again at the profusion of rich small articles with which the old castle was provided. It was possible that he had fallen among a band of thieves, but the loot with which the castle was furnished was not the sort of thing travelers habitually carry with them. That Sir Theodore and his little following could attack the Eastern caravans, which were the most likely source of all the Oriental merchandise, was absurd on the face of it, for nothing but a crusade was quite so heavily armed as the long, strong trains of camels with their hundreds of followers that came out of the depths of Asia to Trebizond. Nor did he believe that the Count of Mesembria lived entirely on the ransoms of captured Frank knights. That would surely have caused comment in time and made bad friends among the Westerners, who were essential to the Trapezuntian economy. Maybe, like Baltha Ogli, the count owned extensive vineyards.

He drank the coffee gratefully. Stephanie's hair was covered with a white, starched headdress that might have come from France, and made his heart thump at the memory of Claire.

"It is late," she said, "and Father is impatient to see you. He has been up since dawn, and I must go in to him now. Eat all your breakfast if you can." She smiled at their secret of the soup and left him to a guard who helped him with the tray. It was not difficult for Pierre to finish its generous contents. The man helped him into his clothes and supplied him with a handsome, light-blue, knee-length Greek tunic, embroidered with silver thread, and gave him a sword belt of Russian leather, but no sword. Pierre smiled at the cautious omission. He ran his fingers through his hair to brush it out of his eyes. His hand, when he withdrew it, smelled strongly of Chadaze's sandalwood. He glanced at his sky-blue tunic of soft cotton stuff and laughed. I'm beginning to look and smell like a Greek! he thought, and he went in to wait upon the count.

Philelphus kept a decent, diminutive court in his great hall, the center of his castle. It was carpeted, tapestried, and equipped with a thronelike chair on a dais under a tasseled canopy. A servant opened both the doors and pronounced, "Sir Peter of France!" and Pierre went to the foot of the blind man's chair and knelt on one knee, as he had been taught to do when being received by great lords. One knee for a lord, two knees for God and a king, a bow and a kiss for a lady's hand. Manners were simple in France. Pierre's behavior, which would have been accounted barbarous at the court of the Great Comnenus, was amply sufficient in the castle of the blind Pontic nobleman, who bent forward, felt his face, and said:

"I am glad to see you, Sir Peter. I trust you will accommodate yourself to our forest ways and our rude hospitality until you leave us."

The corpulent old man wore his Phrygian cap of cloth of gold on his head. An icon in a silver frame, depicting the agony of Christ bleeding in His crown of thorns, hung over his tunic. His small white hands rested lightly on the carved arms of his chair. One of them moved slightly and rhythmically, as if he were beating time to a melody that only he could hear. Sir Theodore, in a cuirass and sword, stood at his right. Stephanie, on his left, had put on a long blue chlamys, or Greek cloak. It buckled with a garnet clasp, and over the shoulder where the halves of the circular garment split, was the *tablion,* or inserted square of embroidery which only an empress ought to wear. All of the family looked serious, and there was nothing in their rich appearance to lead Pierre to believe that his ransom would be a light one.

"I have been courteously treated, sir," Pierre replied.

"You look like a young man, Sir Peter," said the count, "and I see you have a determined jaw. They tell me you have suffered an injury to your sword arm. Perhaps that is not an unmitigated misfortune, since I judge by your face that you might otherwise be tempted to use it. My exuberant retainers sometimes forget their manners. I hope your hand feels better, however."

"I have already given my word that I would not fight with my guards, my lord, and my hand does not hurt this morning. I am very grateful for the care I have received."

"That is good, very good. It has been my hope that your heart could feel gratitude. I shall not remind you that my son saved your life, at a great danger, I might add, to one of the men. The ledge you were lying on fell to the bottom of the gorge an instant after my brave servant rescued you."

"I did not know that, sir." Pierre assumed that this unlucky incident would add a bit to his ransom; he doubted whether the servant would greatly profit by it.

"I can ill afford to lose any of my servants, of course," the count continued placidly. "My appanage consists of only a town or two here near the coast, where the land is not particularly fertile, and my revenues are not great."

"I have been given to understand, sir, that when I go back to the city, you will not be averse to accepting a token of the gratitude which I feel for your hospitality."

"Did you say such a thing, Theodore?" the count asked, raising his eyebrows but continuing to stare with his white eyes over Pierre's head toward the door, "Nay, Sir Peter, not when you get back to the city! I am persuaded that you will not want to put your foot outside the castle grounds until you have expressed your understandable gratitude for the services my family has accorded you, in the solid new French gold. I admired only today how sharp the minting is on a piece of it."

"I see," said Pierre shortly.

"It is my suggestion," the count continued, "that you give me your knightly word, which you have unaccountably refused my son in

284

defiance of all the laws of Christian chivalry, not to attempt to escape until your ransom is paid."

"I cannot give my knightly word, sir, for the simple reason that I am a merchant, not a knight. As far as I know, I am a commoner; the only father I remember is a wonderfully kind man, an armorer, who still lives in Rouen in Normandy in France." Pierre bit his lip, and Stephanie's expression changed a little. Such an avowal came hard, she knew, from a Westerner. A Greek would have spun a fine tale. They all believed him.

The count remarked courteously: "The European noblemen sometimes forswear themselves and never think twice about it. We shall drop the question of your parole for the moment. That you are a merchant makes it easier to talk to you. Whom have you dealings with here in Trebizond, Peter, and whom do you serve in France?"

"In France I am the auditor-general for Jacques Coeur, the minister of finance. I had on my person a sum of the gold which he has recently struck in the king's mint. It was stolen from me, but apparently a coin or two fell into your men's hands. Here in Trebizond I deal, of course, with the French factor."

"Everyone knows that is Baltha Ogli, the Bulgarian prince," the count said casually. "If, as I suspect, my son suddenly looks like a hangman, do not let it alarm you." Theodore was indeed scowling furiously. The count fingered his icon; his face was troubled. "It is not pleasant for one's patrimony to be pledged," he said, "and I shall tell you what my angry son will not: I do not own my lands. Some years ago I sold them to Baltha Ogli. I was in some distress at the moment. He and his secretary drove a hard bargain, and in my weakness I signed the deed. We have paid rent ever since, like peasants instead of the most ancient of the Pontic families. My title derives from the city of Mesembria, far across the Euxine; my family was in Trebizond ages before the Great Comnenus"—here even Philelphus bowed his head as one does at the mention of God—"came with his ten thousand thieving palace guards and made himself king." He paused a moment, and then he said: "Baltha Ogli will be delighted to know that his French colleague has not disappeared."

"He will be astonished to know that I am alive, sir," Pierre said frankly. "He has already tried to have me assassinated. When he discovers that he has failed, he will immediately take steps to murder me again."

The count's face took on a crafty smile, and Sir Theodore said, "The man in the ravine was a Frank!"

"He was dressed like a Frank," Pierre said, "but he was a Greek, and so were the other two."

"Is the Bulgarian in disfavor with the French king?" asked the count.

"He is certain to be if I ever get back to France."

"Why, then," said Philelphus, smiling more and more, "I dare say Ogli would give £1,000 for you this instant. We are on the friendliest terms with him."

"Father!" Stephanie cried. "Would you turn the Frank over to the man who tried to kill him? You know what would happen and who would do it."

"Stephanie, you forget yourself. Theodore will slap your face in front of the servants if you ever say such a thing again. You know better." Pierre thought he had never seen a face so convulsed with fury as Theodore's just at that moment.

"Stupid!" Theodore hissed at the girl. "Father is only threatening. You will spoil everything."

The Greek that was spoken meant nothing in Pierre's ears.

"I venture to guess," he said, "that John Justin might value me to the extent of £2,000. He is the ship's captain."

"Your Turkish and mine come from different provinces," Sir Theodore said quietly. "Did I understand the figure that you mentioned was five thousand?"

"No, sir. I am not so valuable. Another auditor-general could easily be found. The French minister has plenty of able merchants to take my place. It might just be possible for Justin, who likes me, to raise three thousand. But I am not worth a penny more, either to the service or to my friend."

The Greeks were silent. It was a large amount of money.

Pierre added thoughtfully: "You could also be sure that the money would be paid. Perhaps you know Ogli well, but I also know him well. It is my belief that he would not pay if he could help it."

"That is true, Father," Theodore said, but Pierre could not tell from his perfectly controlled face whether he was advising the count to take or to refuse the offer.

The count, smiling gently, fingered his icon, and said: "I accept that amount, Peter. Write a request for £3,000 to your captain, if your hand can hold a pen. Gold, of course. If you cannot write, I shall do it for you. Though, if he knows your handwriting, it is better that you do it for obvious reasons."

"The Italian might think you were already dead and your murderers trying to extract a ransom anyway," Theodore said.

"The same thought occurred to me," said Pierre. "I think perhaps I can write. I did not know you knew John Justin was an Italian, Sir Theodore."

"Of course I know. One of my men happened to notice the great silver collar he wore just before we got mixed up in a turbulent crowd outside the Eastern Star. Sir John was on foot, in a great hurry, and very careless. My man could not withstand the evil temptation. He whacked Justin on the head with his pikestaff and lifted the collar when he fell. He got up shouting Italian; I suppose he was cursing."

"You can be sure he was!"

"It was dangerous and foolish to steal in the city. We are not robbers, Peter."

"It would be unwise to mention the incident in your letter, however," Philelphus observed. "The captain might not trust your hosts. You will be given the collar when you return to Trebizond. If the captain cares to express his thanks for its return, he may send us a small gift sometime, anytime. It is no part of your ransom, and I shall trust you for it. I like to discourage promiscuous stealing on the part of the men."

"I begin to see why my friend did not meet me at the tavern. Are you sure he was not killed, Sir Theodore?"

"A dead man does not wave his sword and bellow. He may have been dizzy for a few minutes, but I know he did not die. Would I let you write to a dead man?"

Philelphus then said kindly: "Though you are baseborn, or think you are—who is ever sure of such things?—and cannot give your word as a nobleman, I am struck with your honest face and I have no doubt that you will keep your word, if you care to give it, on your own personal honor. Promise me you will not try to escape till your ransom is paid, and you will never see a guard again."

"I promise you that, sir."

"Good," said the count. "I may now add something that I did not mention before, lest you think I doubted your honor. You are probably not anxious to meet Ogli's assassins again; my castle is the safest place in the empire from them. Neither he nor his men ever come here."

"That is a practical reason for keeping my word, sir, though I'd have done so without it."

"I do not doubt you for an instant. But there is a saying here that honesty instructed by prudence is doubly honest."

# CHAPTER

## ❋ 26 ❋

PIERRE'S BANDAGE was stuck to his hand, and when he removed it to write, skin and bits of flesh adhered to the fabric. It was very painful, and the letter, when he had finished it, was so bloody that he threw it away and had to write another. Sir Theodore watched him, his hard face relaxed in sympathy. Pierre protected the parchment with a cloth the second time. The writing was recognizable as his own, but awkwardly penned, as if he had traveled back in time to his schoolboy days in Rouen. The young Greek expressed his sympathy; Pierre handed him the missive, which was understandably short, with no very good grace.

"I doubt how Sir John can raise so much money," he said. "Ask me to write no more letters. If you wonder what I have said, show the letter to a priest. I have written it in Latin, which a priest should be able to read."

"I shall trust you, Peter. Our priests dislike Latin. And what could John Justin do, even if you had written, 'Kill this man'? My men will be with me. And if they were not, the Italian would know better than to harm me if he ever expects to see you alive again."

"The captain will probably be aboard his ship," Pierre said. "If he recognizes the man who stole the collar, that is too bad for the man."

"He will not. I shall leave that man here. I wish you would forget about that collar, Peter. I repeat that we are not robbers. I would return it today, except that it would needlessly complicate the collection of your ransom. I give you my word, if you need it in addition to my noble father's promise, that you shall be given the collar when you are set free. In fact," he added sarcastically, "if it will make you feel better, I'll give the bauble to you now. You can stare at it or wear it on your neck for all I care."

"All right," Pierre said.

"All right, what?"

"I said, all right, I'll take it."

"I'll get it at once." His face was a study in disgust as he left the room. When he returned, he threw the collar on the table in front of Pierre. "The merchant is perhaps happier with the silver in his hands. Perhaps you'd like to count the spangles."

Pierre examined the collar carefully, inside and out. Then he pushed it away from him.

"You can have it back now," he said.

Theodore looked hopelessly puzzled.

"What were you looking for?" he asked.

"Blood."

"There is no blood on the collar."

"So I see. I thank God."

Theodore took it back. "I'm sorry for what I said about the spangles, Peter. If Sir John cares as much for you as you appear to for him, I've an idea it won't take long to raise your ransom. I am going to Trebizond at once with your letter."

"Very well, sir."

Theodore rolled the letter and slipped it into his purse. At the door he paused for a moment, grinning. "You are apparently not a very alert merchant after all. Had you counted the spangles you would have found only fourteen. One wrenched off in the scuffle; I am sorry about it."

"Indeed?" Pierre exclaimed smiling. "Nay, I am a reproach to the service!"

Pierre's promise not to try to escape was of great practical benefit to Sir Theodore, who stripped the castle almost bare of men and took them with him to the city. Only the kitchen staff were left, the guards at the bridge, and the count's valet. And John, of course, who had stolen the collar.

A week passed, and Pierre, who had wondered from the beginning how Justin would raise the money for his ransom, began to fear that he had not been able to do so. That the count might then sell him to Ogli he did not doubt for an instant.

Stephanie dressed his hand several times. His removal of the bandage to write the letter opened all the wounds, and they seemed to be healing very slowly. After his first frank admission to Stephanie that he hated

289

pain, like everybody else, he found himself perversely ashamed to admit that the hand still hurt him, and bathed it secretly in the spring when she was not around, sitting on the wall and trailing his hand in the cold, pure water.

A miniature aqueduct ran from the walled spring and tumbled into a trough large enough for camels to drink from in the khan. This was a rectangular structure of stone, with four walls enclosing a great open space in the center. It occupied almost as much ground as the castle itself. The quadrangle within the walls was lined with hitching posts and stables. There were several circular depressions piled round with stones where fires could be built, and there were iron spits over them long enough to roast the carcasses of whole sheep. One end of the khan was set apart from the rest by a low wall, to keep the animals out, and this part was roofed, forming a great room where hundreds of men might easily be accommodated. Suspended on strings from the ceiling were several ostrich eggs, notifying to the heathen that here, as in their own land, the providence of God was ever with them. The egg of the ostrich was a well known symbol of prosperity and plenty, vastly appreciated by the merchants near the end of their journey.

Like all Eastern khans, this one was designed to give shelter and safety to a caravan when it stopped for the night, but it was not an inn in the European sense because there was no proprietor, no cook, no service. The Easterners did their own cooking, which they always preferred to do anyway, supplied their own food from the provisions they carried with them and provided their own beds. Pierre could see how it was a convenient source of income to the count, except that it was situated impractically close to the city.

It had been too dark and he had been too dazed to remember the route by which he had arrived at the castle. He assumed that it was by the road, clearly visible from the khan, over which he had seen several long trains of camels, men, and horses, slowly walking in the direction of Trebizond. None of them had so far availed themselves of the count's hostelry. Perhaps he had his own clientele.

Pierre would have been a welcome guest at the count's table, except that the old man had to be fed by his valet, and he was ashamed to be seen. So Pierre dined after him, when the count had gone back to his rooms. Stephanie always ate with her father. When she dressed Pierre's hand, she was courteous and solicitous, winding the bandage gently. For a day or two she wore her starched French cap, and popped out of the dark rooms and hallways of the castle so often and unexpectedly that he began to wonder if Theodore had appointed her a sort of unofficial guard over him. Then she was less in evidence, and when he did occasionally see her, she was bareheaded again.

Pierre counted the days that Theodore was away. Seven had passed. His chest wound was healing and healthily itching. But for his hand he felt perfectly well, though he was ill at ease and chafed at Theodore's delay. The stronger he became, the more he was inclined to regret his promise not to escape. It looked like the easiest thing in the world to walk out of the castle and up to the caravan route. He knew he had left the city long after dark. He had arrived at the castle just as dawn was breaking, after passing he knew not how long a time unconscious in the ravine. Mules do not walk very fast. The capital could not be too far away.

After supper he went into the yard and sat upon the wall of the spring. He wondered how much the Count of Mesembria relied on his honor and how much on his prudence. Since Ogli must realize that his death was at least problematical and would undoubtedly search for his body, Pierre had to admit that prudence was a consideration. He was unarmed, incapable of using a sword, and absolutely penniless.

He dipped his bandaged hand in the cold water, which instantly made it feel better. The twilight began to fall. This was the hour that the count said his most fervent prayers. The moldering battlements, the dead weeds and shrubs in the walls gave the old castle a curiously soft appearance. Now, as a nearly full moon rose behind it, it lost its depth and became a brown, then a black silhouette against the sky. He and the well were in its shadow. The square, solid walls of the empty khan began to shine, cold and hard in the moonlight. Suddenly a voice spoke to him. Pierre could never get used to the quiet, catlike walk of the Greeks. He looked up quickly.

"I thought your hand was better," she said.

Pierre rose to greet her.

"It is better, Lady Stephanie, but the spring has wonderful curative properties, I think, and it will do the hand no harm to give it a little more treatment."

"You are probably lying. Maybe I should brew you another drink. In my witch's caldron and stir it with my broom. Are all the Franks so moody, Sir Peter?"

"You know I have no right to the 'sir.' "

"I'll drop it, if you drop the 'lady.' "

"Very well, Stephanie."

"Speak to me as a brother tonight, Peter. I am very sad, and I cannot wait for Theodore to return."

"I am anxious to see him again, too."

"I do not mean for that reason. I shall not be glad to see you go."

"You have made my stay very pleasant, but I am naturally concerned with your brother's protracted absence. I have a mission in Trebizond, and I hope Sir John will be able to find the money to enable me to accomplish it."

"Be assured that Theodore is in just as much of a hurry as you are. If I have made your stay pleasant, you have done nothing to make me suspect it. It seems to me that you have kept out of my way as much as you could." She sat down on the wall at his left, because his wet, bandaged hand was now resting beside him at his right. It was no wonder he had not heard her walk. In the dim moonlight reflected from the barren walls of the khan, he saw that her feet were bare.

"It is a pleasant night," he said cautiously.

"Is it? I do not find it so. Theodore never stays long in town if he can help it. The instant your ransom is paid my brother will be here. We are only two hours from Trebizond."

Pierre was silent. Stephanie said:

"I am telling you nothing you will not find out soon enough. Theodore brought you home the long way by the sea. It is very wild there. He had a great deal of money with him, and naturally he wished to avoid the direct caravan route, which is the short way, but is always full of people."

"I see," Pierre said.

"Perhaps you do and perhaps you don't, you cautious Frank." Pierre made a mental note that the Trapezuntian estimate of his wariness was rising. "Theodore had received payment for a great deal of the merchandise he handles. At least I think that's what it was. I know nothing about business myself. But the caravans pass by here all the time. You as a merchant probably understand what it means. I admire how profitably my brother trades. We could never live without him."

The shadow of the castle tower that hid the moon slid off the well as the earth spun and Pierre saw her earnest face. Her words were nonsense in his ears, except to disclose that merchandise rested on the count's estate for a while, and moved off it again, at some profit to the count. He could see that she believed what she said. But it was incredible that the caravans should unload two hours from Trebizond.

"As a merchant," Pierre observed, "I think that is wonderful, and I am very glad for you." He looked more closely at her. "What have you been crying about, Stephanie?"

The girl hid her face in her hands and began to weep again. He could see her body trembling with the intensity of her grief, but she did not make a sound. In a moment, when she could control herself, she whispered: "Do not talk loudly, Peter. Father will hear. He could not see at all today. At noon he asked me when the sun would rise. On a cloudless day, Peter! Never so bright!"

Pierre put his arm around her because it looked as if she were going to fall into the spring. She instantly clung to him, all her black hair cascading down over his chest.

"I am terribly, terribly sorry," he said. He patted her shoulder. "Perhaps it is a temporary manifestation of his blindness. Perhaps he will be able to see a little light when the sun rises tomorrow. Has a chirurgeon treated the count, Stephanie?"

"At first there were lots of them. One great man came all the way from Constantinople. But the eyes were burned out. It was only a matter of time till he would be quite blind. Little Father knew it, but he always loved the light, even though he could distinguish nothing."

"That is very sad."

"He dreaded the day that would be all blackness, and today—. He knows it now."

"I have been cautioned against mentioning his blindness."

"I know." Stephanie leaned her body against him as if she could not support herself. "But my heart is full of sorrow. I do not care what you say or do. He will die now. My brother will kill the eunuch and Ogli will kill my brother, and I shall be all alone."

Pierre patted her shoulder again. "You poor child, I have no idea what you are talking about."

"I dare not tell my brother, and yet I must. Father will tell him at once. The eunuch did it, Peter."

"Did what, Stephanie? Do not sob so."

"A long time ago Father stole something from some stragglers behind a caravan. It was Ogli's caravan, and Ogli found out about it. Ogli could have had father impaled. That is what happens to people who steal from the caravans. They are protected by a savage, imperial law. But instead of denouncing Father, Ogli invited him to his house. He said he would not tell the emperor if Father would sell him his lands for a great sum of money. Then he left the house to go to a ceremony at the court and left his eunuch-secretary to arrange the details."

"I have seen Basil," Pierre said. "What did he do?"

"He is a horrible man. He took Father into the cellars and told him Ogli would not pay him for the land until Father signed something which meant the money had already been paid. Father refused, of course. The eunuch had him gagged and bound. A slave heated an iron plate red hot. They kept my father's eyes open with thorns from a desert plant and pushed his face close to the plate so that he had to look at it. Father was helpless, and he offered to sign. But the eunuch began to scream and laugh as if he were crazy, and Father fainted."

"Horrible!"

"When Father woke up, they were throwing water into his face. He offered to sign again, and Basil let him. The thorns were still in his eyes. But then they made him look at the plate again."

"After he signed away his lands?"

"Yes."

"I can hardly believe such a thing."

"Then the eunuch put vinegar into my father's poor eyes, and they brought him home on a litter. The eunuch gave him nothing at all. Ogli sent a few pounds by a page a week or so later."

"Was there no one the count could go to for justice?"

"He could have denounced Ogli. But Ogli is a great lord, related to the sultan. He would only have been reprimanded. Father suspects he left the house so that he could blame the eunuch if anything were ever found out. But Father never dared tell anyone, because, of course, he was still guilty of robbing the caravan."

"Ogli knows his servant," Pierre said. "I have heard him talk to him. He undoubtedly knew Basil would torture your father."

"Father thinks that, too. But what can we do? Now Ogli has built that khan, and his caravans sometimes stop for a night here."

"That is an odd arrangement, Stephanie. Can they not go on the hour or so to the city?"

She did not directly answer his question. "I never inquire about business matters, Peter."

"Then I shall not. But in France, Stephanie, if your father had done such a thing, he could go to the king and say 'Your Grace, I did a bad thing, but another man did a worse thing. Judge which of us is the guiltier.' "

"This is not France, Peter. If the caravans are molested, the heathen nations all around us will fall on us with their swords. We are woefully outnumbered. That is why the laws that protect them are so strict. Father has never dared say a word, and Ogli knows he never will. But I am terribly afraid of what Theodore will do now. He has a demon in him. He hates the eunuch with a hellish fury. Ogli knows it, and though he is our landlord he never comes here, nor do any of his men."

"I think he very prudently wishes to avoid an incident," Pierre said. He glanced toward the giant, puzzling caravansary, so close to the city. "Probably he has his own reasons for avoiding your brother, and your land, too, for that matter."

"Poor Father!" She covered her face and began to weep again. "It is dreadful to be blind. He has feared it for so long."

"Is he all alone?"

"He will not suffer anyone near him. He has not eaten all day. He has been praying on his knees ever since I told him—I had to tell him; nobody else would—that it was daylight."

"I think that if I were your brother, I should feel exactly the way Sir Theodore does. I have never heard such a horrible story."

Some complex of female emotions that Pierre did not pretend to understand sent her arms around his shoulders and her wet face tight up against his cheek. He comforted her like a child. But there was strength in her arms greater than any child's, and he winced a little when she pressed the wound in his chest a little harder than he could bear. She instantly relaxed her arms, but she did not move her face away.

Pierre's name in all its versions in every Christian tongue, from the isles of Greece to the Scandinavian peninsula, meant 'a stone.' But he was not a stone, and the moon was very bright. A brother would have patted her shoulder, he assured himself, and stroked her tear-stained cheek. Whether a brother would have hidden his face in her musky, black hair and held her solicitously round the waist to keep her from falling into the well, he did not bother to ask his conscience.

"I am sorry if I hurt your cut, Peter."

"It's another of Ogli's little mementos. You did not hurt it, Stephanie."

"How did it happen?"

"I was talking to a Greek, dressed up like a Turk, in the Eastern Star. Three more Greeks, dressed up like Franks came in and we had a fight."

All the disguises amused the girl and she smiled for the first time since she had come to sit beside him.

"Theodore said there was a fearful melee in the street. How did you know who the dressed-up men were?"

"The false Franks were sent by Ogli. They admitted it when we had another fight outside the town."

"I am glad they did not kill you."

"I don't know who the false Turk was, but he was obviously a Greek. I could tell by the way he spoke. They struck him on the head and at first I thought he was dead. But he had a steel cap under his turban, and the blow only stunned him. I saw it just as I went down myself. I'm afraid I didn't last very long in the fight, Stephanie. He had on red buskins under his desert shoes, I think."

"What did you say, Peter?" She sat up straight and looked at him in astonishment.

"I say I think he had on red shoes. Nay, I am sure he did. There were pearls on them, too. He was probably a rich young man on a lark. He said he was very anxious to watch a tavern dancer named Irene."

"There are only two men in Trebizond who wear the purple shoes. Any shade of red is strictly forbidden here. It is the imperial color."

"I have heard something like that. I never paid much attention."

"Peter, I think you were sitting with the emperor!" She was overwhelmed.

"Perhaps I was. He drew his sword very fearlessly, now that I think of it, and ordered the men out of the tavern as if he were used to being obeyed. But is it customary for the Emperor of Trebizond to wander in and out of places on the waterfront all alone?"

"You can be sure he was not alone. David, the younger Great Comnenus, is known to go disguised among the people sometimes. He is always guarded, of course. His friends say he keeps the common touch that way. Most of us Pontic families think he is a little silly, always racing his horses and playing polo and watching theatrical performances. It will be a bad day for Trebizond when such a weak man rules alone."

It was a wonderful thing to have sat with a Great Comnenus, and the girl had momentarily forgotten the terrible tragedy of her father's blindness. But she was not vitally concerned with Trapezuntian politics.

"What was the tavern dancer like, Peter?"

"Oh, she was a very accomplished dancer. Very precise."

"What did she wear? It is several years since I saw the city. I always liked the pretty clothes."

Pierre thought of the seaweed.

"Why, let me see; she had on a long billowy skirt, and a kind of silver jacket, and a sort of Turkish veil. . . . I don't remember exactly."

Stephanie's volatile Greek mood changed swiftly. Her eyes were laughing at him. "These stones are awfully hard to sit on, Peter. Take me for a walk where I can feel the grass on my feet."

Pierre's conscience was melting in the moonlight. France was two months, three fights, four seas in the past, and a ransom away in the future. There was a large greensward beyond the khan, outside the gravelly castle yard, rimmed in by the forest trees. She hung on his arm and they walked toward it.

"I asked you to speak to me as a brother," she said, "and you have marvelously accomplished it. Now you will tell me that the dancer wore the thick kind of Turkish veil that nobody can see through. A likely costume! Do you ever walk barefoot in the grass, Peter? It is wonderfully cool."

Pierre laughed so loudly that he startled himself, and instantly restrained his voice so the count would not hear, if the poor man were still awake.

"My dear girl, don't you realize that a European cannot bare his feet without taking off his hose?"

"Saints! I forgot! What a dreadful thought. Why don't you people dress like Greeks! But you're not talking like Theodore any more. I can imagine what the dancer wore."

Pierre sat down beside her. "You need work your imagination only a little to picture her costume in its entirety."

"Were there any women in the audience?"

"Not on the waterfront, Stephanie."

"Did the men applaud her?"

"They roared."

"Did you applaud, too?"

"I suppose I did."

"I think the whole thing is disgusting."

"Now you are talking like my sister, Stephanie. I haven't any, but if I had, she would say just that."

"Then I shall stop, or you'll talk like Theodore again, and preach me a homily on covering my hair. He thinks I am dreadfully immodest."

"Your hair is lovely, Stephanie."

"Yours is a miracle in Trebizond. I touched it while you were asleep to see if it were real. Many men wear wigs here."

"Do they? Mine is real enough."

"There was a scent of sandalwood in it. That's common enough for a Greek, but Western men do not perfume their hair. I asked Father. Did the tavern dancer put that in?"

Pierre laughed softly. "Stephanie, you almost frighten me. Your brother asked me a lot of questions when he picked me out of the ravine, but not half so savagely. As for the sandalwood, I had to smell prettily to please the infernal nose of Baltha Ogli at a dinner where his fat eunuch did a juggling feat."

He had forgotten Basil's cruelty for an instant, and remembered him only as the entertainer. Stephanie trembled and caught Pierre's hand.

"Do not fall into the clutches of those dreadful men, Peter. Ogli tried to kill you once. Next time he will be careful not to fail. It would break my heart."

Pierre put his arm comfortingly round her again. "I did not mean to mention them," he almost finished saying. But she kissed the sentence to a stop on his lips with her own. "It would break my heart," she repeated, without removing her mouth. Both Pierre's arms went round the girl. If his hand or his chest hurt, he did not feel it.

When, in a little while, he let her go, her eyes were open and laughing at him.

"Did I make you forget the girl in France for a moment, Peter?"

The Greek mind was a mystery to Pierre.

"Yes, Stephanie."

"What is her name?"

Pierre did not answer.

"Of course you will not tell me. She's a yellowhead, I know, and a great lady! I don't care, Peter. I wanted you to kiss me. Nobody ever did before."

Pierre could hardly believe her.

"You will remember me when you kiss her again."

Pierre felt a tingling up and down his spine, as if the strange, jealous girl were cursing him. He was much too bewildered to speak for a moment. Stephanie began to sob again, covering her face with her hands. Suddenly her body grew perfectly rigid and still. Her hands parted and slid slowly off her face. Pierre saw her turn her head a little. There was not a sound from the castle yard except the almost inaudible bubble of water from the spring, and nothing moved in the moonlight.

"There are people on the road," she whispered. "They are coming this way."

She was up on her feet in an instant. He saw her flash across the greensward like a fairy. She crossed the gravel-strewn castle yard without a sound. Her running bare feet did not displace a pebble. Stephanie's silent flight gave Pierre the eerie feeling that she had never been there.

He saw her again for an instant, a speck of white on the drawbridge of the castle. Then she disappeared into the gloomy interior. Almost immediately the bridge rose, like the lower jaw of a giant beast. Pierre had seen and heard many castle bridges raised, slowly, jerkily, rattling and squeaking on their hinges. The Count of Mesembria's went up without a sound, very quickly. It was apparent that the little garrison was taking no chances with whoever was on the road.

Then he heard all the little silver bells on the harness of the lead camel of a caravan. There must have been hundreds of them, for the caparison of the lead camel was always in direct proportion to the strength and wealth of the whole caravan. Since there were so many bells, he was prepared for the long string of stately, laden brutes, tied head to tail with their hair ropes, progressing silently and majestically toward Trebizond.

The unladen ass, whose function was to fall into a hole if there was one, preceded the camel train as usual, proclaiming by his continued existence the smooth safety of the route. Men-at-arms rode on mules or walked beside the camels. There were lanterns here and there, and a few torches carried before important officials, but there was little need for artificial illumination in the bright moonlight.

Pierre thought the entire caravan had passed. And then a separate string of perhaps twenty camels appeared. There were no lights at all on this silent, detached remnant of the train. They turned off the main route, and took the little path that led a few paces beyond where Pierre continued to sit on the grass to Baltha Ogli's caravansary.

It was unlikely that Ogli's Eastern merchants knew anything about the auditor-general from France. But Pierre decided it would be wise to avoid them. The castle, now isolated behind its moat, indicated that Stephanie and the count felt much the same way. The presence of a Frank on the greensward so close to the khan would surely appear a suspicious circumstance to the members of the caravan, who, judging from the total absence of light, were anxious to be as inconspicuous as possible.

As soon as he saw them leave the main route, he ran to the edge of the forest and hid himself in the bushes. He was not ten feet from where they would pass. He was glad they were carrying no lights. Two men on horse-back led the little caravan, and a dozen others followed. They were all on horses and all armed.

The khan had been a puzzle to Pierre since he first laid eyes on it, gaunt, new, solid, and functional. But what its function was he did not know. The ancient, decaying castle had character: impotent, decrepit, mellow with evil grown old and forgotten. But the arrogant, featureless khan was not so easy to understand.

The two mounted leaders were Turkish guides, as might have been expected. The men-at-arms, surprisingly, were Greek soldiers, and what they were talking about Pierre could not have understood if he had listened, which he did not. His ears tingled with the astonishing conversation of the Turkish guides.

"Ogli Pasha should promote us," said one of them. "Not a man lost, not an asper paid in taxes on the way."

"Nor an asper to pay! Wouldn't the collectors in Trebizond love to be here tonight. But I do think the prince could give us some decent beds in his filthy khan out of the money we labor to make for him."

Pierre did not need to listen any more, though the men continued to talk freely. They congratulated each other that they had almost reached the end of their long journey. In the quiet seclusion of their master's estate, completely confident that they were safe from prying ears, they joked about the taxes they saved, the money they earned, where they would spend it, and the promotion they thought they might expect in something they termed Ogli's service.

His corruption is well organized, Pierre thought. It was pellucidly clear to him that Ogli, who had smuggled jewels and opium into France, had also built a khan on the land he had stolen by torturing a man, so that he could store tax-free merchandise until somehow, he smuggled it out of the empire. Pierre was not astonished that Ogli would do such a thing, but he was amazed that he dared to. Only an immensely powerful lord, with friends among the heathen nations and enormous influence in the empire, could have conceived and executed such a project. Pierre wondered whether Charles of France or the Great Comneni of Trebizond lost more through Ogli's daring peculations. From the size of the khan, it was undoubtedly the Great Comneni.

He walked slowly back to the castle and looked up at the drawbridge. He apprehended no danger now from the caravan. But he had nowhere else to go, and he was willing to return to the castle. The irony of being locked out of his prison made him smile. He knew he did not need to shout, for he was sure he was observed at the edge of the moat in the full moonlight. Perhaps the timorous guards would open the castle when they satisfied themselves that the caravan was immured for the night in the khan. A glow appeared over its walls now, as if the men had lighted fires within. Pierre dangled his feet over the edge of the moat and stared at the reflection of the moon in the water. Claire's face swam there. The revelation by the Turkish guides of such dangerous information rendered all Pierre's senses extraordinarily sharp and alert. He could feel his heart thump in his ears. Stephanie's kiss, which he had so vehemently returned, unaccountably framed the floating image of Claire's sweet face in long, raven hair. The vision was disturbing.

Then he heard horses on the road, far away and running fast. Apparently the guards heard them, too. Perhaps they guessed who it was. The bridge began to creep away from the wall, ever so slowly, and it stopped cautiously about halfway down.

In a very few minutes a group of hard-ridden horses, bearing men whose armor flashed in the moonlight, galloped past the khan and up to the castle gate. Theodore reined in his foaming horse and leaped off. Pierre got to his feet. The bridge settled noiselessly into place.

"What are you doing here?" Theodore asked suspiciously.

Pierre answered insolently, "I thought I'd go swimming."

"Were you snooping about the khan?"

"I did notice you had visitors. It is full of Greeks, Sir Theodore. Camels and Greeks."

"How do you know they are Greeks?"

"I heard them talking. I was wondering how to get back into the castle. My jailers appear to have forgotten their prisoner."

"Your jailers rely on your word, Peter. I am glad for you as well as for the family that you were sensible enough to avoid the caravan. We never interfere with our landlord's commercial activities: it's Ogli's khan, Peter. I heard in town that he is looking for you."

"Is he? I am not surprised."

"So are the city police. At least, I think it's you. There cannot be many tall, blond, Turkish-speaking Franks named Peter. Why are you sought by the police?"

"I have no idea."

"What else did you do besides fight with Ogli's men?"

"Nothing that hurt anyone."

"You are a very uncomfortable person to have around. You must leave here at once. Now. Tonight. Your ransom has been paid. I am almost afraid to keep it."

Theodore gave an order in Greek to one of the men, and took Pierre by the arm and hustled him over the bridge.

"The city is alive with rumors. Go to your room at once. I was never so anxious to get rid of a guest in my life."

"How did Sir John raise the money?"

"He will tell you."

Theodore left him. In a little while the count's valet arrived. He had with him a sword, three purses, a cloak, and a cup of coffee. The cloak swished a little when he set it down, like a thin stream of water splashing over a stone. Pierre was amazed at the bewildering assortment of articles that burdened the bearded Trapezuntian. He drew the undecorated sword from its scabbard and flicked the blade with his finger nail. It sang prettily. The temper was true. It was a good, honest sword. Of course, he could not use it with his crippled right hand, and he could not fight with his left, but it gave him a feeling of confidence. He drank the coffee, which made him sweat and set his brain to galloping; perhaps the Greeks made more sense than he thought, with drugs to wake them up and drugs to put them to sleep. He had never felt more alive, and from Theodore's cryptic warnings, he was glad of it. He examined the purses. One of them held Justin's collar. He had assumed that it would. The others were filled with gold pieces. That astonished him. He buckled on the good sword, and felt more like a Frenchman again.

Theodore arrived at the door with a steel cuirass in his hand. He stood for a moment, his face absolutely stricken. Pierre thought he knew why. But he did not tell Pierre the sad news that Stephanie had just whispered into his ear.

"Try this on, Peter," he said. "You may need it."

Pierre eyed the cuirass doubtfully.

"I appreciate your kindness, Sir Theodore."

Theodore threw it on the bed. "Never mind trying it on. I see you could never squeeze yourself into it. The Franks are built to a different measure. But I shall feel better in my mind, knowing that I have done all in my power to keep you from being killed. The cloak is lined with very fine, Persian chain mail, though it looks like any other cloak. I've often worn it myself. Take it as my gift. And go away, in God's name!"

"What is the gold for, Sir Theodore?"

"It is not gold, though there is a little money for you in the smallest purse. The rest is counterfeit. If you are set upon, drop it in the road. Be sure you spill it so that it is seen to shine. If I know your enemies, it will delay them for a moment. Then ride like the wind." Theodore's hard mouth twisted into a ghost of a smile, though his eyes continued to look inexpressibly sad.

The valet tied the purses to Pierre's belt, and said something in Greek. Theodore said: "This good man asks me to call your attention to the skillful knot he has tied on the purse of the false gold. He mentions your bandaged hand, and he asks me to say that all you have to do is to pull the little cord. The purse will spill open and fall."

"You are being very courteous, Sir Theodore."

"My father is indisposed, or he would say farewell to you personally. My sister bids you Godspeed."

"Make my adieus to the lady Stephanie, Sir Theodore. Your father shall have my prayers."

"Father likes to be prayed for. Thank you, Peter."

A man held a horse ready for him in the courtyard.

"Turn to the left at the highway and follow it in to the city," Theodore informed Pierre. "Avoid the little paths that lead off from it. Trebizond is less than two hours away if you hurry. But spare your horse for a spurt of speed if you need it, which I pray you shall not. God keep you, Peter."

Pierre felt the straight back and the lean, strong sides of the good animal under him. He walked him past the khan, seeking the dustiest, quietest parts of the path, and galloped up onto the road. The horse was fresh and had a good stride. Pierre could not complain of Theodore's parting attentions. He wondered again how Justin had raised the money.

From the caravan route on the high ground, the castle looked very small, almost unreal. Its watery moat shone like the coil of a silver serpent wrapped tightly around it.

He had gone only a little way—the castle had scarcely disappeared as he rounded a bend in the highway—when he found the road blocked by a mounted figure on a horse. He had not expected interception so soon, in spite of Theodore's oblique reference to people looking for him. He cursed his bandaged hand and drew his protective cloak around him. He had never heard of such a garment. It was light as a feather on his shoulders. He crouched a little behind his horse's neck and approached the figure cautiously. It was dressed in peasant's trousers and a light peasant shirt.

Suddenly Stephanie's voice called softly to him: "Do not take me for an assassin, Peter, and hurry up." Pierre instantly rode over to her.

"What in the name of all the saints, Stephanie, are you doing here?"

"Theodore is sending you to your death," she said bitterly. "He doesn't mean to, but he is terribly overwrought by some gossip he heard in town, and, of course, I told him about poor Father. Follow me, Peter."

She turned off the well defined caravan route into a little path that led into the darkness of a gully in the direction of the sea. "This is the longer, slower, safer way. I'll show it to you." Pierre followed her.

"You are very foolish," he said. "Does your brother know you are doing this?"

"You will never be a Greek, Peter. Of course he does not know, but he is no fool, and he'll guess soon enough."

They did not pass the weird, high, old monastery in the mountain. Pierre, of course, had no idea where they were, but Stephanie guided him as if she knew the way well. They were in the forest a great part of the night. The moon rode high for an hour or two, and then began to slip down the other side of the heavens, splashing the path with patches of silver light. After a long interval the land grew flatter, at a lower elevation than the plateau, and the path widened somewhat. A cold wind, probably from the sea, rustled the leaves in the branches that soared above their heads and bent the high grass that grew on either side of them. They had passed no one, seen no houses or buildings of any kind since they left the castle. Pierre thought how lightly the bare-headed girl was clad, and was ashamed of his manners. He urged his horse alongside her own and took off his cloak.

"I have been stifling in this while you froze, dear Stephanie," he said. He threw it around her shoulders. The cloak made its curious splashing noise again as it settled around her body. Pierre did not immediately remove his arm, and she looked up at him in surprise. He drew her close to him and kissed her again. She did not put her arms around him; her hands rested lightly against his chest.

They rode on again in a moment. When Stephanie spoke, her voice was low and troubled. "That I did not expect or ask for, Peter. I know I surprised you the first time, but this you did of your accord." She was silent again. Then she laughed a little. "I don't care, Peter. Now I am glad. We are nearly to the city. I think I shall show you all the wrong paths so that we never, never get there. Let's run our horses!" She felt as if she would not breathe again unless she could feel a wind in her face. They galloped for a time, and when Stephanie pulled up her horse, her voice was clear and strong. "The yellowhead doesn't bother me any more," she said.

They came out of the forest and approached the wooden bridge that spanned the great ravine, beyond which rose the hard, stone walls of Trebizond, red and high in the rosy light that had begun to color the sky. Pierre had not realized that the night was so quickly gone. The grayness of the early dawn had not been visible through the forest trees.

Suddenly Stephanie's body grew rigid, the way it had done when she heard the caravan.

"Hush!" she whispered.

Pierre heard it, too. There was a furious galloping sound behind them. Theodore and another man rode up. Their horses were foaming and nearly spent.

"What is the meaning of this, Stephanie?" he cried angrily.

"I didn't want Peter to die."

"Neither did I. But this is dreadful, dangerous nonsense on your part, sister."

"Well, it's done, and I'm glad I did it."

"You must come home at once."

"Look at your horse, Theodore."

Her brother sputtered. "My sister is a willful girl, Peter. Maybe you are a wizard and conjured her out of the castle to guide you."

Stephanie said: "You could have sent a guide yourself, Theodore. That is what you should have done. But you were in no mood to talk to, and so I went out myself before he had a chance to get too far away."

"It is true that we cannot go home till our horses have had a chance to rest." Then he said, rather shamefacedly: "Peter, now that the way is safe, observe that you have plenty of company. I dare say I should have thought more clearly but for some sad news that Stephanie gave me about Father."

"I told him," Stephanie said.

"Then perhaps I am forgiven. I am glad you know, Peter."

"I am anxious to see the captain," Pierre said. "There are stables near the ship, as you undoubtedly know. If you care to come aboard, you can rest till you and your beasts are better able to make the trip home again."

Theodore smiled. "And sail away to France, no doubt, and be hanged on the way! No thank you, Peter. Perhaps my sister would not mind a little trip." He looked shrewdly at her. "But I think we shall stay off your ship, if it's all the same to you."

"Very well," said Pierre.

"Would you take us to France, Peter?" Stephanie was teasing her brother, who did not laugh at the joke.

"I might."

"I think I was away too long," Theodore observed rather sourly. "The next Frank I hold to ransom will be very old and fat. And bald, if I have my choice. I am more than ever glad to get rid of you, Peter."

The alert, courteous guards at the bridge eyed Pierre very curiously. One of them started to question him.

"He cannot speak Greek," Theodore said, "but you can talk to him in Turkish. I doubt if he will tell you anything. He has been my guest for a week, and I know hardly anything about him."

"That's because you have not been home for a week, Sir Theodore," the guard said pleasantly. Then he addressed Pierre. "What is your name, young man?"

"Peter."

"Is that so?" It seemed to the guard that every Frank in Trebizond had been named Peter for some days. "May I inquire whether you are wearing a wig?"

Pierre bent his head. "See for yourself," he said.

"Permit me," said the guard, and gave his hair a firm yank. "It is either real or well glued on," he observed.

"You have curious customs here," Pierre said. "May I ask the meaning of this singular welcome?"

"Certainly you may ask. I am not, however, authorized to reply. Under the circumstances I trust that you will not object to a small guard of men."

"Do I understand that I am under arrest for some crime?"

"I am instructed only to guard and treat courteously a tall Frank named Peter who speaks good Turkish, and conduct him to the chief of police in the palace. There have been several so far. They have all been released. I am perhaps exceeding my instructions a bit, but it is my belief, not my positive knowledge, that the man sought is not accused of crime. Our instructions are usually a little different when a crime is involved."

"Must I go to your chief of police at once? I am very anxious to see the captain of the French ship, *Sainte-Eulalie*."

"That is perfectly all right, sir. It is very early for the chief of police to be awake."

They passed over the bridge, and half a dozen armed men took up a formation at a respectful distance behind them.

"You are certainly not under arrest," Theodore said, "but we should all be this minute if you had mentioned our little business transaction."

"I knew better."

They rode through the gate in the walls, where the sentinels, at a signal from one of the bridge guards, who seemed to have considerable authority, did not question them.

There were bales of goods alongside the Lady. Two men, dressed like workmen, already loitered among them. Pierre thought perhaps they were stevedores who had arrived early for work.

306

"That's the ship I came from France on," he said to Stephanie, pointing to the Lady.

Stephanie urged her horse up to his side to take a better look.

Suddenly there was a whirring in the air, and the plop of a crossbow quarrel in something soft. Stephanie screamed and fell from her horse with the missile in her throat. Theodore and the other Greek leaped down to pick her up. Pierre saw them raise her.

There was a shout from the decks of the Lady. Jacques of Bourges saw Pierre and cried: "Behind the bales! Look out, Pierre!" Pierre saw the man who had looked like a stevedore quickly fitting another bolt to his weapon. His companion, similarly armed, raised his arbalest to shoot. But the companion instantly collapsed with an arrow, which one of the bridge guards let fly, quivering in his chest.

Pierre cried out in rage and pain as if he himself instead of Stephanie had been struck. He kicked his horse so hard that the animal reared on its hind legs and dashed toward the bale behind which the man had suddenly ducked for safety. Pierre drew his sword with his bandaged right hand and leaped off the horse as it arrived at the bale. He landed on top of it and jumped to the ground. He could not swing his sword. He could hardly hold it. He grasped the blade with his left hand as if it were a pike, steadying it with his right by the hilt. He thrust the point into the man's face with the wickedest thrust that La Salle had ever taught him. The guards watched him, astonished at his tears, his cries, and his amazing speed. The point of the sword entered the man's mouth and passed up into the base of his brain. Pierre did not immediately withdraw the weapon. He held it there till the man grew limp. A sword will bend laterally; held with the cutting edge pointing to the earth, the blade will support a great weight. The man was dead in a second or two.

The bridge guards gathered around the dreadful scene and one of them said to another: "Observe that the murderer's feet do not touch the ground. The Frank fights with a sword in a new way."

Pierre flung the man away from his swordpoint and rushed back to Stephanie, but the bolt had slit a vein in her throat and she had bled to death in Theodore's arms.

"Now I shall go aboard your ship, Peter," he said heavily. "It is a matter of utmost indifference to me whether I am hanged or not."

The quiet guards noted the remark, and decently laid out the bodies of the dead men. Justin appeared on the deck of the Lady. Theodore carried his sister tenderly, like a sleeping child, wrapped in her cloak of hidden mail.

A strange Italian guard on the dock stopped them and said, "You cannot come aboard this ship." But Pierre swore at him savagely in Italian and threatened him with the bloody sword. In the presence of the murdered girl and the furious shouting man, the strange Italian drew back ashamed and let them pass. Justin recognized Theodore.

"You've brought the brigand back with you! Good lad! How did you manage it? What happened to the poor girl?"

"She's dead, Sir John. The bolt was meant for me, I have no doubt." Pierre walked heavily. Tears streamed down his face and he did not brush them away.

They laid her on the bunk in the sailing master's cabin. Crispin came, but of course he could do nothing. Theodore closed her eyes and knelt, weeping silently, and prayed beside her. Pierre put his hand on her brother's shoulder, but Theodore shook his head and motioned him away. The other Greek stood outside the door. Pierre went into the great cabin with Sir John.

# CHAPTER

## ❊ 27 ❊

OUTSIDE ON THE DOCK the bridge guards were joined by a large number of the city police, and the strange Italian watchman soon had a group of armed Italians with him. It would have taken a great company of soldiers to have forced a way through all the armed men to the Lady just at that moment.

Pierre's face was still wet when he finished telling the captain about his sojourn in the forest castle. He also whispered into Justin's ear what he had found out about the khan. And in a rush of words he told about Ilderim, the Turkish pilot, and how Jacques Coeur had found the opium and the jewels under the sand at the bottom of the cook's barrel.

"I had intended to tell you my real mission the night we escaped from the factor's house. Of course, I never had a chance."

Justin fingered the collar of his order. "I understand. Your Greeks cannot be all bad, or they would never have given this back. The death of the brave girl is a dreadful thing."

He put a cup of brandy in front of Pierre, but Pierre refused it. "You'd better, lad. I think I know partly how you feel." Pierre drained it then; it might have been water in his throat. For a long time he sat staring at the empty cup. "It's my fault, Sir John. But for me Stephanie would be still alive."

Sir John filled the cup again.

" 'Tis not your fault, boy. You are not to blame. Not for any part of it." He continued to talk in a low sympathetic voice, absolving Pierre over and over again, often repeating himself and not caring much what he said, for he knew Pierre was not listening. At length Pierre drank the second cup of brandy. It strengthened him somewhat, for he raised his head and said:

"Who was the Italian on the dock, Sir John?"

"A Genoese. I sold the ship, Pierre. I had no right to, of course, but I was able to convince the Genoese that I owned her. I went to them because they are not popular in Trebizond and I had a plan for getting the Lady back. They fought the empire, you know, some years ago. Won the war, too, such as it was. The Great Comneni had to pay a token tribute of nuts and wine for a while. But their trade has suffered ever since, and the Trapezuntians do not like them. They gave me £20,000 for the ship, or they said they would. Only half of it has been paid. What did not go for your ransom, I have been spending in bribes to have the ship inspected, overhauled, reinspected, and re-overhauled. They wanted to sail her away at once, of course." He smiled. "The Trapezuntian inspectors have been very cooperative. They have discovered the staunchest ship in the minister's service to be unseaworthy. But my money will not hold out forever. Sooner or later they'll have to certify her. But now you are off my mind, and I have no doubt that we shall be able to go to the authorities and have the sale invalidated in some way. I doubt if we shall get the inspectors' bribe money back, however. There is blood on your hand, Pierre."

He rang his little bell. Henri, the page, was sent for a bucket of sea water and a rag. Pierre cleaned his hand and his sword, which was bloody all the way to the hilt from the blood that had run out of the man and down the blade while Pierre had him on the tip of it.

"I never killed a man before, Sir John. But I'm glad I killed that one."

There was a soft knock on the door. Justin bade the man come in. To his considerable surprise it was Theodore.

"Is it your intention to let this robber go free?" Sir John asked in French.

"I invited him aboard the ship. He did not accept before Stephanie was killed. I do not see how I can be less hospitable after what has happened."

"But the Greek has your ransom. France is at peace with Trebizond. He had no right to hold you. If I ever get the ship out of the hands of the Genoese, and if we ever get safely back to France, don't you think the minister will consider your services a little costly? You've exposed his precious De Coucy, of course, and Baltha Ogli. Maybe he'll think it's worth it. But £3,000 is a lot of money, added to what I've spent bribing the marine inspectors. The face of the young man here looks as if he might be willing to give the money back. He looks scared, Pierre."

"Perhaps he is, as well as grief-stricken, poor man. I have some questions to ask him. I can speak to him only in Turkish, Sir John. It's about Ogli's caravansary on his property."

"Talk to him by all means. The scoundrels were probably mixed up in the smuggling together."

Theodore said: "Peter, a priest has got through the crowd outside. But he is the only one who has been allowed to pass. I have summoned a litter, and it is my intention, if you give me leave, to take Stephanie home. The captain of the guards, however, says that nobody can leave the ship, alive or dead, till after you return from the palace." His shoulders slumped; he spoke like a man who had been sentenced to death.

"They should certainly let you go with your sister."

"Perhaps if you speak to the captain of the guards, he will change his mind. I have no doubt that you are a great lord, Peter. My saving you, and my greedy ransoming of you has brought death and shame to my family. Perhaps you intend to reverse the ransom now. I shall willingly return yours and add to it whatever my father and I are able." The dreary, hopeless face of the Greek was painful even for Sir John to witness.

"Please sit down, Sir Theodore. I am aware of the sorrow you feel. Believe me, I feel it, too."

"When Stephanie died," Theodore said in a choked voice, "it is my belief that she tried to say your name. Stephanie knew very few men. Perhaps she conceived a great affection for you. You do not know it, but when my father threatened to turn you over to Baltha Ogli, Stephanie instantly remonstrated with him. Even the servants heard her."

"Your sister was so brave and good, Sir Theodore, that I do not trust myself to speak of her. About Baltha Ogli I must speak, however, and I beg you to listen to me if you can. I am not a great lord, or even a knight, but I do hold some authority from the French minister of finance. I was sent on a special mission to Trebizond to discover, if I could, the source of certain smuggling of jewels and opium that originated here. I can tell you that Baltha Ogli is the criminal. But last night I found out that there is smuggling going on on your property, too."

"I don't know how you discovered that, Peter." There was utter resignation in Theodore's hopeless voice. "Even Stephanie could not have told you. She never knew anything about it. It is perfectly true that there is a great deal of smuggling, but Father and I are not involved in it. Ogli built the khan, but he rents it from us because it is part of the estate. He uses it for his own purposes, and pays handsomely for it, sometimes in gold, often in merchandise from his caravans." He made a hopeless gesture. "You probably know all this."

"Are they his caravans?"

"They are consigned to him. Every so often, as last night, a string of camels turns off the main route instead of going on to Trebizond. They leave the merchandise in the khan and rejoin the train when it returns to Asia. When the khan is full, Ogli sends a ship to a little cove on the coast. When the goods are safely aboard, he pays us the rent. The goods never reach the city; neither import nor export taxes are paid. The ship is usually Genoese, sometimes English. Mules take the merchandise over the trails that you have twice seen. You know how obscure they are. It is all quietly done, and I imagine that Ogli and his servant, who arranges most of the details, make immense amounts of money by the business."

"Why did you never say anything?"

"Because I never dared. Ogli knew something about us. It is a dreadful thing to steal from the caravans." Theodore told him what his father had done. "And now we would be accused of defrauding the emperor as well as of Father's old crime, for, of course, Ogli would blame us as accomplices. Perhaps we are, in a way, though unwilling ones. Ogli does not know how much I know about him. I have discovered this little by little over a period of years. You seem to have found it out faster. I don't much care."

"If the import taxes are as high as the export taxes, with which I am familiar," Pierre said, "Ogli makes himself a princely income by avoiding all of them. That is stealing from the caravans too, is it not? Isn't he just as guilty as your father?"

"It is certainly stealing a vast amount from the emperor. The laws that regulate all kinds of taxes here are very strict. The empire lives by trade."

"Sir Theodore, if I told you that I have a letter in my possession which conclusively proves that Ogli smuggled goods into France, would you go with me to the authorities here and tell about what you know of smuggling on your own land? I already have proof that Ogli is a thief. You will be believed."

The Greek thought a moment.

"Yesterday I should have said No. I should have been too frightened. But today my heart and spirit are broken. It is Ogli's fault that my father is blind. It is his fault, too, that my sister is dead, for I have no doubt that the man who shot her was an assassin sent by Ogli. Peter,

I tell you, if I live to be avenged on Ogli and his eunuch, I do not care when or how I die after that. If you have the slightest evidence against him and his unnatural servant, I shall welcome the opportunity to go to the authorities and tell them everything I know." Some of the old hardness came back into his face. "The men will sleep late in the khan. It is possible to surprise them if soldiers can be sent quickly enough."

It was still early in the morning when the eparch, or chief of police, of the city of Trebizond began his official day by admitting to his headquarters in the palace three men whom he had never seen before. But he knew something about them.

During its two and a half centuries of precarious existence, Trebizond had evolved the prototype of all the secret police organizations of the world. On land the empire was surrounded on three sides by overwhelming numbers of potential enemies. The fourth side faced the sea, which at any moment might be covered with hostile fleets. The national nervousness amounted to a mania. The result was the secret police.

When the important official who headed this great, silent service saw Pierre, he assumed that he had before him the young Frank whom the Grand Duke Alexius had so unaccountably sought eight days before. He also assumed that Pierre was the man who had been observed in the custody of Ogli's three disguised servants, whose activities had been quietly looked into.

Justin was known to the chief of police as a Frank sea captain of impeccable reputation, except that he had lately been seen much in the company of certain Genoese merchants. That was always a suspicious circumstance in Trebizond.

Sir Theodore, of course, was a well known Pontic gentleman, son of the blind old Count of Mesembria, who had once been under suspicion as a common robber. But nothing had ever been proved against him, and everybody knew that he now lived in retirement on the estates that, having sold to Baltha Ogli, he now rented from that great Bulgarian prince. He assumed that Theodore had come to complain about the death of his sister, a very legitimate reason. Every circumstance in connection with her murder had been reported. Her assassins had been identified as two of Baltha Ogli's guards. He observed that both Pierre and Theodore appeared utterly exhausted; Sir John was very serious.

Turning to Theodore, the eparch said: "I am informed that your party was attacked this morning by two robbers, and that the lady Stephanie was brutally murdered. I am exceedingly sorry, Sir Theodore.

Both assassins are now dead, as you know. I am at a loss to know why they should have shot her."

"Peter will tell you," Theodore answered. The chief of police looked quizzically at Pierre.

"They were shooting at me," he said. "I am sure that they were Ogli's men. Baltha Ogli would be delighted at my death. Three others in his service nearly accomplished it a week ago." He told how the three Greeks, disguised as Franks, had assaulted him in the Eastern Star. The chief of police looked troubled. He knew from the reports of what happened that Pierre was telling the truth.

"The two assassins on the docks have indeed been identified as Baltha Ogli's men. And it has been reported to me that three of his guards, disguised as Franks as you describe, took you, or someone like you, out of the city a week ago. It would appear that the prince is desirous of your death. But attempted murder is a serious charge against so great a lord. Perhaps his wicked servants were simply trying to rob you."

"That is not the case, sir. Baltha Ogli has ample reason to want to kill me." Pierre placed De Coucy's letter on the table. "When you can conveniently have this letter translated, you will learn that Baltha Ogli, careless of the great trust placed in him by the French minister of finance, has abused his important position as our Trapezuntian factor and greedily conspired with a corrupt countryman of mine to smuggle into France quantities of jewels, which defrauds the French king of his rightful import taxes, and also thousands of pounds worth of the rare and costly medicine, opium, so that not only is the king cheated of his taxes, but many unfortunate sufferers are deprived of the benefits of the drug. Obviously, merchandise that is smuggled into France must also be smuggled out of Trebizond. Your own government is being cheated, too. My understanding is that the laws against smuggling here are very strict."

"They are. You are bringing a heavy charge against Baltha Ogli, though I think the French king is more directly concerned than we are. But if this letter substantiates your charge, the grand duke will undoubtedly want to hear about it. The thing is beyond my jurisdiction, of course. Baltha Ogli enjoys the highest sort of diplomatic immunity. He is a relative of the sultan through his kinship with the sultana." The chief of police smiled. "We are very careful to be polite to our heathen neighbors, whose armies are so powerful, and whose trade we live on."

Pierre said bitterly: "I can understand that a few jewels and a little opium smuggled into France might not interest the emperor very deeply.

But I bear no love for the wicked man who tried to kill me and who actually did kill the good lady who was the sister of my friend. Do not assume that Baltha Ogli was satisfied to flout the laws of France and the empire only to the extent of this minor rascality that I have described. Sir Theodore will tell you more."

Theodore did, at great length, and in Greek. Neither Sir John nor Pierre understood a word, of course, but Theodore's resigned countenance, his frequent pauses, his heavy sighs, and the expression of stern gravity on the face of the chief of police, that grew sterner as the recital continued, bore ample testimony to the importance of the communication. At one point the chief of police gave a sharp order to a police captain, who immediately left the room. Sir Theodore smiled, with half of his hard, set mouth. It was as grim a sneer as Pierre had ever witnessed. When, some time later, he finished speaking, his head slumped forward, his shoulders drooped, and he said: "I told him everything, Peter, even about the ransom."

The chief of police addressed Pierre. "This is a bigger thing than I imagined, and much more complicated. First, I should like to know whether you intend to prosecute Sir Theodore for holding you to ransom. You have every right to, though he has informed me that he has offered to return the money. Trapezuntians do not hold citizens of friendly nations to ransom. It was simple, stupid banditry."

"I was treated kindly by his family," Pierre said. "Sir Theodore saved my life by pulling me out of the ravine. His sister nursed me back to health with great skill and tenderness. The count, his father, led me to believe that some Trapezuntian nobles have a foolish, ancient grudge against us Westerners. It is my belief that Sir Theodore is genuinely sorry and intends to return the ransom. As far as I am concerned, nothing more will ever be said about the matter. I hope he does not suffer for his mistake."

"The police do not judge such things. That is a matter for the courts. If you do not prosecute Sir Theodore and the count, his father, I doubt if anybody else will, though, of course, the whole circumstance will have to be reported to the grand duke. Sir Theodore, you are at liberty to go, if you wish, and to take your poor sister home."

Theodore turned to Pierre: "The cloak of mail that did not protect Stephanie is yours; I gave it to you. Shall I leave it aboard your ship?"

Pierre shook his head sadly. "I could not bear to see it, Sir Theodore. It would reproach me to the end of my life that I did not send her home instead of letting her guide me to the city."

"She meant to save your life, Peter. And she did, though not the way she planned to. Very well, she shall wear it to her grave."

No one hindered him from leaving the palace or the city. He went back to his father, with the other Greek and a litter slung between two mules bearing the body of Stephanie in her cloak.

But his father had already heard the news from the captain of the police, who had been dispatched in a considerable force and at great speed during the conversation. Long before Sir Theodore and his sorrowful burden arrived at the castle, the khan had been surrounded, the guides and the men taken and sent back under guard toward the city, and an efficient clerk left behind to make a written record of the merchandise that had been unloaded from the twenty camels and stored there.

As soon as Theodore left the room the chief of police said to Pierre: "We have been looking all week for a Frank who answers your description and who speaks Turkish. We have taken some pains to conceal the fact that the Grand Duke Alexius himself is making the search, and you can believe me when I tell you that my men are not idle gossips. But somebody has talked. It cannot be the grand duke either, for a more cautious man never breathed. I dare not hazard a guess who started the rumor that a great honor is in store for the man we seek. But the rumor exists, and I have been deluged with blond young Franks trying to talk Turkish. They are all named Peter. They all tell me, 'There is no God but God,' and so forth, as an example of their Turkish learning. Only one of them could speak more than a dozen phrases such as any sailor might pick up in the course of a voyage or two, and his hair was dyed. Now you speak Turkish better than most of us Greeks, and I have been informed that your hair is real. It is believed that the man we seek has a wound on his chest. Do you have such a wound?"

"I do, sir. It is nearly healed."

"I am glad it is. But I have annoyed the grand duke with so many Franks that he has ordered me to keep the next one—I am not arresting you, young man—in protective custody for a week or two. We want to be sure his hair is not dyed. By that time it will grow somewhat, and then, if it is black around the roots, of course, the man is just another fraud. I trust you will accept our hospitality as graciously as it is offered."

Pierre could hardly believe his ears. He was very tired, and for the moment he forgot his manners.

"I am exceedingly weary of Trapezuntian protective custody," he said. "Do I understand you to say that I am to be kept here until my hair grows so that you and the grand duke can convince yourselves that it is not dyed? And in the meantime have Baltha Ogli murder my friends? And let the Genoese sail away with our ship?"

"Sail away with the ship? I know nothing about that. As for Baltha Ogli, I cannot touch him. You do not understand the police here, sir. We listen; we report; but we do not act without orders. At this moment your letter is in the hands of His Highness, the grand duke. He reads and speaks French perfectly. Perhaps your charge is serious enough for him to act upon it immediately. If he wants to see you, we will be informed. He is undoubtedly interested in our conversation so far."

"How does he know our conversation so far?"

"As I told you, you do not understand the police of Trebizond. What would happen if you went to a prefect of one of your own French cities with intelligence of a nature such as you and Sir Theodore have put before me this morning? I think I know. A squad of men-at-arms would go raging into the prince's castle, muddying up the floors, spitting on the carpets, and hauling the man off to a dungeon. Then, if he were innocent, there would be terrible reprisals. We do things differently here. A clerk has transcribed every word we have spoken. He will read a summary of your charges to the grand duke. If His Highness is interested, the clerk will read the charges verbatim. The clerk is very skillful at shorthand—it is one of the few things of any importance that we Greeks have learned from the Romans." Pierre had never heard of shorthand.

The chief of police also told him that a number of men had been sent to the forest castle to look into the matter of the khan. "We act very quietly and very swiftly, but very cautiously," he said. Then, turning to Sir John, he added through an interpreter: "It has been reported to me that, contrary to your usual custom, you have been seeing a great deal of your Genoese competitors. Does that have any bearing on your impulsive friend's fear that they will sail away with your ship?"

Sir John cheerfully admitted that he had sold the ship to raise money for Pierre's ransom.

The chief of police smiled. "It is unusual for people to confess so many crimes right after breakfast," he said. "Usually we have to persuade them to talk. But today a Pontic gentleman tells me that he stole a Frank and held him to ransom. I knew nothing about it and the Frank did not denounce him. Now a French sea captain admits that he stole a ship and sold her to the Genoese. Surely, Sir John, if you could convince your fellow Italians, who ought to know better, that you owned the *Sainte-Eulalie*, you should now be able to convince them that you

317

did not, and get your ship back. My department is not concerned with commercial chicanery among foreigners—at least, not until they begin to fight each other. You cannot sell stolen goods and then go to a policeman and ask for the goods back again. Go to a lawyer, Sir John. I understand your position, of course, and I can see why you did what you did. But whatever I may personally think of the Genoese, the laws that protect you also protect them. In any case, it is no business of the police department."

"The inspectors have declared the ship unseaworthy," Sir John observed. "She has been several times overhauled. My hope is that they will continue to find her unsafe."

"Oh, well now. That is quite another matter. It is within the jurisdiction of my department to protect the lives of foreigners. You should have said that at once. Quite obviously, no Genoese shall be allowed to risk his precious life aboard a ship that our inspectors have declared unseaworthy. If your own French crew care to remain aboard, to man the pumps or whatever they have to do, that is their own concern. But you have persuaded me that it is my duty to keep the Genoese off her till our inspectors declare her safe. It was a happy thought to have the inspectors look at the ship, Sir John. If the Genoese cannot get aboard her, they cannot sail her away. And in the meantime, after our young friend's hair grows a bit, and perhaps even before, I dare say the grand duke will see you, too, and help you out of your difficulty."

Pierre remembered Stephanie's amazement when he mentioned the red shoes of Abou Ayub. He decided to force the issue of a conference with Alexius if he could.

"I can make a good guess," he said, "who has started the rumors about me. I think it is the young man who very courteously approached my table that night at the tavern. Is it possible for me to send a message to the grand duke?"

"Of course it is."

"Then tell him," Pierre said, "that the man who seeks me wears a shooting star on his head."

The chief of police looked puzzled. "It is one of the qualifications of a good policeman here to carry messages accurately. I must admit that your words make no sense to me, but I cannot believe that you are joking. Kindly repeat your message. Perhaps I misunderstood."

Pierre did.

"Very well," said the chief of police. "Your message will be given to the grand duke exactly as you have phrased it." He was too familiar with elaborate codes and passwords to say anything more about it. Pierre had been speaking French through the interpreter. Sir John, of course, understood the words, but his face was perfectly blank, and the chief of police had a shrewd notion that the captain did not understand the import of the message any more than he did. He began to wonder what sort of secret plenipotentiary he had to deal with. Most people did not ask him to relay code messages to Alexius, Grand Duke of Trebizond, Paradynast to David, the son of the emperor. The chief of police was a little uncomfortable.

He was more uncomfortable still when the message returned with the startling news that Alexius, still at breakfast, not even having had his bath, commanded the Frank and Sir John to wait upon him immediately.

# CHAPTER

## ❋ 28 ❋

WESTERNERS KNEW very little about eunuchs, and what little they knew was often obscene and inaccurate. It was commonly supposed that they were stupid, unemotional, gluttonous and depraved.

Depraved they sometimes were, but no more often than other men. If Basil liked to see people suffer, what was to be said of the Baron de Retz, who was called many things before they hanged him, but never a eunuch? The depravity was mental.

Nor were eunuchs always gluttonous. The food they ate did indeed transform itself into pads of fat upon their bodies strikingly dissimilar to the distribution of flesh on an ordinary man. But that was a glandular manifestation of their affliction. It had nothing to do with their appetites. Many of them ate very sparingly.

The charge of stupidity is totally refuted by the recognition of their intellectual abilities by all the great Eastern nations. In Turkey they trained the Janizaries, the elite of the sultan's soldiers. That absolute monarch was not foolish enough to confide the discipline of his most trusted warriors, who were the safety of his person and the terror of his enemies, to stupid men. For ages in Constantinople, all but three great posts of the empire were open to eunuchs; eight could be held by eunuchs only. And to put their sons in the way of such lucrative, honorable careers, many parents had their boys, before they were men, made incapable of ever attaining manhood. It is not recorded that a eunuch ever gloried in his affliction. The absurd fanatics, and there were a few, who had themselves made eunuchs for religious motives, were discredited by the Church, which pronounced, logically enough, that grace ought not to be expected for withstanding a temptation which no longer exists. Neither did eunuchs universally lament their peculiarity, though they sometimes wondered wistfully what it would be like to be otherwise. So do children wonder what it will be like to be grown up.

It was the childlike quality of their emotions that made eunuchs so valuable to their masters. They reasoned with the clarity of mature men. But their fidelity was immature, unquestioning, like a dog's; their affection, and they felt affection deeply, was undemanding, like a child's. They were brilliant teachers of youth, patient, untiring, sympathetic, devoted, yet strict and impartial disciplinarians.

The eunuch, Alexius, the grand duke, had been such a preceptor to David, son of the Emperor John of Trebizond, ever since the imperial child's birth. David was already an emperor, but he was not expected to reign until his father died, and a good many people wondered what sort of active emperor such a lightheaded young man would make.

But David was not the first heir to the golden throne in the great hall of the old palace that people had had their doubts about. Many amiable scions of the Comnenus family had been much less able men than the events of their prosperous reigns would seem to indicate. When a weak or silly Trapezuntian prince ruled wisely, there was always a shadowy unofficial figure, often a eunuch, in the background. It had happened often enough for the figure to have a name. He was called the "paradynast," which has never been translated out of the Greek because there was never a position quite analogous to it in European monarchies. The name meant "by the family's side"—not the emperor's, but the family's. Nobody but a Comnenus had ever ruled the empire of Trebizond. The imperial name was incredibly sacrosanct. The ruling family was virtually worshiped—except on Sundays, and on Sundays the exacting ceremonial was relaxed somewhat out of deference to God. The paradynast who advised an emperor actually ruled the empire. So it was thought Alexius someday might rule—in David's name, of course. Except for the grand duke's age, John of Trebizond, old himself, need have worried little about his son's future and the empire's. But Alexius was past middle age when David was born, and that was twenty years before.

For all his advanced years, however, the grand duke was a tireless, busy, devoted servant of the state. The great secret police was entirely in his hands. He knew more about more people than anybody else in the empire, and, naturally, he had some enemies. His position was unofficial; he held it only so long as he pleased the Great Comneni. But he had pleased them so long, and made himself so indispensable, that he could afford to laugh at his enemies.

His honors had increased rather than diminished with age. One of the highest distinctions in Trebizond was an appointment to the supreme court of the empire. Twelve men, called the twelve divine judges, were appointed for life by the Great Comnenus to administer the laws and aid in their framing. They were not ordinarily eunuchs, because both military and judicial activities were traditionally held to be beyond the scope of a eunuch's ability. But Alexius' profound scholarship and serene good judgment were so universally acknowledged that, when one of the twelve divine judges died, the emperor appointed the paradynast, and even the eunuch's enemies had to approve.

Alexius was a bulky man of commanding stature. His skin had begun to wrinkle a bit on his high, intelligent brow and around his mouth, as if constant smiling had worn a crease into his flesh.

But there was no smile on his face when Sir John and Pierre were conducted into his bedchamber. A secretary with a mass of papers in his hand was reading to him. A servant held a breakfast tray over his bed. Alexius was eating and listening to the secretary at the same time. When Pierre and Sir John approached the foot of the canopied bed, Alexius greeted them in excellent French. To Pierre's astonishment the secretary continued to read, in a low voice, one paper after another.

"I am glad to see you again, Sir John," he said, "and I am glad that Pierre is safe and sound after his troubles. Pray sit down, gentlemen." The two Franks found chairs under them which the silent, and apparently polyglot servants, softly slid up to them. "Perhaps you will have a cup of coffee, Pierre. I am told that you have acquired a taste for it," and there appeared out of nowhere a cup of coffee in the hand of a servant who bowed very courteously. Even after his interview with the eparch, Pierre could still be surprised that the grand duke knew the trivial detail of his beginning to like coffee.

"I doubt whether you will want breakfast after what has happened," Alexius said sympathetically to him, "but if you do, pray tell me. I seldom have company for breakfast. It will be a pleasure. I understand that Sir John ate aboard his ship and never takes coffee. Do not mind the presence of my secretary here. I always like to hear what has happened during the night. To tell the truth, I listen with only half an ear, but sometimes I hear something of importance."

Pierre sipped his coffee. Alexius continued with his breakfast, and the secretary continued to read.

"I should have sent for you even without your message, Pierre. The letter from Bernard de Coucy, coupled with the information which you and Sir Theodore gave the eparch earlier this morning, throws a strong, clear light on a number of the activities of the Bulgarian prince that I have had under surveillance for some time. I am delighted that someone has been brave enough to expose him. The French smuggling was bad, of course, but it appears to have been only a part of Ogli's unlawful activities. Do you know what happened to the men who abducted you from the Eastern Star, Pierre?"

"I do not, Your Highness."

"You will not have to wait to find out at the trial. . . . . Ogli must be tried, of course, and his servant, too. There was a sergeant named Leo. Either you killed him or the landslide did. He was pulled out of the gorge the other day. His back was broken."

"The eparch did not mention that, Your Highness."

"The eparch never mentions anything if he can help it. Thirty years in the service have taught him to forget things the minute he reports them. The other two men fled with your money, Pierre—£17,000 of new French gold pieces."

"I am astonished that you know the amount, Your Highness."

"It was easy to count when the man was found. His name was Manuel. He confesses that he killed his companion. He was apprehended at the border trying to cross over to the Turks. He and his companion had divided your gold between them, but, of course, Manual had it all when he reached the border alone. You appear to have thrust him through the sword arm. We are not sure how he managed to kill his companion, but probably Manuel will remember before the trial. Baltha Ogli has some very wicked men working for him. Before I ask you a question that has thoroughly baffled me, Pierre, I want to tell you how indebted the family is to your presence here in Trebizond. Whether you meant to or not, your visit to us has been the means of exposing a monstrously wicked man. The money that was stolen from you will be returned to you today. I understand that you can use it to good advantage. Sir John has been engaged in some very shady dealings with the Genoese in order to pay your ransom to that greedy Pontic nobleman." Alexius smiled. Justin looked very uncomfortable.

"What could I do, Your Highness? I doubt if even your secret police know that Pierre cracked a mutinous sailor over the head on the voyage here. The fellow was going to heave me overboard! I certainly wasn't going to let any Greek keep him if I could contrive to pay the ransom!"

"No, I did not know he saved your life. My men do not police the high seas. You could have come to me, Sir John "

"Your Highness is not an easy man to see. And I had to work fast."

"Perhaps I am easier to see than you realize. But hindsight is always clearer than foresight. You did wrong, of course, but to my mind such an act is the noblest sort of wrong. Before I leave the subject, however, I must caution you to cease corrupting the marine inspectors."

"Saints! Your Highness knows everything!"

"Your ship is perfectly sound, Sir John. Buy her back as soon as you can. Pierre can give you the money now. You will make the marine inspectors dissatisfied with their very ample wages." Justin was blushing furiously.

Alexius sent his tray and his mumbling secretary out of the room. When they were alone, he said to Pierre, "And now, if you will be kind enough, tell me: I am intensely curious to know how you happen to be aware that the little steel cap which David, His Imperial Majesty, wore when you beat off his assailants in the tavern, was made of meteoric iron. His Imperial Majesty sometimes speaks too freely for his own best interests, but it is impossible that he should have mentioned such a thing when it pleased him to sit down with you in the assumed character of Abou Ayub. To the best of my knowledge, I am the only one who knows where that important part of His Imperial Majesty's disguise came from."

"I helped to make it," Pierre said, "and Your Highness is too kind. I remember being worsted in that fight."

"You lasted until my men could save the person of His Imperial Majesty. That is the main thing. It is no wonder that he wants to reward you. But if you helped make the cap—I assume you are telling the truth—you must be an armorer."

"I was reared in the home of Hugh of Milan, the armorer who made the cap originally for Jacques Coeur, long before he became so great a man as he is now."

"Now I know that you are telling the truth, for it was from Jacques Coeur that my master got the cap. He was a little boy then and he used to play with it."

"It rings prettily," Pierre said. "I shall never forget the sound it made the morning after I quite inadvertently aided in tempering it. I was a boy myself, as Your Highness must realize. It was a long time ago."

"It probably seems so to a young man. David has always been a spirited boy." It might have been a father speaking. Nobody but a paradynast would dare call an emperor by his first name. "I remember how proud he was when he grew big enough to have it fit him. But tell me,

324

Pierre, is it not a curious thing that an armorer should have worn such a gaudy sword with so wretched a blade?"

"That dreadful sword was not my own. It was given me by Bernard de Coucy, the French counterpart of your Baltha Ogli, but not quite so wicked, I think."

"It will be exhibited at the trial, Pierre. After that you can have it back. There is a great flaw in the blade."

"There must be. It broke as soon as I used it. I never want to see it again."

"The jewels are valuable."

"Are they? I should believe you if you told me they were false."

"No, they are real. A merchant would be foolish to give them away. In any case, the broken sword will be returned to you after it has served its purpose at the trial. Perhaps if you decide to return to France, you will want to keep it as a memento of your trip to Trebizond."

"If I decide to return to France, Your Highness?"

"I think I should denounce myself as a very bad head of the secret police. I have inadvertently divulged a part of what His Imperial Majesty may speak to you about. If I have correctly read the honest face of Sir John, who appeared very astonished at my mention of your supping with the emperor, you told him nothing about the identity of Abou Ayub, your Turkish friend. You will teach me to hold my tongue, Pierre."

"Pierre never tells me anything," Justin grumbled.

"I meant to conceal nothing from Sir John. I returned only a few hours ago from Sir Theodore's castle. My heart is heavy at the death of his noble sister."

"Nay, of course it is. And you look tired. His Imperial Majesty has commanded me to send you to him as soon as your identity is established. But surely he will forgive me for letting you rest a few hours after your exhausting ride and the tragedy on the docks. If you care to remain here, I shall have an apartment prepared for you in the palace."

"I think I should rest easier on the ship, Your Highness."

"I think so, too. It is sinful vanity, Pierre, which I cheerfully confess to, but I pride myself on sometimes being able to anticipate my guests' preferences. I am foolishly pleased that I guessed that you would prefer the ship. A man at the gate has horses for you both."

He nodded his head graciously to signify that they could retire. A secretary appeared and began to read to him again. A servant, obviously a bath attendant, also approached, silently, like all the Greeks, with towels on his arm and jars in his hand. It appeared that Alexius would be read

to as he was being bathed, just as he had been read to as he was break-
fasting and conversing. Pierre thought, rather groggily, that such an
existence must be very confusing. But he had to admit that the paradynast was wonderfully well informed.

During the day, while Pierre slept, the Emperor David was informed
that the Frank who had defended him the week before had been found.
He was also told of Baltha Ogli's treason and thieveries, but these concerned his father rather than himself, and though he was interested, he
characteristically left the details of Ogli's tedious trial and punishment
to the paradynast and John, his father, the conscientious, hard-working,
senior emperor.

Early next morning Justin awoke Pierre with the news that a messenger, a guard of honor, and a priest had arrived from the palace, and
he had better get up if the glittering assembly were not to be kept waiting, which he hurriedly did.

Then, on a deck of the Lady, a French-speaking herald read from a
Greek parchment, green as an emerald and lettered in vermilion and
cinnabar, a summons to the presence of David, Emperor of the Faithful
Romans, Autocrat of All the East, the Iberians, and the Transmarine
Provinces. The guard of noble knights bore on their shields the ancient
double eagle of Byzantium, signifying their descent from the ten thousand palace guards who had fled from the terror of the Fourth Crusade
with the first Comnenus and founded the empire of Trebizond. The
herald wore over his green tunic the chain of the Order of the Raven,
which was composed of links of silver, and from each link was suspended
a silver wing inlayed with copper to outline the design of the feathers.
The copper had been blackened, and, seen from a little distance, the
wings looked black and shining, like real wings of a living bird. They
signified the speed with which heralds were supposed to fly to the accomplishment of their missions.

The herald himself was not a young man, like the adventurous
European heralds whose business was to deliver challenges to cities
and carry messages in the heat of battle, but rather a dignified court
functionary, whose sedate and honorable mission in life was to convey the commands of the emperor to such of his subjects as were to
be honored, or imprisoned, or executed. The written summons was
short. The titles of the emperor took more words than the command
to appear. But the herald was authorized to inform Pierre verbally
the reason for his coming and to tell him, which he did very tactfully,
what to do and how to behave.

326

"The Great Comnenus intends to honor you," he explained, "but simply and informally, as is his wont. He will receive you in one of the antechambers of the palace. The triple prostration will not be required; you have only to walk with Sir John to the foot of the throne and kneel on two knees as you would to your own king, though, of course, it will be necessary to touch your forehead to the hem of his robe."

"Oh, of course," said Pierre.

"So that nothing will surprise you, or mar the ceremony in the eyes of the Trapezuntian officials and foreign nobles who will be present at the little gathering, I should tell you that His Imperial Majesty, thankful of the service you performed in respect of His Sacred Person, will confer upon you the Order of the Eagle of Trebizond."

"It is a wonderful honor," Justin observed. "Trapezuntian knighthood is accredited everywhere, in Europe no less than in the East. It's no more than you deserve, Pierre. The Eagle is the highest order in the empire. I cannot tell you how happy I am for you."

The herald continued: "I myself shall have the honor of reading to the assembly the reasons which incline His Imperial Majesty to bestow this honor upon you." Then he said very seriously: "I have read the manifesto privately already so that I might memorize it and not have to look at the scroll while I read, for that, of course, would be contrary to custom and a great breach of etiquette."

"Why is that?" Pierre asked.

"Why? I haven't the slightest idea. I never thought about it. When a herald reads a scroll, he simply doesn't look at it; everyone knows that. It will be in Greek, of course, and I am aware that you do not speak Greek. Let me tell you that it is couched in general terms, and no mention is, or by you should later be, made of the tavern or the waterfront. It is sufficient to have protected the Sacred Person. Where such protection was effected should not be gossiped about."

"I understand perfectly, sir."

"Pierre never gossips," Sir John said.

"Except in battle," the herald continued, "knighthood in all Christian countries is bestowed only upon the pure. You are known to have killed, through no fault of your own, one man, and perhaps two. That is why the priest is here; we shall stop at the Cathedral of the Panaghia Chrysocephalos where the metropolitan himself will administer the Blessed Sacrament to you."

327

Pierre nodded and was glad he had not had his breakfast.

"You are not to wear a sword, and, of course, you will not be covered at any time. Any costume of your own country will be acceptable. You are to say nothing except what His Imperial Majesty commands you to say. Try to pronounce the Greek words as well as you can and, if you have difficulty, lower your voice. It will add to the dignity of the proceeding and impress everyone with your sincerity."

"What will the Greek words mean?"

"Why, it is nothing but the oath of fealty to His Imperial Majesty and a promise to protect His Person against his enemies. Since you have already done so, you can pronounce it with a clear conscience. I am seldom asked so many questions, young man. I do not say you are wrong, however, to know what you are doing. You will also swear homage to him for all the lands of Trebizond which you hold from him, and the formula ends, as usual, in your profession of the Christian faith. You will recognize even in Greek the words, 'I, Peter of Trebizond,' and so forth. You have no prejudice against the Christian religion, of course?"

"Naturally not."

"At the end of the ceremony you will again touch His Imperial Majesty's robe with your forehead. You will rise and walk backward four paces: one for the Father, one for the Son, one for the Holy Ghost, and one for the Great Comnenus. Then you will turn on your heel, or on the ball of your foot if it is more convenient for you—the ceremonial is liberal here—to the right, the direction which the Eagle, which you will then have on your breast, faces. Then simply walk to where Sir John is standing. He is your sponsor and will tell you what to do next, but the hardest part will be over. Have I made myself clearly understood?"

"I think you have, sir," Pierre said.

"If you are wondering," Justin interposed, "whether it is proper for a French subject to swear fealty to a foreign prince, be assured that it is. I myself am no less a Venetian for having sworn fealty to Charles of France. Some nobles swear homage to five or six different princes; it is perfectly proper. And as for your Trapezuntian lands, you do not have any."

"You are very penetrating, Sir John. I confess that I was thinking about the question involved in what appeared at first a division of fealty. When Antoine de la Salle taught me a smattering of such things, I never thought I would be fortunate enough to experience them, and I'm afraid I have forgotten most of his teachings. I am glad you are to be my sponsor."

328

"Nay, lad, so am I. Go in now, and tell the Greek priest what a wicked rascal you really are."

"He speaks no French," the herald said smiling, "but it is assumed that a Frank merchant knows the Latin words for a sin or two. He will shrive you in Latin, Pierre. Your guard will wait for you on the docks."

The herald inclined his body exactly forty-five degrees. It was a compromise between the curt nod of the head that a commoner was entitled to and the sixty-degree bow that would be the due of Sir Peter of Trebizond three hours from that moment.

S HAVEN, SHRIVEN, and a little hungry, Pierre progressed in the center of his guard from the cathedral to the palace. Sir John rode beside him, wearing the tunic and collar of his order. Despite the elegant appearance of the mantle in which he had first met Baltha Ogli, Pierre had decided against that stifling garment and had chosen a lighter one. The herald had already left for the palace. Pierre's eyes and ears were still full of the splendor of the Eastern religious rite, which any good European might conform to since the Union of the Council of Ferrara. The scent of the incense, so curiously different from what he was used to at home, still lingered in his nostrils. He felt a sort of exaltation, and he was heartily ashamed of the questions he had asked the herald, and which he now considered flippant. He was very glad that that serious, earnest man had instructed him so meticulously how to conduct himself. He wished for all the world that Claire might magically fly from Montpellier, or wherever in France she was, to the imperial palace of Trebizond and see him made a knight of the empire. The realization that he might now, or in an hour from now, presume to ask her hand of the count, her father, purged all the foolishness out of an etiquette that pompously permitted one the choice of turning on one's heel or the ball of one's foot, and lent the ceremony a kind of sanctity.

Sir John noted his pale, grave face and whispered sympathetically, "Are you frightened, lad?"

"Half to death, Sir John."

"So was I when it happened to me. But it's not in the big court chamber and the herald said it's to be a little gathering. You don't have to do anything at all, you know. Just walk up to the throne with me. It's probably not the big throne that goes up and down. I'll tell you about that sometime; it's terrifically impressive. I am to tell who you are— that's all I'm for. Then you kneel, the way the herald said. It's over in no time. I am curious about only one thing: why the business was set for so early in the morning." He lowered his voice so that the guards could not hear. "The young emperor has the reputation of staying out late. Perhaps he hasn't even been to bed."

It would have been the grossest breach of manners, even in an informal little gathering, for anyone to have entered a room after the emperor or to have left before him. There were perhaps thirty men in the large ante-chamber to which the captain of his escort conducted Pierre and Sir John. They all wore long court tunics and their swords. There were about a dozen Turkish nobles among them. They were the only ones covered, all of them with the green turban that denoted the accomplishment of the pilgrimage to Mecca. Nearly every man in the room wore riding clothes under his tunic. For Sir John had done the emperor an injustice in his thoughts. David was going hunting and might not return for several days. Everyone knew that the young Frank was to be knighted, and they were considerably impressed that the emperor would delay his sport long enough to do it. Pierre did not know it, but he had already made a few jealous enemies among the emperor's hunting companions. The Turks did not care, of course, who he was, and those of the Greeks who were jealous were too polite and too prudent to show it. When Pierre and Sir John entered the room, there was a hum of excitement, and all of the men smiled in a friendly way and several of them nodded, though neither of the Franks recognized any of them.

"They are trying to be friendly already," Justin whispered. "Imagine how they would scowl if you were out of favor."

There was a canopied throne on a low dais at one end of the room and a curtained doorway beside it. A red carpet led over the polished floor directly to its foot. One side of the room opened through a series of arched doorways onto a garden with flowers, fountains, and sculp-tured busts of the ancient emperors, and beyond it one could see the city and the sea. It was a pleasant vista; the day was sunny, and Pierre was a happy man.

An attendant plucked at Sir John's sleeve and whispered something into his ear. Justin nodded his head, and said in a low voice to Pierre: "I am told that Alexius is going to feed us immediately after the cere-mony. Your knighthood is the only business of this gathering. That is very unusual and very fine."

Then all the doors closed noiselessly and simultaneously. There was a peal of silver trumpets, the curtains beside the throne parted, and the young knight with the silver bow of state gravely entered the room and took his place directly behind the emperor's throne. Then the herald entered, a purple scroll lettered in gold in his hand, and finally the emperor himself walked briskly into the room, and every forehead touched the floor.

David wore, over the riding clothes that no one could see, a tunic of red damask embroidered with gold into a pattern that appeared at a distance to be severely geometrical, composed mostly of circles. But closer examination would have discovered it to be intricately wrought into figures of elephants, birds, and forest trees, every one different and every one a work of art. His shoes were deep purple and covered with pearls. The occasion was not sufficiently formal to warrant his crown, but he wore the imperial pallium, which was a scarlet garment of singular construction. It was like a broad band reaching in front to a few inches above his shoes and long enough in the back to have trailed upon the floor, but he bore the after part of it on his left forearm like a train. The sides were cut away, and it looked a great deal like some of the religious vestments of which it was the prototype. The pallium was so covered with golden embroidery and precious stones that hardly any of the scarlet silk which formed its substance was visible. The Great Comnenus of Trebizond, even in informal attire, was a very different man to look at from Abou Ayub of the Eastern Star. The instant he was seated everyone stood up again.

Then a young page came through the parted curtains with a golden object on a scarlet, velvet cushion, and another followed with a sword attached to a belt that shone like silver, wrapped in a red, light transparent veil. The curtains closed, and the herald called in a loud, clear voice, "Sir John of France, come into the court!"

"Steady as you go, lad!" Justin whispered. Pierre kept his face straight, but later he told the noble captain that, more than anything else, that nautical command (which orders the helmsman to keep the course he is on) strengthened his knees and made him able to walk over the carpet, which suddenly seemed to stretch a dozen leagues, up to the foot of the distant throne.

Both men knelt and touched their foreheads to the hem of the pallium. Pierre remained on his knees, while Sir John rose.

"Whom have you brought to the foot of David, Emperor of the Faithful Romans, Autocrat of All the East, the Iberians, and the Transmarine Provinces?" the herald asked.

"Pierre," said Sir John.

Surely it was the shortest title ever heard in the palace. The roomful of noblemen craned their necks for a better look at the monosyllabic young Frank, who was so great or so small that, like a servant or the Holy Father, one name was all he needed. Most of them assumed it was some new fashion among the incomprehensible Westerners.

Having spoken the name of his charge, which was all that was required of him, Sir John backed the prescribed number of steps away from the throne, turned on his heel and retired to an empty space near the door by which they had entered.

The herald then began to read in Greek from his scroll, holding it before him, but never once glancing at it. Pierre studied an elephant in the pattern of the pallium where it folded over the knee of the emperor. Its body was gold, its eyes were red, the tusks were silver, and on each of its feet tiny green toenails had been worked in stitches too fine to be seen ten inches away. The sonorous voice of the herald continued for quite a while. Pierre thought that even the dance of Irene in her seaweed had not taken so long. He knew that the herald, though he was informing the spectators why he was entitled to knighthood, was not talking about Irene and her multiple shipwrecks. In the complex emotional state that so often accompanies grave events in one's life, he was wondering whether "Goldie" or "Greenie" would be the better name for the elephant, with whom he was beginning to feel quite friendly. Suddenly he was aware that the emperor was speaking to him, in Turkish.

In Trebizond, where nothing was left to chance, it had been realized that a graceful political gesture might be made to the Turks if the emperor were to take upon himself, in the Turkish tongue, some of the ceremony which would ordinarily have fallen to the herald. Pierre's proficiency in Turkish made it possible. The emperor leaned forward on his throne.

"Place your hands in mine," he said.

Pierre did.

The Turkish noblemen began to beam at the sound of their language being employed in the creation of a Christian knight.

"Now say after me—"

Then followed a series of Greek words which Pierre had no difficulty in pronouncing, and Sir John smiled like a father whose boy does well at school.

Then the page approached with the golden object on the scarlet cushion. It was the badge of Pierre's knighthood, the Eagle, symbol of the empire. It had one head, in contradistinction to the double-headed eagle of Constantinople, which Trapezuntians derided as facing two ways. It was about as big as a man's hand and beautifully wrought, the feathers sharp, the claws minutely defined, and even the fierce little eyes so deftly sculptured in the pure, precious metal that they seemed to have lights in them. The gold chain links of the collar alternated with miniature icons, painted on ivory and framed with seed pearls. The emperor passed it over Pierre's head, and the Eagle came to rest over the cut in his chest.

"Rise now, Sir Peter," the emperor said.

Pierre did.

The page brought the sword. It had been blessed to holy deeds by the bishop that morning in the cathedral, and not touched since. The emperor removed the veil and buckled the leather belt, full of little silver eagles, around Pierre's waist. He had to stand up to do this, and for a moment the two men looked each other in the eye, for Pierre on the floor was almost as tall as David on the dais.

"We should ask you to come hunting, Sir Peter," the emperor said cordially, "but you have serious business here in town. Also, we doubt whether you could do much hunting with a hand that has suffered torture in our service. It has come to our ears only today how the wound was inflicted. The matter has received the attention of our father, who is greatly concerned." That was for the world. Then he lowered his voice so low that even the sharp ears of his courtiers could not hear, causing Pierre to make a few more enemies. "For the first time in my life, Sir Peter, I am virtually commanded to get out of town and go hunting, to please our heathen neighbors. Alexius will tell you why." Then, more loudly and formally again: "We express our gratitude for your service to the family, and we trust that when we return from our sport in the fields with our friends and our friendly good neighbors, we shall see you again and perhaps command wholly the allegiance which you have sworn in part today to ourself." That, too, was for the world, the heathen world in particular.

The friendly, good-neighborly Turks looked at each other, smiled, nodded and appeared more pleased than ever.

Alexius, to whom the speech from the throne was instantly reported by a runner whose feet did not make a sound behind the curtains, blessed the statesmanship of the young emperor, and sent a corps of his noblest police officials to surround the house of Baltha Ogli with orders to prevent the prince, under pain of instant public arrest, from poking his nose outside the pink stone walls of his splendid mansion.

334

The emperor sat down again and inclined his head briefly to Pierre. Pierre knelt and again touched the hem of the pallium with his forehead, rose, backed away, followed his Eagle in a semiturn to the right and joined Sir John, whose face was proud and shining.

"You walked as if you'd been born with that bird on your chest, Sir Peter," he whispered. The new title came naturally and seriously to his lips, as if he had always called Pierre that. "The emperor talked so long that some of the Greeks began to look jealous. But the Turks appeared jubilant."

The trumpets sounded again. The men in the room again touched their foreheads to the floor, and the procession left in precisely the reverse order from which it had entered, the knight with the silver bow being last, walking backward through the curtains, holding the weapon before his face, lest anyone forget the power of Trebizond.

CHAPTER

❊ 30 ❊

THE APARTMENTS of the grand duke occupied one of the upper
floors of the palace. On a balcony overlooking the garden which was
outside the antechamber where the Great Comnenus had given the Eagle
to Pierre, Alexius had a sumptuous breakfast spread for the new knight
and Sir John. Alexius himself had already breakfasted, but out of politeness he sipped a goblet of fruit juices. The red, tiled roofs of the houses
in the city, and the sea beyond the walls of the lower town made a pretty
sight.

Pierre was getting used to eating from porcelain dishes. He had
acquired little skill, however, in feeding himself with his left hand. Ogli's
servants, the Count of Mesembria's servants, and now the servants of the
paradynast, seemed to take it for granted that a guest's fingers should
be delicately dabbed at with a fine linen napkin if the least sign of a spot
should appear on them.

"I think I am turning into a baby again, Your Highness," Pierre
said. "Perhaps when I get back to France, I shall forget myself and
hold up my fingers to be wiped."

"If Sir Peter did that there, he'd get as many cups of wine as he
held up fingers," Justin said.

"Our customs are different here I know, gentlemen. Perhaps in time
you may come to prefer them. I am told that His Imperial Majesty
touched on the subject of your remaining here in Trebizond, Sir Peter.
That is practically a command to stay here. Most of his speech was
imperial flattery to the Turks. I refer, of course, to his public words. His
private communication to you does not, perhaps, concern me."

Pierre smiled at the polite way the grand duke expressed his curiosity.
"As a matter of fact, it does, Your Highness. He suggested that I ask

you why he is at such pains to be pleasant to the Turks. You undoubtedly know all the flattering things he said about them, and now he is going hunting with thirteen of them."

"Did you count them, Sir Peter? The number is fifteen. Two were not able to be present at your knighting. You have a sharp eye, sir. I can tell you that the trial of Baltha Ogli will be a ticklish business. It is no light thing to punish a sultan's kinsman, no matter what he has done. Only this morning, after the speech from the throne, did I dare place Ogli under a mild sort of house arrest. But he cannot get away. His chimneys were observed to smoke, and, of course, he is destroying all the evidence he can get his hands on. The servant Manuel has remembered a few more details and for the edification of the Turks your tortured hand was mentioned. When Ogli is tried, it will be a great shock to the Turkish national pride. Every means must be found to ingratiate ourselves beforehand to them. That is why His Imperial Majesty mentioned your hand, and why he is hunting with them."

"This is the first I have heard that Sir Peter's hand was tortured," said Sir John. "By now I suppose I should know better than to expect my friend to confide in me."

"It is nearly healed," Pierre said, "and the imperial notice of it has magnified the incident out of all proportion. The sergeant hit me with a rock when I would not tell him where De Coucy's letter was. I do not pretend it was not painful, but I was already so stunned that it did not hurt so much as you might think."

Alexius said: "If His Imperial Majesty made it sound worse than it really was, that does no harm. It is good for Trebizond to have the Turks start thinking evil of the man who did it. I wish you had mentioned the circumstance to me, Sir Peter. Legally it will be advisable to have every possible scrap of character evidence against the Bulgarian. His guilt is obvious and even the Turks have stringent laws against thieves. As far as the tortured hand is concerned, the story of the rock will sound very good at the trial. It would be more dramatic, however, if the hand had belonged, say, to a pious old Moslem with a green turban."

"What does Your Highness mean?"

"What do you know about the Turkish slave Mousa, with the cactus spines under his nails?"

"*Gesù!* Nothing. Nay, Your Highness, perhaps I do. The poor old fellow spilled a drop of cordial when he filled my glass. Basil asked permission to inflict the punishment for his carelessness. Ogli gave it to him."

Alexius said: "Mousa stole out secretly to a chirurgeon a few days ago to have a number of cactus spines removed from under the nails of his right hand. He claimed to have had an accident, but it was obvious that he had been tortured, and the incident came to my attention."

"So that is how Basil was sure he would leave no scars! He is worse than his master. I heard Ogli himself caution him not to hurt the man. At least not to the extent that he could never serve at table again. Is it not against your laws to torture slaves?"

As one of the twelve divine judges, Alexius could answer his question with some exactitude. "Under imperial Trapezuntian law, slaves have no legal rights of any kind. They are property, like any other property, and a man may do as he pleases with what is his own. The old Roman laws, however, from which our Trapezuntian jurisprudence derives its spirit, accorded a great many rights to slaves.

"Probably the most specific answer to your question, Sir Peter, is the edict of the Emperor Marcus Aurelius, who gave the owner of a slave the legal right to take the slave to court and institute criminal charges against him. You may think it odd that a master should bother to go to court against a slave. The purpose of the paradoxical law was to discourage just the sort of private punishment that Ogli inflicted and bring the master-slave relationship into the jurisdiction of the courts and before the judgment of public opinion.

"The whole spirit of the Roman Corpus Juris, especially after the establishment of Christianity, is progressively in the direction of greater liberty and more humane treatment. Here in the empire the old Roman law can be invoked, not as finally authoritative, but, in the absence of specific imperial laws, as at least an indication of how a civilized state ought to be governed.

"Thus, it is not illegal to torture a slave, Sir Peter, but the better element here is against it. I am glad you told me about Mousa's hand. The evil character of the servant Basil is well known to the police. Mention will be made in court of Ogli's permission to his servant to punish the slave. My colleagues will not like so cruel a servant and so careless a master.

"I must also add that, politically speaking, the evidence is of great importance to our relations with the Turks. The fact that an elderly Turkish slave, who had made the pilgrimage to Mecca, was tortured by having cactus thorns brutally driven under his fingernails will go far toward justifying Baltha Ogli's and Basil's punishment, if they are found guilty. Without prejudging the case, I can say that I am confident they will be."

338

The grand duke smiled slightly. "It was not my intention to deliver an oration on the laws of the empire, Sir Peter. But Baltha Ogli's trial and punishment have been much on my mind, and you can believe me when I say that the Emperor John is concerning himself with the minutest details of how it can be accomplished with the least possible offense to the Turks. The thing will not be easy. But every new scrap of evidence augments the mass of guilt against Ogli. The Turkish guides, whose conversation you overheard, and the Greek soldiers have all been interrogated. The contents of the khan have been weighed, numbered, catalogued, and described. The merchandise was immensely valuable. Sir Theodore has given us an enormous amount of data, both in regard to the caravan which you saw and a number of others over a period of the last two years. He candidly states his motive and the deplorable circumstances in connection with the blindness of the count, his father. Naturally, I believe him. You yourself, Sir Peter, will be an important witness at the trial. It will be conducted in public, and there are certain to be scores of high-ranking Turkish noblemen and officials in attendance. You will probably be asked to testify in Turkish, since you cannot speak Greek. The use of the Turkish tongue will have the best possible effect on the Turkish audience. I hope you will agree."

"Of course, I agree, Your Highness. I hope no action will be taken against Sir Theodore and the Count of Mesembria."

"That is hard to say, Sir Peter. It is very unlikely, however. The unfortunate victim of Basil's cruelty has expiated his old crime for a dozen years. Nobody but Baltha Ogli would bring a charge against him. No such charge will be permitted at the trial of Baltha Ogli and his servant. We try one thing at a time here in Trebizond. And after their trial it is my belief that neither of them will be in a position to bring an action in law against the Count, not of Mesembria, but of Thalassopolis. That is his true Trapezuntian title."

"I never heard it, Your Highness."

"He seldom uses it. The title of Megaskyr of Thalassopolis is the right of the lord of the small city of that name lying on the coast near his castle. It has no harbor, but there is a small protected cove near it. Sir Theodore tells us that Ogli used the cove as the base for his smuggling. Actually, Baltha Ogli is now the Megaskyr of Thalassopolis, since he owns the estate. But many of the old Pontic families, who were in the empire long before the Byzantines came and civilized it, cling to their ancient titles as a sort of perennial protest against the emperors. Most of them have never seen the foreign cities and provinces whose names sound so grand in their titles, and a great many do not even know where they

339

are. It is all very harmless and nobody ever pays any attention to them. When the unhappy blind man dies, Sir Theodore can style himself the Count of Mesembria, if it pleases him to do so; most of his neighbors will approve, and nobody in the city will care. But neither Sir Theodore nor the count, his father, can ever be the Lord, or Megaskyr of Thalassopolis until they regain title to their land." The grand duke looked very seriously at Pierre.

"The possibility of such a thing is extremely remote. The disposition of Baltha Ogli's property, if he is found guilty, is entirely in the emperor's hands. John of Trebizond is a just prince, well advised, fair, serene, and capable of wise and noble decisions. I am betraying no secret when I tell you that his heart is full of gratitude for what you did for his son, though, of course, he cannot thank you for extricating His Imperial Majesty from a dive on the waterfront. It might imply a criticism that his son ought not to have been there. It would be unseemly for me to say anything more about the equitable plans now under advisement with regard to the fiscal aspects of the scandalous affairs, that you, Sir Peter, wittingly or unwittingly, but always bravely, have been instrumental in unmasking, and will, by your testimony at the trial, be the means of setting right again."

All the words began to sound alike to Pierre. Later, on the deck of the Lady, he asked Sir John: "What in the world was the grand duke talking about? He was hinting something."

Sir John slapped him on the shoulder, rattling his icons and setting his Eagle to flashing in the sun. "Sir Peter," he said, "you do not know the Greeks as I do. To me it sounded like degradation and confiscation. Ogli is bad, but it seems to me that he is also too rich. If my Italian mind is not wholly asleep, I think I see something even better than your Eagle in store for you."

# CHAPTER

## ❊ 31 ❊

THE TRIAL LASTED a month. The imperial hunting party returned and were present at most of the sessions. There could have been only one verdict in a trial so carefully planned. Ogli and his servant were declared guilty of treasonable larceny. Corruption of the friendly Turkish caravans was conceived to be robbery and held to endanger the peaceful commercial relations of the empire. They were also found guilty of defrauding the Trapezuntian government of vast sums in taxes.

The torture of Sir Peter and Mousa, the Turkish slave, was made mention of as demonstrating the bad characters of the defendants, shortly, without undue emphasis, and with telling effect on the Turkish spectators.

The loss of the right hand and death by impalement was the sentence pronounced upon both Baltha Ogli and Basil. And, in addition, Ogli was subjected to an enormous fine that stripped him of all his Trapezuntian properties. His titles and honors were declared forfeit to the person of the Great Comnenus, John of Trebizond. Basil was discovered to have no property and he was not fined.

It was freely rumored that Ogli would not actually be impaled, but Ogli, in strict solitary confinement in a silent dungeon deep under the palace, believed that he was lost. Guards, who could not repeat the comforting rumors because they had no tongues, continued to serve him delicate meals, and his dungeon, for a dungeon, was comfortable. His anxiety was dreadful, however, and he could not eat his meals.

The hippodrome at Trebizond was an enormous structure built to accommodate thousands of people at the horse races, the chariot races, the polo games, and the archery contests that were held in its spacious

341

arena. It was the most popular place of entertainment in the empire. And for this, the most noteworthy spectacle in a decade, it was crowded to overflowing. Spectators of the last great occasion, when half a dozen highwaymen had been buried in the sand up to their necks and wild horses run over them, speculated that, though this impalement might not cause the death of so many persons, more details were almost certain to be seen.

Impalement was common enough in Turkey, Persia, Arabia, and in a number of other Eastern nations, but it was rare in Christian Trebizond. In Europe it was almost unheard of. Some people, like Mousa and Pierre, were commanded for political reasons to be present. Most people needed no command. By imperial fiat Mousa had been declared free and given a sum of money and permission to go home to the sultan or remain a subject of the Trapezuntian emperors. He had elected to remain. The brilliant green turban of the former slave was observed in an exceptionally favorable position in the audience, so that he could see and be seen. Sir Peter likewise, with Justin beside him in a loge reserved for the higher orders of Trapezuntian knighthood, found himself not twenty yards from the stake and close to the purple, canopied loge of the emperors.

The rulers of Trebizond sat motionless and expressionless on their elevated guilded chairs, the backs of which were bodies of eagles and the arms of which were eagles' wings, folding round the sacred persons of Their Majesties. High-born officials, two to each emperor, had the honor of fanning them gently with long, white-plumed ostrich fans. For the emperors were the slaves as well as the fountainhead of Trapezuntian ceremonial. It was not seemly for them to wipe a drop of sweat from their faces or brush away an annoying fly. The day was hot, and two pages stood ready to present to their lips goblets of iced lemonade, which they did, from time to time, at some minute signal which was not observable to the populace.

Ogli, pale and frightened, dressed in court costume, was conveyed to the hippodrome in a rough farm wagon. It was not fitting for a prince of his rank to walk, even to his own death—or to stand, for that matter. One of his beautiful chairs had been placed in the wagon and he sat upon it, so hopeless and quiet that he appeared dignified. He was not bound. A man-at-arms with a pike stood at either side of his chair.

Basil, clad in a rough, gray tunic, followed at the cart tail, sweating and leaning against the wagon for support. There was a rope around his neck. If he had slipped, and he wished he would (but he could not bring himself to stumble purposely), he would have been dragged over the pavement of the street and probably strangled. It would have been a much easier death.

Basil was to be executed first.

There was only one stake.

Ogli in his thronelike chair in the common cart leaned over and retched. The dreadful thought had struck him that the stake would still be warm and wet with Basil's blood and bowels.

Those in Europe who had heard vaguely of impalement had an idea that the stake was thrust laterally through the body, much as a man was pierced in battle by the lance of a knight, or as a flounder is stuck through by a fisherman with a spiked pole. But the savage who thought of impalement, long before the dawn of history, knew anatomy better than that. A man dies more slowly if he is pierced below the navel. Above it lie the heart and the lungs. Correctly impaled, a man was pierced by a tapering, pointed wooden stake, firmly planted in the ground. It entered the body from the lower end of, and parallel to, the spine. The height of the point above the ground determined the length of time that the man would live. As Basil stood beside the stake, it was observed that the point reached just to the outermost bulge of his huge belly. People wondered how long he would be able to stand. With the point a few inches lower, condemned men had been known to whirl like dervishes around the stake in a desperate futile effort to free themselves of the thing that was killing them. The diameter of the stake was also an important consideration. If too slender, it might snap. When that happened, men had been known to pull out the point. If too large, it was difficult for the guards to place the victim on top of it, and there was danger of his dying before they could thrust him down to where his feet could touch the ground. Since Basil was a heavy man, his own weight could be counted on to effect the introduction of the stake into his body. The stake was, accordingly, at its thickest part just as big around as a man could encircle with the fingers of his two hands.

Basil was not executed naked. After his sentence of death was reread to him by a court officer, the back of his tunic was cut away with a sharp dagger to facilitate the operation of the impalement, but his tunic was not removed. Basil tottered in a faint before the reading was concluded.

It would have been merciful to have impaled him at that moment, and had simple impalement been all of his sentence, the guards would have done so. But the loss of the hand, which was conceived to have stolen from the caravans and robbed the Great Comneni, had not yet been accomplished. The guards who supported the fainting eunuch held

343

out his limp right arm. An executioner with a sharp sword struck the hand cleanly off at the wrist, and Basil revived instantly, to see his own hand on the sand before him, slowly closing its fingers.

Ogli's wagon had been sent away so as not to obstruct any part of the view. The Bulgarian prince sat in his chair, which had been placed upon the ground, and watched his servant suffer. He showed so little emotion that a great many people, especially those who had seen him vomit, suspected he had been given a drug to quiet him and reduce his pain, as was customary when great lords were executed.

Basil was restrained from waving the stump of his arm, which had begun to pump arterial blood in a stream onto the ground. Terror stricken and wholly conscious now, he screamed at the top of his high, penetrating, eunuchoid voice and struggled against his guards with all his enormous strength, but a dozen men held him fast. They lifted him off the ground, over the point of the stake, and brought him down upon it, hard. And when, on tiptoe, he touched the ground, they instantly retired to the sides of the arena, leaving the unfortunate victim to writhe and howl alone. He faced his master and screamed at him in Bulgarian. The very few of the spectators who could understand that wild tongue reported that he was not cursing Ogli, but imploring him, for the love of God, to lift him off the stake. Such a thing would not have been possible or permitted, of course, and in any case Ogli made no move to help his servant.

In his agony Basil forgot that his hand had been cut off. He bent slightly forward and reached down with what he thought were his two hands. Instinct kept him from bending too far, lest the point of the stake, which was now in his belly, puncture more of his organs. Instinct compelled him also to remain on tiptoe, lest the point penetrate further upward. In this position he beat at the stake under his tunic, already crimson with his blood, as if he thought he might break it off or grab it and lift himself away from its point. But he was not able to grasp the stake. For a moment he held up the stump of his right arm in astonishment that there was no hand there; he could not remember losing it. The pain of his two wounds, the great loss of blood, which was collecting in a pool at the foot of the stake, and the fear of certain death made him delirious. Still on tiptoe, holding out his handless arm, shrieking and working his shoulders, he stepped slowly round his stake, so that it appeared to the spectators viewing him from the back where the tunic had been cut away, as if he were walking on two legs around a third one between them.

Presently he was observed to be walking on his heels. The stake had

344

penetrated several inches more. Then it pierced his heart; his cries became moans, and he began to die. He happened to be facing Ogli. With the haemorrhage pouring out of his heart into the interior of his body, he rapidly lost all control of his muscles. His head slumped forward on his breast, his arms hung lax, and his knees slowly buckled under him, as if he were kneeling to his master. And as the heavy body settled down, the slender point of the stake struck up through his neck. It pierced his brain and caused Basil, now dead, to raise his head, from every orifice of which blood suddenly spurted. His bulging, staring, bleeding eyes appeared to look at Ogli.

Basil's body was not removed that day.

Immediately after the eunuch died, a herald, clad entirely in white, with a white document in his hand and something in a bag of cloth of silver, rode a white horse into the arena. From the shining bag he released a snow-white pigeon, symbol of the clemency of the Great Comnenus.

Ogli's curious apathy left him. He knew that he was not to be impaled. With hope, fear returned. His mouth became dry, his body began to tremble and sweat.

Having released the pigeon, the herald faced the emperors and proclaimed in a loud, clear voice that the Great Comnenus, prompted by the profound mercy of his compassionate heart, was pleased to spare the life of the Bulgarian, Baltha Ogli.

But, in order that the empire might not seem to truckle to the Turks, Ogli was simultaneously banished from Trebizond, his attainder and the confiscation of his property were confirmed, and he was sentenced to be beaten forthwith with one hundred strokes of a golden rod.

This was instantly done. Ogli was stripped before all the people, a degrading shame in the eyes of the Turks. Then, with a rod which had been painted gold out of respect for his rank, he was given twenty resounding whacks across the back, and then the executioner stopped.

It was immediately remarked by perhaps two hundred members of the secret police, sprinkled scientifically throughout the audience, that the rod was quintuplicate, so that Ogli had received his hundred strokes. Ogli roared like a beast, but more in anger than in pain. At the end of his punishment, he prostrated himself at the feet of the emperors and thanked them for his life. On the same day, surrounded by a guard of honor and apparently perfectly able to ride his horse, Baltha Ogli left to seek refuge and revenge at the court of the sultan. Pierre, thinking of Ogli's angry, contorted face, had an eerie, premonitory feeling that it would have been better for Christendom if Basil had gone over to the Turks and Ogli been impaled.*

Sick to his stomach, Pierre took Justin on a businesslike tour of the warehouses. For there was now no French factor in Trebizond.

"The minister will not thank us for bringing back an empty ship, Sir John, and I have no appetite for supper anyway. Technically, we have no authority to buy a good salable cargo, but I think we should at least look into the possibility. The minister had no idea that our trip would lead to the banishment of Baltha Ogli."

Justin was not hungry for supper either.

* Baltha Ogli, a renegade Bulgarian prince, is, among others, a historical character. He is known to have been the military adviser to the next sultan, Mohammed II, "the Conqueror," whose enormous cannon breached the walls of Constantinople in 1453, nine years after the events related here.

# CHAPTER

## ❧ 32 ❧

IN THE TRAPEZUNTIAN commercial world, the results of Baltha Ogli's degradation and banishment were immediate and devastating. His counting house was deserted. Many of his clerks disavowed his service completely, claiming that they had never worked for him, or had worked only part of the time, or that they were now tired of being merchants. For they all feared that they might be involved in his guilt and suffer the loss of whatever fortunes they might possess.

The warehouses, which were privately owned and bulging with desirable merchandise, suddenly had nothing for sale except at prices which would have precluded any profit to Pierre. No cargo was to be found for the Lady. The Genoese merchants, who had no love for Sir John after he had forced them to return his ship, declared that their goods were all consigned to trading companies in Genoa. The Venetians, despite their friendliness for Sir John, their countryman, clung to their goods as if each bolt of silk and each length of velvet were worth a king's ransom. The English belatedly remembered that there had been a war with France for some hundred years, and doubled their prices out of patriotic motives.

Looking at Pierre, the auditor-general who was now the ranking French fiscal authority in Trebizond, everyone concluded from his youth that such an inexperienced merchant might easily be imposed upon. Justin, of course, was not a merchant, and was not expected to be.

To make matters worse for Pierre, the *Sainte-Marie*, another of Coeur's ships, put into the harbor. Her captain had no one to whom he could deliver his manifests. Police kept the grumbling crew aboard till the cargo could be cleared and taxed. But the cargo could not be cleared until the manifests were opened. When Pierre attempted to find storage space for the cargo, he was solemnly assured by the owners of the warehouses that space was more costly now and there was no room anyway.

During the few days that followed Ogli's banishment, every shrewd merchant on the waterfront decided to take advantage of the confused state of French shipping and make a fortune.

So Pierre simply bought nothing at all and the angry crew of the *Sainte-Marie* had to stay aboard their ship.

The *Sainte-Marie's* captain, however, came aboard the Lady with a letter from Jacques Coeur to Sir John. It wished him good health and virtually nothing more.

"But here is a curious thing," Justin observed to Pierre: "the minister hopes you are not dead. It appears that De Coucy has taken great pains to tell everyone that your mission was very dangerous and might well end fatally for you. The minister is only half convinced that you are in heaven so soon, but certain of De Coucy's relations think they will never see you again. Read it for yourself."

Pierre read the formal, courteous note. It directed Sir John to come home at once after the delivery of his cargo, and not to wait too long to load a new one, so that he might report what Pierre had done in Trebizond. It concluded:

I know not on what strange intuitive reasoning my secretary bases his assumption that the auditor-general, whom you took with you on your voyage, has met his death. Naturally I hope De Coucy is merely concerned for him, as, I confess, I am myself. Sir Bernard has told the Count de la Tour-Clermont, his kinsman, that Pierre of a surety, is dead, and apparently some of the count's family believe him. I am told that one of his daughters, the younger one I believe, has retired to Port-Royal. I shall reproach myself if Pierre has come to harm. He might have distinguished himself in the matter of the pilot fees.

Justin said to the *Sainte-Marie's* captain: "You will note that our cautious master refers to the pilot fees. He does not think fit to tell even me that Sir Peter was sent here on a confidential mission."

"De Coucy started a good deal of gossip about Sir Peter," the other captain said. He knew all about Pierre's Eagle, of course. It was the first thing he had heard in Trebizond. "De Coucy said he knew Trapezuntians better than the minister. He said he was sure the auditor-general would get into a scrape and get himself killed by the Greeks, who do not like to have people prying into their affairs. I don't know what else he may

348

have said. In the meantime, would one of you gentlemen advise me who has the authority here to relieve me of my manifests?"

Justin nodded to Pierre. "The auditor-general can take them. If Sir Peter accepts the cargo, that will at least authorize the inspectors to go aboard and get the cargo taxed so that your men can go ashore."

Pierre had not been listening very attentively. Port-Royal-des-Champs, outside of Paris, was the most famous convent in France. Sir John said sympathetically: "You'd better break the seals, my friend, and let the sailors go to town and spend their money."

Pierre did, and the sailors went ashore. The tax collectors, after a cursory examination of the cargo, accepted the manifests as the basis for the collection of the import taxes as usual. But there was no warehouse space available to store the *Sainte-Marie's* merchandise. It remained on the ship. And after a week the *Sainte-Marie,* like the *Sainte-Eulalie,* began to incur high wharfage charges.

Justin and Pierre were in the great cabin earnestly discussing the complex state of affairs that the sudden elimination of the French factor had brought about. Henri, the page, announced that a Greek gentleman had come aboard and requested permission to speak to Sir Peter of Trebizond—Henri was practicing the new title, looking popeyed every time he did so.

"Who is it, Henri?" Pierre asked.

"The guard on the dock says it is the same man who came with you that first morning, sir. But he looks different, and I cannot understand his speech."

It was Theodore, but he was a changed man. He had been in the hippodrome among the thousands of spectators of Ogli's flogging and Basil's dreadful death. The howls of the two men had sounded like music to him. He was clean, fresh, rested, and beautifully dressed. It was the first time Pierre had seen him since the trial. He had a spectacular blue cloak over his arm.

"This was my father's," he said simply. "He wanted you to have it. When I told him how you had refused the cloak Stephanie was murdered in, he bade me give you his own. Little Father is now with Stephanie, and with God."

Pierre crossed himself reverently. Justin, who could not understand the Turkish, did the same.

"I had not heard of the death of the count, your father," said Pierre. "I am sorry."

"Father died very peacefully a week ago. Nobody expected him to live long. In the dark, Sir Peter, without Stephanie's voice . . . It is better as it is."

Pierre murmured in Latin the beautiful prayer of the Church for the dead. For no one had it ever been spoken more meaningfully. "Eternal rest give to them, O Lord; and let perpetual light shine upon them." He told Sir John whom it was for. Justin earnestly repeated the prayer, asked Theodore to sit down, and rang for Henri and a cup of wine.

Theodore said: "I am summoned to the Great Court tomorrow, Sir Peter, and so will you be if you have not already been. Everyone knows your honors are not at an end." He smiled frankly and cordially. "But I am absolutely the only one in the empire, except for the officials, who knows precisely what the Great Comnenus will do for you. I am directly involved, as it were. I am breaking custom, perhaps, but I am doing nothing dishonorable, when I acquaint you a bit in advance of old Ravenwings, who will take an hour to tell you, that Ogli's property is being split up and redivided in the manner that a great many statesmen have decided will do the empire the most good. Among many other beneficiaries you are to be given a small estate that formerly belonged to Ogli. It is the one my father sold to him some years ago."

Pierre could hardly believe his ears.

"Isn't such a thing out of all proportion to what I did, Sir Theodore? It was your testimony, more than mine, that told so heavily against Ogli."

"The authorities do not look at it that way. And anyway, Ogli was the richest man in Trebizond. No matter how his fortune is divided, plenty remains for the personal use of the emperors. My little estate is not a thousandth part of Ogli's fortune. This is a very practical country. It is thought wiser to honor an influential Frenchman than a powerless Pontic gentleman. But, as a matter of fact, if I must pay rent, I should rather do so to you than to Baltha Ogli. I have no fault to find with the decision of the authorities.

"Father did not know how fitting it would be for you to have this cloak. He gave it to you with his blessing, out of the generosity of his heart. It is lined, I might mention, with the same fine, light, Persian mail as—the other one. It is fitting that you have it because it carries the motto of Thalassopolis upon it in this embroidered insert, as nearly like the imperial *tablion* as a private gentleman can decently assume. To us the motto 'I Remember' means, of course, Mesembria, and Thalassopolis before the coming of the first Great Comnenus. You will be the lord, or megaskyr, of that city, Sir Peter, and perhaps the motto will mean something to you, too. Most men have something to remember. Wear the cloak in good health—it is freely given, as the other was.

"And my first request of my new landlord is: give me leave to tear down that ugly, dreadful khan, which is associated in my mind with misfortune, dishonor, and death."

Pierre shook his head so violently that Justin thought Theodore must have said something insulting. Theodore looked puzzled and disappointed.

"Surely you don't mean to keep that dismal, useless structure?"

"It is dismal, but it may not be useless, Sir Theodore."

Pierre told him something of the shortage of warehousing space on the waterfront, the high prices of all the merchandise, and the other difficulties that, in the absence of healthy competition, a Frank merchant had to face.

"Does the title of Megaskyr of Thalassopolis lie in your land?" he asked. "The words are hard to say and mean nothing to a Frenchman,"

"They are beautiful to a Greek. Yes, the 'Great Lord of the Sea City'—it's a tiny place, Sir Peter—is any man who holds title to the estate. The megaskyr was formerly my father. Ogli had the title while he had the land. The Great Comnenus has it now. Tomorrow night you will have the title."

"Would you like it back?"

Sir Theodore's eyebrows shot up in surprise. "But of course! That is—"

"Then do not tear down the khan. One of the French minister's ships put in today with a valuable cargo. I can neither find space for it, at reasonable prices, nor can I dispose of it immediately. All the merchandise has been legally entered into the empire; all the taxes have been duly paid. What is to prevent your accepting the cargo at Thalassopolis and storing it in your khan?"

"Nothing at all, Sir Peter! Absolutely nothing at all, either in honor or at law. It would be a good lesson to the vultures on the waterfront. I know them well."

"Your khan can hold the cargoes of half a dozen ships. If things turn out as you say, what is to prevent any or all of my master's ships from unloading at Thalassopolis rather than Trebizond? Except, of course, that the cargoes will have to be handled twice. That costs money."

Theodore began to see great possibilities in the scheme. "You will find labor cheap in your little Sea City, Sir Peter. And, due to Ogli's wicked efficiency, many of the so-called 'fishing boats' are actually lighters, capable of handling cargo. That is what they were built for. The 'fishermen' of Thalassopolis must be stevedores at heart. They can load and unload a ship in the dark. They've done it often enough." He laughed. "I can imagine how astonished they will be to be working in broad daylight. You will make your smuggling village honest and prosperous if you send enough ships, Sir Peter. The idea is marvelous! Indeed, I shall not tear down the khan. And there are plenty of mules: you will make them fat again, for the beasts are kept expressly for the purpose of carrying the goods from the cove to the khan. Now their owners will keep them, and keep them healthy."

Pierre said: "Should I be summoned to court and actually given your estate, Sir Theodore, you and I can conclude an agreement that we both think fair. I shall want you to buy back your land and the lordship of the Sea City as well, as soon as you can. And I have a plan that may enable you to do it quicker than you think. You speak Turkish. Do you know any other Eastern languages such as might be helpful in dealing with the caravans?"

"I speak Persian as well as Turkish, and I know enough Armenian to haggle with the merchants, and Arabic, of course, which is the mother language of half the Eastern tongues. Naturally, I am not as adept in them as I happen to be in Turkish. As you know, nearly every one in Trebizond has some Turkish."

"Perhaps you even know the personnel of some of the caravans?"

"I do. I have had to get to know them. And their merchandise, too, for that matter. For years Ogli paid us in merchandise rather than in gold, whenever we were not absolutely penniless, and sometimes even when we were. Naturally, I had to sell the goods, and I became something of a merchant. It was be a merchant or starve."

"From the appearance of your castle, you trade shrewdly. I have asked you these questions, because, if Jacques Coeur consents, I intend to recommend that you be appointed the French factor here. You seem qualified for the position. Certainly your castle and khan are ideally located. Indeed, if Ogli had worked a little harder and a little more honestly, he could have made a great deal of money, perfectly legally, by setting up Thalassopolis as a competitor to Trebizond."

Theodore's face began to shine, but he cautioned: "Many men will aspire to the lucrative post of French factor, Sir Peter. It is a position of great honor and importance to the empire, as you know. The grand duke, as well as Jacques Coeur, will have to approve the choice. I confess that I am ambitious for the distinction. You yourself, in so generously offering me the opportunity of buying back my estates, have given me the strongest possible motive to work diligently and faithfully for you and your master." He was silent a moment and turned his head in a manner that was painfully reminiscent of Stephanie when she heard something. Then he said: "You Westerners act with a forthright, almost brutal kind of efficiency. I am sure it never occurred to Ogli that the khan could be put to profitable, legal use. Unless I am mistaken, Sir Peter, old Ravenwings has come aboard the ship to summon you to court."

Henri announced the herald, but somewhat more respectfully than the Pontic gentleman.

"How did you know it was old Ravenwings?"

"Everyone knows his limp. He got it years ago fighting the Genoese."

"Stay and hear what he says, Sir Theodore."

But the herald spoke in French, and at very great length. He did not mind Theodore's presence, because he knew that he could not understand French. The herald did summon Pierre, and Sir John as well, to court. He confirmed everything Theodore had said, saving Pierre a good deal of explanation to Sir John, and when he left, he favored Pierre not with a sixty-degree bow, but with almost the ninety-degree bow that would be the due of the Megaskyr of Thalassopolis, when everybody walked backward out of the Great Court the following day.

"I shall surely be jealous of you if that herald pays you another visit," Sir John observed smiling. "But I told you Alexius had something in mind when he talked about—I think he said 'the equitable plans now under advisement regarding the fiscal aspects' of Ogli's trial. Do not think they are burdening you with too many honors, Sir Peter. The emperor will never miss the revenues of the little village of Thalassopolis, and he will be sure of your loyalty by giving you the place. Ogli could take a chance, but the emperor knows you cannot. At least I assume he knows. They know almost everything here. You'll lose your town, if, for example, you start smuggling. The emperors of Trebizond are merchants and good judges of men. I'm bound to say I'm happy for you. Even your friend here doesn't seem to mind. Alexius told us he wouldn't get his land back, but I never saw a pauper look so happy at the prospect of his continued pauperdom."

"Maybe he's not to be the pauper you think," and Pierre told Justin of his plan to utilize Ogli's khan, and the rest of the conversation.

"Nay, now. That makes good sense even to a sea captain! Ask your new tenant if he has a pilot up the sleeve of his pretty Greek tunic. I'll order the *Sainte-Marie* out of this high-priced city tonight!" Which Justin, as senior captain of the minister's fleet had a perfect right to do, even without the fiscal authority of the auditor-general.

It appeared that Sir Theodore knew an excellent pilot, who would take the *Sainte-Marie* to Thalassopolis for a very reasonable fee.

There was a good deal of speculation among the waterfront merchants when the ship sailed with every ounce of her cargo still aboard. Nobody knew what had happened. It seemed to the Greeks incomprehensible that the unpredictable Westerners should choose to put into Trebizond, pay their taxes and sail away again with their merchandise. It was all perfectly legal, of course, but things of that sort made it very difficult for an honest warehouse owner to make any money. A number of the more prominent merchants spoke to each other after supper and resolved to ask the French about such a singular proceeding.

"I think we should receive them," Justin said, when Henri, who was beginning to feel very important, announced the delegation.

Pierre said: "I am reminded of how Cantacuzene acted when he discovered that the Lady's cargo was all consigned to Baltha Ogli. If we really have difficulty, Constantinople is a source of cargo for us."

"I don't think we'll have much trouble. Your prices will probably start tumbling tonight. I think we ought to wear our collars and be very formal with the Greeks, Sir Peter."

So the delegation were told that some new plans had been worked out with regard to French shipping. No warehouses were needed. No cargoes were required. It was a new Western idea. And the knight in the silver collar and the knight in the gold collar sent the Greeks back to their warehouses with every mark of courtesy, a number of sailors carrying lanterns and torches before them over the planks of the wharf to the shore.

"Let them worry themselves out of a cargo or two," commented Sir John. "I think we owe Cantacuzene a courtesy for his fifty-year pilot-free arrangement anyway."

"So do I," Pierre said. "But I've a notion we'll get at least one good Trapezuntian cargo. Unless I am mistaken, the grand duke will hear of the unorthodox departure of the *Sainte-Marie.*"

"He certainly will. You're getting to know the Greeks."

# CHAPTER

## ❋ 33 ❋

THE WIFE of Baltha Ogli emerged from her retreat in the monastery of Saint Eugenius only to witness the degradation and banishment of the prince, her husband. The son of Baltha Ogli returned from Magnesia, having failed to reduce by an asper the troublesome Turkish tribute. Together they fled from the empire and went over the mountains to the Turks, where the sultan, whose remaining years were to be full of bitterness against the Christians for their disregard of certain solemn treaties, slowly relaxed his absolute power and let fall into the hands of Mohammed, his warlike son, the direction of Turkish polity and power. It was this Mohammed, a forward-thinking, fanatical prince, who sheltered Baltha Ogli in his disgrace and encouraged him to experiment with cannon and gunpowder, those new and dreadful weapons of war, by which he hoped to humble the pride of Christendom, and with which, before Pierre's golden hair was white, he did.

The heathen world was full of secret, ambitious plans, but while the old sultan was to live, Turkish policy confined itself to courteous threats rather than open war against Trebizond. Thus there was every reason for John to have sent his imperial son hunting with the Turkish emissaries and to pursue a commercial policy calculated to appease their greed. The immense wealth that poured into the imperial treasury from the confiscated estates of Baltha Ogli enabled the Trapezuntian government to reduce sharply the taxes on Turkish imports. The arrangement proved satisfactory for many years.

The new, low Turkish taxes were announced in the full and splendid ceremony at the same Great Court which invested Pierre with the considerable revenues of the small coastal city of Thalassopolis and granted him the title of megaskyr, or seigneur, or count, of that place. The title

355

was almost untranslatable into French, but the extent of the estate was as great as many a county in France.

Alexius, the grand duke, in recognition of his many years of service to the family, and because it was known that the infirmities of age were certain to manifest themselves in a few years, was given the magnificent, pink, town house of the Bulgarian prince. Alexius, when he grew old, would not have to climb all those stairs up to his apartments in the palace.

Other portions of Ogli's enormous holdings were given to other nobles or officials, whose services in the past or whose fidelity in the future were deemed worthy of imperial notice or cultivation. And when all the gifts were made, there remained a tremendous, though unpublicized, residue for the privy purses of the Great Comneni.

No court can ever be so happy as one where great grants of honors and lands are made. The musical hums by which the Trapezuntian Greeks made known their approval sounded through the court like a melody at each reading of the Herald of the Raven, whose voice grew hoarse as vineyards, forests, ships, houses, cattle, lands, and titles were bestowed upon fortunate recipients. The Emperor John, in his jewel-encrusted pallium, wearing the heavy imperial crown with its shoulder-length strings of pearls and sitting on his golden throne in a cloud of incense that burned in tripods at his feet, looked and felt like a god come down to earth to distribute a great bounty.

At the end of the allocation of Ogli's wealth, to the astonishment of Pierre and everyone else who had never before been to the Great Court, the golden throne began to rise from the floor. The crowd of courtiers prostrated themselves. The fan bearers crossed their great feather fans before the sacred person of the emperor. When, in a moment, the fans parted again, those among the recumbent courtiers who, in defiance of ceremonial, dared to glance up observed that the throne was empty. The glittering emperor had disappeared down a little stairway hidden in the rear. But the effect was one of a new and glorious mechanical Ascension, while a band of musicians struck up a mournful hymn, signifying that the Presence had elected for a time to remove Itself from their midst.

Immediately after the disappearance of the emperor, which the more gullible were always encouraged to believe was miraculous, the entire roomful of people, facing the still elevated throne, rose to its feet and walked backward out of the room, while a group of functionaries, clad in somber black, placed golden covers over the tripods to extinguish the burning incense.

356

A messenger approached Pierre and the captain. He had a serious face, and he summoned them to the apartments of the paradynast.

Addressing Pierre, Alexius said: "Your thanks for the generosity of the Great Comnenus have taken a curious twist, Sir Peter. Pray tell me where you have sent the French ship *Sainte-Marie?* Is it your intention further to disrupt the trade which we have enjoyed so long with the kingdom of France?"

Pierre laughed. "I have done nothing illegal, Your Highness." He explained the sudden outrageous prices of space and goods among the waterfront merchants, as well as his plans for the future of Thalassopolis and his conviction that Sir Theodore would make a good French factor.

Alexius listened attentively. There was a humorous glint in his eye when he observed: "I am not a merchant, Sir Peter, but unless merchants differ from the rest of mankind, which I doubt, you appear to have taken drastic and effective means of assuring a continuance of profit to your master and yourself. With no great loss, I might add, to anyone except a few rich traders along the waterfront. The revenues of the empire will not suffer. That is the main thing. As long as they do not, you are at liberty to make any arrangements you please with private Trapezuntian merchants.

"As for the appointment of Sir Theodore, I am not sure." Theodore was sent for. "I shall have to refresh my memory. I shall look at his record for the past few years."

One of the silent servants, who never needed an order, placed on the table before him a small, bound volume of what appeared to be a great number of carefully written Greek pages. The same servant deftly and gently placed upon the paradynast's nose a pair of spectacles, and Alexius opened the book and began to read silently to himself. Theodore appeared and stood by the door. There was absolute silence in the room.

At length Alexius closed the book. "Come hither, Sir Theodore." Theodore approached the table. He had no idea why he had been summarily snatched from a group of his Pontic friends and called before the grand duke. He was relieved to see Pierre and Justin, but he did not dare speak until Alexius spoke to him.

Alexius pronounced to the three at large: "There is nothing in the record of Theodore, sometime Megaskyr of Thalassopolis, to warrant imperial disapproval of his appointment as a commercial representative if, in the opinion of the French minister of finance, he should be so designated." Theodore instantly realized why he had been summoned.

357

Justin and Pierre began to smile at him. The grand duke spoke directly then to Theodore. "There is only one entry in the police record dealing with you, Sir Theodore, which I find suspicious or perhaps incomplete. Three years ago you are known to have sold to an Armenian merchant, Hovakim of Kars, 4,632 Mohammedan prayer rugs, of Persian manufacture. The transaction was legal, of course, and there is no question of evasion of taxes, since religious articles, both Christian and Moslem, are tax-exempt throughout the empire. But how did you come by so vast a quantity of heathen prayer rugs, and what in the world did a Christian Armenian plan to do with them?"

"He didn't want them at first, Your Highness," Theodore answered. "Baltha Ogli gave me the rugs. He thought them valueless. They were lovely things—short pile, tightly woven, the best wool, and, of course, the double knot. But through some stupid error of the designer, the pattern, which Your Highness must realize is usually severe in rugs of this sort, was quite floridly decorative. Moreover, the pattern of the border, when seen from a distance—perhaps the designer had worked too close to his material—actually suggested the Christian Cross. Ogli was furious. No Mohammedan would ever have prayed on such a thing. Ogli gave them to Father and me. It was rent for the khan, he said."

"What did you do then?"

"I sought out Hovakim of Kars, Your Highness, and I told him I had a great quantity of prime material for camel bags."

"Camel bags?"

"With a little sewing they made excellent camel bags, Your Highness. Many of them are still in use, and they are said to wear like iron. Hovakim paid me handsomely and I am told he made a good profit for himself as well."

Alexius thought a moment. Then he chuckled. "Sir Peter and Sir John, if your master consents to the appointment of this man as your factor, it is my opinion that the French interests will be well served. I consider it something of an accomplishment to sell even one rug to an Armenian. Sir Theodore seems to have sold thousands of them."

Through Theodore's activities the contents of the khan, having been subjected to import and export taxes, were loaded aboard the *Sainte-Marie*, and that ship, with one of the most compact and valuable cargoes ever to come out of the empire, was dispatched back to France.

Pierre courteously refused every invitation to remain in Trebizond, and Sir John, rather than Pierre, privately told the grand duke why.

"Only my young friend's body is here, Your Highness," he said. "His heart and soul are in France, where the great lady he loves has foolishly shut herself up in a convent at some rumor of his death. No doubt he will want to return and visit his city. But all the cities in Trebizond, just now, are not worth one strand of the hair on the pretty head of the girl who may or may not have covered her locks forever with the black veil of the holy women of the Cistercian Order."

Alexius, the eunuch, nodded his wise old head wistfully.

"That is understandable, Sir John. Then we shall wait to welcome Sir Peter again till God or his lady have cooled his blood and instructed his ambition. He would do well here. Few men have found such favor in the eyes of the Great Comneni. And no one," he chuckled, "ever so completely confounded the merchants on the waterfront."

In the cooler weather and shorter days the Lady set her prow west toward Constantinople and the Mediterranean. She had just enough Trapezuntian cargo, purchased at rock-bottom prices from the chastened warehouse merchants, to enable her to sail smartly. Her flags snapped in the stiff autumn breeze, and there was in her waist with the other shields, the shield of Sir Peter, with the Eagle of Trebizond fiercely glaring over its right wing, and below its golden claws the Greek device of the Megaskyr of Thalassopolis, "I Remember."

# CHAPTER

## ✳ 34 ✳

THE MAN in the land of Uz, whose name was Job, smitten with sores from the sole of his foot to his crown, scraping himself with a potsherd and sitting among the ashes, did not deserve his boils.

Contrariwise, it could be argued that Pierre did not deserve his honors, or that they were extravagantly great in relation to his services. But the age rewarded lavishly, just as it punished with unspeakable cruelty.

An English poet, living long after Sir Peter, observed that there is a tide in the affairs of men, which, taken at the flood, leads on to fortune. Pierre did not consciously take the tide at its flood. It lifted him up and carried him along.

And there were certain eminently practical forces, beyond Pierre's ken or control, that worked in his favor. Many of the savage, factious lords, whose outmoded notions of feudal independence had troubled the French king in his efforts to unite the realm, had died in the two, quick, bloody campaigns in Lorraine and the mountains of Switzerland during the summer. A new generation, Pierre's generation, full of French pride and a new concept of national unity, was taking their place. The thinned ranks of the nobles were being filled again; the monarchy grew in strength every day; France was full of new men.

Jacques Coeur, himself an ennobled commoner whom Pierre had served so faithfully and with such good fortune, cheerfully brought all his great influence to bear upon the French College of Heralds to accomplish the ratification of Pierre's countship. Pierre's knighthood, of course, needed no ratification. The scholarly French nobles searched the ancient rolls in vain for a European counterpart of the exotic Greek title of "megaskyr." Coeur then pointed out that it should be "count," since the Trapezuntian estates of Sir Peter were larger and more remunerative than many a county in France.

And Coeur shrewdly observed to the king one day that it would cost the French treasury not one sou to create Sir Peter a count, since his revenues were drawn from the Empire of Trebizond. The king lent a sympathetic ear to the cogent economic advice of his minister of finance, and Sir Peter was duly invested with the title of Count of Thalassopolis and the style of "My Lord."

The *Sainte-Marie* had left Trebizond a week before the Lady, and the Lady spent forty-eight hours in Constantinople completing her cargo. But the Lady sailed faster than any ship in France, and Justin brought her into Montpellier only a day later than the *Sainte-Marie*.

The *Sainte-Marie's* captain, of course, had cautioned his crew not to gossip. But the wine in the waterfront taverns loosened the sailors' tongues, and soon all Montpellier buzzed with the news, greatly elaborated, of what Pierre had done in the distant Greek empire.

Pierre's landlord, the guilty Friar, whose sanctimonious little inn had so long been used as a hiding place for smuggled goods, rushed panic stricken to De Coucy. Bernard had had plenty of time to prepare an orderly retreat for just such an eventuality. On that same night, with a comfortable fortune stolen from the coffers of Jacques Coeur, De Coucy fled into the Spains, where, at the court of the amiable, indolent John of Castile, with witty stories and ample means, he lived in opulent exile and comparative peace of mind. It rather hurt his pride that nobody ever prosecuted him or even tried to bring him back to France. Actually the king felt that he was well rid of one more corrupt nobleman. De Coucy was later heard to have become a great favorite, especially with the Castilian sovereign's young son, whom history inelegantly calls Henry the Impotent.

# CHAPTER

## ❧ 35 ❧

PIERRE HAD RIDDEN up to Paris on a younger, faster horse
than the one Claire had given him. That middle-aged beast was
now fat beyond all thinning, and Pierre was in a hurry. Jacques Coeur
was in Paris with the king, whose court was exceptionally festive that
winter. It was there that Coeur told Pierre of the final action of the
College of Heralds in the clarification and ratification of his title.

"Unless you intend to retire on your revenues," the minister told
him, "which I realize you could easily do, I shall ask you at your
leisure to consider remaining in my service. De Coucy's disappearance
has left me with more detail than I can efficiently handle."

It did not appear to the minister that the new nobleman with the
spectacular Eagle on his chest was duly impressed. Coeur quickly
added: "Not as my secretary, you understand, though De Coucy once
told me that you were doing almost all of his work. It was proper for
me to summon an impecunious knight to my room with a little jade
gong, but I could not ring for a noble count, with greater rents than
most counts, in such a manner. I was thinking of your proficiency in
the Eastern tongue and the diplomatic finesse that you evinced in your
intercourse with Cantacuzene." He began to chuckle and rub his hands.
"No pilot fees! No head taxes! Truly that amazed me. Your talents
would be wasted as my secretary, Sir Peter. It is a diplomatic post which
I have in mind. God was surely with you when you exposed the wicked-
ness of Baltha Ogli, but your own sharp wits outwitted the factor in
Constantinople." Then the minister stopped and said severely: "You
are not listening to me. My offer would make the fortune of a man who
did not already possess one. Have money and titles so quickly gone to
your head, Pierre?"

"My lord," Pierre answered, flushing crimson up to his hair, "you honor me too much. I should not be ashamed to answer the jade gong. But I confess I have heard you with only half an ear. The trouble is not with my head, but rather with my heart." He told the minister why he had hurried up to Paris. "It was not to seek ratification of my title, which I have offered to sell back to Sir Theodore, nor to gloat over the success of my mission, which I firmly believe you rightly attribute to divine aid. Nor do I forget Sir John, without whom I could have accomplished nothing."

"God and Sir John and a slave girl and a monkey all helped, Sir Peter. I do not minimize the other elements in your success. My offer still stands, however. And do not too hastily throw away your title. Honors are hard come by and easy to lose. One clings to them when one grows accustomed to them. Believe me. I am in a position to know. We shall speak of your future plans again, when your heart and your head are at peace with one another. As for the daughter of the Count de la Tour-Clermont, I know nothing beyond what I wrote to Sir John: she has retired to Port-Royal. Church affairs do not lie within my jurisdiction, though it may interest you to know that a friend of yours is in Paris. The Austin friar, Isambart de la Pierre spoke to me of you only the other day."

"What is Father Isambart doing in Paris, my lord?"

"Father Isambart is becoming a famous ecclesiastic without even trying. He has no ambition in this world, but the Church is heaping honors upon him. It is curious how those who were against the Maid have fallen upon evil days, and those who were for her have prospered. Nicolas Midi, who preached the funeral sermon at her martyrdom, is dead of leprosy. The Bishop of Beauvais, who presided at her trial, died in midcareer without ever achieving the archbishopric he coveted, and there are rumors of a posthumous excommunication. Isambart, who appears to have been an unwilling official witness of her death, is now busy with the reversal of her sentence. The highest dignitaries of the Church consult with him all the time. The correspondence with Rome is said to be heavy and frequent." He smiled. "Frequent, that is, for the Church. Perhaps one dispatch every six months, which is frequent for an organization which differs from a merchant's in that it exists for eternity. People are beginning to say that Jeanne d'Arc will one day be a saint. I do not know. But that is why Isambart is in Paris. He has a miter now, and they call him Eminence. Perhaps he will help you, Sir Peter."

# CHAPTER

## ❧ 36 ❧

MAHAUT, THE LAY SISTER, rose every day of the year three hours before dawn. Such early rising was necessary because the reverend mother herself always rose two hours before dawn. The extra hour was not too long a time in which to rouse a husband, feed him, clothe and feed three lusty youngsters and oneself, and then hurry across the fields to the Convent of Port-Royal.

Mahaut always let herself into the enclosure with a great old iron key that opened the little postern gate. She wore it like a talisman attached to her belt. Her key gave her enormous prestige in the village. Today it turned hard in the frozen lock.

The spiritual day for the nuns of Port-Royal started with Matins, but the physical day started with Mahaut and the diabolical clatter she made with her wooden shoes when she walked down the long corridors to the chambers of the mother abbess. The dreaded, punctual noise of the lay sister's steps over the ancient stones shattered the sleep of the nuns, the novices, and the boarders, as well as a considerable corps of servants, cooks, and cleaning women, whose labors were essential to the cloistered community of perhaps two hundred women.

The ecclesiastical rank of Michelle de Langres, the mother abbess, was high, being roughly equivalent to that of a bishop.

At the door of the abbatial chambers, Mahaut would knock, wait a moment, put off her noisy shoes and enter. She would dust the chairs and the abbess's table, taking care not to mix up the letters and papers that were always arranged there in neat, orderly little piles. She dusted the statue of the Virgin in its niche and put a new candle into the votive light at the statue's foot. On winter days, like this one, just before the Feast of the Holy Nativity, she would light a taper from the votive light and ignite the peats that had been carefully laid the night before in the fireplace so that a little warmth might permeate the room before the abbess got out of bed. It often seemed to Mahaut that the reverend mother's chambers were the coldest in the building. The dormitory of the nuns, directly over the kitchens, was much more comfortable.

It was more comfortable still, of course, to sleep next to one's husband. There one never got cold. Once Mahaut had actually said as much to the abbess. It was during a particularly severe winter; Mahaut was carrying her third child. With an earthy directness that would have been insulting from anyone but a simple peasant woman, Mahaut had contrasted her pregnant condition, about which she was very happy and proud, with the barren body and lonely bed of the reverend mother. Instead of rebuking her impertinence, the abbess had gently replied: "Mahaut, do you not answer a call from your children during the night? When the babe in your body is born, if he calls you, will you not stop whatever you are doing and go tend him?"

Mahaut had said: "Certainly, Madame l'abbesse. Any mother does that. You can always hear a baby cry, even when you're dead tired in the middle of the night."

The abbess, gravely smiling, had indicated the Virgin with the Holy Child in her arms in the niche above the *prie-dieu*.

"Some of us have heard another Call, Mahaut. If you do not understand me, say so, and I shall explain further."

But Mahaut had understood.

When the fire in the little study was blazing, Mahaut would knock at the abbess's bedchamber. It was her duty to enter whether the abbess answered or not, since there is always the possibility that death may come while one is asleep. When the abbess answered, Mahaut would go in, take down a clean wimple from the closet shelf and, if she were asked, aid the abbess in dressing.

Today, however, the abbess was already dressed. She was praying before the statue and she did not look up when Mahaut entered. Mahaut peeked into her bedchamber. Either the reverend mother had kept a vigil all night, which was unusual, or else she had made her own bed, for it did not appear to have been slept in. Mahaut shook her head; the floor was so cold it made her teeth chatter. She glanced at the wimple the abbess was wearing. It was wrinkled. It was obviously yesterday's. She noticed that the candle in the votive light was nearly exhausted. If the abbess had simply arisen a little earlier than usual, she herself would have put in the new candle, as she had often done. Yesterday's wimple and yesterday's candle could only mean one thing: the reverend mother had prayed all night long. It was amazing how rested she looked. Mahaut wondered whether she ought to go away and leave the abbess at her prayers. But the cold of the stone floor made her decide against it.

If the reverend mother elected to pray all night that was her concern, but the temperature of the room was Mahaut's. Mahaut boldly lit the taper from the votive light, not three feet from the Abbess's eyes, carried the flame across the room and started the fire in the fireplace.

It was difficult to ignore the lay sister, Mahaut.

The abbess rose from her knees, and at the same time Mahaut dropped her the deep courtesy that was due her rank.

"Why have you come here at night, Mahaut? Is something amiss? Is someone ill?"

"It is not night, Madame l'abbesse. It is morning and a very cold one. The fields are white with frost. There is frost in here, too, if you don't mind my saying so. It isn't good to stay up all night in so cold a room. May I fetch you a cup of hot broth from the kitchens?"

"I did not realize the night had passed so quickly." The abbess looked perfectly refreshed. She might have slept instead of prayed the night away. She seemed to have even more than her usual energy. "Send to me at once the sister prioress and the sister mistress of the novices. And the cook. And see that both fires are lighted in the common room."

"Both fires, Madame l'abbesse?"

"Both. Then open the sacristy doors so that the church will be warm."

The abbey church was connected with the building where the nuns had their living quarters and dormitory.

"Yes, Madame l'abbesse. You have never ordered both fires before."

"I never wanted the church so comfortable before. And you may bring me the broth, Mahaut. It was kind of you to think of it."

When Mahaut returned with the broth, she found the reverend mother putting on a fresh wimple. It was exactly like the clean one she changed to every day, except that this one was so new that it had never even been laundered. Hidden behind her wimple and under her long black veil, the hair of the reverend mother was nearly white.

In the absence of specific orders, when several people were summoned to the presence of the abbess, they waited upon her, much as an ecclesiastical procession forms, in the reverse order of their rank. Therefore the cook was first.

"The house is being descended upon," the reverend mother pronounced to the cook, "by thirty men."

"Thirty men," answered the cook, like a response to a litany, nodding her black-veiled head sagely, as if she knew all about men. "Thirty men means sixty extra meals, Madame l'abbesse. And meat, will it not?"

"Certainly."

"Men are always hungry. Like the locusts in Egypt, I always say, devouring everything in their path. What will the nuns eat, Madame l'abbesse?"

The reverend mother did not hesitate an instant. She recalled to her mind the second, the third, the twenty-seventh, and the sixty-fourth chapters of the rule of Blessed St. Benedict under which they all lived: how an abbess is not to overdrive or sadden her nuns, or give them cause for just murmuring. The tempting odor of the roasting joints would fill the cloister. It was the holiday season. She was not a monster.

"Meat, too," she said. The cook went away with a broad happy smile on her comfortable face and gave an order in the kitchens that set the great fires to roaring. The convent grew warm and began to smell wonderfully toothsome. When a few of the nuns asked the reason for the unusual, welcome, secular incense, the cook maintained, on her honor as a cook, which served only to deepen the mystery, that she knew nothing, no, not a thing, about it.

The sister mistress of the novices was next, and with her the abbess had a long, serious talk. It was always a delicate business to inform a novice of anything that had happened in the outside world that might affect her decision to be or not to be a nun for the rest of her life.

"I do not know how Claire will take this news, Madame l'abbesse. Last week I had to tell her how her kinsman had disappeared in disgrace. It had a salutary effect, I thought, and the girl spent much time in private devotions. Of course, she has always been gentle and prayerful."

"It is not always possible or proper to know what a novice is praying for," observed the abbess practically. "Excuse Claire from all religious duties today. Let her spend her time in meditation, or in any reasonable way that she likes. The men will arrive shortly after noon, I imagine. That is little enough time for her to make up her mind on so important a subject. Let Sir Robert, the Count de la Tour-Clermont, interview his daughter in the common room. I am given to understand that he has agreed to the marriage, but he is a wise man and he knows that everything depends on Claire herself. Then Claire is to see this Pierre, this Sir Peter, this rich Megaskyr of Thalassopolis."

"What in the world is a Megaskyr, Madame l'abbesse?"

"It is some sort of count in the Empire of Trebizond."

"Probably one of those swarthy foreigners, Reverend Mother. Perhaps Claire will remain with us."

"A man's country and complexion do not determine his effect on a young girl. The heart is sometimes very empty and sometimes very full when one makes one's final profession, as you well know. The main thing is that the head be clear. We do not know what Claire de la Tour-Clermont will do. But I am persuaded," she said positively, "that it would be safest for the girl and the man to see each other not in the common room but in the open air in front of the church. There is less chance for a scandal if, for example, he should embrace her."

"Heavens!" murmured the sister mistress of the novices. Suddenly another thought struck her. "And in her habit, too! It would be sacrilege, Reverend Mother."

The abbess sighed. "It would not, of course. But it would certainly be unbecoming. I have pondered the question seriously."

"I could easily borrow a secular dress from one of the boarders," the sister mistress suggested. "One or two of them at least are slender enough for their gowns to fit Claire."

"No doubt. And suppose Claire elected to renounce the world and her Megaskyr? How foolish we would look. How mean a thing our faith would appear. Such things have happened. I conceive that we ought not to influence Claire's decision one way or another, and I think perhaps we are unable to; surely such things are in the hand of God. If the Holy Spirit whispers in her heart, she will listen. If the Calling is for her, she cannot but obey. The good name of the cloister, however, is a wholly different consideration, and it is my thought that it would be scandalous for us to dress Claire as if we were already convinced that she would leave us. Do not, therefore, borrow a dress from one of the boarders."

The sister prioress, next after the abbess in dignity and authority in the convent, was the last to wait upon the reverend mother.

"Go to the chaplain," the abbess ordered. Michelle de Langres held in her hand the letter that had kept her up all night. Neither her hand nor her voice was quite steady. "Tell the chaplain that . . . His Eminence may want to conduct Vespers."

"His Eminence, Reverend Mother?"

"His Eminence, Isambart de la Pierre." The abbess had not said the name with her lips for thirty years. Even to one's confessor, of course, names are never used.

PORT-ROYAL WAS only half a day's journey from Paris. A little
after noon, exactly as the abbess had predicted, the courtyard in
front of the church began to fill with the mounted retinues of the old
Count de la Tour-Clermont and the young Count of Thalassopolis.

Sir Robert went in at once to talk to his daughter.

Pierre walked slowly back and forth under the frosty branches of the
high, old, winter-bare trees. In spite of the cold that made the frozen
grass snap under his footsteps and turned his breath into a palpable
cloud, he was so agitated that he felt uncomfortably warm. He took off
his hat, and in a little while he flung the long blue cloak that Sir Theodore had given him off his shoulders and carried it over his arm.

The sister mistress of the novices, peeking from a window in the
dormitory, made a mental note that if that were a Megaskyr, not all
foreigners were swarthy.

Most of the other nuns, the novices, and even the secular boarders
were peeking out, too. It was years since so many men had been within
the walls.

The reverend mother, like a general who has planned a good battle,
waited now for the battle to be fought. Isambart, in a sense, was her
opponent. On neutral ground, under the arches of the cloister, by a
garden where next year's roses slept under their blanket of straw, the
two elderly ecclesiastics awaited the outcome of the opposing forces
they had set in motion, but they did not immediately mention Claire.

"The work of Your Eminence in the rehabilitation of the Maid of
Orleans is becoming famous," the abbess said pleasantly.

The reverend mother was still too much of a woman to admit that the sight of his signature on a letter had caused her to spend a sleepless night exorcising the ghost of a handsome young man, infinitely below her station in life, who, years before, had taken holy orders. Or perhaps it was not necessary any more to mention it. The instant she saw the man, the troublesome ghost of the boy was laid forever. She thought what a dreadful mistake she might have made.

"It is a work of justice, reverend mother. Though it takes me much in the world and sometimes I miss the seclusion that you must enjoy in your more cloistered conventual duties."

Isambart, too, was rid of a ghost, for there was nothing in the respectable appearance of his colleague, Madame l'abbesse, that resembled the image which had persisted so long in his imagination of the noble, impulsive Lady Michelle de Langres, whom at first he had been a little reluctant to meet again. He put it down to an exaggerated memory of youthful infatuation.

Their walk had brought them close to the side door of the abbey church. The habits of a lifetime drew their steps toward it. Their meeting after so many years, which each of them had somewhat feared, was an easy, natural thing, concerned, like their lives, not with themselves but with others. Sober contentment, that eventually fills a life of devotion and sacrifice, where nothing ever changes, poured into their hearts like a power from an inexhaustible source.

"I conceive it to have been no sin," said the abbess, as if they had been talking about it, which they had not, "to have been so happy as I have been. I should like to pray a moment, Reverend Father, that the young people, in whose lives you have interested yourself, shall be as happy."

Isambart understood her perfectly. He found himself repeating the beautiful words he had spoken thousands of times, softly at the entrance into the sanctuary: "I will go in unto the altar of God." The abbess, whose hair under the veil was nearly white, made the response, "Unto God who giveth joy to my youth," and together they went in and knelt for a few, restful moments.

They happened to emerge from the great west door of the church just behind Sir Robert and his daughter, who had finished their talk in the common room and chosen the most direct route to where Pierre continued his walk under the trees.

Claire's decision was already spectacularly manifested.

She had put off her novice's veil. Her hair tumbled in a golden cloud around her shoulders.

Sir Robert, whose leg the healing waters of Lamalou had done no good whatsoever, remained at the top of the church steps with Isambart and the abbess.

The sister mistress of the novices, peeking out of the dormitory window, breathed a sigh of relief that the veil, at least, was gone, when Claire flew down the steps to meet Pierre.

The reverend mother shook her head.

There was no trace of resignation in her proud voice when she said, "The Calling is not for everyone."